SIX MILE CREEK

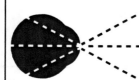

A JUDD WHEELER MYSTERY, BOOK 1

SIX MILE CREEK

RICHARD HELMS

KENNEBEC LARGE PRINT
A part of Gale, Cengage Learning

GALE
CENGAGE Learning·

Detroit • New York • San Francisco • New Haven, Conn • Waterville, Maine • London

GALE
CENGAGE Learning·

LIBRARY OF CONGRESS CATALOGING-IN-PUBLICATION DATA

Helms, Richard W., 1955–
    Six mile creek / by Richard Helms. — Large print ed.
        p. cm. — (Kennebec large print superior collection)
    ISBN 978-1-4104-4781-4 (pbk.) — ISBN 1-4104-4781-2 (pbk.) 1. Large type books. 2. Murder—Investigation—Fiction. 3. North Carolina—Fiction. I. Title.
PS3608.E466S59 2010
813'.6—dc23   2012001029

Published in 2012 by arrangement with Tekno Book and Ed Gorman.

Printed in the United States of America
    1 2 3 4 5   16 15 14 13 12
FD123

For Elaine
Just because . . .

CHAPTER ONE

Hector Ramirez paced my office, waving his hands as he spoke. He had a heavy Mexican accent. My head hurt as I tried to follow him.

"I cannot believe you arrested Vicente," he railed. "Vicente is a good boy, Chief Wheeler."

"He went after Seth Kramer with a tire iron," I said.

"And for this you put my son in jail?"

"When a citizen swears out a complaint for assault, it's my job."

"A schoolyard fight. Boys do these things."

I sipped from my coffee cup. It was cold. The artificial creamer had started to congeal on the surface. I really didn't care. I wasn't into aesthetics. I just wanted the caffeine.

And something to do with my hands.

"Mr. Ramirez," I said. "Schoolyard fights I can understand. Tire irons are another matter entirely. If Seth's buddies hadn't held Vicente back, we might be talking about a lot worse than assault here. Let's face it. Your kid really lost control."

"And who can blame him? Did Vicente tell you what this Kramer boy said?"

"Yes, he did."

"He called my son a *beaner.*"

"I know."

"And you don't care?"

I sighed and set the coffee cup back on my desk.

"As a human being and a citizen of the world, I care. As chief of police here in Prosperity, it's not an issue. There's no law against calling someone a name. I talked with Seth's father. He's willing to drop the charges. You can take Vicente home any time."

"And what happens tomorrow?"

"I'm not psychic. Tomorrow will have to take care of itself."

"When Vicente shows up at school, and word gets around that he was arrested, how is he supposed to deal with that?"

"Graciously. Now, if you don't mind, I have work to do."

"Of course. White man's work. Anglos' work. Maybe you would not be in such a hurry to run me off if I were to file a hate crimes complaint against Mr. Kramer's son."

I really did have other work to do. On the other hand, Hector needed some advice before he dug himself in a lot deeper than he could dig himself back out.

"Come with me to the break room so I can talk some sense into you, Hector."

He followed me down the hall to the break room, which was actually not much more than an oversized storage room at the back of the police station, which itself was actually just a storefront in Prosperity's three-acre commercial district.

I dumped the mess from my coffee cup into the sink and rinsed it out before refilling it from the pot sitting in the coffee-maker.

"Here's why filing a hate crimes lawsuit would be a bad idea," I said, without looking at him, as I spooned in some sugar and creamer. "You file a suit, and you're going to bring a lot of attention on yourself. First thing you know, you'll be on the front page of the *Ledger-Telegraph,* maybe above the fold. There will be pictures, and a lot of people asking questions. Now, unless you have magically sprouted a green card in the last day or so, what do you think happens next?"

"Are you threatening me, Chief?"

"I don't have to. Hector, I'm not a Federal agent. I don't work for the INS. Frankly, I don't give a shit about your illegal status. Since you don't vote for or against the people who sign my paycheck, you're pretty much neutral so far as I'm concerned. You start making waves, though, and sooner or later someone's going to wonder how you came to reside in this little slice of heaven. If you can't explain that, the next stop is south of the border, and I don't mean South Carolina. Dig?"

"What is this *dig?*"

"Do you understand the words I'm saying to you? Because, the way I see it, you have two choices. You can collect Vicente, take him home, and teach him not to settle his differences with a tire iron; or you can start packing your bags for a one-way flight to Oaxaca."

I sipped from the coffee cup and stared over the top of my reading glasses at him as he digested his dilemma.

Hector was basically a decent guy. So was his son, for the most part. Like a lot of illegals, he had come to this country to try and knock off a piece of the American dream. He just hadn't bothered to do all the paperwork first.

The Hispanic population had tripled in Prosperity over the last year or so, drawn by the lure of relatively high-paying jobs on the local farms and as housekeepers and the like. Despite the fears of the Anglos, I didn't see any more lawbreaking from the Mexicans than I did from anyone else. In fact, there was more tension between the recently arrived upperclass professionals from nearby Parker County and the farm families that had populated Bliss County for nearly two hundred years than I had ever seen between Hispanics and whites. It was my job to keep it that way.

"There will be no charges?" Hector asked.

"Like I told you. Mr. Kramer prefers to keep this all quiet. He's willing to drop the charges on the condition that Vicente stays away from Seth."

Hector nodded.

"It seems fair."

"And I'll drop by the Kramers'; have a discussion with Seth about this *beaner* talk."

"That would be very kind, Chief," Hector said, extending his hand.

"Just keeping the peace," I said as I took it.

CHAPTER TWO

Prosperity had two bubbletops, one old and one new. They were shared by the three cops hired by the mayor and city council — which also had three members — to serve and protect Prosperity's eight thousand residents. I told Sherry, my civilian office assistant, that I was going out, and I took the new squad car.

Prosperity used to be a very quiet wide spot in the highway between the Parker County line and Morgan, the Bliss County seat. Ten years or so earlier, it had been mostly farmland, rolling hills of cattle farms, and a few widely spaced houses.

Then, some idiot in Parker County figured out that the property tax rate in Bliss County was a quarter of that just across the line, and before you knew it Bliss County — and Prosperity — began to fill with upper-class tax refugees eager to get away from it all.

Word spread, and one by one the farms began to fall to the outrageous offers from land developers. They flattened the gentle hills, bulldozed the old-growth hardwoods, and replaced them with the serpentine roads of bedroom communities and the ubiquitous "Carolina box" transitional houses.

I grew up in the "old" Prosperity. My father was a farmer. I decided to become a cop. Then I decided I didn't want to be a cop anymore after a decade of riding the crime-infested streets of Atlanta, and I came home just in time for my father to die of a brain aneurysm. So, I took over the farm and tried to make a go of it.

The population in Prosperity grew, and before long it became difficult for the Bliss County Sheriff's Department to handle all the calls. The sheriff suggested to the mayor that maybe it was time to think about hiring a couple of full-time cops and open a town police department. Someone put a bug in his ear that I had been a cop in Atlanta, and he approached me about being chief. I told him to ram it, but after a few months I realized that I was a really shitty farmer, and I changed my mind.

That was seven years ago. I've been chief of the Prosperity Police Department ever since. Reckon I will be until I retire, unless

I piss off the Town Council.

I drove the cruiser past the upfitted Prosperity Glen High School, with its new two-story brick facade, and turned left onto Deep Crick Road. On one side of Deep Crick was a seemingly unending series of housing developments where the homes started at a half million and arced steeply upward from there. On the other side of the road, stashed judiciously way back in the trees, were the rental homes populated by the mixture of legal and illegal Hispanic aliens who did most of the scut work in town.

I drove through the entrance of High Shoals, one of the ritzier neighborhoods in Prosperity, and turned left onto Ebenezer Church Road. About two-thirds of the way down the road, I pulled into Kent Kramer's driveway.

Kent's trophy wife Crystal greeted me at the door.

"Judd! How nice to see you. Do come in."

I stepped into the marble-tiled foyer.

"I'm here on business, Crystal. Is Seth home?"

"No, but he'll be here in a few minutes. I just sent him out to the store. Kent's here, in his office. Why don't you visit with him for a few minutes while you wait?"

"That'll be fine."

I knew where the office was. I'd been in Kent Kramer's house a number of times since he had moved to Prosperity from Parker County.

I walked through the kitchen and den to the double glass doors that separated Kent's office from the rest of the house. Kent saw me as I reached the door, and waved me in.

He was on the telephone, sitting behind his oak desk in a button-and-tuck leather office chair.

I took a seat in the corner, on a matching leather loveseat.

"I don't care about that," he told someone on the other end of the line. "I told the Cub Scout pack here that I was going to take them to a Pythons football game, and I sure as shit don't want them sitting in the nosebleed section. What kind of experience is that for a boy? I need ten seats in the lower section, preferably somewhere between the twenty-yard hash marks, you get me? Hell's bells, boy, I don't give a shit how much it costs. You just get me the seats. Call Jack Cameron. He owes me a big favor. Yeah, just get back to me by Friday . . ."

As he spoke, I looked up at the framed picture on his bookshelf. A teenaged Kent Kramer stood proudly under the goal posts of Pooler High School over in Parker County. He was decked out in a sparkling new uniform, holding the helmet that had been hand painted in Pooler's blue and gold school colors by the wives of the football team boosters. Young Kent grinned from ear to ear, full to bursting with the confidence that you can only feel before life just kicks the living bejeezus out of you.

I remembered that Kent, very well. He and I were the same age, and it seemed only a couple of years ago that I was the starting quarterback for Prosperity Glen. We blew Kent Kramer and his Pooler High Patriots off the field at their senior homecoming game. At that age, I probably looked a lot like the kid in the picture, except that Prosperity Glen could only afford new uniforms every five years or so, and my three-year stint there fell right between them.

Kent dropped the receiver back in the cradle and stood to walk around his desk.

"Judd, good to see you. Did you talk with Hector Ramirez?"

I grasped his extended hand. "Yeah. He won't raise a beef. You'll drop the charges against Vicente?"

"I ought to call the fuckin' INS on the little wetback. Don't want to make too

16

much of a fuss over this thing, though. Got some scouts from Clemson dropping by his week to catch Seth's game. It'd be nice to avoid any unpleasantness."

"I don't suppose it would help things if they were to find out he got his clock cleaned by Vicente Ramirez, either."

"There *is* such a thing as bad publicity. Hell, Judd, it was just a schoolyard fight."

"Something it appears Seth knows a little about, judging by his record this year. When I checked at the school, I was informed that he's been in four fights this year, only two of which were reported to the principal."

"Damn, you get around, Judd. Kids, you know? Whatcha gonna do?"

He circled his desk and sat in his chair.

"So, when you gonna sell me that farm of yours?" he asked.

"When you become a farmer."

"Oh, come on, now. A hundred acres? I'll make you a multimillionaire. Parcel like that, I could put sixty houses in there, and still have room left for a little pond."

"I already have a pond."

"The location's all wrong. We'd have to move it."

I was becoming impatient.

"Do you know when Seth's getting back?" I asked "I need to talk with him."

"Any minute now. Hey, got something to show you."

He walked over to a display case, and pulled out a football that had been resting on a pedestal.

"Take a look," he said, tossing it under-hand to me.

The ball was signed in an indecipherable scribble.

"What's this?" I asked.

"Lennie Stockwell! He signed the ball."

Lennie Stockwell was an NFL first-round pick, and the current quarterback for the AFC Pooler Pythons franchise up in Parker County.

I underhanded it back to Kent.

"Pretty cool. How much did he charge?"

"Not a thing. That's the ball he used to throw that sixty-yard touchdown pass to Jermaine Coltes last year in the playoffs. I'm working on a deal to get Lennie to move out here to Bliss County, maybe bring along a teammate or two, get 'em to buy houses in one of my developments. Stockwell's on board, so I'm giving him a break on the house. The ball's part of the deal."

"Playing all the angles," I observed.

I heard the front door swing open and closed, and Seth walked by the double doors to the office.

"Hey, Seth, come in here for a minute," Kent called.

Seth backtracked to the doors, and stood there, waiting to be asked in. He was a big kid, went maybe six-three and two hundred pounds, most of it shoulders and neck. He had the kind of fine wheat-colored hair that just shouted *future Heisman candidate,* and deep blue eyes that registered only the slightest reflection of intelligence and insight. He had been bred for seventeen years for one purpose — to fulfill the athletic promise his father had squandered. He was all reflexes and reaction, with very little room left for deliberation or reason.

"Chief Wheeler," he said.

"Sit down, Seth," I said. He took the chair across from mine, and Kent sat in his own chair. I remained standing.

"As you know," I said, "I arrested Vicente Ramirez following your little dust-up the other day, because you complained that he attacked you with a tire iron. Your father has agreed to drop the charges."

I think it took a moment for the term *drop the charges* to register. Then his brows knit angrily, and his face reddened.

"What? You mean that beaner is gonna get off scot-free?"

"That's right. And I have a few things to

discuss with you. I've been informed that you've been in a number of fights this year. As best as anyone at the school can recollect, this is the first time Vicente's been in any trouble at all."

"What are you saying?" Kent asked from behind the desk.

"According to witnesses, Vicente was alone in the parking lot when Seth and a couple of the other guys from the team confronted him," I said, before turning back to Seth. "According to Vicente, you confronted him about a conversation he had with a junior cheerleader in the cafeteria."

"She's dating Gary Tomberlin, our wide receiver," Seth said. "She's wearin' his ring. He had no business hittin' on her."

"Maybe we should let Mr. Tomberlin handle his own problems," I said. "That notwithstanding, Vicente says you got in his face, and poked him in the chest. You told him to stay away from, and I'm quoting here, *decent white girls.'* Is that correct?"

"Sure. I told him to stay away from her. Beaners need to stay with their own kind."

"Yeah, well, here's the deal on that, Seth. Confronting Vicente with your posse could be construed as making a threat. When you poked him in the chest, in the course of threatening him, you technically committed an assault."

"Like hell!"

"Under the law, touching him in a threatening manner is assault. If Vicente had wanted to file a complaint, I'd have had both of you in the slam. How would that look to your Clemson recruiters?"

"I don't believe this!" Seth said, and he turned to his father. "Do you believe this?"

"There's more," I said. "You admit calling Vicente a *beaner* to his face. Under the school rules, that constitutes racial harassment, and is punishable by a suspension of up to five days. Also, under the school rules, people who are suspended for five days or more in one semester are not allowed to participate in extracurricular activities."

He stared at me, his mouth open, eyes wide.

"Like football," I added.

"You're takin' *his* side?" Seth squawked.

"I'm not taking any sides. Your father agreed to drop the charges against Vicente, and Vicente has agreed to stay away from you. Based on what Vicente told me, though, I'd say that — in the interest of keeping the peace — you'd probably bear a little closer supervision. It would not be a good thing for you to get yourself into any more fights this school year. Understand?"

"What if I get jumped?" His voice had risen almost an octave.

"Then the person jumping you had better have some kind of record of behavior problems, unlike Vicente Ramirez. Keep your nose clean, Seth. It's that simple."

"Is that all?" Seth asked.

"It'll do for now. You can go."

Seth jumped from the chair, and stomped out of the room. I could hear the clumps as he continued to stomp all the way up the stairs.

"A little harsh, don't you think?" Kent asked.

"I didn't tell you the whole story. There was no need. Seth knows what happened. Let's just say that, according to reliable witnesses, Seth picked that fight, and targeted Vicente because he thought he could beat him. Vicente was acting in self-defense when he pulled that tire iron. I'd have been surprised if Judge Burrell over in Morgan would have convicted him in a fair trial. Seth got off easy. I just want to see to it that he keeps it cool for the rest of the year."

Kent settled back in his chair, and clasped his hands behind his head.

"You are a piece of work, Judd. Always were. I reckon you're a good cop, but maybe you should remember who pays the lion's share of taxes in this town. It sure ain't the Mexican wetbacks."

"No. They pay in other ways. And I don't forget who wields the real power in Prosperity. I just don't care. I can hand in my badge any day you and the Council want, and walk away from it. I make enough from sharecropping to support me and my son. You want my badge, Kent?"

I unpinned it from my shirt, and held it out to him.

He stared me down, until it became painful.

For both of us.

"Keep the badge," he said. "Damned if I know where we'd find another cop dumb enough to take your job for the pay. I, uh, guess I should thank you for not running Seth in to the station."

"Old times' sake," I said. "Keep it in the road, Kent."

I let myself out.

CHAPTER THREE

I turned out of Deep Crick Road onto Morgan Highway, a two-lane commuter track between the county line and Morgan, the county seat.

My farm was on the far side of Prosperity. That sounds like a long way, but it amounts to no more than a five-minute drive, if you don't catch the two town stoplights just right.

It was the middle of fall, and the local farmers had just plowed under their fields and fertilized them in preparation for the spring planting. The air was dank with the bite of processed cow manure as I drove the roller-coaster hills separating my farm and the miniature hell wrought by Kent Kramer and his fellow developers, my driver-side window down, my left elbow cutting the crisp dry air like a khaki wing.

Within a minute, I had crossed Six Mile Creek, the imaginary boundary between the interlopers and the long-time Bliss County residents. The fractured landscape smoothed and healed itself, became fragrant and fertile. The wet summer had yielded a bumper crop of scarlets and ambers and oranges in the hardwood trees. The farther I drove away from the Parker County line, the less accessible were all the creature comforts that Parker represented, and the less attractive the land became for the invaders from the Big City. This was the Prosperity I recalled from my childhood, and I treasured it, even as I knew its days were numbered. Sooner or later, the demand for new parcels would grow and the incursion would jump the banks of Six Mile Creek. The life I had always known was doomed.

I pushed the thought from my mind as I pulled through the fieldstone gate into my family farm.

Somehow I had never inherited my father's genetic yearning for the soil. He would dig his hands deep into the wet tilled earth just after plowing, raise the clods to his face, breathe in the musty aroma, and proclaim it to be God's own perfume. All I saw was detritus and worms and decayed manure. I suppose I was just never meant to be the farmer my father had wanted.

Oh, I love the land well enough, I suppose. I just never wanted to get *too* intimate with it.

We owned a hundred acres, which my father had once rotated every several years between tobacco, when the prices were up, to corn when the Feds had their backs turned and he could make a buck selling to the moonshiners over in Mica Wells. Now I rented it out in twenty-acre parcels to folks who couldn't afford their own land to farm, many of them the same hard-working illegal Mexican immigrants that Seth Kramer claimed to despise as lazy and undeserving of a chunk of the American Dream.

I pulled up in front of my house. My grandfather had built it in 1920. Bought the whole damn thing out of the Sears catalog. Plunked down his money, and several weeks later the train stopped in Morgan with our house on a flatbed car, just a stack of lumber and shingles and bricks, which the porters offloaded onto the trucks and horse-drawn wagons my grandfather had arranged to borrow, his friends driving, so that they could caravan back down the rutted dirt Morgan Highway and build a damn fine house. I still had the catalog from which it was selected. My father had enshrined it in the china cupboard he built for my mother with planks he milled from the tulip poplars and box elders he felled to clear the west forty, the year after Granddaddy died.

It was a quaint Craftsman house, with a deep front porch, pyramid columns, and a tin roof. The exterior was covered in finely mortared field stone turned up over the course of years of plowing, and stacked in a heap next to the shack my grandfather had lived in while waiting to save enough money to pay the $1,300 price for his Sears house kit. He had kicked in an additional $30 for the custom hearth, a Mexican tile affair that had always been my favorite place in the house as a kid, perhaps because it was the warmest during the brief wintry months in the south.

My own son, Craig, the fourth generation of Wheelers to live under the roof of this house, lounged in one of the wicker settees on the front porch as I drove up. He was deep into his grunge period, all oversized plaid shirts and slouchy pants and hair and attitude. He read a comic book as I climbed from the cruiser and shut the door.

Hell, at least he was reading.

"Hey," he said.

"Hey, yourself. Don't you have homework?"

"I did. It's done. Can I go to Morgan

tonight?"

"No."

"Aw, Dad . . ."

"School night, Craig. We've had this discussion."

"We're just going to the Burger Shack, grab a bite."

"We who?"

"Steve Kling and Brian Slayton and me."

I sat in the wicker chair next to his settee.

"Steve Kling got pulled over last Saturday night on Stone Valley Road," I said. "He was driving that ricer hot rod of his. Had it going about seventy in a forty-five zone."

"He told me. He said he got popped by Slim."

Harvey "Slim" Tackett was one of my two patrolmen on the Prosperity police force.

"I don't want you in the car when Steve Kling's driving. He's going to wrap himself around a telephone pole one of these nights, and I don't want you there when he does it."

"What if Brian drives?"

"What if I drive you guys over there and drop you off? I can pick you up after an hour or so. That should give you plenty of time to wolf down a burger and harass some of the Morgan girls."

"What are you going to do in Morgan?"

I unstrapped my duty belt and draped it over the back of the chair.

"I dunno. Wolf down a burger. Harass a couple of Morgan moms."

He tried to give me the Teenaged National Sneer, but he couldn't hold it for long before laughing.

"You'd do it, too."

"Bet your ass. Your homework's really done?"

"I finished it an hour ago. You can check if you want."

"Donna Asher's coming over for dinner tomorrow night. I don't want to spend half the supper hour discussing your missing work."

"Me neither," he said. "Not again. You know, it's kind of gross, you dating my teacher."

"Gross?"

"Well, yeah. How d'you think I feel, sitting in class, watching her lecture us on Steinbeck and shi . . ."

I shot him a warning look.

". . . Steinbeck and *stuff,* knowing that you've seen her . . . you know."

I knew.

"It can't be helped," I said. "The heart wants what it wants."

This time he really did roll his eyes, and

then he tossed one of the throw pillows at me. I caught it, one handed, and tossed it back at him.

"For real," he said. "Can I go?"

I thought it over.

"Brian's driving?"

"Yeah. He's really safe. He's scared to death of cracking up, on account of what happened to his brother."

I thought some more.

"You'll be back by nine," I said.

It wasn't a question.

"Nine-thirty at the latest."

"Nine at the latest. You can keep late hours in Morgan on the weekend, but not on a school night. Back by nine, or you can't go."

"Damn, you're strict."

"You eat with that mouth?"

"You kiss my teacher with *that* one?"

If he only knew.

Maybe he did. It was a small house.

"Okay," he said. "Nine o'clock."

"Take your cell phone. Just in case."

He nodded, just as my walkie-talkie chirped.

"Chief?" The voice was my other deputy, Stuart Marbury. I toggled the microphone.

"Yeah, Stu. I'm code seven to the house."

"Sorry to disturb your evening, Chief, but I

think you're pullin' some overtime tonight. I need you over to Donnie Clift's place."

"What's he done this time?"

"Gone and got himself killed. Looks like some kind of ritual thing. I think you better come."

"Ten-four." I closed the phone.

"Jesus," Craig said.

"Don't say a word to anyone," I warned him. "At least not until I know what's going on."

I didn't really need to tell him this. Craig knows the rules. It isn't always easy being a cop's kid, especially when your dad is the chief in a three-cop town.

I pulled myself out of the wicker chair and strapped the duty belt back on. I dug my money clip from my pocket, peeled a ten off the roll, and handed it to Craig.

"That should cover dinner," I told him. "Nine o'clock, you hear?"

CHAPTER FOUR

It took me about five minutes to drive to Donnie Clift's mobile home. Donnie had inherited a tract of fallow land from his mother, and had promptly planted his doublewide there on cinderblock piers, bricked in the foundation, and added a deck and a front porch to the trailer to make it seem a little more permanent. It looked pretty much the way you'd expect, like a cheap trailer with a bunch of shit nailed to it. He'd also installed an above-ground pool he'd bought from Morgan Salvage in the back. In all, it constituted his little estate.

Donnie didn't hold a regular job. He drifted from employer to employer when he needed a buck or two to augment the disability payments he received after falling off the roof of one of Kent Kramer's Carolina boxes under construction. His back had long since healed, but Donnie's home was paid for and his overhead was low. He had decided that the disability payments were all he needed. Once in a while he'd crave something special, like a new color television, and he'd take some part-time work helping one of the local farmers during harvest season, or pull a few shifts behind the counter at the Stop and Rob on the Morgan Highway when the owner, Gwen Tissot, wanted to run off to the beach for a few days for a shag dance contest.

The rest of the time he'd hang out in his trailer, or lie by his pool during the warm months, swatting at bluebottles and horseflies, drinking beer, and listening to a lot of right-wing talk radio. Donnie tended to believe what he heard on the radio. Some fast-talking loonie from the West Coast railed for a solid hour one day that taxation was theft, and that property owners weren't bound by local law to pay tax for stuff they'd already been taxed on when they bought it in the first place. Donnie took it to heart.

He sent a stamped, self-addressed envelope to the radio loonie, along with a generous donation, and received a detailed ten-page screed outlining why the county had no right to confiscate its share of Donnie's hard-earned disability pay once a year in return for all the services it provided.

Mine, for example.

Donnie had erected a large plywood sign in his front yard, and had painted on it much of the faulty reasoning in the ten-page diatribe, and declared that he would no longer pay property tax.

In doing so, he not only found himself in violation of the county ordinance on property tax, but also of the zoning ordinance for billboards.

The property tax delinquency was none of my affair. That was county business. The sign ordinance, though, was a Prosperity town issue, and I had been called on several occasions to remove the offending message. It was always back up two days later. Apparently, Donnie had an endless supply of plywood and latex paint.

I pulled into the gravel driveway leading up to Donnie Clift's pre-fab estate. Stu's cruiser was already there, its light flashing alternating reds and blues that reflected eerily off the metal flashing of Donnie's trailer. One of the fire department's rescue pickups had arrived, and its dash light was also rotating.

I reached through the window and cut off Stu's light as I walked by his cruiser, and did the same with the fire truck. No point in drawing a crowd.

Just as I walked up the steps to the front porch, another car rolled into the gravel drive, tossing up errant rocks as its rear end skidded slightly.

Slim Tackett shoved open the door of his Buick GS and climbed from the car. He was in his civvies, since he wasn't on duty, and looked like he had just come from a barn dance. He was wearing his finest red plaid flannel shirt, a new pair of jeans, and his snakeskin boots.

"What are you doing here, Slim?" I asked.

"Stu called me. Said Donnie's been murdered."

"We haven't established that yet. You're off duty. Go home."

"Don't worry, I won't clock in or nothin'. I just thought I ought to see how you go about this kind of thing. We haven't had a murder in Prosperity in ten years."

Both Slim and Stu had marveled at my stories of my beat days in Atlanta. I'd probably seen more crime there in three hours than Prosperity ran across in a year.

"All right then," I said. "Just don't tramp around in here. I don't want you fucking up the crime scene. Got it?"

"Ten-four, Chief."

He clambered up the steps behind me. The front door to the trailer was open, and a faint scent of corruption wafted through it as I hit the top step.

Stu was inside, with Wally Pons, from the fire department.

Donnie Clift lay on his back on the all-weather carpeted floor. A ginger-colored stream flowed across the floor from what was left of the top of his head, which looked as if someone had stuffed a cherry bomb in it. His arms were splayed out, so that he formed a fleshy cruciform on the floor. He was naked. There was a greenish-gray mass sitting on his chest.

"You checked his pulse?" I asked Stu.

"Oh, yeah. He's dead. Been dead for a day at least, from the smell."

"Okay. You can leave, Wally. We'll have no need for the Rescue Squad this evening."

Reluctantly, Wally turned and left the trailer. He stopped at the door and took one last lingering look at the body.

"And don't tell anyone what you saw here tonight," I told him, without looking back. "If I hear accurate descriptions of this scene, I'll come looking for you first."

"Yessir, Chief Wheeler."

Moments later, I heard the big Mopar engine in the truck roar to life, and the crackle of tires on gravel as he pulled out of the drive.

"Tell me about it," I said to Stu.

"Well, Huggie flagged me down at the grocery store parking lot about an hour ago. He told me that Donnie had put that damned sign back up, and he wanted me to drive by and pull it down again."

Fletcher "Huggie" Newton was the mayor of Prosperity. He signed my paycheck, though I really only reported to the Town Council.

"Was the door open when you arrived?"

"No. It was unlocked, though. I saw that Donnie's truck was parked behind the trailer, so I thought I'd let him know I was here to pull down the sign before I set about doing it. You know Donnie. If he's liquored up enough, he might think I'm some kind of tax-and-spend Democrat vandal, and come after me with his bird gun. Anyway, I knocked on the door a couple of times, but nobody came. I took a peek through the window and saw Donnie lying on the rug, so I came on in."

"Have you moved anything?"

"Not a hair," he said. "I only touched him to check his pulse."

"You call anyone besides Wally?"

"I put a call in to Billy Wade over in Morgan."

"Now why in hell did you do that?"

37

"Well, he's the coroner, Chief."

I didn't bother to remind Stu that Billy Wade was a tire salesman who had run for coroner because he knew that nobody would ever vote him into an office with any real responsibility. He was about as qualified to rule on cause of death as Donnie, but the damage was done. I pulled my walkie-talkie from my belt, and switched to the sheriff's department's frequency.

"Hey, Judd," the dispatcher said.

"Marlene, who's on rotation for death cases from the hospital this evening?"

"That'd be Neerjah Patel. Why, something happening down your way?"

"One of those evenings. Could you page Dr. Patel and have her come to this address?"

I recited Donnie's address, and signed off.

I took a good look around the room. Nothing was missing. The place was shabby, but clean for the most part. Donnie had not been a neglectful housekeeper. The stream of blood running across the floor from the top of his head was the only large flow I could see. There was no evidence of gunshot or stab wounds to the body.

"What in hell is that on his chest?" I asked.

"I wondered about that, too," Stu said. "Then I realized it's his brains."

38

I stepped back. It took me a moment, but I saw it. It looked as if someone had excised Donnie's brain from his skull and laid it on his chest.

"That's what I meant," Stu said. "Like it's a ritual or some sort of thing. You don't think we're dealin' with Satanists here, do you, Chief?"

"What makes you say that?"

"Well, they got him posed like he was crucified, and they took out his brain. I read once that some of those Mexican tribes a thousand years ago used to do human sacrifices, and they could rip your heart out and show it to you before you died. You think maybe they tore Donnie's brain out and showed it to him?"

I didn't say anything, mostly because I didn't want to make Stu feel like an idiot. Instead, I walked around and peered down the gaping hole in the top of Donnie's skull. Sure enough, it was practically empty.

"I don't get it," I said. "If you were going to take out someone's brain, how would you do it?"

Neither of the deputies answered.

"Come on. Stu? How would you?"

"I suppose you'd have to saw off the top of his skull, like in them Frankenstein movies," he said.

"That'd be my guess," I said. "But that's not what they did with Donnie here. It looks like someone took a blunt object and broke off the top of his head. Look at these jagged bone fragments."

"If it's all the same to you," Slim said, "I'd just as soon beg off."

"Thought you wanted to learn."

"This is just gross. Takin' people's brains out and layin' them on their chest. I figured it was just going to be some kind of shooting, like on TV."

"Things are seldom the way they're portrayed on television," I said absently. My mind was still occupied with the scene. Something was out of kilter.

"I've got it," I said. "I know what's wrong. Look at those skull shards lying on either side of his head. There's nothing inside his skull. They didn't break *in.* Those are exit wounds."

I stepped back and surveyed the scene again, more carefully this time. I had been working on an assumption to this point that had colored my perceptions. Now, I turned the scene around a hundred-eighty degrees, and looked at it from a different angle.

I walked over to the wall and flicked the overhead fluorescent lights on, and suddenly the trailer was almost as bright as daylight.

The lamps cast a greenish yellow glow on Donnie's body. I stood next to him and slowly turned around. It took me a minute, because of the dark wood they'd used on the interior of the trailer, but then I saw what I had expected. I looked up at the ceiling. There was an ochre smudge there, in the fiber ceiling tiles, right over the middle of Donnie's body.

"Well, I'll be damned," I said. "I've heard of it, but I never . . ."

"What?" Stu asked. "You figured it out, Chief?"

"Don't touch anything," I ordered, and walked back out to my car. I retrieved my halogen maglite, just as Billy Wade pulled up in the drive in his champagne Caddy Seville.

"I got here as fast as I could," he said, as he struggled to pull himself from behind the wheel. Billy was built like a balloon held upside down. His doughy pear shape was almost wedged underneath his steering wheel.

"Don't know if we'll need your services. Neerjah Patel is on her way to make the death declaration."

"Whose place is this?" he asked.

"Guy named Donnie Clift. Local character."

41

"Got any idea who killed him?"

"I think I know exactly who did it."

He followed me into the trailer, and looked down on Donnie's slowly bloating body. He lasted almost ten seconds before darting back out the door. I could hear him retching in the bushes at the side of Donnie's home.

"So much for a pristine crime scene," I said. "Doesn't matter anyway. You guys wanted a lesson? Let me show you something."

I flipped off the overhead light, and then the table lamp that provided the only other illumination for the room. Then I hit the switch on the maglite.

"Look at the walls." I swung the beam from the light around the room very slowly. "About every foot or so. You'll see a drop."

"What is that?" Stu asked.

"It's blood," I said. "All around the room. Projected in an even circular pattern, almost all at the same height."

"I don't get it," Stu said. "It's only about two, three feet off the floor."

"Which means that Donnie was sitting."

"You mean when they knocked off the top of his head?" Slim asked.

"Nobody knocked the top of his head off," I said. I walked back to the wall and flipped on the overhead lights.

"Look under the furniture. Don't touch anything you see. Just get down and look."

They divided the room into halves and started crawling around it, being very careful not to run across the now-dried stream of blood from Donnie's head.

"Holy shit," Stu said, as he shone his flashlight under an unmatched easy chair. "Here it is."

"Don't touch it," I said again.

I walked back out to my car and grabbed an evidence kit from the trunk. I pulled on a pair of latex gloves, working the elastic over my thick fingers, and returned to the trailer.

"Lean that chair back," I told Stu.

He did, and I reached under to retrieve the gun he'd found, careful to touch only the barrel. I stood and held it up in front of me.

"Murder weapon," Slim said.

"I don't think so. Can you identify it?"

"I can," Stu said. "Colt ten millimeter automatic."

"Right," I said. "This is a new model. Just came out last year."

I laid it on the counter, and pointed at the ceiling.

"Notice the stain on the ceiling?"

"Water leak?" Stu asked.

"Too dark," I said.

I walked to the door.

"You finished barfing out there, Billy?" I called. "I need to tell you how Donnie died."

In a moment, Billy Wade reappeared at the door. He was pale, except for his bloodshot, teary eyes.

"You know who killed him?" he asked.

"Yeah. He killed himself."

Nobody said a word for a moment. Then Slim snorted.

"Bullshit! Ain't no way Donnie could have yanked his brain out and laid it on his own chest before he died."

"In a way, he did," I said.

I stepped back a bit, and set the scene for them.

"You do a BAL on Donnie here, and I bet you'll find he was drunk as a skunk. He got all despondent, and he stripped down to his skin and sat in the middle of the floor here with that cannon, trying to decide whether it was a good day to die."

I knelt down next to Donnie's head and flashed the maglite at his right temple.

"Most people who kill themselves with a gun do it all wrong. They shoot themselves in the temple, blow away their frontal lobes, and forget what they did. They usually don't die, though, unless they use some little .22 piece of shit that splinters inside their skull and ricochets around some. Even then they might survive. Look here. It's small, but there's an entry wound on his scalp, just about ten millimeters in diameter. You can also see a ring of burned tissue around it.

"Before you take Donnie down to the morgue, you're going to want to bag his hands. Have the Medical Examiner do a paraffin test during the post on his right hand, and you'll find GSR."

"GSR?" Billy asked

"Gunshot residue. Donnie shot himself in the temple."

"I don't understand," Stu said. "What about the positioning? And how did his brain get placed on his chest?"

"I've heard stories about this happening, but I've never seen it in real life," I told them. "When Donnie shot himself, he was very anxious about it. He wanted to do it right, not miss. So, he pressed the barrel of the Colt very tightly against his temple. Now, with an automatic like this, there's no place for the gases to go when you pull the trigger, like in a revolver. There's only one way out, and that's through the end of the barrel. Remember, the barrel is pressed tight against Donnie's head, right?"

They all nodded. Even Billy, whose nausea appeared to be forgotten, replaced by a sort of grim fascination.

"Okay," I continued. "When Donnie pulled the trigger, the bullet exited the barrel first, and drilled a hole in his temple. Then came the explosive gases, which blew up his skull like a pig bladder. In an instant, the gas pressure blew off the top of his head. The reduction in pressure sucked his brain out the hole, and snapped it off at the stem. The escaping pressure blew Donnie's brain out the top of his head, like an air cannon. It flew up and hit the ceiling."

I pointed at the stain on the panel over Donnie's body.

"In the meantime, he threw out his arms in a startle response, and fell over backward. When his hand hit the floor, he let go of the gun, and it skittered under the chair over there. By now, the brain is on its way back down from the ceiling, and Donnie is lying on his back. The brain hits his chest and sticks there, held in place by the membranes that used to connect it with the skull. And that's how Donnie Clift died. No Satanists, no ritual murders. Just a dumb drunken fuck with too much firepower."

"I'll be damned," Billy said. "Now I have seen ever'thing."

Billy and I walked out onto the tiny porch as Dr. Patel's car stopped behind the Caddy, and she got out of the car. Slim and Stu stayed inside the trailer and replayed the suicide, pointing out the steps to each other over and over, as they tried to digest what had happened.

"Who's dead?" Neerjah said as she walked up to the steps.

"Hot damn, Dr. Patel!" Billy said. "You got to see this. Damnedest thing I ever heard of . . ."

CHAPTER FIVE

North Carolina had passed a Safe Schools Act about five years earlier, after one of the major newspapers in the state ran a series of stories about fights and bullies and drug traffic in a couple of big-city high schools following the Columbine massacre. Part of the Act required that each high school maintain a staff of what they called "school resource officers."

Some systems used sheriff's deputies, and some hired their own rent-a-cops. In Prosperity, coverage was provided by the police department. Since I was on duty during the day, and Slim and Stu rotated on and off days every two weeks, I'd usually assign one of them to do the school duty, while I handled the mundane patrol and administrative chores for the department.

After the incident between Seth Kramer and Vicente Ramirez, though, I thought it might be a good idea to hang out at the school for a few days, maybe take the edge off any potential aftershocks.

School duty was made up largely of sitting around in an office near the Guidance Department, and strolling around the school once every hour or so looking officious and mean. That, and drinking a lot of coffee.

I parked the new cruiser in front of the school and locked my Browning in the safe in the trunk. School resource officers were not allowed to carry firearms in the school.

The kids could bring all they wanted, as long as they didn't mind being expelled for them.

"Chief!" Elsie Carpenter said as I walked into the office. "Didn't know you were going to be here today."

"Decided I needed a change of pace," I said, as I headed for the coffee pot. "Vicente Ramirez comes back to school today, doesn't he?"

"His suspension was over yesterday, so he should be here. You aren't expecting any trouble, are you?"

"He promised me he'd stay away from Seth. Got any new magazines up here? Gets boring back in that office."

About halfway through the day, there was a rap on my door.

"Come in."

The door opened, and Donna Asher peeked inside.

"I heard you were here today," she said.

"Slumming. Decided to see how hard my deputies have to work. Come on in."

She slid in through the door and closed it. Then she walked around the desk and sat in my lap. We kissed a couple of times. She smelled like citrus and rosewater. It was nice.

"Teacher's pet," I said. "Not a bad gig."

"It's a preview. I'm looking forward to dinner tonight."

"Me too."

"And dessert."

"Me too."

She sealed the veiled promise with another kiss, and then slithered off my lap.

Donna was in her mid-thirties, about five years younger than me. She was shorter than I thought I liked my women, but you have to remain open-minded about these things. Her hair was long and wavy and very, very dark, almost black. There were only a couple of stray strands of silver invading the ebony cascade. I thought of them as character.

She had attended Appalachian State on a tennis scholarship, and still maintained the strong thighs and calves of a marathoner. The rest of her was pretty taut, too. She had considered a pro tennis career during college, but realized that all the middle school students would eat her shorts, so she settled on teaching instead.

She sat on the edge of my desk. Her skirt rode up her thighs. I don't think she was aware of it, but I was.

More preview.

"Craig tells me he has a hard time concentrating in your class," I said.

"Oh? Why's that?"

"He can't seem to banish the mental image of us doing the nasty."

She blushed.

"Oh."

"Is that a problem?"

She shook her head.

"Occupational hazard. After a while, as a teacher, you get used to it. I'm young yet, and I'm still in good shape, and these high school boys bone up in a stiff breeze. Three-quarters of the boys in my classes sit there mentally undressing me."

"And the rest?"

"They're mentally undressing the other boys."

"Oh," I said. "Then I should count my blessings with Craig."

"We've been discreet. Craig's a bright kid, with an active imagination. It just happens he may have a little more to work with when it comes to fantasy, in my case, but I don't see him as being any more distracted than the rest of the boys. If it's a problem, though . . ."

"He'll adjust," I said. "If not, we'll just transfer him to another English teacher. Someone old and crabby."

She leaned over and kissed me again, and then hopped off the desk.

"I'm on planning period. Got lesson plans to write. I'll see you around six, though. Can I bring anything?"

"A toothbrush," I said.

The principal at Prosperity Glen dropped by the Resource Office about an hour later. I was leaning back in my chair, reading a pulp novel I'd picked up during lunch.

His name was Hart Compton. He was an okay guy, but we weren't close friends. For one thing, he was a Democrat, and the entire Town Council — my employers — were all Republicans. Hart had made a couple of futile runs at the Council. Despite the prevailing political winds in Bliss County, he'd probably make one or two more before giving up.

"Busy?" he asked, nodding at the book.

"Just catching up on modern detecting methods. What's going on?"

"Checking in. I was at a meeting when you arrived this morning."

"You check in with the Resource Officer every day?"

"Only when he's also the Chief."

"Do tell?"

"You being here on the same day that Vicente Ramirez returns from suspension piqued my curiosity."

"Coincidence," I said. "Nothing to worry about. Vicente and I came to an agreement. Same for Seth."

"I was thinking about . . . larger issues."

I put the book down on the desk.

"Anything I should know about?"

He nodded.

"I've caught an undercurrent over the last month or so. Nothing overt, you understand, but it's there. You run a school for a few years, and you get attuned to this sort of thing. There's a tension in the hallways."

"Racial tension?"

"Seems that way. Things are polarizing here at the school. I'm seeing more bands of the Hispanic kids walking around, all in groups. It can be a little intimidating. So, the white kids start hanging in groups."

"Safety in numbers," I said.

"That's it. The wealthier kids, you know, the new kids here in Prosperity, seem to have arrived with some preconceived notions. We don't have a lot of black kids — less than twenty in the whole school — but we have a healthy population of Latinos."

"Mexicans. Let's call 'em what they are."

"Only in here, behind the closed door," he said. "Political correctness, you understand. Anyway, the kids that've spilled over from Parker County are almost all from wealthy families. In this state, that means conservative, with a capital *K*. They think the Mexican kids are put here mostly to serve the white kids' needs. Probably because so many of the Mexican kids' parents work for their parents. We like to think we have a classless society, but in reality there's a pecking order. For the newcomers, our Mexican kids are the peckees."

"Does that make the rich white kids the peckers?"

He chuckled.

"You didn't hear me say that, Chief. Let's just say there's some tension. That fight the other day, between Seth Kramer and Vicente Ramirez, was only a symptom. I suspect there's a lot of covert harassment going on in the halls that we don't see, surreptitious

54

stuff that really gets under the Mexican kids' skins."

I drummed my fingers on the book I'd placed on the desktop.

"Vicente Ramirez says he was confronted by a group of white kids in the parking lot," I said. "Seth Kramer was the leader."

"Seth's a BMOC. A lot of the kids look up to him. Wherever he goes, there's a crowd."

"Hangers-on."

"It's warm in the spotlight. Lots of kids who don't get attention enjoy being in his company."

"You're saying that just because he wasn't alone when he accosted Vicente, doesn't mean Vicente was jumped."

"I heard the same story, Chief. You should know that there's been some bad blood between Vicente and Seth for a while now."

"It wasn't just over this girl?"

"I heard that one too. The girl may have been incidental. Vicente is a talented baseball player. He has a wicked curve ball and a decent slider for his age."

"I hear he swings a mean tire iron, too."

"Seth is a three-letter man. Want to guess which position he plays on the diamond?"

"This can't be just about sports," I said.

"For some of these kids, everything is just

about sports. Seth Kramer can go anywhere he wants for college. His dad can write the tuition check for Duke and never bat an eye. The only way Vicente goes to college is on a scholarship. On the other hand, Seth likes being adored. If Vicente's on the mound, Seth's on the bench."

"There are other positions."

"Not for Seth. For him, there's quarterback, starting pitcher, and power forward. Vicente threatens him. Seth found an excuse to threaten back."

"And was surprised when Vicente didn't back off."

"Precisely."

"Which means that Seth lost face."

"You're catching on."

"I'll bet that ratcheted up the tension a little, didn't it?"

He smiled.

"Nice to have you here today, Chief," he said. "I wouldn't mind seeing you here on a regular basis."

CHAPTER SIX

Craig sat on the front porch picking out a tune on an unplugged Strat copy electric guitar when I drove up that afternoon. As I got out of the car, I could hear the faint, tinny twanging of the muted steel strings.

"Homework's done?" I asked, as I walked up the steps.

"Didn't have any."

I arched an eyebrow at him.

"Really!" he said. "On account of the football game Friday night. There was a pep rally at the football field after school, and they decided to make it a no-homework day."

"Shouldn't you be at the field, then?"

"What? Hang out with a bunch of preppie a-holes and scream and yell to support the local blood sport? No thanks. Not my scene."

"Blood sport? Football?"

"What would you call it?"

"Well, it's not exactly gladiators in the arena."

"Pretty close to it. What's for dinner?"

"Donna's coming over," I said, as I loosened my duty belt. "Thought I'd grill some ribeyes and corn, bake some potatoes."

"That's cool. Are you two going out after dinner?"

"Thought we'd stay in."

"All night?"

I hung the duty belt on the back of the chair, and sat, stretching my legs out.

"Maybe. Is that a problem?"

"Besides the fact that it's probably scarring me for life? Not at all."

"You'll survive."

I sat and watched the breeze kick the fallen leaves around on the drive, while Craig ran through the opening sequence of *Stairway to Heaven* over and over, making a different mistake every time.

"Tough riff," I said.

"I'll get it."

"I talked with Principal Compton today."

"About me?"

"Why? Something I ought to know?"

He pushed his hair away from his eyes. "Hey, I'm the Chief's kid. If I screw up, you'll read about it on the front page of the *Ledger-Telegraph*."

"I just consider that one of the perks of the job."

"What are the others?"

"That pretty much covers it. Mr. Compton says there's been a lot of tension at the school lately, between the Mexican kids and the whites."

"Uh-huh," Craig said, and hit a clinker.

"You hear anything about any gang activity at the school?"

"Gangs? You mean like the Bloods and the Crips?"

"Yeah."

"No, there's none of that stuff here, at least not yet. I hear things about that stuff up in Parker County, but not here."

"There are a lot of kids at Prosperity Glen who were in Parker last year."

He chuckled.

"Yeah, and I'll just bet they were Bloods up there. The gangs are well known for their khakis and Topsiders. No, I don't hear much about gangs here, yet. Of course, if I did I might not tell you."

"Why's that?"

He placed the guitar back in a stand next to his chair.

"Because I'm seventeen, and I have to go to that school. I'm already singled out because you're the Chief of Police. All I need right now is to be labeled a snitch."

He picked up the guitar and walked into the house, allowing the screen door to slam behind him.

I tried to remember back when I was twenty, and why I had wanted to be a father.

Craig left with some friends to go to a movie right after dinner. Donna and I seized the opportunity.

Afterward, we lay next to each other on the bed and let the ceiling fan dry the sweat off our bodies. The light from the bathroom played off her muscular frame and baseball-sized breasts as they rose and fell rhythmically with her gasps. Within a minute, the gasps subsided, replaced with normal breathing. She was a consummate athlete — compact, flexible, and oh-so-energetic.

"The things I do to get a speeding ticket fixed," she said, after basking in the afterglow for a few minutes.

She rolled on her side, facing me, and draped one damp arm across my chest.

"Are you staying?" I asked.

"Do you want me to?"

"Every time."

"I have a change of clothes in the trunk of my car. I have everything I need. I wouldn't

have to go back home before work tomorrow."

"I hear a lot of silent *buts*."

"Just tentative ones. What about Craig?"

"Let him get his own girl," I said.

"You know what I mean."

I did.

"If he were eight or ten, I'd worry," I said.
"He knows how things work, though."

"So do I, I'm afraid. He's my student,
Judd. It isn't easy for him."

I didn't say anything.

"Hasn't been easy for you, either, has it?"
she asked.

"You know."

"You don't talk about it much, though."

"There isn't much to talk about. I talked
about it for two years afterward, with Dr.
Kronenfeld. Finally got talked out. Came to
the conclusion that there are things you'll
never be able to explain, and sometimes all
you can do is accept them and move on."

"So you don't talk about it. About her."

"Talking about it isn't moving on. She
wouldn't want me to stagnate because of
her. We discussed it."

"You didn't."

"Yeah, we did. We had long conversations
about it. *What would you do if . . . ?* That
sort of thing. She asked me once whether

61

I'd get married again if anything happened to her. I told her I wouldn't. It wouldn't be fair, to make another person live their life being compared with her, to spend a lifetime comparing one marriage with another."

"And now?"

I thought for a moment, mostly about changing the subject.

"I try not to make comparisons," I said, finally.

She snuggled even closer, if that was possible.

"Good."

"You aren't bothered by that?"

"Lord, no," she said. "Who'd want to marry a cop? Now shut up and let me sleep."

CHAPTER SEVEN

A couple of kids who'd skipped school to walk down in the woods and smoke a joint ran across Gitana Camarena's body lying next to Six Mile Creek. She had been dead for a while.

Within an hour, we had sealed the area, and closed the section of the Morgan Highway appending the creek to through traffic. Both of the Prosperity police cruisers sat by the side of the road, their lights flashing in near-unison with that of the ambulance that had been summoned to remove the body to the medical examiner's office in Morgan.

As it happened, Neerjah Patel was on rotation again with the Sheriff's Department. Since Prosperity had such a small police force, and a limited operating budget, we had a reciprocal agreement to share services with the sheriff in Morgan, who handled most investigations out in the county.

Neerjah knelt next to the body, and inserted a long needle thermometer into the right side.

"She's been dead at least a day and a half," she announced. She reached out and gently grasped each side of the girl's head.

"We have rigor, but I can move her head readily. I can feel bones grating. I'd say cause of death was a broken neck, but we'll know more following the post in Morgan."

Neerjah and I were alone on the east bank of Six Mile Creek with the body. I had taken care to keep everyone else back up at the road, in an effort to avoid contaminating the scene. The sheriff was sending a CSI team in from Morgan. I could hear their siren in the distance.

A small crowd had begun to gather at the roped-off area on the Morgan Highway. I keyed my walkie-talkie.

"Slim, I want those people as far away as you can get them," I said.

"Ten-four."

"This one didn't kill herself, Judd," Neerjah said. "And I'd say she wasn't killed here."

"That was my thought. Someone dumped her here, hoping she wouldn't be found for a while."

"Looks like she was a pretty girl. Any idea who she is?"

"No. We haven't found any identification in the area. She looks Hispanic, which might make things even more difficult. If she's illegal, we won't have much to go on. We'll just have to wait for a missing persons report to match up with her."

"Shouldn't take long. Everybody in town will know we found a body by the end of the day. You'll probably be flooded with calls from anxious parents wondering whether she's their daughter."

The wail of the siren ended abruptly as the crime scene guys pulled to a stop up on the highway.

Moments later, I heard two of them picking their way down through the trees toward our position. I turned and waved.

I recognized the man. He was a former deputy named Clark Ulrich. I'd never seen the woman before.

"Clark," I said, extending my hand as he walked up.

"Judd. Good to see you, except for the circumstances."

He nodded toward his partner.

"Sharon Counts," he said. "Chief Wheeler."

I shook her hand. She was plain and thin and very serious-looking. Her hair was pulled back in a severe bun, and she wore very little makeup. I could make out the lines on her forehead and under her eyes. I could recall seeing pictures of Okies during the Dustbowl days who looked a lot like her.

"So, what do we have here?" Clark asked.

Neerjah took over.

"Teenaged Hispanic female. Time of death probably sometime during the last forty-eight hours. Hard to say for certain because of exposure, but rigor has set in. Looks like a fracture of the second or third cervical vertebra. She was probably killed somewhere else, and dumped. We'll depend on you guys to confirm that."

"Okay. If you and Chief Wheeler can step off about thirty or forty feet, we'll do our magic, and then you can transport the body."

Neerjah and I watched for an hour as they photographed, marked, and drafted the entire scene. They bagged and logged a number of articles — mostly trash, as far as I could tell from a distance, but you never know what will turn into a clue down the road. Finally, they roped off a perimeter about sixty feet across, by wrapping yellow crime scene tape around various trees.

It gave me a lot of time for a little bit of self-torture, as I surveyed the scene. The very path we had scrambled down from the highway had a history. I could recall the night it had been carved from the living forest. For a long time after, it had been a red clay scar leading from the road to the creek, a freakish eight-foot wide swath of naked soil on which nothing would grow. I don't know when it happened, but slowly the flora had finally returned. The gash of dirt was closing from the sides. Fall leaves of every hue had covered the mud and the tire tracks. For the casual observer, it looked for all the world like any other forest path.

I saw it for what it was — the dividing line between one life and another.

"We think we got everything," Clark said, as they trudged back up the hill to us. I willed myself back into the present and turned to face him. "It would be nice if you could see to it that nobody gets inside that perimeter, though. We might need to come back at some point."

"I can't promise," I told him. "We only have three officers in this town, you know. We can keep an eye on the area during patrol."

"Probably about all I can ask for. You can remove the body now."

Neerjah called for the ambulance personnel to come down with a stretcher, since the hill was way too steep and uneven for a gurney. Together, the four of us rolled the body onto the stretcher and each took one corner for the trek back up the hill.

Once they had the body in the ambulance, Neerjah signed off on the transport, and let them go.

"I'll give all the information I have to the ME," she told me. "You should hear something in a day or so. If you put a call in to Billy Wade, you might be able to speed things up a bit."

"Can you ask the ME to put a priority on identification?"

"Goes without saying. I want to know who that little cutie was as much as you do. Her family may be out there worried sick."

She climbed back into her car and drove off toward Morgan.

I keyed my radio.

"Slim, Stu, go ahead and open up the highway. We're finished here."

I climbed into the new cruiser, and headed back to the barn. The paperwork on this one was going to be back-breaking.

CHAPTER EIGHT

Two things happened very quickly.

First, the press caught wind of the murder and decided they saw an angle for a story on the front page, above the fold.

Second, I found out who the dead girl on the bank of Six Mile Creek was.

I had been back in my office for about fifteen minutes when a kid named Cory True walked in. Cory had graduated from the journalism school at Chapel Hill about fifteen minutes earlier, and the Morgan *Ledger-Telegraph* was his first gig out of school. He didn't look much older than Craig.

"Chief Wheeler?" he asked as he walked into my office. "Got a minute?"

"Come on in, Cory." I pointed toward a chair. He sat.

"Seems you've had an interesting day," he said, his pad ready to write.

"Not so much out of the ordinary. Started

out pretty much like usual. Two eggs, bacon, toast . . ."

"I'm talking about the murder."

"I know, Cory. I know."

I tried to be patient with Cory. He had a lot to learn, but he wasn't going to learn it if I shut him down every chance I got.

"Have you identified the body?"

"No. And before you go shouting murder, you should know that the autopsy hasn't even started. We don't know that she was killed intentionally."

"So it was a girl?"

I winced. I had forgotten that we hadn't released any specific information about the victim.

"A female. Don't know her age or name. No identification on or around her."

"Any idea how long she was there before you found her?"

"Not really. Maybe a couple of days."

"Any leads?"

I just stared at him. I hoped the stare was enough for him to figure out that if I had any leads, I sure as hell wouldn't be sitting in my office jawing with him.

"Okay," he said. "No leads at this time. Tell me, Chief, how long has it been since the last murder in Prosperity?"

"About ten years. I wasn't living here

then. As I recall, though, it involved a drunken blowout between a husband and wife who lived over off Old Village Road. The husband pulled five to fifteen for voluntary manslaughter. Before that, I have no idea. A long time."

"Murder comes to peaceful little town," Cory said, as if trying out headlines.

"Not murder," I cautioned again. "Not yet, at least."

"Could this have been anticipated?"

"What?"

"As the population in Prosperity and Bliss County increased. Should we have anticipated an increase in violent crime?"

"Your reasoning being, I presume, that higher density leads to increased criminality."

"Oh, that's good," he said, scribbling.

"Hold your horses. First of all, that only applies to extremely high population densities, on the order of one person per ninety square feet. Read your social anthropology, Edward Hall in particular. Now, Prosperity has a town charter specifying that residential areas be confined to lots of no less than one acre in size. Last time I looked, an acre was around forty-three thousand square feet. Not exactly a recipe for breakdown of the social contract, kid."

"What about the problems of racial and economic inequality, especially between the whites and Hispanics?"

"What about it? Are you trying to stir something up, Cory? There is no reason to believe this death was racially linked. Nor, at this point, do we know it to be murder. If you go around tossing out words like *racial inequality,* we could have a real problem on our hands. So, in order to at least partially satisfy you, here's the best dope available at this time.

"One: We have discovered a body along Six Mile Creek. Two: We don't know who she is. Three: The ME will complete a post-mortem in the next couple of days and release any pertinent data. Four: I have nothing further to add to One, Two, or Three. I'll keep you posted."

"Who's doing the autopsy?"

"Ask Billy Wade. He's the coroner. Thanks for dropping by, Cory."

"Just a couple more ques . . ."

"Thanks for dropping by, Cory," I said, more firmly this time.

I risked pissing off a member of the Fourth Estate, but when it came to things like felony behavior, the Council preferred that Prosperity suffer as little exposure as possible.

About an hour later, Sherry poked her head into my office.

"Do you have a minute, Chief?"

I had just finishing the report on the recovery of the girl's body, and my eyes were bleary from looking at the computer screen.

"What is it?"

"I have some people in the outer office. They . . . they think they might know who that girl was."

"Show them in."

She ushered a couple into the office. The man was in his early forties, short, brown, and dark-eyed. His chocolate-colored hair was cropped close to his scalp. His hands were rugged, with discolored nails. I could see the calluses on his palms as he removed his baseball cap.

The woman, slightly shorter, also appeared to be in her forties. She was dressed in jeans and a flannel shirt, with worn sneakers. Her hair was pulled back and gathered with a rubber band.

Their eyes harbored a fear I could read from across the room. I had seen the look before, in my shaving mirror. I pushed that memory back and stood to greet them.

"I'm Chief Wheeler. Please, have a seat."

"*Gracias,*" the man said. He said something to the woman, and they took the seats directly across from my desk. The woman cast her eyes toward the floor. The man struggled to meet my gaze.

"My name is Roberto Camarena," he said, in halting English. "This is my . . . *mi esposa.*"

"Wife," I said.

"Thank you. My wife, Alfonsa Reyes. I do not wish to trouble you, Chief, but we have heard that you found a body today."

"That's right. The medical examiner is doing an autopsy."

He looked at me the way a cat looks at a doorknob.

"A doctor in Morgan is examining the body, to figure out how she died."

Roberto Camarena translated what I had said. His wife stiffened, and then shuddered slightly.

"This body," Camarena said, "was she a teenager?"

"I can't say. She was young."

"And was she . . ." he struggled for the word.

"She was Hispanic."

He nodded, and translated again for his

wife. She seemed to deflate a little next to him. I saw her eyes tear up.

Camarena put one gnarled arm around her shoulders to comfort her. I had a feeling she was going to need a lot of comforting.

"Is someone missing?" I asked.

"*Sí*. Our daughter, Gitana. She is a student at the high school."

"Just one moment." I pulled up the missing persons form on the computer. "I need to get some information from you. You say her name was Gitana?"

He spelled it out for me.

"She is sixteen, but she looks older," he said. "She went out with a friend three days ago. She never came home."

"Can you describe her?"

He got that confused look again.

"What does she look like?"

"She is about my height. She is pretty, with long hair."

"How long?"

"Half the way down her back."

"Any identifying marks? Scars, broken bones, unusual birthmarks?"

Camarena talked briefly with his wife. She nodded, and said something to him.

"She has a tattoo. She got it on a trip to the beach. We didn't know about it until later, and by then it was too late. It's on her right . . ." He thought about it for a second, and pointed toward his back.

"Her right shoulder?" I asked.

"*Sí.* It is a rose."

I made some notes.

"Date of birth?"

He told me. She would turn seventeen in a month.

"Do you know what she was wearing when she left three days ago?"

"No. She left a note, saying she was going to the city with her friend Anita. We called Anita, who told us they did go, but only stayed for a few hours, and then came back. Alfonsa and I were at work at the time. We did not see her."

I filled in a few blanks on the form, and then slid the keyboard aside.

"I'm sorry your daughter has gone missing, but I do have a question. You say she's been away for three days, but you're just filing a report now. Why did you wait so long?"

Camarena translated for his wife. They looked at each other for a long moment. Camarena looked back at me. He didn't say a word.

"You're illegal?" I asked.

They both looked at the floor.

"I'd like you to know something and I

hope you can help spread the word about this. The police department isn't involved with the Immigration Services or Homeland Security, at least not directly. Nobody should be afraid to come here just because they're undocumented."

"We are sorry," Camarena said. "We hear things."

"I know you do. That's why I'm hoping you'll help spread the word. Do you have any pictures of your daughter?"

Camarena reached into his back pocket and pulled out his wallet. He opened it and showed me a picture in a plastic sleeve.

"Her high school picture, from last year," he explained.

The body on Six Mile Creek had probably lain there for up to two days. Amazing things happen in a body after death, including some very disfiguring bloating. In addition, lividity around the victim's face had made half her features uncertain.

There was something about the picture, though, that looked familiar.

"May I have that?" I said. "I just need to copy it."

He pulled it delicately from the sleeve, as if it were a leaf, and handed it to me across the desk. I arranged for Sherry to copy it, and then returned to my seat.

"I need both of you to come to Morgan with me," I said. "I'd like to think that the body we found today isn't your daughter. On the other hand, we need to rule out every possibility. Is it all right to go there now?"

Camarena nodded readily, even before he spoke with his wife.

The Bliss County Morgue isn't listed in the local telephone book, because it really doesn't exist as a separate entity. While Prosperity is a relatively affluent community, at least since the mass migration from Parker started, the rest of the county is largely rural and poor. The tax base is skimpy at best, and some services have to be combined in order to be provided at all.

A small wing in the basement of the Bliss Regional Hospital had been set aside for use by the medical examiners, to conduct autopsies. A room on the fifth floor constituted the Coroner's Office, where he conducted his inquiries into untimely and messy death.

Likewise, while the North Carolina Chief Medical Examiner is required to be a forensic pathologist by training, county MEs only have to be a licensed physician. In fact, if there is no actively licensed physician in a county, the role of ME can be filled by the locally elected coroner.

I'd hate to think what might become of Bliss County if Billy Wade also served as a medical examiner. Billy's a nice guy, but he's not real sure where his own butt is, and I sure wouldn't like to depend on him to find a cause of death in a young girl like the one we found along Six Mile Creek.

I held the front door of the Regional Hospital open for Roberto Camarena and Alfonsa Reyes, and showed them to the elevator to the basement. With each step, their bodies seemed to gain ten pounds. They reminded me of a guy I'd once seen being shuffled down the last mile to the gas chamber. Their faces betrayed feelings of both awe and terror.

We reached the morgue, and I rang the bell.

"It's Chief Wheeler, from Prosperity," I said into the speaker. "I have a couple here who might be able to ID that body we found earlier today."

The door swung open, and I gestured to my charges to walk through. We faced an empty desk, with several chairs set up along the opposite wall on each side of the door. After a moment, a young woman walked into the room from another door to the side of the desk.

"Chief, I'm Carla Powers, the Acting Medical Examiner," she said, extending her hand.

I introduced Gitana's parents, and explained how they had come to me at the police department in Prosperity.

"We haven't started the autopsy yet," she said, after asking us to take a seat. "My medical assistant has just finished prepping the body. Do they speak English?"

"Mr. Camarena does," I said.

She turned to Mr. Camarena.

"Sir, the body Chief Wheeler sent here today was in the woods for as much as forty-eight hours before it was found. It had already begun to undergo decay. I can't show you the body itself, until I complete the autopsy. We do take pictures during the preparation process, for use in identifying unknown victims. I'm going to ask you to come over to the desk with me so I can show you the picture. Are you ready?"

Camarena repeated what Dr. Powers had said to his wife, and she nodded, tentatively. They stood, and followed her to the desk, where she used the mouse to select a picture from a file in her computer.

"Before I show you this, I need you to understand something. It may be difficult to recognize the person in the picture. She was apparently moved after death, and she was found lying on her side. One side of her face is somewhat swollen. The blood pooled on that side, so she will look bruised. We don't know whether there are any injuries that caused the bruising, and we won't know until we examine her. Do you understand?"

They both nodded, after Camarena translated for Alfonsa.

She clicked the mouse, and turned the monitor toward them.

Alfonsa Reyes gazed at the picture for a moment, and then let out a small cry. She buried her face in her husband's chest. He tried to hold her close as she sobbed, even as his own eyes brimmed with tears.

He nodded once.

"It is Gitana," he said. "I wasn't certain at first, but it is her."

"Dr. Powers, did you find a tattoo on the right shoulder while preparing the body for post?" I asked.

"A rose," she answered.

"Okay. That does it, I guess."

I passed her a copy of the missing persons report I'd written up at the department, and a copy of the picture from Camarena's wallet.

"Here's the information I have available. You'll have trouble finding medical records on her."

"Illegal?"

I nodded.

"I've seen a lot of those lately," she said. "I'll try to get this post done today or tomorrow. I'll get you the results as quickly as I can."

She turned to Camarena and Alfonsa.

"I am very sorry for your loss. I'll do my best to find any clues I can that will help Chief Wheeler's investigation. If someone killed your little girl, we'll do whatever we can to find them."

She closed the picture file on the computer and stood.

"If you'll excuse me, I have to get to work."

She left me with Gitana's parents. Alfonsa was still sobbing, and saying things I didn't understand. I had heard the inflection before, though, far too many times. Their entire life had just come to a sudden and horrifying stop. They would spend the rest of their time on earth in recovery.

All in all, it had been a really shitty day.

CHAPTER NINE

I waited in Hart Compton's office at Prosperity Glen High School, while he attended to some problem or other down a distant hallway. I didn't know what it was, and I didn't care. Slim was working the high school that day. I figured he could handle it if things got nasty.

Compton walked into the office after I'd waited for about ten minutes.

"Chief," he said. "Twice in one week. Must be some kind of record."

"I'm going to need your help."

He sat behind his desk and pulled out a legal pad.

"Taking notes?" I asked.

"All the time. I'm over fifty now, and I can't remember everything as well as I used to. If I don't take notes, things will just start slipping away."

"This won't. We identified that body your two students found along Six Mile Creek.

She was another one of your students, a girl named Gitana Camarena."

He stopped writing.

"Gypsy," he said.

"Her nickname?"

"*Gitana* was a bit of a mouthful for some of the students. She decided to call herself something easy, and Gitana means *gypsy* in Spanish. Jesus. What happened to her?"

"We're not totally certain yet, but it looks like someone snapped her neck and then dumped her along the creek."

Compton leaned his chair back. He ran a hand across his forehead.

"Damn, Chief. This is the first student I've lost at this school. This is terrible. You'll want to see her records, I guess."

"That'll be part of it. What kind of student was she?"

"Fair to middling. She wasn't in line for a Morehead Scholarship, but she wasn't failing, either. As I recall, she spoke reasonably good English, but she wasn't — how should I put it? — exceptionally studious."

"Was she popular?"

"How do you mean?"

"Did a lot of students like her?"

He drummed on his desktop with his pen as he studied me carefully.

"You're looking at a student for this?"

"I'm looking at anything that can give me a clue as to how this girl wound up lying in the mud next to Six Mile Creek with her head twisted around a couple of times. If she was popular with the other students, it means running down a lot more loose ends."

He tapped the pen a few more times. If he kept it up, I was probably going to feed it to him.

"Maybe I should assemble her teachers. I really didn't know Gypsy all that well. She wasn't a discipline problem, so we had very little official contact."

"How much *un*official contact did you have?"

"What are you asking?"

"You knew her nickname, and you were aware of her scholarly acumen, but you had very little official contact. You had to become aware of her somehow."

"I'm not sure I like your insinuation, Chief," he said.

His face was reddening quickly.

At least he had stopped tapping the damn pen.

"How quickly can you get her teachers together? As you may or may not be aware, we're most likely to figure out who killed this girl in the first day or so. After that, it gets more and more difficult."

I had known Compton for several years. I could always tell when he was pissed off, because he became more officious and his voice became clipped.

"School ended a half hour ago," he said. "They should all still be here. I'll call them up to the conference room."

"Thanks," I said. "Do me a favor. Don't tell them why they're being called in."

Ten minutes later, Gypsy Camarena's four teachers sat around the oak-veneered conference table off the main office.

Donna Asher was among them. I hated dropping the news on her like this, but I couldn't see any alternative.

Prosperity Glen High School ran on a block schedule system, which meant that each student had only four classes a day. Besides having Donna for English, Gypsy had been scheduled for History with a hyperthyroid man in his mid-twenties named Henry Scragg, Algebra with a rotund middle-aged woman named Brenda Rollings, and Earth Science with a fellow I knew from Craig's soccer days, named Mike Thurman. Thurman had been a coach for the Prosperity Youth Soccer program. I vaguely recalled that he was also one of the football coaches for the high school.

"Thank you for staying a little later this afternoon," I said, trying not to look too longingly at Donna. "I'm afraid I have some bad news. As you've probably heard, a couple of your students found a body down by Six Mile Creek this morning. We've completed the first stage of the investigation process. We've identified the body as that of Gitana Camarena."

All four registered various degrees of shock and dismay. Brenda Rollings, in particular, gasped and began crying immediately. Donna tried to comfort her, even as she worked to hold back her own tears. She stared at me, and I couldn't tell whether it was in amazement or rage for keeping her in the dark.

Mike Thurman leaned forward, his hands clasped, and said, very softly, "Oh, my God. Gypsy."

Henry Scragg tried to maintain a stiff upper lip, but I could see it quivering. He put his hand to his face, as if to ward off a headache. I saw him furtively wipe away a tear.

"I'm sorry to drop this on you without much warning," I said. "Fact is, we've been busy all day. I just returned from taking Gypsy's parents to identify the body. I only informed Mr. Compton about fifteen minutes ago. I was hoping that, as her teachers, you could fill in some of the blanks regarding Ms. Camarena's life here at school."

Brenda Rollings was still sobbing. Donna tried to hold on to her the way a rodeo rider grapples with a bucking longhorn.

"She was a beautiful girl," Henry Scragg said. "So many of the Mexican girls have that squashed Inca facial structure, but she was genuinely gorgeous. I'd imagine her family lines contained a great number of the Castilian invaders."

I glanced over at Compton. He shrugged. I guess he was used to strange things coming from Scragg's mouth.

"She was a challenging student," Thurman said. "She had the ability to do extremely well, but she never seemed to put forward the effort. Wouldn't you say?"

He directed this to the other teachers. Brenda Rollings apparently had reached an intermission in her crying jag, and she nodded, as she dabbed at her eyes with the tissue Donna had handed her.

"I liked Gypsy," she said, each word broken off by a half-sob. "She always said hello to me when she came into class. I do wish she had applied herself a bit more, but I don't suppose it matters much now, does it?"

"I guess it's fair to say that she wasn't a model student?" I asked.

"She wasn't a behavior problem," Donna said.

"No," Henry Scragg added. "Not at all. She usually sat quietly in class. She was never a disturbance, but neither did she participate much."

I pulled out a chair and sat at the table.

"Look," I said. "I'm not really interested in eulogizing Gypsy Camarena right now. What I really need to know is who she hung with. Who were her close friends? Who did she trust?"

They all looked at each other, and then back at me.

"I'm sorry," Thurman said. "I only really saw her for a couple of hours a day, and my class is pretty structured. She may have been friendly with one or two of the students there, but beyond that I really don't know who she associated with."

"Well," Donna said. "There was the Ramirez boy."

"Vicente?" I asked.

"Yes. I saw her sitting with him at lunch from time to time."

"Did she sit with anyone in particular during lunch most of the time?"

"Not that I can recall," Donna said. "But

I really didn't monitor her lunch hour very often, except when another teacher was out sick. It conflicted with my planning period."

Henry Scragg raised his hand.

"Yes," I said. "You really don't have to raise your hand to speak, Mr. Scragg."

"Sorry." His voice was tremulous and timid. "I saw her sitting with Vicente Ramirez. But I also saw her with some of the other Hispanic kids. They like to sit together, because they're allowed to speak their own language at lunch."

"Could you give me any names?"

"Oh, I don't know," he said. "There are so many."

"I do recall that she was friendly with Anita Velez," Donna said. "Their lockers were just down the hall from my classroom. I saw them talking there often. Excuse me, Judd, but do you believe that one of our students might have killed Gypsy?"

I noted that she had called me by name. I let it ride. I wasn't certain how much the other teachers knew about us.

Probably everything. It's a small town. People like to talk.

"I don't have any suspects at this time," I said. "That's how investigations work. You start asking questions, and you wait for patterns to emerge. You say the girl's name was

Anita Velez?"

"That's right."

"The girl's parents mentioned a friend named Anita. Mr. Compton, could you get me some information on her? Home address, telephone number, that sort of thing?"

"I'll see what I can do," he said.

"Anyone else you can think of that Gypsy might have associated with?" I asked the group.

Slowly, one by one, they each shook their heads.

"Okay. If you do think of someone, just call me at the station. If I'm not there, leave a message with Sherry or one of the other patrolmen. We'll take it from there. Also, once word gets out that Gypsy's dead, you're likely to hear a lot of whispering about her in the halls. Anything you overhear — no matter how unlikely it seems — I'd appreciate it if you'd pass it along. This is a murder investigation. I can use all the help I can get. Don't worry whether it might get someone into trouble. If the person is innocent, we'll find out. For the time being, though, I need to know everything you hear."

I thanked them for their time, and remained seated as they filed out of the room. Donna lingered behind for a moment.

"You'll be at home this evening?" she asked.

"Damned if I know," I said. "Give me a call."

She nodded, and then followed the rest down the hall.

I sat for another couple of minutes, jotting down everything I could remember from the discussion on a legal pad. It wasn't much. I stowed the pad in my duty folder just as Hart Compton walked back into the conference room.

"Here's Anita Velez's address and phone number," he said flatly, handing me a sheet of paper. "I checked. Anita wasn't in school today."

"Really?" I said, as I stowed the paper in my breast pocket. "Now, that's interesting. I think I'll drop in on her on the way home."

"You'll keep us informed?" he asked.

"As much as I can."

I walked out to the cruiser and unlocked the front door. I was just about to slide behind the wheel when I heard someone call my name. I turned and saw Mike Thurman jogging my way.

I dropped the duty folder onto the car seat and straightened to face him.

He stopped by the side of the car and

caught his breath. I waited.

"I didn't want to say this back in the conference room," he said, wheezing a little more than I might have expected for a football coach. "This place is nothing but a big gossip machine. You know I'm an assistant coach on the football team? Well, the boys talk, the way boys will, and sometimes I overhear them. A couple of the guys last week were discussing Gypsy Camarena in the locker room."

"Really," I said.

"Oh, yeah. Now, most of the time I just disregard this kind of thing. I was a teenager myself, and I remember how I'd blow things out of proportion. I hear it, though, and some of it is hard to forget."

"Pretty raunchy stuff?"

"Oh, man, like a *Penthouse* letter to the editor. That's how I know most of it is bullshit, you know? These guys, though, acted like they knew what they were talking about."

"Who were they?"

"Garrett Aalst and Justin Warfield."

"I don't know Aalst. Justin Warfield is Fred Warfield's boy."

"They're big-time jocks, multiple-letter guys. Garrett was talking about some girl from over in Morgan that he'd had sex with, and Justin laughed and asked whether he'd had Gypsy yet."

"Do you recall exactly what they said?"

"Not word for word, but the gist of it was that Justin was just one of several kids who'd had sex of one kind or another with Gypsy at a party the weekend before. Apparently, Gypsy came to the party with this Anita Velez girl Donna talked about, and they both set up shop in one of the bedrooms. According to Justin — and I don't mean to sound crude here, you understand — but according to Justin, Gypsy could 'suck a basketball through a soda straw.' He said she really pulled the train that night."

"Did he say who else was at the party?"

"You know, the usual jock crowd. He didn't use a lot of names, but these guys don't float far from their comfort zone. You ask around, and I'll bet someone can give you the complete list. Maybe Anita Velez. You going to talk with her today?"

"Tell you what," I said. "You keep all this quiet, okay? Don't tell anyone else what you just told me. I'll follow up on it discreetly, and I'll keep your name out of it. Thanks for the tip, though."

I shook his hand, gave him a conspiratorial wink, and climbed behind the wheel to drive off.

I had always liked Mike Thurman, more or less, though we had never been particularly close friends. Something about the way he came on to me in the parking lot, though, had set off a lot of alarms in my head. I could understand why he'd been cautious about dropping his little bombshell in the conference room. Prosperity is a small town, and it seems as if the main hobby here is everybody else's business.

On the other hand, he had actually seemed gleeful about sharing his tawdry little secret with me. Here I'd just informed him that one of his students had been murdered, and it seemed he couldn't wait to tell me what a skank she had been.

Maybe being a coach was the way he avoided leaving his own adolescence behind. Maybe he liked hanging around the teens because he could revel vicariously in their stories of debauchery, true or not, and pretend he was their confidante. Who knows how people like Thurman get their jollies? I sure don't.

There was something about him, though, that just made me want to stop somewhere and wash up.

CHAPTER TEN

Anita Velez lived in a two-bedroom ranch house off Mount Zion Church Road on the other side of Six Mile Creek from the school. I knew the neighborhood fairly well, and knew that much of it was now rental property owned by one of several developers over in Morgan. The illegal Mexican population tended to gravitate toward rentals, since they couldn't get a mortgage through the traditional bank outlets. Even if they could have gotten a mortgage, they would probably have trouble avoiding foreclosure due to the ridiculously low pay they received for doing all the jobs the white folks wouldn't touch.

The street on which Anita Velez lived was tidy and well maintained, though, with closely cropped lawns and colorful flower gardens interspersed with the vegetable plot each family appeared to have planted in the spring, now going fallow as we nosed over toward the winter months.

I pulled into the Velez driveway, and walked up to the front door. When the door opened, a man in his late thirties peered out at me through the screen.

"Mr. Velez?" I asked.

"*Si.*"

"Do you speak English, sir?"

"A little," he said.

"I'm Chief Wheeler, Prosperity Police," I said. "I would like to talk with Anita."

"Ah," he said.

He didn't do anything, though.

"Is Anita home?" I asked. "*Anita esta aqui?*"

He nodded and opened the screen door, gesturing for me to come inside.

Someone had put a lot of effort into sprucing up the inside of the house. The walls and ceiling were freshly painted, and the furniture was new. The living room, which was all I could see from the doorway, was spotless, with Spanish-language magazines arranged on a coffee table in perfect rainbow arcs. The television was on, tuned to a cable soccer channel.

Mr. Velez toggled a remote control to mute the television.

"I get Anita," he said, and walked to the hallway at the back of the living room. I heard him knock on a door, and say something softly in Spanish. Several seconds later, he led a teenage girl back into the living room.

She was garishly made up, in the way that teenagers do before they learn moderation in cosmetics. Her jeans rode down her pelvis, to a point that I expected to see wisps of pubic hair, and her top ended at mid-torso, exposing an expanse of deeply tanned skin. Her hair had been mercilessly teased until it sat on her head like a dead animal. I thought I saw fear in her eyes.

"Anita?" I said.

"Yes."

"I need to give you some bad news, and I need you to translate for your father. We found Gypsy Camarena's body along Six Mile Creek this morning. Somebody murdered her."

Her eyes grew wide, and she bent over at the waist, crying suddenly. She sat heavily on the sofa, and covered her face with her hands.

"*Que?*" her father asked, alarmed.

"*Gitana fue asesinado, Papa!*" she said, her words interspersed with sobs.

"*Gitana? Gitana Camarena? Como?*"

Anita looked up at me.

"What happened to her?"

98

"All we know is that her neck was broken. She was dumped along Six Mile Creek after she died."

"Su cuello estaba quebrada," she told her father.

"Mi Dios!" he exclaimed. *"Cuando?"*

"When did this happen?" Anita asked.

"We're not sure. Probably within the last two days. I need to ask you some questions, and we should be alone when I ask them. Would your father let me talk to you by yourself?"

"El desea preguntarme sobre Gitana," she told her father. *"Con mi solamente."*

Mr. Velez looked at me, his gaze mixed with concern and suspicion.

"Esta mi hija en apuro?" he asked.

"He wants to know if I'm in trouble. Do you think I had something to do with her murder?"

"I don't have any suspects at this time. I'm just trying to find out everything I can about Gypsy."

"No," she told her father. *"El ahora esta preguntando solamente."*

He looked back and forth at us, and then nodded somberly.

"Usted puede preguntarla. Estarle en el dormitorio."

"He says you can ask your questions. He

99

will wait in the other room," she said as he turned and walked down the hall. "Who found her?"

"A couple of kids from the high school. Apparently, she was left by the side of Six Mile Creek within the last day or so. When was the last time you saw Gypsy, Anita?"

"Three days ago. We wen' to the mall in Morgan to shop for some earrings. This is just terrible."

She started to cry again, but this time it was more controlled. I could tell she was still shaken by the tragic news, but she was more worried about why I was in her house, questioning her about the dead girl.

"Did someone drive you there?" I asked.

"Yes. Jaime Ortiz. He's a senior at the high school."

"Did this Jaime Ortiz take both of you home?"

"Yes."

"Who'd he drop off first? You, or Gypsy?"

"Gypsy. I . . . we . . . Jaime and I wen' somewhere else after. He took me home later."

"This was three days ago? What time?"

"We lef' for the mall jus' after school. Jaime bought us somethin' to eat at the Food Court, and we shopped for a couple of hours. It mus' have been about six when he dropped Gypsy off at her home."

"What time did he bring you home?"

"Around eight-thirty."

"What did you do for that two and a half hours?"

She began to flush noticeably.

"Anita, I need to know where the two of you were during that time. You may need to establish an alibi."

Her eyes shot upward at me.

"What is this . . . alibi?"

"You may need to be able to account for your time. Were you and Jaime with any other people during that two and a half hours between the time he left Gypsy at home and the time he brought you here?"

I thought I saw a flash of anger on her face, but she quickly suppressed it.

"No."

"You were with this boy alone the entire time?"

"Yes."

"Where were you?"

"In his car."

"For two and a half hours."

"Yes."

I jotted down a note.

"Anita, I have to tell you this. I've received reports about you and Gypsy. You need to understand that I'm not interested in judging you. I have to check these things out, because Gypsy may have been murdered by someone she knew. I've been told that you and Gypsy attended a party last weekend. According to my sources, you and Gypsy had sex with several of the high school boys at this party."

"Who tol' you this?"

"I have to keep my sources confidential. Is the report true?"

"I don' have to tell you that."

I stopped writing, and looked down at her.

"May I sit down?" I asked.

She pointed at a glider rocking chair near the sofa.

I settled into the chair and stared her down.

"Here's the thing. I have a dead girl on an autopsy table over in Morgan, and you and this kid Jaime may have been the last people other than the murderer to see her alive. Right now, I'm just looking for some background information. You want to make this official, we'll make it official. Of course, that means we take it down to the police station, and I'll have to read you your rights, and the next thing you know I have to make all these reports. Maybe these reports make their way to Homeland Security, who'll ask a lot of questions about what you and your family are doing in the country illegally, and how you're bound up in a murder case. I don't want to be a bad guy here, but cooperating with me would be in your best interest."

I felt a little like a louse, laying heavies on a sixteen-year-old girl, but it had been a long day, and I was becoming impatient.

"So, here's what I need to know. Were you and Anita at a party last weekend, having sex with some of the school athletes? Yes or no."

She was furious, but she put a lot of effort into not showing it. I couldn't imagine what was going through her mind. Her father was only twenty feet or so away, possibly listening to our conversation. I wasn't sure just how bad his English was, but she knew exactly what he did and didn't understand. I was asking her to give up some intimate details about her life. She didn't like it a bit.

"We were there," she said, finally.

"And the rest of it?"

She chewed anxiously on one well-worn thumbnail.

"Do I have to talk about that?"

"I need to know who was there and how they interacted with Gypsy."

She nodded, but didn't say anything.

"Let's try this," I said. "Why don't you tell me what Gypsy did at that party? You don't have to admit to anything you did."

She started to cry again. Grief I could understand, but this was beginning to irritate me.

"You won' tell anyone?" she asked, through her tears.

"I might," I said. "I can't promise to keep any secrets. If you tell me something, I might have to tell someone else that you said it later on."

"I see," she said. "She's dead, though, right? Nothin' can hurt her now."

"It would seem that way."

"Yeah. Okay. Wha' you heard about Gypsy was right. She and I wen' to this party, at a house in a nice neighborhood over near Deep Crick Road."

"Who was there?"

"A bunch of boys. I don' know all of them. I heard that a couple were from over in Mica Wells, and go to Allenwood High School."

"Which ones did you know?"

"Eddie Place, and Jason Phipps. Justin Warfield. Seth Kramer. Everyone knows who they are."

"All Anglos?"

"Yeah. I never thought about it that way,

but Gypsy and I were the only Latinas there."

"Who invited you?"

"I don' know. Gypsy called me and said she been asked to come, and she could bring another girl if she wanted. So we went."

"What happened after you got there?"

"You know. People were drinkin'. A little weed. It was a party."

"At which point did Gypsy start having sex with the boys?"

"It wasn't very long. Justin Warfield started by taking her into the basement. We were hangin' around the pool, and there was this slidin' door to the basement. There was a bedroom off the basement, and they wen' in there. I didn't see them go, but a few minutes later another guy and I wen' looking for a place to hook up, and we ran across them."

"What did you do?"

"It was a party. We were stoned. When you stoned, you don' care who around. Gypsy and Justin pulled some covers off the bed and went on one side of it, and this guy and I went on the other."

"Who was the boy you were with?"

"I don' know. He was one of those Allenwood guys."

"What happened next?"

"It's kind of a blur. Several boys came in, several went out."

"Can you recall the ones who had sex with Gypsy?"

"Justin Warfield, of course. Kevin Byrne. Gary Tomberlin. One of the Allenwood boys, I don' know his name. Seth Kramer. Maybe Steve Kling, I'm not sure."

"You remember who you were with?"

"I thought this was about Gypsy."

"It is," I said. "You know boys, though. They talk. Maybe one of the guys you were with could remember everyone Gypsy was with."

"You think one of those guys killed Gypsy?"

"It's possible. Somebody did. Maybe he's going to kill someone else. The more I know, the better the chance I can catch him before he does."

It took a few minutes, but she finally gave up three names. I knew all of them. They were jocks, but not troublemakers. So far all I had was a list of Prosperity's most spoiled teenagers. I had a feeling she had actually screwed a few more, but my list of people to interview was already growing larger than I might be able to manage.

"Just a couple questions more. I heard

that Gypsy dated Vicente Ramirez."

"Sure. She dated a lot of guys."

"Did Vicente know what happened at this party?"

"I don' know," she said. "Why? You think he be angry at her for humpin' a bunch of Anglos?"

"You think he wouldn't?"

"Chief, you don' understand kids. You were a teenager a long time ago. Today, we hook up, we break up, we go on to the next guy. Same for the boys. If Vicente or Jaime had been invited to that party, they'd have been in that bedroom right next to the Anglo boys."

"But they weren't invited."

"The Anglos, sometimes they a little scared of Mexican boys."

"But not the Mexican girls. Tell me something. Were there any Anglo girls in that bedroom?"

"What are you saying, Chief?"

"Why do you think Gypsy and you were invited to that party?"

"I don' know. Gypsy invited me. She didn't say why they invited her."

"According to my source, one of the boys said that Gypsy had sex with almost every boy there."

She shrugged, and stared at the floor.

"I don' want to talk about this no more," she said.

"Just a couple more questions. You know that Vicente Ramirez and Seth Kramer got into a fight the other day?"

"Sure. Everybody knows about that."

"I heard it was because Vicente was coming on to an Anglo girl, and Seth's posse didn't like that."

"Yeah. So?"

"Is that the way you heard it?"

"That's part of it."

"Tell me the other part of it."

She sighed and heaved her shoulders a little. When I had entered the house, she had looked defiant and a little intimidating. Now she just looked like a pouty little girl.

"Vicente heard about Gary Tomberlin screwing Gypsy, and he didn' like it. He didn' care so much that Gypsy was doing it with another boy, but he don' like Gary at all. So, Vicente figured it would be okay to try and hook up with Gary's girlfriend."

"It wasn't okay with Gary, though, was it?"

"I don' think Gary gave a shit, you know? It's that Seth Kramer asshole who made a big fuckin' deal out of it. Gary wasn't even there when they got into the fight."

"They weren't fighting over Gypsy,

though."

"No. Every boy got a piece off Gypsy started fightin' each other, you'd have a fuckin' riot in this town."

CHAPTER ELEVEN

There was a message on my desk when I got back to my office.

Call Carla Powers. It was followed by a phone number in Morgan.

I dialed the number.

"This is Chief Wheeler," I said when she answered.

"Thanks for calling," she said. "I have some preliminary results on the autopsy."

"Preliminary."

"Well, the toxicology samples will take a while to process, and the DNA will take longer."

"Maybe you'd better start over."

"The cause of death, as we expected, was the fracture of the second cervical vertebra. It's hard to tell, exactly, but it looks like a crushing injury rather than a twisting injury."

"How would that happen?"

"From the looks of it, with the posterior

damage to the vertebral surface, she could either have been hit very hard from behind, or someone could have sat on her back and pulled her head backward until the spinal cord snapped."

"She couldn't have been hit in the head, snapping her head backward?"

"This injury isn't consistent with that. I'd expect to see more facial bruising. Even in the instant between the impact and death, you'd see some kind of capillary oozing."

"You mentioned toxicology and DNA."

"Well, the tox screen is standard in unknown deaths."

"You'll probably find THC metabolites. I've discovered that she was a pot smoker, at least occasionally. Do you suspect any other substances?"

"No suspicions, but thanks for the heads-up. There was something else, though. She'd had sex not long before she died."

"Did it appear forced?"

"No. There was no vaginal tearing or excessive bruising of the labia or vaginal walls. It doesn't look as if anyone made her do it. I found seminal vestiges in the vagina and around the cervix. There were still a few active sperm in there."

"What does that mean?"

"She hadn't been dead more than forty-eight hours. That's about the limit for sperm survival. I took a sample and sent it off for DNA testing. Who knows? Maybe we're dealing with a known sex offender with a DNA profile on record."

"That would be almost too easy. Besides, I've discovered that Gitana was . . . well, if not promiscuous, at least very sexually active."

There was a short pause on the other end.

"This is turning into a sad story," she said, finally. "Drug use, heavy sexual activity, and only sixteen years old."

"Think how I see it. I have a kid that age."

"There was something else. I found some epithelial skin underneath the fingernails of both hands. I did a scrape and sent them off for typing and DNA too."

"You think she fought off her attacker?"

"Could be. If she had sex shortly before death, though, she might just have been a back scratcher."

"So, if the DNA of the skin residue matches that of the sperm, we still won't know for certain if we have the killer."

"No, but if we can get a match, we will know who one of the last guys to see her alive was."

"Yes," I said. "There is that."

■ ■ ■ ■

I was finishing my report on the contacts with Anita Velez and Carla Powers when Donna Asher walked into my office. I had left standing directions with Sherry that if I was not otherwise engaged with a dangerous felon, she should be allowed open access. It's good to be Chief.

"A little warning next time?" she said, after giving me a peck on the lips and taking a seat next to my desk.

"Sorry. You were in class, and I had to run some things by Compton. Hope it wasn't too much of a shock."

"It was, but I'll recover. I'm not so sure about poor Brenda Rollings, though. She might have to go on life support. Any more information you can share?"

"Nothing for public release. Broken neck. That's about it. You'll probably read about that in the paper tomorrow. I've been asking around about Gypsy all afternoon, though, and I'm not happy with what I'm finding. Maybe you can help?"

"I'll try."

"What was your take on her? As a person, I mean, not as a student."

She thought about the question for

a moment.

"She was gorgeous, but you already know that. The boys liked her."

"Mexican boys?"

"And some Anglos. There isn't a lot of line-crossing, you know, but Gypsy seemed to get along with the white boys, too."

"What about Anita Velez?"

"She isn't one of my students. I only know her by reputation."

"Which is?"

"Not a good student. A little wild. She's been suspended a couple of times, but not for anything overtly dangerous. She isn't very strong, academically. She's boy-crazy. I suppose that would go for Gypsy, too."

"Unusually boy-crazy for a sixteen-year-old?"

"Maybe a little more open about it. I've heard one or two of the white boys talk about her as being a tease."

"They still use the word *tease?*"

"Well, that's half the term."

"We're talking about Gypsy now?"

"Gypsy and Anita both, I suppose."

I tried to think of what to ask next. I was running out of questions. It had been a long time since I'd run a genuine investigation. Too many speeding citations, not enough murders.

I considered that a good thing.

"Did Gypsy seem particularly close to any one boy?" I asked.

"Not for any length of time. Permanence isn't a particularly salient value for these kids. They hook up, hang for a while, and then float away from each other."

"That's what Anita told me."

"There you go. Independent corroboration."

"Have you heard anything about sex parties among the students?" I asked.

"Sure. Everyone does."

"Funny. I haven't."

"You wouldn't. Orgies don't violate any of the town ordinances. We live with these kids for a third of their lives at the school. We hear things."

"Like what?"

"Like I said, Judd. These kids aren't into permanence. They want thrills — quick, vivid, and varied. They're the video game generation. Attention spans among these kids are measured in seconds."

"Immediate gratification," I noted.

"And how. The STD rate among high school kids is going through the roof, more among the girls than the boys, but that's just because a lot of these new diseases don't produce overt symptoms in boys.

They don't consider blowjobs to be sex, so the girls hand them out like we used to pass notes in school."

"Really?"

"Please tell me you already knew about this."

"I guess I'm just an ignorant old fart. Blowjobs aren't sex?"

"Not for the kids today."

"Damn. Go figure. What else isn't sex?"

"Handjobs. Sometimes anal."

"Keep talking, teacher-woman. You're turning me on."

She smiled. I liked her smile. It was one of the things that had drawn me to her.

"You old goat. Everything's sex to you."

"Everything you've mentioned so far. I figure if I'm getting off and there's someone else in the room, that's sex."

"Well, not for teenagers today."

"That's disheartening," I said.

"Sounds kind of prudish, coming from you."

"No, that's not it. I'm just feeling a little left out. I think I was born twenty years too early."

She stood, came around the desk, and kissed me, the way I like it. Then she stood behind me and wrapped her arms around my neck. She rested her head on my shoulder.

"You do okay," she said. "Are you hungry? I'm hungry."

"I could eat."

"Let's go grab dinner, then. Maybe later we won't have sex."

CHAPTER TWELVE

Donna rolled over and placed a hand on my arm.

"What is it, Judd?"

My eyes jerked open. My heart was pounding. I had a hard time catching my breath.

"What?" I asked.

"You were thrashing in your sleep, and moaning. It scared me."

"Nothing," I said. "Bad dream."

"About Six Mile Creek?"

"Yeah."

"I was worried about that."

I rubbed my palm across my brow. It came away damp.

"You were?"

"Come on. A body lying along Six Mile Creek? Right at that point off the highway? It was bound to dredge up . . . stuff."

"It's nothing. A long day. Too much misery. It'll pass."

"Do you want to talk about it?"

"We've had this discussion, dear."

She didn't say anything for a few moments. My pulse slowly dropped back to a level where I could actually count it, and I found myself breathing normally. I allowed myself to lie back on the pillow, but my eyes refused to close. I stared at the ceiling, afraid to go back to sleep. I didn't want the dream. Anything but that damned nightmare.

I almost forgot about Donna. She was lying on her side, her head crushing the pillow. She was watching me. She reached out and crossed my chest with one delicately muscled arm.

"Can I do anything?" she asked.

I shook my head.

"It's fine. I'm fine."

"Well, go back to sleep then."

I nodded. I closed my eyes. Moments later, I heard her breathing flatten and deepen. Shortly, she was snoring ever so softy.

I didn't sleep, though.

I didn't dare.

The first clash erupted between first and second periods at the high school the next day.

Word had filtered through the student body during the night that Gypsy Camarena had been murdered. By the time teachers arrived at the school around seven-thirty, the huge boulder sitting in the grassy strip between the parking lot and Morgan Highway had already been painted red, white, and green, with the words *"We will miss you, Gypsy"* near the top, and *"Usted Estara En Nuestro Corazones, Gypsy"* underneath.

Teachers reported that small groups of Hispanic girls began to gather in the commons area near the cafeteria as soon as the buses started to arrive. Many of the girls were tearful. They consoled each other on the loss of their friend.

More troubling were the clumps of Hispanic boys who gathered in the parking lot and milled about restlessly, talking loudly amongst themselves, their voices becoming increasingly animated as the Mazdas, Acuras, and Beemers belonging to the wealthy Anglo youths began to file into the lot for school.

Most of the white girls seemed somehow oblivious to the fact that one of their classmates had been murdered and dumped only a few hundred yards from their hallways. This seemed only to distress the

Hispanic girls more.

Slim arrived at the school about fifteen minutes before the first class. Slim's a wiry, hillbilly-looking guy, but he's no dummy. He recognized the tense atmosphere almost immediately, and radioed me for backup.

I drove into the parking lot ten minutes later, and Slim and I decided to divide the school into zones. I'd patrol Zones One and Two, and he'd keep an eye on Zones Three and Four. It was thin surveillance at best, but I didn't want to inflame the situation by summoning more backup from the Sheriff's Department in Morgan.

Everything went well until the end of first period. A boy named Jeffrey Skelton went out to the parking lot to retrieve a math book he'd left in his new Mustang, only to find that the windshield had been smashed. He returned to the school in a fury, just as the halls were packed solid with students changing classes. He ran into a group of Anglo boys clustered around a drink machine, and managed through his tears of rage to communicate, in his words, that some *greaser* had broken his windshield with a tire iron.

All he had to say was *tire iron* and, despite the fact that he never actually saw a tire iron, the boys all associated this imagined instrument of destruction with Vicente Ramirez and his recent assault against Seth Kramer.

As fate would have it, I was patrolling Zone One at that moment, and Slim was in Zone Four. We couldn't have been farther away from each other.

The gang of privileged Anglos started to roam the halls, looking for Vicente Ramirez. As it roamed, it grew like a snowball rolling down a hill, gathering steam and hatred in its path.

A Mexican girl overheard that the miniature mob was looking for Ramirez, and she waited for them to pass before she ducked into the auditorium and took a shortcut through the backstage door to the far hallway.

She found Vicente at his locker. She warned him about the growing crowd of vigilantes.

Within minutes, he had assembled his own posse of brown-skinned protectors. They weren't looking for trouble. They just wanted to ensure that they had safety in numbers if the two juggernauts collided.

By the time the Anglos rounded the corner to the far hall, they numbered maybe fifteen youths. The Mexican kids had about twelve. Mob mentality took over, fueled by teenage testosterone that you could almost smell in the air like a fetid swamp.

The two groups faced each other down for a moment, waiting for any signal of aggression. Finally, Skelton stepped forward.

"Ramirez!" he yelled.

Summoned by his voice, a history teacher named Arnold Jantz stuck his head out his door. He appraised the situation instantly, and shut his door to protect the twenty students or so who had already arrived for class. He grabbed the telephone in his classroom and dialed the two-digit code for the front office.

"That was a cheap shot," Skelton said. "My dad just bought that car."

"What are you talking about?" Ramirez said.

"You broke my windshield. You know you did."

"Somethin' happen to your car?" Ramirez said. "Why the fuck you think I did it? You fuckin' *loco,* boy."

They had reached critical mass. The only thing holding them back was the expanse of ten feet or so of linoleum floor and the air they were expending at an increasingly alarming rate.

"You and me," Skelton said. "Right here. Right now."

"Forget it," Ramirez said, even as he stepped two feet forward of the gang of posturing Hispanic youths. "I had nothin' to do with whatever happened to your car. I'm not going back to jail over some *perdador rico* like you."

"Hey," said some kid from the white gang. "I know what that means. He just called you a rich loser, Jeff. Go on. Get him. Show him now!"

Jeff Skelton stepped forward a couple of feet and assumed a kung fu stance.

"What the fuck is *that?*" Ramirez asked. "You goin' to fight like that? Get your ass kicked, boy."

"Get him!" one of the white boys said, and then he made a fateful mistake. He pushed Skelton toward Vicente.

Vicente's mob saw Skelton charge, and pushed forward, driving Vicente into Skelton. Within moments, the hall was full of writhing bodies, grappling at each other and swinging wildly, mostly missing, but still drawing enough blood to slime the floor in spots.

Overhead, the fire alarm blared. Some alert girl halfway down the hall had realized what was happening, and had decided to help by clearing the building. All she accomplished was to fill the hallways with more scared kids.

By this point, Hart Compton had found me over in Zone One, half the school away from the fight. He grabbed me just as the alarm klaxon began to wail.

"One of my teachers says there's a rumble over on D Wing!" he shouted over the clanging bell.

I didn't wait for an explanation. I thumbed the radio at my shoulder and told Slim to meet me on D, and Hart and I ran down the hall toward the battle.

Slim met us at the middle of the school, as I slipped a little on the newly waxed floor while turning a corner. Ahead I saw girls and boys fleeing toward the fire exits. We charged against their current, taking care not to bowl anyone over, and then turned onto D Wing.

The scene was like some kind of macabre orgy, as boys grappled with each other and rolled around on the floor. Further down the hall, a Mexican kid sat, his back to the wall, a reddening tee shirt stuffed to his face as he tried to stanch the flow of blood from his broken nose. Across the hall, another youth, an Anglo, glared at him as he cradled his bruised ribs.

Slim and I waded into the maelstrom, grabbing boys by the shoulders and dragging them away from the eye of the storm. We jacked them up against the lockers and told them to stay. For the most part, they stayed.

It took a couple of minutes, but we finally got the battle broken apart, and had separated the two groups of combatants. Slim and I stood in the middle of the hallway, daring them to leave their places next to the wall.

"Right now, you're all under arrest!" I bellowed. "Anyone wants to spend the night in the slam, you just go ahead and leave the wall. I'll cuff you on the spot."

I looked over at Hart Compton.

"Will someone turn off that damned alarm?"

Almost instantly, the bell stopped clanging.

"That's better," I said, trying not to smile at the coincidence. Far off, I could hear the sirens of the VFD trucks charging down the Morgan Highway toward the school.

"Mr. Compton, you might want to call off the fire department," I suggested. "Slim and I will handle this."

Slim and I wrote down the boys' names from their school ID cards, and herded them into separate classrooms as we cleared them. We told them to take a seat and shut up, read them their rights, and reiterated the threat of cuffs and the clang of slamming cell doors.

As if coming down from drugs, the kids all became wide-eyed and incredulous as they saw what had happened. Rage was overwhelmed by fear — mostly fear of what havoc their parents would wreak when they found out what had happened.

When we had corralled them, I turned to Slim.

"You know what to do," I said, and turned to enter the Anglos' classroom.

Slim interrogated the Mexican boys while I worked over the whites. A half hour later we met in the hallway and compared notes.

"It sounds like Vicente was getting ready to get jumped," Slim told me. "He was minding his own business, hanging at his locker, when some girl told him there was a lynch mob hunting for him."

"That gibes with what I've heard," I said. "Skelton says he didn't intend to fight with Vicente. He was upset and angry that someone had smashed his windshield, and he just fell in with a group of buds who were ready to bang some brown skin."

"Man, this place was a war looking for an excuse."

"I was afraid of this. What do you want to do?"

"We could run 'em in," Slim suggested. "We'd have to add a wing to the jail first."

"Does Vicente want to press charges? He was an innocent victim, after all."

"I don't think there was anyone innocent on this hallway, Judd. I think these kids are itchin' for a fight. And you know what else?"

"What?"

"I don't think it's over . . ."

We finally decided to turn them over to Hart Compton. We had their names, and I had a feeling I'd be taking a lot of telephone calls from angry parents later in the day, but in the end nobody wanted to file any complaints. It was just a schoolyard fight gone way out of control. We figured the school discipline code would handle it.

I briefed Hart on our findings, and left Slim to watch over the proceedings in the school office while I patrolled the hallways. As I walked, I realized I had come to the school that morning with more than one purpose. I toggled my shoulder mike.

"Slim, let me know when Principal Compton winds down in there. I need to do a couple of interviews."

"Ten-four."

My hand itched, and I held it up. A long, angry scratch ran from just behind my thumb to the base of my middle finger. I couldn't recall cutting it in all the commotion. I ducked into a hallway bathroom and washed it under hot water and lots of soap. I needed an infection like I needed a third ball.

As I left the bathroom, I saw Donna walking up the hall toward me. As she saw me, her pace quickened.

"Are you all right?" she said, even before she reached me.

"I'm fine. Just a scratch."

We were alone in the hall. She reached out and hugged me, hard. I didn't mind it a bit.

"I heard what you and Slim did, taking on that rumble."

"Not much of a rumble. Just a bunch of worked-up boys wrestling each other in the hallway. They didn't put up much resistance once they saw the uniforms."

"Is what I heard true? Was it a race riot?"

"I don't know if it rose to quite that level, dear. Some kid got his car messed up, and he immediately jumped to conclusions. The rest of it just sort of evolved. There's tension here, though. I can feel it. Have you heard anyone talk about what might have happened to Gypsy?"

She nodded.

"Just whisperings, but they're getting louder. Gypsy wasn't as popular among the Mexican girls as the rock outside indicates. A lot of them were angry at her for being a little . . . well, wild. Word was getting around even before she was killed that she was having sex with the white boys. Some of the girls are saying she was getting paid. Do you know anything about that?"

"A little. Not much I can talk about. I have to do some interviews in the office for the rest of the day. Why don't you check by before you leave?"

"I'll do that. You be careful, Judd. I have a feeling the unrest is just beginning."

"Not if I have anything to say about it."

She glanced around to make sure no one was watching, and then she stood on tiptoe to kiss me. I met her halfway.

CHAPTER THIRTEEN

I finally got use of the conference room in the main office around lunchtime. The first kid I wanted to talk with was Justin Warfield.

He was a rangy boy with short hair and very little acne. He wore a Prosperity Glen letter jacket over a blue oxford cloth buttondown and a pair of jeans, the jock national uniform. He wasn't a bad-looking kid for seventeen, but I could tell from his hands and his neck that he was going to gain a lot of weight before he reached thirty.

"Have a seat, Justin," I said as he walked in.

He sat across the table, but he didn't say anything.

"You know who I am?" I asked.

"You're the Police Chief. Mr. Wheeler."

"That's right. Before I start, Justin, I want you to know that you are not under arrest. Because you're a minor, you do have the right to have a parent here in the room while I interview you. Do you understand?"

"Sure."

"Great. Some fight this morning, huh?"

"I wasn't there."

"I know. I was. Just making conversation. Some of your buddies were there, though, weren't they?"

"I guess."

"Guys like Eddie Place, and Jason Phipps."

"I didn't know Jason was there. I saw Eddie in the lunchroom. He got roughed up a little."

"Did he tell you what the fight was about?"

"Not much. Something about Vicente Ramirez trashing some guy's car."

"Yeah. Well, for the record, Mr. Ramirez had nothing to do with that. A bunch of your buds jumped to conclusions. You might want to spread that around."

"Whatever."

He was trying hard to appear aloof and unintimidated, but I knew better. After I left the Atlanta force, and before I took this gig as Prosperity Police Chief, I was still intimidated by cops, and I had *been* one.

"I'm not here to talk about the fight," I said, looking over my notes. "You know

132

about Gypsy Camarena getting murdered?"

"I heard about it on the news last night."

"You knew her, right?"

He shrugged.

"Is that a yes or a no?" I asked.

"We'd met."

"When did you last see Gypsy, Justin?"

"I don't know. A few days ago."

"At school?"

"I guess."

"It wasn't at a party over off Deep Crick Road last weekend?"

I tried to suppress a smirk as the color rose in his face.

"Tell me about that party," I said. I put a lot of effort into making sure it didn't sound like a request.

"What do you want to know?"

"Where it was, first of all."

"It was at Kevin Byrne's house. I don't know the street address."

"That's okay. Who else was there?"

"A bunch of guys. Some of the football team, a couple of basketball players."

"Names would be helpful, Justin."

"Well, Kevin, of course. Seth Kramer. Eddie Place. Um . . . Gary Tomberlin. Some guys from over to Mica Wells."

"Allenwood High boys?"

"Yeah."

133

"Do you know their names?"

"Not really. One of them was Mitch Biggers. I know him on account of he plays opposite me in football. I'm a lineman."

"Offense or defense?"

"Offense. Why?"

"Just curious. Mitch Biggers, you said?"

"That's right."

"Any other names you can give me?"

"Jason Phipps. I remember him being there. There were some others, but I can't recall right off hand."

"No girls?"

"No white girls."

"You make a distinction?"

He shrugged again. I'd seen that shrug before, from my son. It was the worldwide adolescent gesture for *fuck off.*

"Who were the girls that *were* there?"

"Gypsy. That Anita chick."

"Any others?"

"No."

"Any of the Mexican boys?"

"Yeah, right," he snorted.

"You had Mexican girls, right? Why not the Mexican boys?"

He just stared at me.

I stared back.

His neck reddened a little, to match his ears.

"Here's the deal, Justin," I said. "I've already talked with some of the people who attended this party, and I know that you guys had Gypsy and Anita pull the train. Know what I mean?"

"That's why Kevin invited them," he said. "Don't mean I was involved with that stuff."

"That's not what I heard. In fact, according to at least one source, you were the one who took Gypsy back to the bedroom in Kevin's basement. When it comes to hauling the choo-choo, you got to be the coal car. Everybody else just got sloppy seconds."

"Who told you that?"

"Someone who was there. Are you denying it?"

"Hell, no. What difference does it make? She was just this beaner skank. Hell, she probably wouldn't have minded getting knocked up. She has a baby in the States, she gets to stay."

I wasn't prepared for his sudden outburst. I took a moment to draw back my impulse to twist his head around a couple of times.

"Someone killed that *beaner skank*, Justin. You'd better hope she *wasn't* pregnant when she died, and you'd better hope that if she was the baby's DNA doesn't match yours, because if it does I'd call that a dandy motive. Wouldn't you?"

"Well, you can forget about that. You think I'd stick my dick in some wetback without a rubber? God knows what she might have been carrying."

"You used a condom?"

"We all did. Kevin had a bowl of them right next to the bed. We damn near backed up his septic tank flushing them all down the john. Is this what you wanted to talk about? You think maybe someone at that party killed Gypsy? If I were you, I'd take a long look at one of her Mex boyfriends. Maybe Jaime Ortiz. I saw them together at the mall the other day. Maybe he found out about her and Kevin's party, and lost control."

"Jaime has an alibi," I said. "Nice try. And I know Vicente didn't do it, because I had him locked up at the time. Make another guess."

"You're the cop. All I know is nobody at that party could have gotten Gypsy pregnant, and I didn't kill her."

I nodded.

"You stay close by," I said. "No extended out-of-town trips, okay?"

"Hey, I watch TV, Chief. I know my rights. If you don't arrest me, I can go wherever I want."

■ ■ ■ ■

I summoned Kevin Byrne next. He juked
into the room as if listening to an unseen
hip-hop group. He was wearing a sweatshirt
and jeans. His neck was as big around as
his head, and the rest of him was obviously
the product of countless hours in the gym.
Despite this, he had a choirboy face. His
beard was almost nonexistent, and he
peered at me through clear blue eyes
perched over the pug nose of a preschooler.

"I'll get right to the point," I told him,
after I reminded him that he could have a
parent present. "I know you tossed a party
at your house last Saturday night. I know
who attended, and I know you and a bunch
of other students had a little gangbang with
Gypsy Camarena and Anita Velez. You with
me so far?"

His eyes clouded, and his forehead
wrinkled. I couldn't tell whether he was
distressed because he'd been ratted out, or
because I'd used too many words in one
breath.

Then he started crying.

It was like he went from zero to sixty with
the tear-works in about three seconds.

"Oh, Jesus, Chief, you gonna tell my

parents? If they find out about this, I'm gonna be grounded for life."

"Where were your parents?"

"They were out of town. Went to the beach for a golf weekend. Jesus, I didn't know someone was gonna kill Gypsy. If I'd known she was gonna be murdered, I'd have never asked her to come to my place. Jesus, you don't think I did it, do you?"

I picked up a box of tissues and slid it across the table to him.

"Calm down. Right now I'm just trying to reconstruct the last several days of Gypsy's life. Pull yourself together and we'll talk some more."

He stopped crying fairly quickly, but he kept snuffling and snorting for another several minutes. I realized that the choirboy look was no ruse. I wasn't dealing with a master criminal here.

"Okay," I said. "I want you to tell me why you asked Gypsy and Anita to your place."

"One of the other guys suggested I do it."

"Who?"

"Seth Kramer. He told me to ask them to come over while my folks were away. He said they'd do anyone."

"How did he know?"

"I didn't ask. All he said was if I asked them two girls over to my place, I'd get my ashes hauled."

"Did you?"

He nodded. His face turned red.

"I never done gone all the way before, Chief. I didn't know what to expect. Seth told me to ask these girls over, and I figured this was my chance."

"You didn't worry about catching some disease?"

He shook his head.

"Seth brought three or four boxes of rubbers. He said just to make sure I used one if I got with one of the girls, because he said they been with dozens of guys, some of them Mexicans, and they got diseases down in Mexico that will just eat your junk plain away."

"So this was all Seth Kramer's idea?" I asked, dreading the answer.

"Yeah. He found out my folks were going out of town, and he figured we could have us a real party."

"And you did."

He nodded.

"I was scared, though, on account of I never been with a girl before, not like that."

"Your folks still don't know what happened?"

"No. We stayed out around the pool and in the basement. Nobody went upstairs."

"Okay. I need a list of all the guys at this party, including the ones from Mica Wells."

"I'm not sure I know 'em all, Chief. Seth Kramer got a lot of them to come."

"Of course he did," I said.

Seth Kramer and I hadn't parted on the best terms at his house several days earlier. He was still copping an attitude when he walked into the conference room. He sat across from me, but he didn't say anything.

"This is an informal interview." I told him. "Nobody's under arrest, and you don't have to answer any questions. If you want, you can have a parent present during the interview. Do you have any questions?"

He slumped in his chair and stared out the window for a moment.

Then he stood up and walked out of the room.

Chapter Fourteen

I finished my interviews by the end of the school day, and didn't learn much that was interesting. Just about everyone I spoke with confirmed Justin Warfield's story. Most of them thought Kevin Byrne had organized the party. Most of them, given an opportunity to reason this impression through, realized that a kid like Kevin could never have organized an evening that cool.

Surprisingly — or perhaps not — none of them appeared overly distraught regarding Gypsy Camarena's murder. Maybe their lofty positions in the student body hierarchy didn't allow them to empathize with the plight of those they considered lower-born. Maybe their only interaction with Gypsy had been as a community fuck-buddy, and they regarded her with all the emotional attachment they'd have had with a milking machine.

Maybe they were just a bunch of spoiled jerks.

Whatever the case, all I got from my day of interviews was confirmation of what I knew going in. I was going to have to settle for that.

I was packing my materials when Cory True walked into the room.

"What's up, Chief?" he asked.

"Does Hart Compton know you're in here?"

"I checked in at the front desk. Why?"

"Didn't know he allowed reporters in the building. What do you want, Cory?"

"Someone from the school phoned the City Desk at the *Ledger-Telegraph* a little while ago. Said there was a race riot at the school this morning. I'm just following up on it."

"And what have you found out?"

"Not much. Can you fill me in?"

"Nope."

He sat and waited for me to continue. I really wasn't in a mood to accommodate him.

"Uh, mind telling me why?"

"Because your caller was mistaken. There was no riot here."

"You didn't intervene in a hallway fight between two gangs of kids. Whites on Hispanics?"

"There was a fight. Slim and I broke it

up. I don't think it rose quite to the level of a riot."

"But it *was* between a group of white boys and a group of Mexican boys?"

"A small group. On each side."

"How many?"

"Hell, Cory, I don't know. We didn't arrest anyone. Ask Mr. Compton. They were all referred for school discipline."

He scribbled something down.

"Do me a favor and edit out that *hell* part," I said. "Don't want my son reading about me using profanity in the newspaper."

"Did this, uh, *fight* have anything to do with the murder of Gitana Camarena?"

"I don't think so. Some kid got his car damaged, and he mistakenly thought another kid did it, and things got a little out of hand. We broke it up in about two minutes."

"I see," Cory said, still writing notes. "Anyone have to go to the hospital?"

"Not that I know of. One kid got his ribs stove up a little. Another had a bloody nose. Other than that, it was mostly just some scrapes and bruises."

"Do you have any new information on the Camarena murder you can share?" he asked.

"The investigation is ongoing."

"Getting nowhere, huh?"

I resisted the urge to impale him on my billy stick.

"I didn't say that. And don't try to bait me, kid. I'm not that easy."

"Speaking of easy, I heard that this girl Gitana got around a lot."

"Really? Where did you hear this? I'm looking for my next person to interview."

"A source told me she was promiscuous."

"Don't print that. Her parents don't need to read that."

"It's background. A sixteen-year-old girl with hot pants. Kind of widens the field of suspects, doesn't it?"

"Right now everyone except me is a suspect. You seem to know a lot about this girl, Cory. Maybe I ought to run you in to the station and sweat you a little. Maybe *you* did it."

He chuckled as he kept writing.

"That's why I love talking with you, Chief. You never lose your sense of humor. Gotta run. Thanks for the information."

I drove back to the station and retreated to my office to write up the report of my interviews that day. There wasn't much to write, since I hadn't learned much new, except that Seth Kramer had organized the party at Kevin Byrne's house.

I finished my report, and pulled out a legal pad. I started three days before the last time Gypsy was seen, on the night of the party at Kevin Byrne's house. Then I used one page for each day, and listed the hours down the side of the pad. On the Saturday night before the murder, I marked through the times from about seven until about midnight, and wrote out to the side *Pulling the Train. Kevin Byrne's.*

Then I moved to the page for two days before we found the body, and marked out the slots from three in the afternoon until six in the evening, and wrote out *Jaime Ortiz/Anita Velez-Mall.*

I had already gotten Gypsy's attendance records from Hart Compton, so I could mark out some pretty large portions of the weekdays for the last week and a half of Gypsy's life, because I knew she was in school.

I could be relatively certain from Carla Powers's autopsy that she had been dead about forty-eight hours before we found her, so I marked those hours out, and simply wrote *DEAD* on those two pages.

I knew she had been in school on the Monday before she was found, so that left a fairly small margin between the end of the school day on Monday, and her murder.

I still had a bunch of empty yellow space on the pad. I still didn't know how she had spent the majority of her last three days on earth. That was depressing. Somewhere in all that yellow space she came into conflict with the person who broke her neck.

I shoved the pad into my desk drawer, pulled on my hat, and headed over to High Shoals.

Kent Kramer was mowing the lawn when I drove up. It was Friday afternoon, and Prosperity Glen was scheduled to play Morgan High that night. Maybe Kent wanted to spruce the place up in case some of those Clemson scouts wanted to come back to the house to knock back a few and discuss scholarships.

He shut down the mower when I pulled into the driveway. Kent was the original hail-fellow-well-met guy, the kind of man who never met a stranger. He could sell rubbers to monks. When he saw me park my cruiser in his driveway, he looked like he wanted to tear my head off.

He walked over to the cruiser.

"You can't talk to him, Judd."

"He has to cooperate sometime."

"You don't understand. He has to play tonight. You want to fuck up his head with this murder shit right before he goes out to play in front of the Clemson scouts?"

"I don't understand? You think? Gee, Kent, I wonder what it must be like to be the starting QB for Prosperity Glen."

He shook his head and looked around. Maybe he was worried about being seen talking with the police chief in his own front yard.

"That was a quarter century ago, Judd. It's different these days."

"Not so different. What has he told you?"

"Just that you were grilling some of the other team members at the school this afternoon about this girl who got killed."

"Did he tell you why?"

"No. Give him a break, Judd. This is a big game. He needs to keep his head screwed on straight."

I fiddled with the headlight controls, and considered running both Seth and Kent in for obstruction.

"Give him tonight. I'll bring him in to the station tomorrow. How about that?" Kent asked.

"I only work until one tomorrow."

"I'll get him up. We'll be there, okay?"

I thought it over.

"All right," I said. "I'm working the game tonight. All three of us are. After that shit at the high school today I've asked the sheriff to send me a few more guys to help keep things under control. Maybe I'll see you there."

"Hey, if I'm sitting with guys in orange jackets, do me a favor and wave at me from a distance, okay?"

Jesus. He had to get up early on a Saturday morning to take his kid in for questioning, and he still couldn't pull his head out of his ass.

CHAPTER FIFTEEN

I took Craig and Donna over to the fish camp in Mica Wells that night. We stuffed ourselves on Calabash-style fried flounder and oysters, and about a gallon of lemony sweet tea each.

Around seven, I headed back to Prosperity to oversee security at the football game. Craig begged off, so I dropped him by the house. Donna, as a faculty member, wasn't expected to be at the game, but she probably would have attended anyway. She loved football. Just one more thing we had in common.

Slim was patrolling the parking lot when I got there. It was half an hour before game time, and the lot was filling fast. I parked the cruiser in the yellow zone in front of the school, and joined a group of four sheriff's deputies who had gathered there.

"Here's the deal," I told them as I assigned placements. "We had a fight involving about thirty kids this morning, half and half Anglos and Mexicans. We don't usually get a lot of the Mexican kids show up for the football games, but they might decide to put in an appearance. I'd like three of you to be highly visible along the walkway at the top of the home grandstand. The fourth can hang out over at the visitor side. My deputy and I will patrol the sidelines, and keep an eye on the crowd from the field level. Does that work for you?"

The highest-ranking deputy, a mid-twenties kid named Shaklee, nodded.

"This is your territory," he said. "You're the boss. You tell us where to go, and we'll do it."

"Great. You can keep your guns holstered, but I need you to leave the magazines in your trunk safes."

"We do the same at the Morgan games," another deputy named Hartwig said. "Just one thing, Chief . . ."

"Yeah?"

"My kid brother plays for Morgan High. Is it all right to cheer if he scores a touchdown or something?"

"Anybody else have relatives playing for Morgan?" I asked.

The rest of them shook their heads.

I turned back to Hartwig.

"Let's put you on the visitors' grandstand," I told him.

For the first two quarters, it looked like it was going to be a quiet evening. The temperature had dropped after sundown, and by the end of the first quarter it was down to about forty degrees. There was a light wispy fog over the field, but it didn't threaten to descend and ruin the game. I excused each of the deputies one by one to go back to the parking lot and retrieve their jackets.

Forty seconds before the end of the first half, with the game tied at zero, Seth Kramer faded back on the snap with the line at Morgan's twelve-yard hash, and executed a perfect draw, pulling Morgan's left line in even as Prosperity's left line was decimating the visitors' right flank. Justin Warfield hit a defensive lineman so hard that he flew backwards through the air and landed with a thud on his back, just shy of the goal line. It was all the opening Seth needed, and he sprinted through the hole to score a touchdown and put Prosperity up six-zip.

I glanced up at Kent Kramer, who was sitting with two men in orange Clemson University jackets. Kent glad-handed both of them, and they nodded appreciatively.

Seth was scoring points both on and off the field.

Prosperity easily speared the extra point, and the rest of the first half ran down as Morgan tried vainly to move the ball beyond their fifteen-yard line following the kickoff.

I took the opportunity at the half, when the crowd would be its most active, to leave the sidelines and walk up the grandstand steps to check in on my sheriff's deputies, who had been stationed about every fifty feet along the top of the concrete grandstand.

I sidled up to Shaklee.

"Maybe I had you guys come out here for nothing," I said.

"Shoot, even if it stays quiet I'd rather go to a football game than hang around the house watching TV. Your quarterback's a monster."

"You have no idea," I said.

A moment later, the noise level in the stadium dropped to about half. There's something in the human genome that still reacts to the herd instinct, and everyone seemed to realize that a change had descended on the crowd. For some reason, everyone looked over to their left, toward the miniature suspension bridge over Six Mile Creek that connected the parking lot with the football field.

A solid line of students, over two hundred feet in length, marched across the bridge. They were easily visible by their brilliant white tee shirts. As they walked under the mercury lamp on the pole at the end of the bridge, we could see that they were almost all Hispanic kids from the school.

"Stay alert," I told Shaklee. "I'm going to see what they want."

Stepping almost in perfect cadence, the phalanx continued over the bridge and toward the home grandstand. The football field had been carved out of a valley between two natural hillsides, and the concrete stands were set into the hillsides. There was a long concrete incline leading up to the breezeway behind the stands, and the parade started toward the top of the stands using that incline. I met them halfway up the hill.

Vicente Ramirez led the group. Right behind him were Anita Velez and Jaime Ortiz. As I walked up to them, I could see that the tee shirts were printed with a copy of Gypsy Camarena's school picture from the previous year's Prosperity Glen annual, and the words *No Nos Olvidaremos,* in bold script.

I could have stood in their way, but that would have made it two hundred to one,

153

and I didn't like those odds. Instead, I fell into step with Vicente as he trudged up the incline.

"It's cool, Chief," he said, interdicting my question. "We're not here to cause trouble."

"What *are* you here for?"

"Just a show of solidarity. Gypsy was one of us. We want people to know we won't forget."

"Where'd you get the shirts?"

"Some of us work in a screen-printing shop over in Morgan. We ran them off this afternoon. I mean it, Chief. We'll stay peaceful."

"See that you do," I said, and trotted up ahead of them.

"What's going on?" Shaklee asked when I got to him at the top of the grandstand.

"Peaceful demonstration. You speak Spanish?"

"Some. Why?"

"Mine's rusty. What's it say on those tee shirts?"

He squinted at Vicente's chest.

"*We will not forget.* That picture. It's the dead girl?"

"Yeah."

"Looks like she had a lot of friends."

I watched as Vicente passed by us, leading the group toward the back of the grandstand, where a chain-link fence separated them from the rest of the school property.

"Maybe more than she knew about when she was alive," I said.

They lined up against the fence and linked arms, forming one long human chain, a breathing billboard from which Gypsy Camarena's beaming face stared out at the home crowd over and over and over. Spectators milling about to grab a snack from the concession stand or to visit the bathroom were confronted with multiple images of Gypsy in far happier times. There was no way to escape her picture, or the declaration that the protesters would not forget.

The line of grim-faced Mexican youths stood silently. They stared straight ahead, not even daring to make eye contact with the crowd. A couple of girls had streams of tears on their cheeks, but most of the group simply stood rock-still, breathing slowly, with that thousand-yard stare. It was spooky.

Some of the more nervous Prosperity Glen spectators quietly left their seats and made their way back down the ramp toward the parking lot. I had a feeling they wouldn't be back that evening. As if they had waited for someone to trump the retreat, several more left in their wake.

I could hear the murmur running through

the crowd. Individuals kept turning around to glance at the line against the back fence, and then whispered furtively to their neighbors.

Within minutes, the grandstand was half empty. Spectators who had already left their seats to visit the snack bar or the bathrooms simply never came back. The flow of people walking back down the incline toward the bridge grew from pairs and small groups to dozens at a time.

On the field, the two teams ran back out from their respective dressing rooms, pumped up and ready to start the second half. They got to midfield before the first Prosperity Glen player noticed the change in the home grandstand. People walked up the steps instead of back down to their seats.

All the while, Vicente Ramirez's silent, stony-eyed demonstration remained locked arm-in-arm, immobile against the back fence, avoiding all interaction with the dwindling crowd.

The two orange-jacketed Clemson scouts stood and stared somberly at the back fence. Then they leaned down to say something to Kent Kramer. Kent seemed to try to reassure them, but they simply shook his hand, and then walked up the steps to join the exodus from the stadium.

The officials took the field to find both teams just standing near the fifty-yard line, staring dumbfounded up at the top of the grandstand. Where almost a thousand people had sat through the first half of the game, only a few more than a hundred now remained, and they looked itchy. For the first time in Prosperity Glen history, there were more spectators in the visitors' stands than on the home side.

The officials blew the whistle to start the second half. I didn't watch the kickoff, because I had joined with Stu and the three sheriff's deputies at the top of the grandstand, keeping an eye on the protesters to ensure — in whatever meager way we could, realistically — that their demonstration continued in a peaceful manner.

I felt a hand grab my shoulder.

"Judd, what in hell is going on?" Kent Kramer demanded.

"They're making a show of solidarity over Gypsy Camarena's death."

"Well, can't you make them go do it somewhere else?"

"These people have a right to be here. They're Prosperity Glen students."

"But they're ruining the game."

"The game's continuing. I haven't seen any disruption on the field. You think maybe you're upset because they ran off your Clemson scouts?"

"You know better than that."

"Chill out, then, Kent. It's just a game. These people have promised me they won't disturb or molest anyone. They're demonstrating peacefully. I'm glad you came up to visit, though. I'm coming in to the office a little late tomorrow morning. I wanted to let you know. Probably won't be in until nine-thirty or so. Probably leave around one. You can bring Seth in anytime in there. Okay?"

"What?"

"I still need to interview Seth. I couldn't do it this afternoon. I need to see him tomorrow. If you'd like, I can cruise by your place instead . . ."

"No. That's all right. I . . . I'll try to get him in before one."

I shook my head.

"If I don't see him by one o'clock," I said, "I'm putting in some overtime at your house. Understand?"

He didn't say anything. His face said it all.

He seemed to waver for a moment, caught between his own discomfort and his desire to drink in one of the few remaining moments of high school glory his son would provide. He finally turned and walked back down the grandstand steps to his seat. He was the only person left on his row. He sat grimly and watched the game grind itself out, as two hundred Mexican immigrant kids stood at the back fence, staring off into space with pictures of Gypsy Camarena on their chests.

CHAPTER SIXTEEN

"Chief, this is Wylie Ford at the fire station. We just got a rescue call. Sounds like a coupla cars went head-on near Six Mile Creek . . ."

I willed myself awake, and desperately tried not to lurch out of the bed.

It was always in the deepest hours of the night that the dream hit, and I slammed into the panic wall. There was something about the night that brought it on. Maybe I was too busy during the day to allow my mind to contemplate, or maybe it was the similarity of the blue-black hours to the gloom and silence of the crypt. It was at night that I was most aware of my own mortality, and the certainty that my days were numbered. It was the time when my deepest dread made a house call.

Like most people, I suppose, I spent a lot of time denying the certainty that I would someday die. Sometimes I envied the truly devout among the people I knew, those who stated with absolutely no reservation that at the instant of their deaths they would be transported miraculously to paradise and the presence of God. I thought it must be great comfort to them, deep in the bleakness between sundown and sunrise, and that surely they never awoke with the pangs of desperation and terror that I often felt.

Then, as it always did, my panic subsided, and I realized that this was just part of the human condition. The price of our sentience is the awareness that we are, for better or for worse, only temporal beings, and there's not one thing we can do about it.

In the absence of the faith that I imagined spared my more spiritual neighbors, I usually reminded myself how lucky I was to have been alive at all. I considered how vast the odds were that, in that moment of coupling between my parents, the single seed out of all the millions that contested for life found its way home, and that seed was *me.* Then I considered all the countless generations that had come before me, and how it was necessary for them all to have been conceived just as they were for me to exist at all, and I marveled at the very unlikelihood of it. I contemplated how each of the infinite pyramid of my ancestors had to have lived their lives in exactly the way they did, all the way back to my hairiest, most primordial forebears, just descended from the trees of the forest primeval, and how a single instant of indecision or a momentary distraction was all that would have been required in all those eons of human history, and I never would have breathed the sweet air of life.

Life was a gift. It didn't matter that it was for only a sparkle of reflected moonlight off a whitecap in the ocean of eternity. For one brief gasp of time I could behold the richness and the joy of existence, and it was worth an eternity of corruption and moldering to seize that moment and hold it as tightly as I could, and to be very, very certain that I did not take it for granted.

It was also essential, I realized, that I never take for granted the lives of people whose own equally unlikely existence had been snuffed out by evil.

If Susan had left me with nothing else, she had left me with that.

I must have drifted off sometime before daybreak, for maybe an hour, because I woke to yellowish sunlight on my face, and the tinny blather of the clock radio on Donna's side of the bed.

It was always a little disorienting to wake up at her house. With the exception of my stint as an Atlanta beat cop, I had lived almost my entire life in the house my grandfather had built. I knew the bed there like an old, comfortable friend. Donna said my mattress hurt her back, that it was too soft and that I should replace it with some modern, ultra-quilted, compartmentalized, NASA-designed affair that would cost me a week's pay and a month's sleep while I adjusted to it.

My solution was somewhat more elegant. Whenever she began to complain too much about my old mattress pal, I'd just sleep over at her house for a few days.

I heard her hand slap at the clock, and the noise was cut off in mid-screech.

"Now why in hell did I set that damned thing?" she mumbled through her pillow. "It's Saturday."

"My fault. I have to work. Remember?"

"Oh, yeah."

She rolled over and faced the ceiling.

"You had nightmares again last night," she said.

"Yeah. Did I wake you?"

"Uh-huh. It's no big deal. I usually don't have a lot of trouble getting back to sleep. I woke up again about a half hour later, though, and you were still awake."

"I was thinking."

"You know, you don't have to go through that stuff alone. If you need to talk to me . . ."

"It's okay. I'm all right. The doctor told me I'd have spells like this. It won't last."

"If you say so. Just as long as you know I'm here. You want breakfast?"

"I can grab something on the way to the station. Go on back to sleep. You deserve to sleep in. It's been a tough week."

"Tougher than facing down those kids at the game last night?"

"That wasn't tough. They didn't intend to cause trouble."

"They did, though. There are going to be repercussions," she said. "Kent Kramer is going to want someone's hide."

"We'll see. He's supposed to bring Seth in this morning for a little chat. I'll get a good idea of what he plans then. Go on, now. Get some sleep. I'll call this afternoon. Maybe we can take in a movie this evening."

"That would be nice," she said, but I could tell that she was already drifting back off to dreamland.

Freshly showered, shaved, and dressed in a crisply pressed uniform blouse and trousers,

I pulled up to the station to find that Kent and Seth Kramer were already there, waiting in Kent's Cadillac.

I had picked up a couple of sausage and egg biscuits from Gwen Tissot's Stop and Rob on the Morgan Highway. I grabbed the grease-stained bag and locked the cruiser before waving at them. Then I walked into the station.

Kent and Seth followed me inside.

"Have a seat, guys," I said from the back. "I'm making some coffee. Anyone want a cup?"

"No, thanks," Kent said.

Seth didn't say anything.

I fiddled with a rubber band while I waited for the drip coffeemaker to finish its duty, and then I poured myself a cup and doctored it with the sugar and creamer.

"Come on in," I said at my office door when I got back to the front.

They sat across from me. I sat at my desk. I blew across the top of the coffee in my mug and ventured a sip. It scorched my upper lip a little.

"I always rush it," I said. "Congratulations on the game last night, Seth."

Seth still didn't say anything.

"Seth told you I tried to interview him at the school yesterday?" I said to Kent.

"Yes," Kent said.

"Did he tell you that he walked out on me?"

Kent glanced over at his son.

"No," he said.

Seth shrugged.

"Why'd you walk out on Chief Wheeler?" Kent asked.

"I didn't want to talk with him," Seth said. "He told me I didn't have to say anything, and I didn't want to say anything. Walking out seemed like the best thing to do."

"Pregame jitters," Kent said.

"Sure," I said. "He's not playing a game tonight, though, is he?"

Kent shook his head.

"You know what I want to talk with you about," I said to Seth.

Seth nodded.

"You want your dad in here when we discuss this?"

"Do I have to?"

"Nope. If you want this conversation to be private, it can be private."

"Wait a minute," Kent said. "What if I want to be in the room?"

"Seth's seventeen," I said. "He's still a minor. You want to stay, there's not a lot I can do about it. He might talk a little more openly if you waited outside, though."

"One thing," Kent said. "I just want to make sure. Seth isn't a suspect or anything, right?"

"Of course he is. So are you. So is just about everyone in town except me, because I know I didn't kill Gypsy Camarena. I can't say that about anyone else. I'm just trying to narrow the field of suspects right now."

"Maybe I ought to have our attorney here."

"Do what you want. At some point, though, Seth and I are going to have this little talk."

He thought about it for a moment.

"I'll wait outside. If you get uncomfortable, son, you just come out and get me. You understand?"

Seth nodded. Kent stood and walked out the door, closing it behind him. I had a feeling he didn't move very far from it. Guys like Kent Kramer hated not knowing the score.

"Here's what I know," I told Seth. "Last weekend, while Kevin Byrne's parents were at the beach on a golf trip, there was a party at his house. I have a list of the Prosperity Glen students who attended, and the name of at least one student from Allenwood High. I also know that Gypsy Camarena and Anita Velez were there, and that you were just one of eight or ten boys who had sex with them."

"Okay," Seth said. "You know all this stuff. Why do you need to talk to me, then?"

"In the course of gathering all this intelligence, I discovered that the party was your idea."

"Bullshit. Kevin set it up."

"No, he didn't. Kevin couldn't set up a circle jerk with an instruction manual. As it happens, you told Kevin it would be cool to have a party while his folks were out, and you suggested to him that he invite Gypsy Camarena."

"Prove it."

"I don't have to. There are no charges against you. I'm making statements of fact, based on the information I've received from the other boys who were there, and from one of the girls. How did you know that it would be fun to invite Gypsy to this party?"

"Lucky guess," he said.

"Uh-huh. Of course, you just tacitly admitted that inviting her was your idea. How well did you know Gypsy?"

He shrugged.

"We talked, sometimes."

"When was the first time you had sex with her?"

"Last Saturday night. Nothing wrong with

168

that. She was over sixteen."

I shook my head.

"Don't lie to me," I said. "You'd had sex with Gypsy before last Saturday night, probably a bunch of times."

He shrugged.

"Here's what I'm doing," I told him. "I'm trying to build a timeline for Gypsy from the night of the party until she died roughly three days later. I'm finding a lot of gaps in that timeline. How did Gypsy get to the party?"

"Damned if I know. She probably drove."

"She didn't own a car, and she didn't have access to one. Who brought her to the party, Seth?"

"How would I know?"

"Okay, here's what I'm going to do," I said. "Just because you're being such a tubesteak, I'm going at this the hard way. I'm going to get a subpoena for your car. You drive that red Grand Am, right? Sweet ride, Seth. I'm going to have it towed to the sheriff's department garage in Morgan, and I'm going to have the crime scene boys go over it with every toy they possess. If they find so much as a hair in that car that matches Gypsy's DNA, I'm going to arrest you on obstruction charges, and you can kiss your scholarship goodbye. How's that sit, pal?"

Seth muttered something under his breath.

"What? I didn't catch that," I said.

"Asshole," he said, just loudly enough for me to hear.

"That's *Chief Asshole* to you, kid," I said, as I picked up the telephone. I dialed my home number. Craig had spent the night with one of his friends, and I knew he wouldn't be home. The machine would pick up. "You know what a telephonic warrant is, Seth? That's where I explain the situation to the judge, and he tells me over the telephone to impound your wheels."

I let him stew for a few seconds. Just to twist the knife a little, I waited until he started to speak.

"Look . . ." he said.

I silenced him by holding up one finger.

"Good morning, Your Honor," I said into the phone, trying to cover the beep as my machine kicked in. "Yes, sir, I'm very sorry to disturb you on the weekend. I have a situation, though, and I may need to request a telephonic warrant. Could you hold on for just a moment? Thank you."

I covered the speaker and turned to Seth.

"Okay," he said, dejectedly. "I'll tell you what I know. Just don't take my car."

I uncovered the speaker.

"I'm sorry, Your Honor. My witness seems to have decided to cooperate. You too, sir. Have a very nice weekend."

I racked the receiver, and faced Seth.

I waited, as he tried to gather his thoughts. For a kid like Seth, that could take a while.

"I brought her," he said, finally.

"Yeah. I know."

"If you knew, why'd you threaten to take my car?"

"I had to hear it from you. What I want to know now is how long you and Gypsy had been having sex."

He rolled his eyes.

"In general terms," I added.

"Maybe a month. She was at a party after the Pooler game in September, and we hooked up there."

"Whatever happened to *'beaners ought to stay with their own kind'*? Remember? That's what you said last week, after I cut the deal with your dad to let Vicente Ramirez off the hook. I would like to remind you that, at that exact moment, your squeeze was decomposing by the side of Six Mile Creek."

"She wasn't my squeeze."

"How would you define it?"

"We just hooked up from time to time."

"So it was okay for you to boff Gypsy Camarena, but it was this big deal for Vicente to talk with Gary Tomberlin's girlfriend?"

"It was a big deal to Gary. I was helpin' out a teammate."

"That's not what Anita Velez said."

"Who?"

"The other girl you and your butt buddies gangbanged at Kevin Byrne's house."

"Oh. Her."

"Anita was one of Gypsy's closest friends. She told me that Gary Tomberlin wasn't all that upset that Vicente talked with his girlfriend. She says you were the one who made a big deal out of it."

"What can I say? Beaners lie."

"I don't think so. I think maybe you were looking for an excuse to deal a righteous ass-whooping to one of the Mexican kids. In this case, it just happened to be the kid who threatened to bench you on the baseball team next spring."

"That had nothin' to do with it," Seth protested.

"Okay, whatever. I'm just jerking your chain, kid. I'm demonstrating to you that, so far, you've lied your ass off every chance you've gotten, and I haven't been fooled. So when was the last time you saw Gypsy Camarena?"

"I told you. At Kevin Byrne's house."

"And you brought her there?"

"That's right."

"So how did she get home?"

"How the fuck would I know?"

"You would if you took her home."

"But I didn't. Yeah, I took her to Kevin's house, her and that other girl."

"Anita Velez."

"I didn't really get her name. I hadn't met her before. Gypsy showed me how to get to her house after I picked her up."

"What time did you pick Gypsy up?" I asked.

"Around six. We got to that Anita chick's house around six fifteen."

"What time did you get to Kevin's house?"

"About seven-thirty."

"It took an hour and fifteen minutes to drive from Mount Zion Church Road to Deep Crick Road? That's only a mile and a half."

"We got something to eat first."

"Why?"

"Because Gypsy wanted something to eat. Her parents weren't home when I picked her up. She said she hadn't had lunch."

"Where did you eat?"

"We got pizza at the shopping center."

"Okay. And you say you have no idea how Gypsy and Anita got home that night."

"That's right. I was wasted. Most of the guys were. We all crashed at Kevin's house. I don't remember seeing Gypsy after about midnight."

"So someone drove her home."

"Maybe she walked. It isn't that far. Maybe an hour."

"Or maybe she didn't go home at all. I know she was at school on Monday, and I know she went out that evening with Jaime Ortiz and Anita Velez to the mall, and I know she came home around six-thirty. Sometime between six-thirty and midnight she was murdered. Maybe the person who took her home Saturday night decided he wanted a replay. Maybe he picked her up, took her somewhere quiet, made his play, and she told him to stuff it. Maybe he got angry and lost control, and next thing he knew she was dead. What do you think about that?"

"I think it sounds like a TV show."

"Maybe it does at that," I said. "On the other hand, if I can find out who took Gypsy home that night, I can fill in at least another hour or so on my timeline. So you know what I need?"

"What?"

"I need you to find out for me who took her home."

174

"Aw, come on, Chief!"

"I think that would be a great way for you to get off my shit list, Seth. You *do* want off my shit list, right?"

In about five minutes, he had gone from haughty and defiant to completely defeated. He leaned forward, his elbows on his knees, his hands hanging limply between his legs, and his head bowed.

"Will it get you off my back?" he asked.

"It would be a start," I said.

CHAPTER SEVENTEEN

"Go sit in the car, Seth," Kent Kramer said after I walked Seth back out to the waiting room.

Seth didn't reply. He just walked out the door, and allowed it to slam back behind him.

"So, what's up?" Kent asked me.

"Just filling in the blanks. I have a lot of time over the last three or four days of Gypsy Camarena's life that aren't accounted for. Seth helped me cover a few hours."

"He knew that girl?"

"He didn't tell you?"

"No."

"I think you ought to talk with your boy, Kent."

"Why don't you tell me?"

"Because it's personal, and this is an active investigation. I go around yakking to everyone about what I find, and the next thing I know I run up against someone who can really help me, but has had time to manufacture a cover story that screws the whole thing up."

"But Seth is a suspect."

"We've been down this road. Everyone's a suspect. Seth. You. That cute blonde girl who checks groceries over at the Piggly Wiggly. Everyone."

"Except you."

"I know I didn't do it. Can't say that about anyone else. I will tell you one thing, though. Even if that boy of yours does somehow manage to shag a college football scholarship, he's going to fuck it up unless he calms down a little. Colleges don't have time to deal with kids who get into fights at the slightest provocation. Thanks for bringing him by, Kent."

"Wait a minute!"

"I'm kind of busy right now," I said. "If you have some pertinent information that will help me find the person who murdered Gypsy Camarena, please let me know. Otherwise, I have to get back to work."

I turned my back on him and walked back into the office. He didn't follow me, so I figured I wasn't going to solve the murder in the next five minutes.

I sat at my desk and ate my breakfast, sipping coffee between bites to keep the doughy biscuits from sticking to the roof of my mouth. When I finished, I walked into the men's room to wash my hands.

I almost surprised myself when I looked in the mirror. The fluorescent lamp over the sink made my skin look jaundiced, and highlighted every line on my haggard face. I couldn't believe how tired I looked. After the intrusion of my nightmare, I had slept for only an hour the night before. The night before that, I had never really gotten back to sleep. The damned dreams were wearing me out.

I heard my telephone ring, so I dried my hands and returned to my desk.

"This is Carla Powers," she said when I picked up the receiver.

"Doctor. Any results from the DNA tests yet?"

"Oh, Lord no. I don't expect those until sometime next week. I just wanted to call to let you know we're finished with the Camarena girl's body. Anytime her parents want to arrange for burial, she can be picked up."

"I have their number here somewhere," I said, fishing through the growing pile of papers related to Gypsy's murder on my desk.

"I already tried to call," she said. "The number is disconnected."

"Happens all the time. Some of these families are lucky to put food on the table seven nights a week. Some of the luxuries have to go begging once in a while. I'll drive by their house in an hour or so and give them the message."

"Thanks. Any leads on who might have killed her?"

"I know I didn't do it," I said. It was becoming a litany. "Beyond that, I'm still guessing. Don't worry, though, something will turn up. It always does."

"I heard you had a disturbance at the high school last night."

"Word gets around quickly."

"Especially when it makes the front page of the *Ledger-Telegraph*."

I pulled my shoes off the desktop and sat upright.

"Say that again?"

"You haven't seen the paper yet?"

"No."

"There's a nice picture of you in there, facing down a line of protesters up against the fence at the football stadium."

"Oh, great. Thanks for calling, Doctor. Sounds like I need to go buy a paper."

I replaced the receiver, and walked out the back door of the station. The business district in Prosperity is limited by town

179

charter to about three square acres at the tee intersection of the Morgan Highway and the highway that stretches between Parker County to the north and Mica Wells to the south. It consists of a grocery store, a Chinese restaurant, a pharmacy, a pizza shop, a dry cleaner, and assorted medical offices, along with the Town Hall and the police station. There was a newspaper box outside the pharmacy. I dropped a half-dollar into the slot and pulled out a copy of the morning paper.

Damned if Carla hadn't been right. Page one, above the fold. There I was, shot from behind, standing with my feet spread and my hands on my hips, facing down a phalanx of Mexican teenagers. The headline read *Hispanic Protest at Local Football Game,* and included a couple of quotes from Vicente Ramirez. It was written by Cory True, who had managed to squeeze in a couple of quotes from our conversation the day before, and who also mentioned the fight in the school hallways. Other than the fact that he got the final score of the game wrong, the story was largely factual and well written.

It was also a pain in the ass.

I returned to my office and read it over a couple of times. Vicente hadn't told Cory

180

much more than he had told me, which was comforting. Even so, this was the kind of publicity the Prosperity town fathers preferred to avoid. I was probably going to catch hell when they returned to work on Monday morning.

Like I cared.

Around eleven o'clock, I locked the station door and climbed back into my cruiser. Roberto Camarena and his wife Alfonsa lived on the other side of Six Mile Creek, in a rental house halfway down Morris Quick Road, an unmarked rural two-lane piece of asphalt that ran between the Morgan Highway and the Old Village Road.

The houses on Morris Quick Road were older than most in the town. They had been built in the 1930s, when the Civilian Conservation Corps engaged in logging and watershed preservation operations in the area. The houses had been conceived as dormitory quarters for the youths who joined the corps. After the beginning of World War II, the houses were converted into duplex rentals. They were hastily built frame affairs, little more than shanties even in the Roosevelt Administration. Each side of a duplex had two bedrooms, a single bath, a kitchen, and an open area that passed for a living room. The amenities were simple, because the stingy bastard landlords wanted to keep the overhead low, the rents high, and the leases ironclad. The population along Morris Quick Road was about ninety-percent Mexican, of which one hundred percent were illegal aliens.

I parked the cruiser on the street in front of Roberto Camarena's house, and walked up the broken concrete walkway to the front porch. There wasn't a doorbell, so I rapped a couple of times on the peeling, dry-rotted wood of the screen door.

Nobody answered. There were curtains across the glass of the front door, so I couldn't see inside the house. I walked back to the cruiser and rechecked the address on my legal pad. I had the right house.

"Ain't nobody home," somebody said.

I looked across the street. A man in a wheelchair was sitting on the meager front porch of a dilapidated frame shotgun house, his legs covered with a fraying tartan afghan.

"Say again?" I said.

"They gone. I saw 'em leave. Loaded up all their shit on the back of a pickup and drove off."

"When was this?" I asked.

"Yesterday afternoon, on into the evening."

"You're talking about the Camarena family?"

"Damned if I know their names. Not much of a family, if'n you ask me. Just the man and his wife. Loaded up and bugged out."

I crossed the street and picked my way up to his front porch by way of a random set of flagstones set into a muddy front yard.

"What's your name, sir?" I asked.

"Puddin' Tame. Ask me again I'll tell you the same."

He cackled at his joke. I could see his pink gums through his open mouth, but very few teeth. He looked somewhere in his seventies, but the people who lived on Morris Quick Road tended to age early.

"You know who I am?" I asked.

"Johnny Law."

"I'm the police chief in Prosperity."

"Hell, I didn't vote for ya."

"Nobody did. I'm conducting an investigation into a murder. I'd appreciate it if you could cooperate a little."

"What if I don't?"

"I might have to run you in. Ask you questions at the station."

"You gonna lock me up, Johnny?"

"I could."

"Bet the food's better there than what I

have to eat. Let's go."

He wheeled his chair toward the splintered plywood ramp someone had installed alongside the porch.

"Hold on, there, old-timer." I walked over and stood in his way.

"Jake," he said.

"Jake what?"

"Jake Wiley. Wiley Coyote. Coyote Ugly. Ugly Pugly."

He cackled again, and his tongue rolled over in his wreckage of a mouth like a drunken worm. I had seen that routine before, mostly in overmedicated mental cases I had transported to the state hospital.

"You taking your meds, Jake?" I asked.

"When I can get 'em."

I nodded.

"So you saw the Camarenas load up and drive off yesterday evening."

"That's what I said."

"You live alone, Jake?"

"Since my wife died, God rest her soul. Had a coupla kids, but they come to no good. Never hear from 'em anymore. No, it's just me and my cat, and sometimes the cat don't come home."

"You know if anyone else saw them leave?"

"Who?"

"The Camarenas," I said, biting my tongue.

"Naw. I prolly wouldn'ta seen 'em myself, but my television's shot, so I got nothin' to do but sit out here and watch stuff. They seemed to be in a hurry, though. They was real nervous-like."

I stood there, trying to think whether I was missing any obvious questions. Nothing came to mind, so I tipped my hat at him.

"You take care, Jake."

"Thought you was gonna run me in, lock me up, feed me a decent meal."

"Can't think of a good reason to do that," I said. "Keep it in the road, neighbor."

I turned and walked back to the cruiser, and after doing a quick turnaround in the Camarenas' drive I headed back out toward the highway. Jake Wiley watched me all the way. It was pretty much all he had to do.

I was halfway back to the station when I suddenly pulled the cruiser off the road, next to the bridge over Six Mile Creek. I flipped on the bubbletop, and pulled on my hat before climbing from the car.

I made my way down the beaten path to the bank where Gypsy Camarena had been found. I didn't really know why I was there, or why I had suddenly decided to pull over and revisit the scene. I guess something drew me there.

The yellow police tape was still in place. I couldn't make out any signs that the area had been overly trampled by sightseers. At first I took care to stay outside the taped perimeter, but after a few minutes I ducked under the tape and walked over to the mossy bank where Gypsy had lain for up to a day.

There was a large rock on the creek bank. I sat on it and stared down into the lazily flowing waters of the creek. The creek was made up of the confluence of a series of watershed runoffs from farms down the line and a couple of local springs, and without a constant supply it had been whittled down to little more than a three-inch-deep trickle of water meandering between smooth stones sticking up from the mud. I knew from my childhood that if I were to turn over a couple of stones I'd find some crawdads, but you'd have to turn over several dozen to collect enough to make a decent meal, so nobody ever really bothered.

During a rainy season, and when the area was hit with the occasional torrential summer thunderstorm, Six Mile Creek would swell and deepen, and even sometimes overrun its banks. I had often seen the Morgan

Highway Bridge over the creek under a foot of water. Every several years the local Boy Scout troop would make a spring project of cleaning out a tangle of loose tree branches, random garbage, and broken vines that would collect on the upstream side of the bridge and clog the underside of it as if it had been specially woven to form a dam.

About five years earlier, some damn fool kid from Morgan had decided to raft the creek during a five-day spring storm. He was tossed from the raft and pinioned against the pile of detritus under the bridge. I tried not to imagine his terror as he struggled against the thousands of gallons of raging water that held him fast against the snarl of refuse, even as it rose up his chest, past his chin, and then submerged him totally, as he fought for breath right up until the last moment when his burning lungs gave out and he sucked in the mire that entrapped him. I had a hard time conceiving a more horrifying end.

Then another death intruded on my reverie, and I again allowed my eyes to follow the scarred path in the earth down the hill and right up to the chewed and gnarled burl of a black walnut tree growing on the bank of the creek.

It seemed that nothing much ever came to

a good end on Six Mile Creek.

If only I had taken the damned telephone call . . .

I jerked my head up, and shook it violently. I realized that I had mentally drifted away, sitting on the rock, lulled into a heart-slamming flashback by the bubbling of the stream as it caromed around the rocks and tumbled over a series of natural six-inch waterfalls leading to the bridge.

I quickly looked up the hill, to where I had parked the cruiser, and was relieved to find that it was deserted. Nobody could see my sudden panic as I broke myself away from the waking nightmare that forced me back to another day on the banks of Six Mile Creek.

I shook it off, rubbed my eyes, and slowly rose from the rock. It was a bad idea to spend too much time down here, where so many people had died.

It might be catching.

CHAPTER EIGHTEEN

Slim was waiting in my office when I got back.

"Your shoes're muddy," he said as I walked in.

"Been down to Six Mile Creek."

"That's not a good place for you, Chief."

"It can't be helped. I was looking for something to help me in this Gypsy Camarena murder case."

"Sheriff's boys cleaned that creek bank off. What'd you think you're going to find?"

"I don't know," I said. "I have an assignment for you while you're out on patrol this afternoon. It looks like Gypsy's parents have bugged out. Maybe they were afraid the publicity surrounding her murder would bring the INS down around their heads. If you drive through the Mexican neighborhoods, maybe you can ask around a little, see if anyone knows where they went."

"Those people aren't going to tell me jack

shit, Chief."

"Ask anyway. While you're at it, let them know that the Medical Examiner wants to release Gypsy's body. Maybe these people won't tell you where Roberto Camarena went, but they might know how to get a message to him. Girl deserves a decent burial."

"Did the autopsy provide any leads?"

"Not yet. Maybe when we get the DNA tests back. I'm taking off. You're in charge for the rest of the afternoon."

He nodded, and started pulling together his gear for the afternoon patrol.

I walked toward the door.

"Hey, Chief," he said.

I looked back.

"You stay away from Six Mile Creek, okay? That place is no good for you."

Part of me wanted to remind him who called the shots in the Prosperity PD. Then I realized that he was probably right. That place wasn't any good for me. It never would be. Slim was just doing what any good friend should, warning me away from the creek.

"Thanks," I said.

I sat on my front porch, sipping a Corona and listening to the Metropolitan Opera broadcast on the local public radio station. I had changed from my uniform into jeans and a plaid flannel shirt, with the sleeves rolled up halfway to my elbows.

The performance that afternoon was *Don Giovanni,* again. It didn't matter what was being performed, actually. Sitting on the front porch on Saturday and catching the opera had been a tradition under the Wheeler roof as far back as I could recall.

I didn't really understand the lyrics, though once in a while I would catch a stray word I could recognize. It was the sense of grounding I received, keeping the tradition alive, that mattered. I urgently needed grounding, after the previous several days.

A little grounding went a long way. By the end of the first act I became restless, so I switched the radio to the Carolina–N.C. State football game. The Tarheels were out front by two touchdowns. I wasn't going to fall sucker for that routine, though. It was early in the second half, and I knew that the Wolfpack could come roaring back.

A car pulled into my driveway and began the quarter-mile trek up to the house, crunching gravel under its tires as it made the long arcing turn around a stand of apple trees that my grandfather just hadn't had the heart to cut down. I watched as it approached, but I didn't get out of my chair.

It stopped in front of the house. The door opened, and Mayor Newton, with some effort, extricated himself from behind the wheel. Like me, he was dressed casually, in a long-sleeved golf shirt and a pair of khakis. He had a Bliss Country Club ball cap pushed back on his brow.

He reached back to his pocket and pulled out a handkerchief, which he used to wipe his forehead.

"New car, Huggie?" I asked from the porch.

"Ain't it a beauty?"

"It's spiffy. What is it?"

"Chrysler 300, the new model. You got the Carolina game on up there?"

"Sure do. Want a beer?"

"No, thanks."

He took the five steps up to the porch and sat in the chair next to mine.

"Who's leading?"

"Heels. You come out here to listen to the game?"

"Not exactly. Saw you on the front page of the *Ledger-Telegraph* this morning."

"Not my best side," I said.

"Not everyone would agree. I talked with Kent Kramer this afternoon."

I didn't say anything.

"He thinks you're riding some of the boys at the school a little hard," Newton said.

"Does he?"

"Is it true you questioned a bunch of the students at the high school without their parents present?"

"They were all told they could have a parent in the interview. They declined."

"You want to tell me why you wanted to talk with them at all?"

"Part of the murder investigation."

"Oh, yeah. That Mexican girl."

"Her name was Gypsy Camarena."

"Yes. Well."

I took a sip of the Corona, and gazed out over the fields to the east of my house. It was one of those crisp, crystal-clear autumn afternoons, and it was a pure shame to waste it on a political hack like Huggie Newton. He did sign my paychecks, though, so I was sort of obligated to let him have his say.

"You think you might find out who killed her anytime soon?" he asked.

"I'm working on it."

"What have you found out?"

"Mostly I'm trying to reassemble the last several days of her life. There are some important gaps I'm trying to fill."

"And you think the high school boys can

help with that?"

"They were among the last people who saw her alive. She was at a party last weekend over off Deep Crick Road. You could say she was the main attraction. I'm still trying to find out how she got home from that party."

"Why?"

"Because I don't know."

"You think it might be important?"

"I think not knowing is important. It's the things you don't know that come back and bite you on the ass. Is there something I can do for you, Huggie?"

He squirmed in the chair a little.

I remembered Huggie from back in high school. He had been a pudgy, bespectacled bookworm throughout his early years. There was no question Huggie was smart, but he had taken a ton of ribbing over the years because he didn't really fit in with the other teenagers in the old Prosperity, before it had been overrun by developers.

It wasn't for lack of trying. I recalled a time back in our sophomore year of high school when he screwed up his courage and tried out for the football team. He had been all of five and a half feet tall, and weighed maybe two-fifty, so the coach had put him on the offensive line — probably thought he'd make a reasonably acceptable speed bump on the path to the quarterback. Poor Huggie didn't even know how to get into a decent three-point stance. On the first series of scrimmage plays on the first day of practice, a big old farm boy name Hack Pressley squared off against him on the defensive line. I was the quarterback, and when I called the snap Pressley lowered his head, then jerked up and rammed Huggie right in his pillow-like midsection. Lifted him right off the ground, flipped him over in midair, and slammed him on his back into the turf. Huggie lay there gasping for breath, looking like a beached whale.

He didn't come back for the second day of practice.

That was pretty much the end of Huggie's football career.

He went off to college and came back an attorney. Somehow that seemed to change things, when he opened his practice in Prosperity and wound up writing wills and contracts for most of the people who had derided him in school.

His self-confidence had expanded almost as rapidly as his waistline. Within a few years, he knew just about everything about everybody in town, including where the figurative bodies were buried. Knowledge being power, the next natural step had been into politics.

Huggie Newton was a great white shark in a minnow pond, and was destined never to rise any higher in office than Mayor of Prosperity. Because of that, he maintained a stranglehold on what power he had managed to acquire, and wielded it like a five-pound brickbat.

"I'll be honest with you, Judd," he said. "I'm getting some complaints."

"Let me guess. You've been talking with Kent Kramer, Fred Warfield, and Elzie Phipps."

"Among others. They don't like their kids getting grilled by the police on school grounds."

"How do they feel about their kids gang-banging teenaged Mexican girls in Kevin Byrne's basement?"

He winced.

"See, here's my problem," I said. "It's entirely possible that one of the boys at that sex party last weekend decided to kill Gypsy Camarena. I can't say why, and I won't speculate on that for the time being. It's a pretty good bet, though, that whoever did kill her already knew her, and you don't get much more knowledge of a person than those boys did. They're suspects, Mayor. As such, they're fair game. I told every one of them that he didn't have to speak with me without a parent or a lawyer present. Every one of them decided against having some- one else present. You're an attorney. You want to tell me I've done something wrong?"

"Not legally . . ."

"Okay. Politically."

"Well . . ."

"Are you afraid of alienating your voting base, Huggie?"

He shook his head. His face slowly turned crimson, and he was sweating profusely.

"I can make you stop," he said.

"No," I said. I could hear the fatigue in my voice. "You can't."

"I can have you fired."

"That you *can* do."

"It isn't out of the question."

"It never has been, Huggie. When you recruited me for this job, though, I told you how things were going to be. You wanted a cop. You got a cop. You want to go find some kind of rubber-stamp that you can send out and yank back when it suits you, you go right ahead. Until then, though, I'll enforce the law and conduct my investigations the way I see fit."

He didn't say a word. His complexion told

me everything I needed to know.

"Now how about that beer?" I asked.

CHAPTER NINETEEN

Donna had planned to go antiquing on Saturday afternoon, but we were supposed to get together at the farm that evening to cook out. Craig had begged off dinner, claiming that he was going to a movie in Morgan with a couple of friends.

As soon as the Carolina–State game ended — Carolina managed to hang on for a three-point win — I buttoned up the house and took my Jeep over to the shopping center to pick up some thick-cut pork chops and fixings at the Piggly Wiggly.

I loaded up the basket with chops, a fresh Vidalia sweet onion, a couple of cans of pinto beans, and a can of collard greens. I also got some cornbread mix, because I was too lazy to make it from scratch. I topped it off with a jug of Chateau Screwtop. I wasn't going to waste good wine on a cookout.

I was headed for the Jeep in the parking lot when Kent Kramer called to me from a couple of rows over.

"Hi, Kent," I said, as I stowed my bags on a hook behind the front seat.

He walked over to me, his hand extended the same way he probably did to every real estate pigeon he met in the course of a business day.

"I was hoping to run across you," he said.

"You were? Was that before or after you talked with Huggie?"

"Oh, that was yesterday. We jawed a little at the football game last night. You cleared a lot of my concerns up this morning. No, I thought you might be interested in some tickets to the Pythons game tomorrow. Maybe take your boy out for a day on the town."

"Craig doesn't like football."

"No problem. I was supposed to take a bunch of the Cub Scouts out tomorrow, and a couple of them backed out at the last minute, so I have some extra tickets."

He pulled them from his jacket pocket.

"Seth doesn't want to go?"

"Oh, he's already going, but he's using our season tickets. They're in another section. What do you say, Judd?"

I hadn't been to a Pythons game in a couple of years. Most of them were shown on television, and a cop's salary doesn't pay for a lot of extras.

They were good tickets, too. Forty-yard line, on the shady side of the field, about thirty rows up. Would have been fun.

"I'd better not," I said, handing them back to him.

"What's the matter? Other plans?"

"No. No plans. I just better pass on it. Thanks anyway."

I started to climb up into the Jeep.

"I'll hold onto them just the same," Kent said. "In case you change your mind."

"Don't reckon I will. No offense, Kent, but it might not seem right to take them, your son being a suspect in this murder and all."

I watched as the blood drained from his face.

"Now, you know better than that, Judd. Seth couldn't kill anyone."

"I hope you're right. I also hope he can find out who took Gypsy Camarena home from that party last weekend, like I asked him to do. That would be a big help. You have a nice evening."

I started the Jeep and put it in gear, then backed up and pulled out of the parking lot. I could see Kent in the rearview mirror, still standing in the middle of the asphalt, the tickets still in his hand. He looked like I had run right over him.

"I think Kent Kramer tried to bribe me this afternoon," I said, as I turned the pork chops over on the grill.

"How?" Donna asked. She handed me the beer she had retrieved from the refrigerator in the kitchen.

"Football tickets. Pythons. Good seats, too."

"Not much of a bribe."

"Yeah. I was thinking the same thing. You don't suppose he really thought he could buy me off with a couple of $50 tickets, do you?"

"You? Not likely."

"He knows me better than that. We both know each other better than that. What do you suppose he was up to?"

"Can't say," she said, and she took a sip from her wine cooler. "Guys like Kent, though, always seem to think they can buy their way into or out of things. What was he bribing you to do?"

"He didn't come right out and say, but I've been leaning on Seth pretty hard the last couple of days. Maybe he wants me to look somewhere else on this Gypsy Camarena thing."

"Is Seth a serious suspect?"

"As serious as anyone else. This is still a fresh case. Every murder you work tends to run by its own rules. I'm still trying to figure out the rulebook."

She sat in a folding chair I had set up out by the stone and mortar grill, and took another sip of her drink.

"I, uh, stopped by Six Mile Creek this afternoon," I said, tentatively.

"Okay."

"I walked down to the spot where we found Gypsy the other day. Sat on a rock for a while and thought."

"What did you think about?"

"This and that. You know where she was found, right?"

"I heard. Is that a problem for you?"

"Seems like a strange coincidence."

"Is it getting in the way?"

"Come again?"

"Are you having a problem seeing past . . . you know? Is that interfering with your ability to get a grasp on Gypsy's killing?"

"I don't know. I don't think so, but it's hard to say."

"You weren't just thinking about Gypsy down there on Six Mile Creek, though, were you?"

"No," I said.

She nodded and crossed her legs. It was

Indian summer, and she had dressed in a pair of walking shorts. Her calves were still tanned from the real summer, and when she crossed her legs I had to catch my breath.

"Maybe it interferes, just a little," I said. "I'm trying to get past that."

"By not sleeping."

"Sleep isn't the problem. If they could make a no-dream pill, I'd be just fine."

"Don't burn the chops," she said.

I glanced over. The fat from the pork chops was falling on the hickory embers, and flaming up. The tongues of fire swiped at the bottom of the chops. I used the tongs and moved them to a cooler part of the grill.

"You know what I think?" she said, when I turned back.

"What?"

"I think you need to go back and talk with Dr. Kronenfeld."

Later that evening, Jaime Ortiz took Anita Velez to the movies in Morgan. After the movie, they hit the drive-through at one of the chain Burger Death restaurants, and ate as they drove back down the Morgan Highway to Prosperity.

Somewhere around Six Mile Creek, Anita pulled a joint from her purse and showed it to Jaime. He grinned and nodded, and turned the car around to head for Morris Quick Road.

Anita lived with her father and Jaime lived with his parents and three sisters in a house that could have fit inside Kent Kramer's garage, so there wasn't a place for them to be alone and private. A car was a perfect place to be together without dealing with prying eyes and parental interruptions.

Kramer Development had bought ninety acres off Morris Quick Road at an estate sale, and had graded and paved roads through it in preparation for a new mid-priced residential neighborhood. Someday it would be overrun with $200,000 cracker box houses, but on that evening it was nothing but a bunch of fresh asphalt and mud, and the centuries-old hardwood forests that had been temporarily spared in the face of encroaching civilization.

Jaime pulled his car into a dark cul-de-sac and killed the engine. Anita fired up the joint with a disposable lighter, and they took turns hitting off it until it was nothing but a glowing roach.

Jaime pulled Anita to him, and kissed her with the rough tenderness of inexperience and impatient youth. Piece by piece, clothes flew from the front to the back seat, and within minutes Jaime was deep inside her, pounding for all he was worth, muttering the only words he could find in his limited vocabulary to tell her that, at least for this night, he was hers and hers alone.

A half hour later, it was all over. Anita fell back against her door, huffing and gasping, as Jaime leaned his seat back and basked in the endorphin-glazed contentment. They looked at each other. Anita laughed first. It was nervous laughter, borne of sexual relief and drug-induced intoxication and youth. Jaime began to giggle, and he ran his hand up Anita's leg in the only gesture he could think of, at that moment, that was intimate and affectionate at the same time.

He slowly became aware of an urge, and he excused himself, saying he would be back in just a few moments. Slipping on his sneakers and nothing else, he left Anita in the car and walked back through some future homeowner's front yard to a stand of yellow poplar, until the darkness enveloped him like a velvet glove, and he leaned back against a tree and urinated.

Anita had almost passed out in the front of the car when she became aware of the engine noise from behind. Another car had pulled into the cul-de-sac, its lights darkened and its engine idling. She heard doors open and slam. In seconds, the door against which she was leaning was jerked open, and thickly muscled arms grabbed at her from behind. She felt herself being dragged from the car, almost too anesthetized to struggle or resist. Another pair of hands encircled her ankles like steel manacles, and she was hoisted in the air. A hand snaked around her head and covered her mouth before she could scream.

"Where is he, bitch?" she heard one voice rasp in her ear.

She tried to struggle, but the vise-like arms holding her off the ground just grasped her tighter. Anita felt herself floating through the air, until her back slammed down onto a cool, solid metal surface. It took her a moment to realize she was on the trunk of the car.

In the inky blackness of the night, she couldn't make out any faces. There was only the perception of restraint, and a strange, sour, violent musk about the men who held her down on the trunk lid.

"Here he comes," she heard one of them say, and in an instant one of the sets of hands pinning her to the car disappeared. She thought for a second that she might be able to free herself, but as soon as she was released, another man stepped in and held her down.

"Pop the trunk lid," someone said.

Seconds later, she heard the *thunk* as the latch underneath her was released. Again she rose up in the air, only to be thrown down again. Her head hit something sharp and hard, and for an instant what vision she had swirled and twisted crazily. Then she heard a slamming sound, and everything was even darker than before. She tried to sit up, but her head hit a low obstruction. It took her a moment to realize she had been locked in the trunk of Jaime Ortiz's car.

"Jaime!" she screamed.

Stu Marbury had the evening patrol shift on Saturday. He was cruising the local neighborhoods, and listening to a college football game on the radio. He turned down Morris Quick Road and into the dark, deserted streets of Kent Kramer's new development, hoping to find a few teenagers to roust. The unpopulated streets were an open invitation to kids who just wanted to hang out and pound back a few beers, or take their girlfriends for a late-night make-out session.

He turned into the cul-de-sac, and saw an empty Buick sitting quietly, its passenger door hanging wide open. He switched on the bubbletop, and *whooped* the siren once, just to make the kids inside jump.

Nothing happened.

He killed the engine and pulled his nightstick from the holder between the seats, then opened the door and walked toward the Buick.

"Anyone around?" he called out. "Prosperity Police!"

That was when he heard a rhythmic thumping from the rear of the Buick, and a muffled voice crying out desperately. He unhooked his pistol, ran to the front of the car, and hit the trunk release under the dashboard. The lid flew up, and a naked girl pounced out. She cried and screamed as she ran around to Stu and grabbed him by the sleeves, jabbering incoherently in a language he hadn't spoken since high school.

He grabbed her by the arms and held her away from him. He could smell her fear and the stink of sex on her, and for a moment he feared that he was being set up for a rape charge. She continued to babble, though, and he tried to calm her by asking what the problem was.

"*Jaime!*" she said, finally. "They came for him!"

Stu shined his flashlight inside the car, and saw the clothes strewn carelessly across the back seat. He opened the door and handed Anita a shirt and a pair of pants.

"Put these on," he said. "What happened?"

She tried to explain to him, but all he could figure out was that someone named Jaime was still around, somewhere, and must be hurt.

"Stay here," he said.

She grappled at him, desperately afraid of letting him go, but he peeled her fingers away, told her again to stay by the car, and stalked off toward the trees beyond the cul-de-sac.

It was a moonless night. There were no lights in the development, and only the faintest glow in the sky from the north and Parker County. Stu moved his flashlight back and forth, trying to catch any random movement. The play of the high-intensity beam cast eerie shadows against the trees, which seemed to dance back and forth as he scanned for Jaime.

He was about to turn back when he heard the raspy, fluid moan. He aimed the flashlight in the direction of the sound, and saw part of a leg protruding from behind a thick-trunked white oak.

The newly fallen leaves crunched under his feet as Stu ran to the tree. The moaning increased as he drew near, and he could tell that someone was sitting on the ground on the far side of the trunk. He circled cautiously, until the body on the other side was fully illuminated in the cone of light that cut through the mist like a golden scalpel.

"Oh, my God," Stu whispered. "Jesus God Almighty . . ."

Jaime Ortiz sat with his back against the tree. He was naked except for one of the shoes he had slipped on before leaving his car. His chest and face were pockmarked with bruises. The flesh from the bridge of his nose to the middle of his forehead had been peeled back like the skin of a banana, and hung down like an elephant's ear over his mouth, which was swollen like a purple flower. His arms were pulled up, as if he were surrendering, but then Stu realized that they were suspended in place over his head by the eighty-penny nail that had been driven through his hands and the bark, into the living pith of the white oak trunk.

CHAPTER TWENTY

It was another sleepless night, but this time it was because of a real-life nightmare.

Stu called the Rescue Squad first, then called me. I was sitting on the couch at the house, watching a movie with Donna, when the phone rang.

I could tell immediately that something bad had happened, because Stu's voice had risen to near-soprano pitch, and he was pounding out a couple of hundred words a minute.

"Hold on," I said. "Slow down. Tell me again, real slow this time."

He explained what he had found.

I didn't bother to put on my uniform. I just strapped on my Sam Brown and pinned on my badge, told Donna that I probably wouldn't be back until morning, and kissed her goodnight.

It was just as bad as Stu had described it. The Rescue Squad boys beat me to the

Morris Quick Road cul-de-sac by about a minute. Their red flashers blended crazily with my blue ones, and the woods took on a life of their own in the dancing shadows.

Anita Velez was wrapped in a blanket, but still shivered as she leaned against the side of the Buick, her mascara running down her cheeks mixed with the hot tears she couldn't seem to stop. She sobbed uncontrollably, and occasionally she wailed as the paramedics tended to her.

"Is she going to be okay?" I asked as I walked up.

"Just a superficial scalp laceration," one of them said. "And she's real upset. You gotta see the other guy, though."

Several other paramedics had joined Stu back in the woods off the cul-de-sac. All of them had high-intensity flashlights. I could see Jaime Ortiz's leg splayed out at a sharp angle, but that was all I could see until I made my way into the crowd.

"Jesus," I said, as I saw him for the first time. "Who in hell did this?"

"The girl said something about a bunch of guys in a car that pulled up behind the Buick," Stu said. "She wasn't sure how many there were, and she never really saw their faces."

"Could she recognize any of the voices?" I

asked, without looking at him. I couldn't take my eyes off Jaime Ortiz.

"She's really not in shape to answer a lot of questions," Stu said. "Maybe after they get her to the hospital . . ."

"Have you guys ever seen anything like this?" I asked the paramedics.

"Not like this," one of them said. "Had a couple of construction workers shoot themselves accidentally with nail guns a few months back, but this . . ."

He shook his head.

"So," I said. "Are we just gonna leave him sitting there, or do you think we might want to get him to the hospital?"

"We were just talking about that when you drove up," Stu said. "That nail's about seven inches long. Thing's damn near a spike. We were tryin' to figure out how to get him loose."

"Hold on," I said.

I walked back to the cruiser and opened the trunk. I took out a heavy-duty bolt cutter, the kind we would use to cut galvanized chain, and walked back to the oak.

"One of you get in there and try to push his hands back toward the bark," I said.

It wasn't easy. The trauma of being nailed to the tree had swollen Jaime's palms. They looked like inflated surgical gloves — puffy, fat, and bloodless. Even so, with a little effort the paramedics were able to give me a half-inch of the shaft to work with.

"Just like when you go fishing," I said, as I worked the jaws of the bolt cutter into the narrow gap between the nail head and Jaime's left palm. "If you catch your finger on a hook, you just grit your teeth, push the hook on through, cut off the barb, and pull it back out."

I squeezed the handles of the bolt cutter, and the nail head popped off into the mud and the fallen leaves.

"I'm gonna need that," I said to Stu, pointing at the nail head. "Now, you guys slowly pull his hands forward, and let the nail shaft slide through the wounds. You be careful. As soon as you lower his arms, those nail holes are going to bleed like a son of a bitch."

Moments later, they laid Jaime on a stretcher, and busily bound his hands. They had already done what they could for his ruined face.

"Let's get them both to the hospital in Morgan," I said. "Stu, you go with them and make the calls to these kids' families. I'll call the sheriff's department and have them send out some crime scene guys, and catch up with you later."

■ ■ ■ ■

The CSI specialists from Morgan didn't finish their work until about four in the morning. By the time they had set up their halogen lights and generators and other equipment, it looked as if a movie company had invaded Prosperity to film a low-budget horror flick.

As luck would have it, the vagaries of shift rotation meant that Clark Ulrich and his new partner Sharon Counts were working that night. Sharon had looked drawn and austere in the daylight at Six Mile Creek. The halogen lamps at night didn't do her any favors.

"What in hell is going on down here?" Clark asked, as he rolled up a cloth tape measure. "You got some kind of Mexican crime wave in Prosperity?"

"Just a lot of victims," I said. "I'm still working on that murder the other day, and the girl who was here when my officer arrived couldn't say for certain who attacked her and the boy."

"We're going to have to cut up that tree to get the rest of the nail," he said. "You think the property owner's going to be upset about that?"

"Let me handle him. You just do what you need to do."

In the end, they felled the white oak with a chainsaw, and then sectioned out the portion with the nail in it.

"Shame to kill that tree," Sharon said, as she watched it fall. "I'll bet it's older than anyone in this county."

I realized that these were the first words she had ever said to me.

"I'll talk to the owner," I said. "I'll see to it that the wood doesn't go to waste. I know a sawyer over in Mica Wells who can quartersaw it. There's a lot of nice furniture in that tree trunk."

She nodded, but her eyes never left the tree.

I guess the conversation was over.

I got to Bliss Regional Hospital just as the eastern sky reddened with the onset of sunrise. Stu was waiting for me in the ER. Anita's father sat in a plastic seat in the waiting area. He was leaning over, his elbows resting on his thighs, and he stared at the random pattern in the linoleum floor.

"The boy's parents," Stu said, pointing with his chin two rows over. A couple in their early forties sat in the chairs. The man had his arm around the woman's shoulders.

She stared off into space.

"How much do they know?" I asked.

"Not much. I had a hell of a time talking with them over the phone. The girl's daddy doesn't speak much English at all, but compared to the boy's folks he's a freakin' expert. I managed to remember enough high school Spanish to get the idea across that they needed to come to the hospital."

"Did you ask the hospital to provide a translator?"

"Not yet. There's not much to tell them. You know how it works here, Judd. Hurry up and wait."

"Okay. Your shift was over hours ago. You need to run back to the station and write up your report. Leave it on my desk. I'll handle things here. Before you leave, radio Slim and tell him where I am, but let him go ahead and do his Sunday morning church traffic chores."

"Ten-four, Chief," he said, and walked out through the automatic doors, which whispered shut behind him.

I walked through the doors to the ER treatment desk and called over the charge nurse.

"You here about the Mexican kids, Judd?" the nurse said. She was a woman named Charlotte. I'd known her for several years.

"Yeah. Any news?"

"The girl should be ready to go in a half hour or so. She had a scalp lac, probably from when she hit her head in the trunk of the car. The boy . . ." She shrugged.

"He's pretty beat up," I said.

"That's one way of putting it. Somebody kicked the crap out of him. So far we have a broken cheek, cracked supraorbital ridge, a possible broken jaw, some major tissue and cartilage damage in his hands along with a few broken metacarpals, some nerve damage in his fingers, broken ribs, and the obvious facial soft tissue injuries. If that boy doesn't get worked over by a really good plastic surgeon, he's going to look like Frankenstein."

"He's going to be here for a while."

"He sure isn't going home today. Beyond that . . ." She shrugged again.

"Can you help me get an interpreter for the families? They don't speak much English."

"I'll find someone. So what in hell happened to you?"

I turned to face her.

"What?"

"You look like shit, Judd. Have you been sick? I could carry groceries in the bags under your eyes, and your color's awful."

"I haven't slept much since the murder," I said.

"Maybe you ought to clock out for a few hours and grab some sheet time. You might think a little clearer."

"I'll consider it. I'm going to hang around here for a few hours. Can you just page me when you find the interpreter?"

"Sure."

"Also, I'd like to interview the girl as soon as she's able."

"They're sewing her head now. She'll probably get a scan, just to make sure she didn't sustain a skull fracture, but I think she's going to be fine."

"You'll call me when she's ready?"

"You bet. Why don't you wait in the break room? There's a couch in there."

I didn't have to be psychic to read between her words. Sometimes it's nice when people are concerned enough about you to look after your best interests. If she had any idea what horrors faced me if I went to sleep, she'd have kept her damned mouth shut.

Even so, I did go to the break room, and I tried to keep myself wired by pounding back a couple of mugs of the radiator fluid they stashed in the coffee urn there. While I chugged my second cup, I sat on the couch she had mentioned. It was very comfortable. It would have been easy to just nod off and take a little somnolent vacation.

I didn't dare, of course. My conscious memories were bad enough. Compared to the guilt trips my mind played on me in my dreams, though, they were a walk in the park. I'd rather face the reality of my personal tragedies than the monsters that had visited me in my sleep since we'd found Gypsy Camarena lying on the banks of Six Mile Creek.

Nobody would look me in the eye . . .

"Chief?" someone said, and I felt a hand shake my shoulder.

It broke through a flashback and, like a sleepwalker suddenly roused, I jerked and grabbed the hand.

"What?" I asked, alarmed.

It was Charlotte.

"Sorry, Judd," she said. "I didn't mean to frighten you."

"That's okay. What is it?"

"The girl. Anita? She's almost ready to check out. You said you wanted to talk with her."

She led me through the ER to a warren of cubbies where the patients settled up with the hospital. Anita wouldn't be doing much settling, though, since neither she nor her father had any insurance, and it would probably take a year for her father to cover the bill. In the end, as was the case with most of Bliss County's illegals, the hospital would eventually chalk Anita's case off as a bad debt, and jack up everyone else's fees to cover it.

They had placed Anita and her father in an empty office in the processing area. Someone had washed her face. Without her makeup, she looked every bit of her sixteen years and change, and not a minute older. Compared to our first meeting, she now looked scared and vulnerable. I was hoping that she would also be a little more co-operative.

There was another person in the room, a woman in her thirties dressed in hospital greens, with a pair of glasses on a thin chain around her neck.

"I'm Chief Wheeler from over in Prosperity," I said to her, holding out my hand.

"Connie Escuela," she said. "I'm not really an interpreter. I'm a surgical technologist, but I speak fluent Spanish. Is that all right?"

"Can you keep a secret?"

"I suppose."

"Good. Whatever is said in this room stays here, Connie. You have any problems with that?"

"I don't think so."

"All right."

The next quarter hour or so was pretty tedious slogging, since I had to ask every question, wait for it to be translated into Spanish, and then wait for the answer to be translated back into English. This is more or less the way the interview went, though.

"Mr. Velez," I said. "Your daughter was in a parked car with Jaime Ortiz last evening, on a cul-de-sac over off Morris Quick Road. Someone attacked them. I'm here to get whatever information Anita can offer, so that I can find the people who did this and bring them to justice."

"I understand," he said. "Ask your questions."

I turned to Anita, and interviewed her. She didn't really need an interpreter, but Connie Escuela droned on in the background nonetheless, so that Anita's father could know what was being said.

"What were you and Jaime doing in that cul-de-sac?" I asked.

She looked at me, and then at her father.

He nodded at her.

"We were on a date," she said. "We went to a movie in Morgan, and then to eat. We stopped on the way home to . . . to make out."

"Did you have sex with Jaime last night?"

I heard Connie stop interpreting behind me suddenly. I turned to her.

"It's your call," I said. "If you think her dad shouldn't hear this stuff, you go with your conscience."

She nodded. Then she said some stuff to Mr. Velez, and he said some stuff back.

"I asked him whether he really wanted to know the details of his daughter's love life," she said. "I told him I could . . . um, edit her story if he wished. He said it was okay for him to hear everything. He said he is aware that Anita is a little wild, and he has not been able to provide constant supervision for her. He said that he could deal with whatever she had to say if it meant that her attackers are caught and punished."

"He said all that?" I said.

"Well, we talked a little before you came into the room," she said, smiling a little.

"I see. Okay."

I turned back to Anita.

"So, Anita, did you and Jaime have sex last night?"

She had a hard time looking me in the eye. Having her father in the room probably didn't help her any. She looked down a little and nodded.

"Is that why Jaime was naked, except for

his shoes?"

She nodded again.

"Okay. We're getting somewhere. So you and Jaime drove to the development and parked on the empty cul-de-sac, and you had sex, and then what happened?"

"He wen' into the woods to piss," she said. "I stayed in the car. We had . . . we had smoked a little weed, and I was real mellow, you know. So I was almos' asleep when someone opened my door and pulled me out of the car."

"Just one person?"

"No, there were several. At least three. Maybe more."

"Could you see their faces?"

"It was too dark."

"Did they say anything?"

"They talked with each other. I think they might have been Anglo."

"What makes you say that?"

"They spoke in English. They sounded Anglo."

"What did they say?"

"They asked me where Jaime was."

"They specifically asked about Jaime?"

She looked up at me, her eyes questioning.

"No, they didn'. They said *Where is he, bitch,* and then they said *Here he comes.*

225

They never used his name."

"You're doing fine," I said. "What happened next?"

"They put me in the trunk, and I hit my head. I screamed to warn Jaime. From inside the trunk, I could hear Jaime yelling at them, and then I heard him scream once or twice. A few minutes later, the other car started up, and I heard it drive away."

"How long was it between the time the other car drove away, and the time my deputy arrived to let you out of the trunk?"

"I don' know. It was dark, and I was scared. It could have been ten minutes. Maybe even a half hour. Is Jaime going to be all right?"

"I won't lie to you," I said. "He's in bad shape. It's going to take him a long time to heal. When these men who attacked you were talking, did you recognize any of their voices?"

"I'm not sure," she said, the tears starting to flow down her cheeks again. "It happened very fast."

"Is it possible that any of the men who attacked you were the same men who had sex with you and Gypsy Camarena at Kevin Byrne's house?"

She shook her head.

"I could not say," she said. "It was all too

fast. I was too scared."

"Another question," I said. "When you and Gypsy were at that party last week, how did you get home?"

"One of the boys there said he'd drive. It was very late. Most of the boys were passed out. I got dressed and went out to the pool to get something to drink. There was a boy there. I think he goes to Allenwood, over in Mica Wells. I don't remember ever seeing him at Prosperity Glen. He said he was leaving, and he offered to take me home."

"Just you?"

"Gypsy had already left."

I sat back, trying to put it all together.

"When did Gypsy leave the party?" I asked.

"Maybe a half hour before I did."

"Who took her home?"

She looked at me strangely.

"Nobody, Chief Wheeler. She was angry, because she asked some of the boys to pay her for what she had done, and they laughed at her. She got really pissed, so she just walked out. Justin Warfield asked if she needed a ride, but she said she wouldn' get in a car with one of those assholes for all the money in the world. She said she would walk home."

"At that hour?"

"She wasn' afraid," Anita said. "Gypsy, she wasn' never afraid of nothin'."

CHAPTER TWENTY-ONE

I didn't get much more from Anita. She was woozy from medication, and looking back on it she probably didn't know much more than she told me anyway.

After her father took her home, I returned to the main ER desk. Charlotte sat behind the desk, updating charts. It was after eight in the morning — Sunday morning — traditionally a pretty quiet time in Bliss County. She looked tired, but happy that Saturday night was behind her.

"I guess I need to talk with the Ortiz kid now," I said. "Is he awake yet?"

She looked at me as if I had antennae.

"Get real, Judd. That kid isn't talking with anyone soon. They had to take him upstairs."

"Upstairs."

"Yes. To surgery."

"What happened?"

"Edema. His brain started swelling.

They're going to drill a couple of holes in his skull to bleed off the intracranial pressure."

"That's bad."

"It sure is. They usually induce a diabetic coma if that doesn't work."

"A coma? For how long?"

"Until his brain stops swelling. There aren't any rules here. The doctors just play it by ear."

"What are you saying?" I asked. "I might not be able to talk with him for — what? Days?"

"Maybe weeks."

I nodded and slipped my hands into my pockets.

"Guess I'll talk with his parents and head on back to Prosperity, then. Will you leave word in his chart that I need to talk with him as soon as he's conscious?"

"I'll write it down, but don't get your hopes up. Sometimes with these head injuries the patients lose their memory. He might wake up with absolutely no idea how he got here. He might never get that memory back."

"I thought nurses were supposed to instill hope," I said. "Thanks for making the note in the chart. You know where to find me."

■ ■ ■ ■

Connie Escuela and I found Jaime Ortiz's parents in the neurosurgery waiting room. Mr. Ortiz was taller than I expected, with an aquiline nose and piercing dark eyes. His mouth was a thin horizontal line. He was dressed in a sports shirt, sweater, and slacks. Jaime's mother was somewhat shorter, but also had a long, angular face, which as I walked into the room was lined with the tracks of her desperate tears.

The conversation, like that with Anita's father, was slow going.

I told them both how sorry I was for what had happened to their son.

"Thank you," Mr. Ortiz said. "This is terrible. How can something like this have happened?"

"I don't know," I told him. "We're still pulling together all the facts. It would help me if I could get some background on your son."

"What would you like to know?"

"Had he spoken to you about any threats against him?"

Mr. Ortiz shook his head.

"Jaime is not a troublemaker, Chief Wheeler," he said. "He goes to school, and after school he does his homework and then he goes to work."

"Where does he work?"

"Specialty Tees, in Morgan. They make shirts, with pictures and sayings on them."

I had heard of the place. Hector Ramirez had told me that Vicente had a part-time job there. It was the place where he had arranged for all the tee shirts the kids wore to the football game on Friday night.

"What can you tell me about the people who hurt my son?" Mr. Ortiz asked.

"Not a lot."

"Were they Anglos?" Mrs. Ortiz asked.

"We don't know, for certain. Anita, the girl who was with Jaime this evening, thought that they might have been, but it's really too early to say."

When I mentioned Anita, the mother's eyes darkened, and her face hardened.

"Anita," she said, almost spitting it. "A *puta.*"

I didn't need Connie to translate that one. I had heard the word before.

I explained to them that the forensics team from the sheriff's department had taken all the evidence from the scene, and that I hoped it would lead us to the people who attacked Jaime.

There wasn't much else they were likely

to be able to tell me, so I apologized again for what had happened, on behalf of the town of Prosperity, and left them to their own worst parental nightmares.

I stopped by the office before going home. Stu had left his report on my desk. It was concise, well written, and graphic. I added the information I'd obtained from Anita Velez, Charlotte, and the Ortizes, and filed it in the cabinet. Then I pulled out my legal pad.

At least I could add a couple of hours to my timeline of the three days leading up to Gypsy's murder. I now knew that she had left Kevin Byrne's house in a rage somewhere around twelve-thirty, the previous Sunday morning. According to Anita, she walked home. I found it interesting that Anita and Gypsy lived only a quarter mile from each other, and yet Anita didn't say she saw Gypsy on the road when the fellow from Mica Wells took her home. The walk from Kevin Byrne's house should have taken her around an hour, even if she were making a decent clip.

That made me wonder. Maybe she didn't walk all the way home. Maybe someone picked her up before she made it all the way back to Morris Quick Road.

Maybe whoever picked her up came back on Monday night.

I grabbed the telephone and dialed Kent Kramer's number. Crystal answered the ring.

"Hello, Judd," she said when she heard my voice.

"Crystal, is Seth around?"

"He's still asleep."

"Is Kent up?"

"Sure. Just a moment."

A second later, Kent picked up the receiver.

"Judd," he said.

Not *Hello.* Not *How are you.* Not *Drop dead.* Just *Judd.*

"I wanted you to give Seth a message for me," I said.

"What is it?"

"Tell him he's off the hook. I know that Seth didn't take Gypsy Camarena home the other night."

"Okay. I'll pass it along."

"One more thing, Kent. What time did Seth get in last night?"

"He never went out. He had a couple of friends over. They watched a movie and played pool until maybe one in the morning."

Jaime Ortiz had been attacked around

234

midnight.

"Do you recall who these other boys were?"

"Sure. Justin Warfield and Gary Tomberlin. Why?"

"There was some trouble last night, and I wanted to know who I could rule out. Don't worry, Kent. Seth's in the clear on that one, too."

"That's nice to know," he said. His voice was still cool.

"Look," I said. "About yesterday . . ."

"Forget it, Judd. You made your point. You thought I was bribing you."

"It was a matter of appearances. I didn't want anyone else to think it."

"Save it, okay? I heard you loud and clear."

I counted to ten, while I tried to measure my next words carefully.

"We've known each other for a long time, Kent. We've had our differences over the years. We've always been able to work them out."

"And maybe we will this time. I have to go, Judd. Have to get ready to take the boys to the Pythons game. Was there anything else?"

"No, I guess not. Keep it in the road, man."

"You, too."

He hung up without saying goodbye.

I got back to my house around ten. Donna was sitting on the front porch, reading the Sunday paper and sipping a cup of coffee.

"Tough night?" she asked, after I kissed her and sat in the wicker chair beside her.

"The toughest. Somebody nailed Jaime Ortiz to a tree over off Morris Quick Road."

"My God!" she said. "Is he . . ."

"He's alive, but he's in bad shape. He was in surgery when I left the hospital. His brain was swelling, and they had to drill holes in his skull."

"Who did it?" she asked.

"I don't have a clue. Anita Velez was with him, but she didn't see any faces. She thinks they were Anglos. Jaime isn't talking. He might never talk again."

She folded the paper and placed it on the table next to her.

"This is getting out of hand," she said after a few moments.

"You think?"

"When word gets out at school tomorrow . . ."

"I was thinking about that. Are you up to some serious talk?"

"This early in the morning?"

"It can wait . . ."

"No. You are one stoic son of a bitch, you know that? If you want to talk, you go right ahead. God knows I don't get many opportunities."

I reached across her and picked up her coffee cup. I took a sip as I gathered my thoughts.

"I'm thinking about quitting," I said.

"Quitting."

"I've been police chief for seven years. Ninety-nine percent of that time has been traffic tickets and neighborhood patrol. Big fuckin' whoop, right? One percent has been real crime. This town needs a police chief like it needs a few hundred more illegal Mexicans."

"You're tired."

"I was tired before Gypsy Camarena got her neck snapped. I was tired before Vicente Ramirez went after Seth Kramer with a tire iron. I've been tired a long time."

"But you haven't been pessimistic, at least not like this. When was the last time you tied together more than two hours of sleep?"

"Maybe four days."

"You're wiped out, then. It's the lack of sleep. I'll bet you're starting to see things that aren't there — little movements out of the corner of your eyes that make you turn and look to see what's happening. Next thing you'll be hearing voices. Sleep deprivation is a bitch, Judd. I don't want you drawing down on something your mind manufactures just to keep you on your toes."

"What do you know about it?"

"I was a tennis star, remember? How do you think I went from tournament to tournament, practiced six hours a day, and still kept up with my schoolwork? White crosses, black beauties, diet pills. Whatever it took. Some weeks I was up four or five days straight. It got to the point I didn't know whether what I saw coming at me was a real ball or something I imagined."

"What did you do?"

"I got off the merry-go-round. I took some time for myself, and I got some sleep."

"I have a case to solve."

"A damn lot of good you're going to be if you can't think straight. Here's the way it's going to be. Either you go into the house and sleep until dinnertime, or you get your ass into town and see Dr. Kronenfeld first thing tomorrow morning."

"That's old territory, Donna. I've been down that road."

"Surprise, darling. You're back in the old neighborhood. You can't sleep because your nightmares and your damned flashbacks won't leave you alone. You need help. You're already staggering around like you're half-drunk. It's a matter of time before you fall asleep at the wheel and wind up . . ."

"What?"

"Forget it."

"No, Donna. Say it. Before I fall asleep at the wheel and wind up *what?*"

She sighed, and drained the last of her coffee. She wouldn't look me in the face. Instead, she gazed out over the fields and the long, winding gravel drive that led out to the Morgan Highway.

"I thought you wanted to talk," she said. "I think maybe what you really wanted was for me to give you permission to quit the force. I can't do that, Judd. You do it or you don't, it's up to you. You didn't want to talk with me. You wanted to talk *at* me. It's not the same thing."

I nodded, and tried to think of something I could say that would prove her wrong. I couldn't.

"I'm sorry," I said.

"You're exhausted. I think maybe I have some stuff to do at home. What you need to do is stretch out on the sofa and nap all day. If you have awful dreams about Six Mile Creek, sweat them out. Or wake up and go back to sleep. If you don't log some sack time, though, you're headed for a major crack-up. I'll see you tomorrow."

She handed me the half-empty coffee cup, leaned over to kiss me, and then walked down the steps to her car.

Before she got in, though, she turned back to me.

"I've got no use for you the way you are right now," she said. "I mean it. Get some sleep. I want my boyfriend back."

I sat and watched as she drove back out to the highway.

I tried to sleep, but it was almost as if I had forgotten how. I crashed on the sofa, but all I did there was toss and turn. I couldn't get the image of Jaime Ortiz nailed to a tree out of my mind. There was something about the image that triggered a distant memory. That image led to another, one that I desperately wanted to avoid.

Donna was right. I was exhausted. I knew it. What was worse, it appeared that everyone else around me knew it.

I flipped on the television around noon. The Pythons game was supposed to start at twelve-thirty. I stared at the set for the next four hours, occasionally drifting off into that hazy dream-like state that isn't really sleep, and so I missed several important chunks of the game, such as the thirty-yard touchdown pass that Lennie Stockwell lobbed to Jermaine Coltes in the third quarter. I didn't care.

The Pythons won by nine, and I still didn't care.

I got off the sofa around four. I made a bowl of canned chili and a salad. It was my first solid food since the cookout Donna and I had made the night before. I scarfed it down so fast that it sat on my stomach like a coiled snake.

I didn't care.

The rest of the day on into the night is a blur now. I don't recall much of anything. I probably sat in my wicker chair on the front porch, watching the leaves fall from the trees and accumulate on my winding gravel drive. I probably tried to think about absolutely nothing. Maybe I thought that if I cleared my head, like some kind of Buddhist monk, I could keep myself from reliving the insistent memories of the worst day of my life, and I could wake up with something resembling half a brain.

She still had the cell phone in her hand . . .

I jerked my head around with a gasp. I was still sitting on the porch. It was almost dark. There was a chill in the air, and I realized that I was shivering.

I went inside and made a pot of strong coffee.

I wasn't going to sleep. Not tonight. As bad as the flashbacks were, I knew I could never face my nightmares.

Donna was right, though.

I had to see Dr. Kronenfeld.

CHAPTER TWENTY-TWO

I was headed out the door to drive to Morgan the next morning, when my radio chirped.

"Chief, this is Slim."

I toggled the microphone on my shoulder. "Go ahead, Slim."

"You better come by the school."

"Why?"

"You want me to talk about this over the radio?"

"Be there in five," I said. "I was headed out the door already."

I telephoned Dr. Kronenfeld's office in Morgan to let them know I had been delayed by an emergency, but that I would come by later. The receptionist there told me that the doctor had a light schedule, and they shouldn't have much trouble shoehorning me in whenever I showed up.

I pulled into the school parking lot about thirty seconds behind the ambulance. Principal Compton was waiting as the paramedics pulled a gurney from the van.

"What is it?" I asked him.

"Justin Warfield. Someone kicked the crap out of him in one of the bathrooms."

He led me and the paramedics down a hallway and across an outside patio to a separate building. We went down another hallway to the bathrooms. The door to the boys' room was wide open.

"In here!" I heard Slim call out.

I led the way into the bathroom.

There was blood everywhere. A mass that I could barely recognize as Justin Warfield lay on the floor, a wet pink towel covering one half of his face. The half I could see was swollen and oddly misshapen.

"What happened?" I asked, as the paramedics went to work on him.

"A kid from the class down the hall had to use the bathroom during first period, so his teacher gave him a pass. When he got here, he found this kid moaning and bleeding on the floor."

"Any guesses how he was injured?"

"I can't find any knife punctures or bullet holes," Slim said. "I could have missed them, though. This guy's a mess. I'd say someone went after him with a baseball bat or a two-by-four."

"Warfield's a moose," I said. "He plays the offensive line on the football team. It would take more than one guy."

"Not if it was a sneak attack," Slim said. "You could come up behind someone with a bat or a stick, whack him over the head, and he'd be so stunned that you could work him over with barely a hint of resistance."

I stared at my patrolman.

"Don't ask me how I know that," he said.

"What's it look like?" I asked the paramedics.

"It's mostly head wounds," one of them said. "He has a broken collarbone, and his ribs are stove in. Probably broke at least two of them, but he ain't coughing up bloody froth, so maybe we got lucky on a lung puncture. Beyond that, it's up to the doctors to work it all out."

They stabilized Warfield, and together we lifted him onto the gurney. Within moments they were speeding him down the hallway toward the entrance to the school and the waiting ambulance.

"I want to talk with the kid who found him," I said.

"I'll round him up," Slim told me. "Are you going to the front office?"

"Yeah."

Several minutes later, Slim ushered a

student into the Resource office at the front of the school. He looked a lot younger than I had expected.

"This is Billy Stack," Slim said. "He found the kid in the bathroom."

"Thanks," I said. "Let me talk to him alone for a few minutes."

The kid was nervous, and he looked small in the chair across from me.

"What year are you, Billy?"

"I'm a sophomore. Tenth grade."

"You know who I am?"

"You're Chief Wheeler. I heard the other policeman call you that."

"All right, then. I want you to know right off that you aren't in any trouble. I'm just trying to find out how this thing happened this morning. I'd appreciate it if you could tell me what all you saw when you went to the bathroom."

"Well, I was in first-period history class, and I had to go to the bathroom real bad. So I asked my teacher for a pass, and she said I could go. I walked into the bathroom, and there he was."

"Tell me what you saw."

"I saw this guy on the floor, and he was bleeding really bad. His face was all swollen and bruised, and it was bleeding from several places. He was making some noises, so I knew he wasn't dead, but I didn't stay around long enough to find out anything else. I ran back to the classroom and got my teacher."

"You didn't see anyone else in the bathroom or the hallways?"

"No. Like I said, it was in the middle of first period. Everyone was in class."

"Okay. You go on back to class now. Thank you for your help."

He stood and left the room. Hart Compton walked in before the door closed.

"I had a call from the hospital. They just brought Justin War- field in. I called his mother. She's on the way to Morgan. What in hell happened, Judd?"

"You know about Jaime Ortiz?" I said.

"Just that he was attacked Saturday night."

"They jacked him up something awful. Nailed him to a tree."

"Jesus!"

"That stays in here," I said. "He's in the hospital in Morgan. They have him in some kind of artificial coma to keep his brain from swelling. If you know about it, I'll bet others do, too. Anita Velez was with him. She was released from the hospital yesterday morning. Twenty-four hours is a lot of time to stir up a little resentment in the Mexican community."

"You think one of the Hispanic kids might have done this to Justin?"

"One or a bunch. I need a list of your kids who didn't report to first period."

"Why?"

"You saw that bathroom, and you saw Justin. You don't fuck up someone that bad without getting a little bit of them on you. The way blood was splattered on the walls, there has to be some on the attacker or attackers. Unless they brought a change of clothes, I'd say they had to go home after the assault. That would mean missing first period."

"What if they had time to get home before first period began?"

"Doesn't play. Justin was attacked after the first-period bell. Otherwise someone would have found him before classes started. No, whoever beat the living sin out of Justin Warfield was also absent from class. I need that list."

"I'll put it together."

He started out of the Resource office, but I stopped him.

"The complete list," I said. "Mexicans and Anglos both. We don't know that this was done by one of Jaime's homeboys, Hart. Got it?"

"I understand."

"Until we know what's going on, it would be best to keep this between us as much as we can."

He nodded. "I'll get you that list as quickly as I can."

Slim walked into the office several minutes later.

"I called the sheriff's CSI team," he said. "They'll be here in a half-hour or so. Some guy got himself shot up over in Morgan, and they're tied up for the moment."

The sheriff only had one CSI team per shift. Sometimes we in the hinterlands just had to wait our turn.

"Okay," I said. "Tape off the bathroom and make sure nobody goes in. Hart is putting together a list of kids who didn't make it to first period. Odds are our attackers are somewhere on it. Get the list for me, and I'll run it down later this afternoon. I'm going into Morgan to the hospital, talk with the Warfields."

"They're gonna be hot," Slim said.

"Maybe I can cool them down a little. I don't have to tell you, this is beginning to escalate. If we can drop a lid on it, maybe we can still control things. Word gets out about Justin, though, we might have to take some measures to keep the Anglo and Mexican kids separated."

"Lion-taming wasn't part of my criminal justice education program, Judd."

I smiled, perhaps for the first time in days.

"You'll do fine, Slim. If you need me, I'll be in Morgan."

If I showed up at the ER in Morgan one more time this week, they were going to start charging me rent.

I saw Fred Warfield and his wife Allison waiting in the chairs as soon as I walked through the automatic doors. Fred jumped to his feet. Allison seemed to plead with him with her eyes, but that wasn't going anywhere.

"How in hell did this happen, Judd?" he demanded.

"We don't know yet. There weren't any witnesses. Allison, I'm sorry for what's happened to Justin. It's terrible."

"Did you see him?" she asked.

"Yes."

"They won't let us back to look at him."

"He's banged up pretty bad," I said. "Sometimes it looks worse than it is, though, what with all the blood and everything."

I heard her gasp.

"Just remember, a little blood goes a long way," I reminded her. "You don't have to lose much before it makes a big mess. I'm not a doctor, so I can't speculate on how long it will take him to recover."

If he recovers, I thought, but I didn't say it out loud.

"Did he say anything about who attacked him?" Fred asked.

"He didn't say anything about anything. He was barely conscious when he was found by another student. I just wanted to come by here and meet with you, let you know what we've found out. It isn't much, but the Crime Scene team from the sheriff's department is working out at the school. Maybe they'll come up with something we can use. I'm also putting together a list of possible suspects using the school attendance records."

"Attendance records?" Fred asked.

"Whoever attacked Justin couldn't have returned to class afterward. He would have been too . . . there would have been telltale evidence on him. We figure that — if it was a student — the attacker had to leave the school after the assault, so he or they wouldn't show up as attending first period."

"You think it might not have been a student?" Allison asked.

"Right now, I don't know one way or the other. I'm going to have to ask you to be patient. We don't want to jump to conclusions."

"You don't seem to know much, Judd," Fred said. There was a clear challenge in his voice.

"Nobody witnessed the attack," I said.

"Word has it that one of the Mexican kids was hung from a tree on Saturday night."

"Word has it wrong," I said. "There was a boy attacked Saturday night, but he wasn't strung up. Beyond that, I can't talk about it."

"Well, that should narrow your search, shouldn't it?"

"How so?"

"Isn't it obvious? That girl was killed the other day, and then this other Mexican boy was assaulted. It stands to reason that Justin was beaten by some Mexican kids trying to get in a little revenge."

"That's just one possibility. We'll be looking at every clue we have. We're going to do this the right way. We aren't going to go off half-cocked. When I know something, I'll tell you, okay?"

"And what are we supposed to do until then?" he said, his chin thrust forward.

"Tend to your son. Let me do my job. I'll be in touch."

■ ■ ■ ■

I called Dr. Kronenfeld's office from the hospital, and rescheduled for the next day. I could already see that this was going to be a fifteen-rounder, and I was in no mood or shape to engage in mental calisthenics with my shrink.

I radioed Slim on the way back to Prosperity. He told me that the CSI team had just arrived. It was lunchtime, so I dropped by the sub place at the shopping center behind the station and grabbed a turkey and Swiss sandwich to eat on the fly.

I was halfway through my sandwich and a quarter of the way through my report on Justin Warfield's ass-kicking, when Huggie Newton knocked on my door.

"You heard?" I asked, as he walked in.

"About the Warfield boy? Yes."

"This is getting messy."

"Yes. Well . . . I was wondering if you have a few moments to step next door."

That couldn't be good. The only thing next door was the Town Council chambers — little more than your average-sized meeting room. Prosperity only had three councilmen. It didn't need an ornate Town Hall. Right off the council chambers was Huggie's office, which was no larger or smaller than mine.

Of course, his law office on the other side of the shopping center was a virtual showplace. Few people could boast an edifice complex like Huggie.

"What's up?" I asked.

"I have some people I'd like you to meet."

"Sure. Just let me finish my sandwich and wash up."

I walked into the chambers several minutes later to find Huggie and the Town Council, along with a couple of guys I had never met.

The Council consisted of Kent Kramer, Art Belts, and Tommy Keesler. Kent, of course, was a major developer in Bliss County, and in Prosperity in particular. Art owned the shopping center behind the cop station, and Tommy was a doctor in Morgan. He was also the only member of the Council who had grown up in Prosperity. He and Huggie, as a doctor and a lawyer, were more or less Prosperity's biggest success stories.

"This is Chief Judd Wheeler, of our local police department," Huggie said to the two strangers.

One of them, a lanky, sallow fellow with great hair and bad teeth, stood and extended his hand.

"Mitch Gajewski, Department of Justice, Civil Rights Criminal Division."

As I shook with him, the other guy, who looked like a retired middleweight prizefighter, complete with scarred ears and a bald head that contrasted with his closely cropped moustache and beard, also stood.

"Jack Cantrell, Homeland Security."

As I shook his hand, I turned to Huggie. "Feds?"

"Yes, Judd. We — that is, the Council and I — met this morning as soon as we heard about this Justin Warfield business, and we thought . . . that is, we *decided* that maybe you could use a little help. You know, with this racial thing in the high school."

"Racial thing," I said. "To the best of my knowledge, the only racial thing I know about is that little rumble last week in the school hallway."

"If you'll pardon me," Gajewski said, interrupting as politely as he was likely able.

"Yes?" I said.

"The Civil Rights Criminal Division is primarily interested in hate crimes and other violations of the civil rights of racial and ethnic minorities."

"Yes, I know."

"Well, in light of this past weekend's

lynching in your town . . ."

"Whoa!" I said. "Lynching?"

"What would you call it?" Gajewski asked. "This young Hispanic boy is beaten near half to death, and nailed by his hands to a tree? That would seem to qualify as a lynching to me."

"Only if you can demonstrate that it was racially motivated. We haven't proven that yet. I can't imagine how we would, at least until we find out who did it."

"The girl who was with him," Huggie said. "I understand she said the men who attacked the Ortiz boy were Anglos."

"She said she couldn't clearly identify them as Anglos or Mexicans. She thought they might be locals, but she wasn't certain. Even if she had been able to finger them as Anglos, that doesn't mean it was a hate crime."

"What else could it be?" Kent asked.

"Any number of things. Gang retribution, for one."

"You have gang activity in Prosperity?" Cantrell asked.

"No, at least as far as I've been able to tell. There are gangs in Morgan, though. And there's a lot of organized crime up in Parker County. Sometimes it flows over the county line."

"Are you suggesting that the attack on the Ortiz boy was gang-related?" Art asked.

"No. I'm not suggesting anything just yet. We don't have enough information. That's my point."

"Yes," Huggie said. "Well, that's where we thought maybe Mr. Gajewski and Mr. Cantrell could be of service."

"The attack on the Ortiz boy, at least by appearance, fits the Civil Rights Division's definition of lynching," Gajewski said. "We're proceeding on the assumption that his attack was racially motivated."

"Which means that you'll find evidence supporting that contention, and only that contention," I argued. "It's my opinion that we should keep an open mind until we have more evidence."

"And how long is that going to take?" Tommy Keesler asked. "It's been a week since that Mexican girl was killed."

"And only five days since we found her," I said. "We've been piecing together her movements over the last two or three days of her life, trying to find out who had access to her last Monday night. We've already been able to eliminate some potential suspects."

"But you don't know who killed her?" Huggie asked.

"If I knew that, I'd be in the DA's office in Morgan right now, getting an arrest warrant. We're making progress. No offense gentlemen, but I am greatly concerned that pulling the feds into this investigation, at least at this point, will only cock things up."

Both Gajewski and Cantrell did that fed thing where they crossed their hands in front of them and stood quietly. They were waiting for me to hang myself in front of the Council, so they could be given *carte blanche* to operate freely in Prosperity.

I realized I wasn't doing such a good job of convincing anyone in the room, so I sat down and waited for another opportunity to make my point.

It didn't take long.

"This Hispanic girl who was murdered last week," Cantrell said. "She was undocumented?"

"Yes. Her parents brought her into the country with them a few years back. They've disappeared."

"Disappeared?" Cantrell asked.

"We think they were afraid that the murder would put the spotlight on them as illegals. They were probably afraid of being deported."

"So they abandoned their daughter?" Huggie asked.

"There wasn't much they could do for her. She was dead. I talked with a neighbor the day after we found her. He told me they packed up and bugged out that night."

"And you have no idea where they are?" Cantrell asked.

"I have one of my officers working on it, but he'll probably get nowhere. The illegal community can get pretty tight-lipped when they want to protect their own. And while we're discussing this, just what in hell does Homeland Security have to do with all this?"

Cantrell cleared his throat and ran his hand across his smooth scalp.

"In 2002, all the activities formerly covered by the INS were placed under the Department of Homeland Security. We're the authorized agency for dealing with illegal immigration in the United States now."

"Dealing with illegal immigration," I said. "And, besides the fact that both Gypsy Camarena and Jaime Ortiz were children of illegals, what does that have to do with this case? Do you intend to deport their parents?"

"We deal with that on a case-by-case basis," Cantrell said. "This administration, as you may be aware, is particularly sensitive to the plight of illegal Hispanic immigrants."

"Of course it is. They're part of the president's voting bloc."

"Be that as it may, the Department is aware that Hispanic immigrants may constitute a special class."

"Okay, I'm with you so far," I said. "Now what does that have to with these two crimes?"

Cantrell sat at the table, and laced his fingers together.

"You have a large number of illegal Hispanic immigrants in Prosperity, don't you, Chief Wheeler?"

"I suppose. These people go where the work is. Ever since Bliss County and Prosperity began being overrun by Parker County residents trying to avoid high property taxes, there have been employment opportunities in town."

"At minimum wage?" Cantrell asked.

"I don't know. I don't employ any of them."

"Isn't it your job to see that the law is enforced in Prosperity?"

"Sure."

"Aren't the Department of Labor's wage guidelines part of the law?"

"Not when it comes to my department. We enforce local and state laws, gentlemen.

We aren't charged with looking out for violations of federal statutes. We have three cops in this town, and I'm one of them. We're busy enough without doing the FBI's job."

"I see. Didn't you arrest one of these illegal aliens a week or so ago for attacking Mr. Kramer's son?"

"Yes."

"Did you verify his immigration status at that time?"

"I didn't have to. I've known Hector Ramirez for some time. I knew before I arrested his son that he was undocumented."

"Yet, you didn't inform the Department of Homeland Security in Parker County that you had arrested an illegal immigrant?"

"No."

"Do you think that was wise? After all, if we had been informed of the activities of the 9/11 hijackers before they could kill over three thousand people . . ."

"Whoa," I said. "That's a bit of a logical stretch, don't you think?"

"We like to know when undocumented foreign nationals break the law," Cantrell said. "That way we can keep track of potential troublemakers."

"Vicente Ramirez isn't a troublemaker. Before the incident with Kent's son, he had a spotless rap sheet and an excellent academic record. Besides that, Mr. Kramer declined to press charges, and I released Vicente. His record is still clean. Now, Mr. Gajewski, if you want to talk about potential civil rights violations . . ."

I looked over at Kent Kramer, hoping he would recall my conversation with Seth the previous week.

God bless him, he picked up on the cue. Kent was always sharp.

"I think we're getting afield," he said. "Our intention in asking these gentlemen to come down from Parker County was that they might help throw some oil on the waters."

"How?" I asked. "By beating the bushes for hooded Klansmen and harassing hardworking undocumented workers? Have any of you considered what your lives would be like if we didn't have the Mexican people in this town handling all the shitty jobs your kids won't touch? Art, do you want to mow the grass on that three-acre yard of yours every weekend? Do any of you want to pay three times what you've been paying to have your houses painted or your roofs reshingled? Hell, most of the backbreaking labor in this county is done by people who don't have a choice because they also don't have a Social Security number. I would be very surprised if any of you would really like to change that arrangement."

"What about that demonstration at the football game the other night?" Cantrell asked.

"Peaceful. Those kids were no threat to anyone."

"But what if it had gone the other way? Someone beat up that boy at school this morning. Maybe your peaceful demonstrators have decided that civil disobedience isn't working fast enough for them, especially after one of their own got nailed to a tree two nights ago."

"And maybe they had nothing to do with the attack at the school this morning. We don't know. Until we do, we're at genuine risk of accusing innocent people of a terrible crime. I thought we had some philosophical problems with that in this country."

Cantrell cleared his throat.

"All I'm saying is that it seems you have a very large illegal population in Bliss County, compared with the average across the state. If they skirted the nation's laws to get here, maybe they're willing to disobey the local laws to stay here."

"Wait a minute," I said. "Just sit tight. I'll be right back."

I walked next door to my office and yanked open my filing cabinet. It took me a minute to find the file I wanted, maybe a few moments longer than it usually would have since I was expending a lot of energy muttering epithets under my breath.

I reentered the antechamber of the Council meeting room just in time to overhear the end of a conversation.

". . . You told me he would be cooperative!" Gajewski said.

"He will. Judd does things his own way. He's a good cop, though," Huggie replied.

"He sounds like he has his head in the sand," Cantrell said. "Has he been in a coma for the last several years?"

"He's a local," Kent said. "They think differently than folks from the city. Different values."

"*Better* values, if you ask me," Tommy Keesler said.

"Well, you'd think so, wouldn't you?" Kent argued. "You're from this town too."

"Are you forgetting me?" Huggie asked. "I'm from here."

"Maybe by birth, but you've been places," Kent said. "Like they say, how are you gonna keep the boy down on the farm . . ."

"All I want to know," Cantrell said, "is

264

whether you people can control your police chief."

"Depends on what you mean by *control*," Huggie said. "I tried talking some sense into him the other day. He as good as told me to shove it. I told him I could fire him. He agreed, but he also made it clear that I couldn't tell him what to do."

"Oh, great," Gajewski said. "A maverick. Just what we need . . ."

I chose this moment to walk back into the room. Everyone looked up at me. I thought a couple of them, especially Huggie and Tommy, looked just a little guilty.

"You were saying?" I said to Cantrell.

"Beg pardon?"

"Just before I left the room. I'll quote you. *It seems you have a very large illegal population in Bliss County, compared with the average across the state. If they skirted the nation's laws to get here, maybe they're willing to disobey the local laws to stay here.* Is that it, more or less?"

"More or less," Cantrell said.

"I'd like to show you something."

I opened the file folder I had retrieved from my cabinet in the police station, and handed Cantrell a photograph.

"I received that from Sheriff Roy Bazewell of Webb County, Texas. For the less geographically astute among you, the county seat there is Laredo, one of the largest entry points for illegal Mexican aliens. That picture you're looking at was taken about one hundred yards *inside* the Mexican border. Sheriff Bazewell thought I might enjoy taking a look at it."

Cantrell coughed slightly, and then handed the picture to Gajewski, who gazed at it uneasily before handing it to Huggie.

"That, gentlemen," I continued, "is a billboard, depicting an outline of the state of North Carolina, with a star placed right in the center of Bliss County. The legend underneath the outline of the state reads *Bliss County, El Carolina del Norte: Un Buen Lugar a Vivir y a Trabajar.*"

"What's that mean?" Gajewski asked.

"My high school Spanish is a little rusty," Huggie said. "But it appears to translate to *A Good Place to Live and to Work.*"

"That is the exact translation," I said. "I did some checking, and it appears that this sign was erected about three years ago, through an advertising agency in Ciudad Juarez, Mexico. It was paid for by the Bliss County Chamber of Commerce."

"So?" Cantrell said.

"So, Mr. Department of Homeland Security, I think maybe you're confusing reality with your agenda. I think the federal government is still smarting because a bunch of Saudi terrorists rubbed its nose in its own complacency a few years back, and it feels the need to do something that at least looks effective. I think maybe this same government has found itself impotent to stop terrorist activities around the world. I think maybe this same government, through your honorable office, has decided to hit hard against one element of border security that it feels it can control.

"Well, here are the facts, Mr. Cantrell, right here in black and white, before your very eyes. These illegal Mexican immigrants you are so concerned about aren't congregating in our lovely county in such large numbers because they have some devious plot to overthrow the American way of life. They are here, simply put, because *we invited them.*"

Nobody said a word. Cantrell's shiny pate began to glow beet red in the overhead fluorescent lamp. Gajewski cleared his throat once or twice.

"And," I added, "I think you could probably agree that, once they made their way here, we gave them one hell of a shitty welcome. So here's the way it is. *I* am the chief of police in Prosperity. I will keep the peace to the best of my ability. If I need help, I will go to the county sheriff, who is an old friend and a damned fine gentleman in his own right. If the Council wants my badge, they know where I live and where I work.

"As long as I am the chief of police in this town, though, I will enforce the laws as I see fit. I will not interfere with any federal investigations you fellows want to pursue. The federal statutes are none of my concern. On the other hand, I will not be handled, controlled, bullyragged, coerced, threatened, or otherwise persuaded to compromise my principles, my standards, or my procedures. Have I left anything to any of your imaginations?"

It took several seconds for anyone to respond. When it did come, it was — predictably — Huggie who spoke.

"I suppose that will be all, Chief," he said. "If we need your assistance further, we'll let you know. You go ahead and carry on with your investigation."

I gathered up the material in the file folder and returned to my office.

Chapter Twenty-Three

In retrospect, I probably didn't do myself any favors pitching a hissy in front of the feds. At that point in a very long week, however, I couldn't have cared less. I had one murder and two major assaults in my town over the course of seven days, and I was becoming irritated.

My mood didn't improve any when my telephone rang and I found Carla Powers on the other end of the line.

"Did you get the DNA report back yet?" I asked, almost before she got the *hello* out of the way.

"No, Judd. I'm sorry. They're doing PCR, and the lab is backed up. I was calling to see if you had gotten hold of the girl's parents."

"Gitana," I said. "Her name was Gitana Camarena."

"I'm not going to spend a half hour apologizing for everything I say."

I stopped and took a deep breath.

"No," I said. "And you shouldn't. I'm the one that's sorry. I just got out of a meeting with the Town Council, and I'm a little prickly. So what's the holdup on the tests?"

"Another case of too many requests and not enough manpower. Once they get started, the PCR will only take a day to process and get the results back to me."

"I'd appreciate a call as soon as you get it. Now, about Gypsy . . ."

"She's getting a little ripe here. She really should get to a mortuary soon."

"What happens if her parents don't surface?"

"We can't keep her here indefinitely. We're not equipped as a storage facility. If I don't have somewhere to send her by Wednesday, I'll probably have to notify the Committee on Anatomy, and ask them to take custody."

"What happens then?"

"They'll see to it that she's embalmed, and then dispose of the remains."

"How?"

"That's up to them. They'll either cremate her or bury her in a county cemetery. They'll do whichever is cheapest. Like everyone else, their budgets only stretch so far."

"I don't know," I said. "A potter's field

grave doesn't seem right for her, somehow. After everything else she's gone through . . ."

"No offense, Chief, but she's not here anymore. All I have is meat and bones."

"Do me a favor and never say that to me again."

"Are we back to the apologizing thing?"

I counted to ten, and tried to think of a way to stall her.

"What about the coroner's inquest? Doesn't it have to take place first?"

"Scheduled for tomorrow morning. It will be cut and dried. It's not like you see on television. I just present my findings and Billy rubberstamps them, and that's it. It doesn't really matter, though. Once I release the body, we don't need it anymore. What I do need is the space."

My eyes felt gritty and swollen. I rubbed my hand over my cheek, and it felt dry, like a molted snake's skin. I needed a nap. I needed time to pull myself together. I needed, more than anything else, not to be saddled with the disposition of Gypsy Camarena's remains right at that moment.

"I'll see what I can do," I said. "Let me make a couple of calls. I don't want her in some unmarked grave, Carla. She deserves better than that."

"You do what you can," she said. "But Wednesday I call the Committee on Anatomy. I can't wait any longer."

I racked the receiver, and pulled out my legal pad with the timeline of Gypsy's final seventy-two or so hours. In the margin, I scribbled *Catholic burial?* and checked my telephone book.

Rural North Carolina, as a matter of course, is largely Protestant, and most of those churches border on the more extreme boundaries of that faith. While the influx of more affluent citizens from the next county to the north had brought along with it a fair share of the more liberal and tolerant Methodist, Lutheran, and Episcopal churches, we couldn't lay claim to many outlets of the Church of Rome in Bliss County.

I found two Catholic churches, one in Morgan and the other in Mica Wells, which kind of surprised me. Morgan had a burgeoning Mexican population, almost all of whom were devout Catholics, but I had a hard time seeing the call for a priest in a fundamentalist hotbed like Mica Wells. Go figure.

The telephone jangled again. It was Hart Compton from the high school.

"I have your list, Chief," he said. "You

want to come by and pick it up?"

"Sure. Could you have Anita Velez brought up to the office before I get there? I need to ask her a question. Also, I need to talk with Vicente Ramirez."

"I can send for Anita . . ." he said, and his voice trailed off.

"Don't tell me," I said.

"You're going to see it for yourself. Vicente was one of the students who never reported to first period."

I pulled the new cruiser into the school lot and parked next to Slim's older one. Slim was leaning against one of the forty-foot-tall aluminum columns holding up the front of the walkway leading to the front door of the school. He was smoking a cigarette.

"Judd," he said as I walked up.

"Have you had any luck finding Gypsy's parents?"

"Naw. Nobody wants to talk to Johnny Law."

I stopped.

"What did you say?"

"Nobody wants to talk to Johnny Law."

"Yeah. Nobody."

I made a mental note to drop back by Jake Wiley's shack on Morris Quick Road later.

"Do me a favor, okay?" I said. "I'll be here

273

at the school for the next hour at least. You go over to Morgan and see if you can find out who owns that piece of shit house Gypsy lived in. Maybe the landlord has a forwarding address for their mail."

"Wilco," Slim said, as he ground the cigarette out on the heel of his boot. "Anything else?"

"No, you can punch out afterward. I'll stay on duty until Stu clocks in."

"You got it."

"One more thing," I said.

"What's that, Chief?"

"Don't smoke on the town's time. It doesn't look good."

I walked into the school and ran right into Donna, as she walked out of the office. She saw me immediately. She stopped and leaned back against the wall. I stood next to her, trying to think of something useful I could say.

"Mad at me?" she asked.

"No. Mad at *me*. You're right. I can't handle this alone. I thought I could. I didn't sleep much yesterday or last night. Right now I'm running on fumes, and they're getting thin. I don't like it much."

"You look like shit, lover."

"I think maybe I've never loved you more than right this moment."

"At least you can say it."

I had to smile at that. It hurt a little on my shopworn face.

"I had an appointment with Dr. Kronenfeld this morning."

"What did he say?"

"I had to reschedule it. Justin Warfield." She shuddered.

"I heard all about it. Hart's been holding meetings with teachers on break all day. It's terrible. Do you have any idea who did it?"

I shook my head.

"I'm meeting with Compton in a moment. He's made me a list of kids who didn't make it to first period. I'll start there. What are you doing tonight?"

"Washing my hair."

"How about tomorrow night?"

"Drying it."

I chuckled.

"I get it. No nookie until I see the shrink."

She looked around, nervously.

"Don't even *think* that in these halls. I have to work here, Judd."

"All right," I said. "Tomorrow morning, I see the doctor. I promise."

She nodded.

"Good," she said. "And for God's sake, get some sleep tonight. You really do look awful."

She looked both ways, up and down the hall again, stood on her tiptoes, and kissed me quickly on the mouth, and then turned and walked toward her classroom. I watched until she made the turn through her door and I couldn't see her anymore.

Good Gawd, that woman can walk.

Hart Compton was in his office when I rapped on the door.

"Got something for me?" I asked.

Compton picked up a computer printout on his desk.

"In all, sixty-three kids missed first period today. I've called some of them, kids I figured would never have anything to do with what happened to Justin Warfield. They were all home sick. I put checks next to their names. That left forty-two names. Some are stoners. I figure they were out in the woods toking up, or in their parents' basements hanging out until after school. A good number showed up later with doctors' excuses. You wouldn't believe how many kids in this school go to the orthodontist on the average day, and they all go at eight in the morning. I checked them off too."

"That leaves these eleven names?" I said.

"The ones I didn't check aren't accounted for."

"How many of these are upperclassmen?" I said, handing the list back to him.

He looked it over.

"About half. Why?"

"Because Justin Warfield is an ogre. I don't see how a freshman or a sophomore could have done to him what was done. Maybe if they snuck up on him and got in one good whack before he knew they were there, but I don't see it that way. Check off the underclassmen. If I hit a brick wall, I'll come back to them later."

He marked off several names, but he seemed distracted.

"You okay, Judd?"

"No. Why?"

"Because you don't look okay."

"Haven't slept much lately. Did you call Anita Velez up here?"

"She's waiting in the Resource office."

"Thanks. Do me a favor and post one of the office workers near the door. I don't want her accusing me of stuff, me and her in there alone."

I took the list from him and walked back to the Resource office. I was met there by one of the school counselors. She stood by the door as I walked inside.

Anita Velez sat in the chair across from the desk. She seemed more subdued than I

277

had previously seen her. She was staring at the floor.

"He's dead, isn' he?" she asked, quietly.

"Who?"

"Jaime. You called me up here to tell me that Jaime is dead."

I shook my head.

"No. The last I heard, there was no change."

She looked up for the first time.

"Then why?"

"I have a few questions. First, do you know where Vicente Ramirez is today?"

She stared at the floor again.

"No."

"When was the last time you saw him?"

"Las' night. He came by the house after he heard wha' had happened to me and Jaime."

"When he left, did he say anything about where he was going?"

"I figured he was goin' home. He didn' say anythin' about goin' nowhere else."

"Okay," I said, looking at the list. "What about Geraldo Orozco? Seen him lately?"

"He was at the house yesterday, but I was asleep. I haven' seen him since the game last Friday night."

"Federico Armand?"

She shook her head.

"I ain' seen him in a few days."

"Did you tell Geraldo or Vicente what happened to Jaime?"

"Of course."

"Did he say anything about getting even?" She shook her head.

"Nobody done said nothin' to me about gettin' even," she said. "Ever'body been very nice to me, tell me how sorry they are I and Jaime got fucked up."

I circled the names *Ramirez, Orozco,* and *Armand* on the sheet. Given what she had gone through, she was probably telling the truth. On the other hand, people have hidden agendas. Sometimes they don't want to overplay their hands. For all I knew, either Vicente or Geraldo Orozco may have left Anita's house with a plan.

"I want to ask you about Gypsy," I said. "Do you know if she went to church regularly?"

"Yeah," she said. "Well, not *regular* regular, but pretty often. Maybe once or twice a mont'. Her mama wanted her to go. Her mama, she knew Gypsy was wild. She hoped the Blessed Virgin would calm Gypsy down."

"What church did she go to?"

"That one over in Mica Wells. The little one. St. Ignatius. It ain' much bigger than a

279

classroom, but she liked to go there. She says she liked the Father there."

"You know his name?"

"Yeah. Father Salazar. That's why she liked him. He's from our country."

"You know what happened to Justin Warfield this morning?"

She nodded.

"I heard. Heard he got fucked up real bad."

"Real bad," I repeated. "I don't suppose you would know anything about how that all happened, would you?"

"No. If I knew, I'd tell you. Justin was nice to me, at leas' when we were alone. I think he was afraid of that Seth Kramer, so when Seth's around Justin treat me like Seth. When it's just me and him, though, Justin was nice. I understan'. It's okay."

"All right then," I said. "That's all I needed. You can go on back to class."

I handed her a hall pass and sent her on her way.

CHAPTER TWENTY-FOUR

I knew exactly where Vicente Ramirez lived, because I had driven out to his place a week and a half earlier to arrest him.

Has it only been ten days?

Seemed like a month, at least. I wished I could turn the clock back ten days, to when the biggest problem I had was a couple of teenage boys letting their testosterone get the best of them in the school parking lot.

Hector Ramirez's house was on the poor side of Deep Crick Road, where the domestics and the day laborers rented their cheap frame houses and tried to scratch an honest day's pay. The house Hector and Vicente rented was just this square, nondescript masonite-sided box, with two bedrooms, a single bath, a kitchen, and a den. Hector was cutting the grass when I drove up. He shut down the push mower and stepped over to the cruiser.

"I need to see Vicente," I said. "Did you

know he wasn't in school today?"

"No," Hector said. "I worked late last night — third-shift janitor at the Piggly Wiggly. I didn't get home until almost eight. He's usually gone by then. Why? What's happened?"

"There was a problem at the school today, and whoever caused it wasn't in first period. Vicente wasn't in first period, so I'm checking him out."

"You think Vicente did something wrong, Chief?"

"Somebody did."

"Maybe he is at work."

"The tee shirt place?"

"*Si.* It is a busy time of year. They hire many of our people."

"I'd like to clear him, Hector. I have to talk with him first, though. You see him, maybe you ought to just bring him up to the station. Whoever's on duty will call me."

"If it will help."

"It would. I'll scoot by the tee shirt shop in Morgan later and see if he's there, and if he was working this morning instead of going to school. Another thing. Did you know that girl who got killed last week? Gypsy Camarena?"

"Yes."

"Her parents have disappeared. If they

don't show up soon, the medical examiner in Morgan's going to have to turn her body over to Social Services. They'll bury her in an unmarked grave, on unconsecrated ground. You understand what that means?"

He nodded, his weathered face stony and grim.

"It's a very bad thing," he said.

"So I hear. If you have any idea where the Camarenas are, you might want to pass along the word that they need to claim Gypsy's body and arrange for a proper funeral, got it?"

"I'll see what I can do, Chief. And I'll bring Vicente to the station as soon as I see him."

"You're a good man, Hector," I said, extending my hand. "I appreciate your help."

I drew a blank at Geraldo Orozco's house, and again at Federico Armand's place.

Orozco's mother hadn't seen her son since the middle of Sunday, and pleaded with me to bring him home if I ran across him.

Federico Armand's parents were gone, but his sister was home with her two-month-old baby. She told me, in severely broken English, that she thought Federico might be in Morgan, working.

On a hunch, I asked her whether Federico worked at Specialty Tees.

"*Si,*" she said, nodding.

I needed to talk with people at Specialty Tees, but I also had to keep Gypsy from a date with the crematorium, so I drove over to Mica Wells to check out the St. Ignatius Church.

Mica Wells is only a few miles from Prosperity. Right after you dust off the Prosperity Town Limits sign on Morris Quick Road, there are a couple of small bedroom communities, which quickly give way to open, rolling two-lane country roads, trees, and pastures. This part of Bliss County had changed very little since I was a kid. I considered that a good thing.

As I drove along, I caught sight of a red-tail hawk circling over the stubble of a harvested cornfield to my right. It glided and swooped on the updrafts, circling lazily in the sky. For a moment I lost it in the orange glare of the late afternoon sun, and then it was there again, almost suspended in midair, as if I was watching a living landscape tableau.

Then, without so much as a flutter of its wings, the hawk pivoted, tucked itself into a projectile, and dove straight for the earth. At the last second, it flared out, belly to the ground, snared some poor creature in its talons, and grabbed at the air with its fully outstretched wings to take off again for the nearby stand of tulip poplars.

I knew what would happen next. I had seen it many times in the hardwood forest on my farm. The hawk would settle on a sturdy poplar limb and proceed to disassemble the animal it had captured with its razor-like beak, tearing whole chunks of flesh as it gorged itself on its prize.

A year or so earlier, a private detective from Virginia had arrived in Prosperity following a lead. He was an ex-cop, so he understood the value of checking in with the local police department before harassing the locals. I recall that his name was Frank, and that he was a falconer. We talked a bit when he presented his credentials and — being from the South — just kept talking for a while.

He told me a story about his hawk, and how he was foolish enough one day to forget to secure the jesses that strapped the bird to his arm after a session of hunting. The bird had captured a healthy field rat, somewhat larger than a mouse but not so big as a gray squirrel or a muskrat, and had returned to Frank with its quarry.

As Frank attempted to secure the bird, a

piece of meat from the field rat dropped to the ground, and Frank absently bent over to pick it up. The raptor, perhaps thinking that the master meant to share the spoil, launched from Frank's arm and intervened the only way it knew how — by grasping its owner's hand with its powerful talons.

As he told me about the incident, Frank showed me the scar, right on the heel of his palm, where the hawk had buried a claw right up to the knuckle. Frank told me that he had never felt pain and pressure that acute, and that he had learned an important lesson that day.

He also told me that it helped him to understand what the prey felt in its last moments, as the predator swooped over and speared it with hundreds of pounds of pressure, crushing spine and piercing entrails, perhaps even killing the quarry instantly, to be carried away to a place of safety and to be eaten without resistance.

Sometimes I felt a little like the poor creature whose violent demise I had just witnessed. It only wanted to get across the cornfield, maybe pick up a morsel of grain along the way, and retreat to the safety of whatever warren it called home, when out of the sun death had descended like a falling missile, and in the instant of clutching and impaling it realized that it was nothing more than a part of the great circle of life.

I had been complacent. I had become comfortable, weathering the invasion of my bucolic family community by the developers and land rapists who had descended on it like dozens of starving raptors. I had fooled myself into thinking that I was safe on my hundred-acre preserve, free to enjoy the sunsets over my fields and the tender warmth of my girlfriend, and that by ignoring everything outside my own skin I could make it go away.

Then, in a single senseless, angry instant, Gypsy Camarena had swooped down and wiped away the protective shell I had woven about me for six years. It wasn't fair, any more than the sudden, unbidden crush of the falcon's talons had been fair for the mouse. It just *was*, and that was all there was to it.

It was just life's way of reminding me.

Nobody had ever promised *fair*.

Anita hadn't been kidding when she called St. Ignatius *little*. The priest, Father Salazar, had apparently arranged to use a storefront at the crossroads in the middle of Mica Wells. The inside couldn't have been more than six hundred square feet, but the ceiling was high and Salazar had managed to cadge some castoff pews and a few dozen hymnals. He had erected prayer stations to the major saints along each wall. I had seen full-sized versions in St. Patrick's on my only trip to New York, and the tour guide there had explained what they were used for. My Baptist upbringing, discarded as it might have been, made it difficult for me to fathom praying to people who had walked the earth for intercession rather than going straight to the Big Guy himself, but I tried to respect other people's faith, even if I had rejected my own.

A man stood at the front of the sanctuary, watering plants that had been placed across the back of the room to hide a series of water and sewage pipes that had been exposed when a wall had been taken out to extend the length of the room.

"Excuse me," I said.

He turned around. He was short and brown and built like a miniature halfback. He was wearing jeans and a Carolina Pythons sweatshirt with the sleeves cut off. It strained against his cabled biceps and light-bulb torso. His face was the color of fresh-hewn walnut, etched with canyons of smile lines, and as open as a cathedral door.

"Yes," he said. "Can I help you, Officer?"

"I'm looking for Father Salazar."

He put down the watering can.

"I am Father Salazar."

I stepped forward, offering my hand.

"I'm Chief Wheeler, Prosperity Police Department."

He shook my hand, and nodded sagely.

"Ah, yes. Prosperity. The murder case. I've been following it in the paper, and on television. You don't look like your pictures, Chief."

"Actually I do, at least when I've had the opportunity to sleep more than an hour at a time for a few days. I probably look a little haggard right now."

"I wasn't going to say it, but there you are. How can I help you, sir?"

I gestured toward the pew next to me. He nodded, and I sat. He sat in the pew ahead of me and turned to talk.

"I understand the dead girl, Gitana Camarena, attended your church."

"Yes," he said. "Not often, but I recall her visiting for Mass a few times."

"Do you know her parents?"

"Roberto and Alfonsa. Yes. They attended more regularly. Lovely people. Such a tragedy in their lives. You know about their son, of course."

I shook my head.

"I didn't know they had a son."

"He was older than Gitana, maybe four years or so. He stayed behind in Mexico when the rest of the family came to North Carolina. He was very close to his grandmother, who was ill, so he decided to stay behind until she passed. After her death, he arranged to come across the border with a band of coyotes."

"Coyotes?"

"Mercenaries who bring Mexicans into the United States for a price. They own trucks or railroad cars. They wait until they have ten or twenty people willing to pay to come across and then they cram them into their vehicles like so many smoked oysters. The coyote who brought Gitana's brother across abandoned the truck at a rest stop in Arizona when he thought the police were about to search it. He left the truck locked, and he never came back. Everyone inside the truck died."

"That's terrible. When was this?"

"About a year ago. Alfonsa was devastated. I'm afraid she was just recovering when Gitana was murdered. Tell me, Chief, have you made any progress in finding her killer?"

"We're working on it."

He stroked his battered face.

"So I thought. You have a hard time getting the Mexican people to talk with you."

"They've been a little reluctant."

"They are afraid, Chief. The legal system in the old country can be oppressive, and the prisons are to be scrupulously avoided, so they shy away from the police. Then they come to this country, and find that many people want to exploit and deport them at the same time."

"Crazy world," I said.

"Just parts of it. How can I help you?"

"Gitana's parents have disappeared. I was hoping you might know where they went."

"Why?"

"Her body has been at the morgue for almost a week. She's been dead for eight days. The medical examiner can only hold her for ten. After that, she has to be turned over to the Committee on Anatomy."

"And what happens then?"

"As little as necessary. A quick embalming, a cheap funeral, or cremation, and an unmarked grave in the county's human landfill. If her parents can claim the body, she may be able to have a decent ceremony and be buried in consecrated ground."

"Consecrated ground," he repeated.

"I hear that's important to you people."

He nodded.

"Where do you bury your dead, Father?"

I asked. "It's obvious your church doesn't have a graveyard."

"No, but you can get a great slushie at the convenience store next door."

We both laughed at that one. Then he became somber again.

"We've made a deal with one of the local commercial cemeteries. They set aside a portion of their property and donated it to the church for the tax write-off. I contacted the bishop, who conducted a service of *Consecratio Cymiterii*."

"I don't know what that is," I said.

"It's a consecration ceremony. Very elaborate. Very old. It provides for the 'hallowed ground' to which you referred. When a member of my congregation dies, they can be buried there."

"I don't mean to sound ignorant. I'm not Catholic," I said.

"Would you like to be?"

I smiled. "Always recruiting, huh?"

"It isn't very hard, you know."

"I think it would require a certain degree of faith that I lack."

"I see," he said. "No harm trying. Tell me, though, if you don't resort to faith, how do you deal with all the ugliness and sin you run across in your work?"

"Right now? I don't sleep much. Like I

said, I'm not Catholic and I don't know a whole bunch about how things work in your church, but I was wondering if you could help me with a little information."

"I'll do what I can — and what I am allowed."

"I'm trying to find out how Gitana Camarena spent her last three days before she was murdered. I want to eliminate as many potential suspects as possible. Did you see her last weekend, or sometime on Monday?"

He shook his head.

"She didn't attend Mass on Sunday. Her parents were here, but she wasn't."

"Do you know whether she had an ongoing . . . um, romantic relationship with anyone in the community?"

He rested his corded forearms on the back of the pew, and lowered his chin to them, then stared at the floor.

"Do you know what happens in confession, Chief?"

"Just what I've seen on television."

"Fanciful imaginings, most of it. The confession is a pact between the penitent parishioner and the priest. It can't be any other way. If the penitents have any doubt whatsoever that the priest would keep everything said in the confessional absolutely and completely secret, then they

293

would never divulge all their sins. The prospect of discovery would seal their lips, and condemn their souls. For that reason, nothing that is said in the confessional box is ever repeated. Ever."

"But, if the penitent is dead, and divulging the confession would help to find her murderer . . ."

"It doesn't matter. Nobody is ever completely dead, Chief. According to the faith, they merely transcend to a confessor of a higher order. And they leave loved ones behind whose lives could be very badly affected by the contents of the deceased's confessions."

"Are you saying that Gypsy told you things in confession that could help me find her killer?"

"I'm telling you nothing of the kind. I'm telling you that I can't tell you anything that I have heard. It is impossible. I carry the cross of my parish's sins. It is a heavy burden, but I cannot lighten it and remain the pastor of my flock. Does any of this make sense to you?"

I leaned back in the pew.

"Frankly, no."

"Then you'll have to take it on face value."

I thought about this for a moment.

"Okay, then," I said, standing. "I guess

that's all I had to ask. I would appreciate any information you can find on Gypsy's parents. I'd hate to see her handed over to the state."

"Why did you ask about our cemetery arrangements?"

"I'm not sure. In the back of my head, I guess, I'm still trying to keep her out of a potter's field somewhere. Tell me. If her parents don't come forward to claim her, how would I go about having her buried in your church plot?"

"Was she given the anointment for the sick and dying?"

"Beg pardon?"

"Was there a priest called when she was found?"

"No, Father. We were a little busy."

He scowled briefly, and then stood and walked up to the front of the room. He gathered some articles and then returned to me.

"Please take me to her," he said.

We arrived at the hospital in Morgan a half hour later. I parked in the police slot near the ER and ushered Salazar inside to the elevators.

"You have a first name, Father?" I asked, as we rode to the basement.

"Enrique. Why?"

"I feel a little awkward calling you Father."

"A lot of people do. Thank you for bringing me."

"Actually, I was about to thank you for your help."

"I'm not sure how much help I've been."

"Day's not over yet, Enrique."

The doors opened, and I showed him to the unmarked double doors leading to the morgue waiting room. Once there, I rang the bell on the front desk. Carla Powers walked in a couple of minutes later.

"This is Enrique Salazar," I said to her, gesturing toward the priest.

"Hello again, Father," she said.

"Oh," I said. "You've met."

"Many times, unfortunately," Salazar said.

"You could have said something," I said.

"Now what fun would that be?" He turned to Carla. "I would like to see Gypsy Camarena. I've just been informed that she was never administered the rite for the sick and dying."

"Follow me," Carla said, seriously.

Father Salazar walked through the doors behind her. I didn't ask if I could come. I simply followed them. Nobody screamed or told me to return to the waiting room.

Sometimes it's good to be the chief.

Carla opened a metal door set into the wall, and rolled the table out. I had expected Gypsy to be covered by a sheet, the way bodies are on television, but instead she lay naked on the cold metal tray. Her skin looked unearthly in the stark overhead fluorescent light, almost milky, but with a waxy cast. Her belly was distended, almost as if she were several months pregnant. The Y-shaped incision in her chest and torso made at the time of the post-mortem had been hastily closed with heavy sutures. Likewise, deep incisions in her neck and the back of her scalp had also been sewn casually. Her breasts lay heavily to each side of the major chest incision, looking slightly deflated and sad. The bruise on the side of her face that had lain next to the earth on the bank of Six Mile Creek had turned black.

Looking at her made me feel self-conscious.

Enrique Salazar appeared oblivious to her nudity as he prepared to administer the rites.

He began by cutting a lemon and rubbing his fingers with it. Then he opened a vial of oil. He made a small sign of the cross with his thumb, dipped in the oil, on Gypsy's eyes, ears, nose, mouth, and hands.

As he touched her, he said, "Through this holy anointing, and His most tender mercy, may the Lord forgive you whatever sins you have committed by the organs of sight, and hearing, and smell, and taste, and speech, and touch. Amen."

When he was finished, he seemed somehow suddenly tired. He closed his eyes and muttered a quiet prayer in Spanish, and then began to put his things away.

"You can roll her back inside now," he said.

"Was that the last rites?" I asked, as Carla returned Gypsy to her resting place.

"Yes."

"What's the purpose?"

"Why do you ask?"

"Curiosity. Natural propensity in cops."

He nodded, as he kissed and folded the stole he had draped over his shoulders, and returned it to the box he had brought in with him.

"The *purpose,* as you refer to it, is to remove any remaining sin from the deceased so that she can enter the Kingdom of God in a pure state."

"I thought people had to be alive to receive the last rites."

"It is preferable. If one is alive, she can make her last confession, and be absolved.

We believe, however, that when a person dies without unction — that is, without receiving the anointment for the sick and dying — that the soul *may* remain in the body for an unspecified time, waiting for release."

"May," I said.

"It is a matter of faith."

"What if Gypsy's soul decided not to wait around?"

"The prayer I spoke for her after offering the last rites was intended to help her if her soul languishes in purgatory."

"So, if the soul doesn't get a decent cleansing before it leaves the body, it goes to a place where it can be purified by other people's prayers?"

"More or less. It is a complicated issue, still under some debate in the church."

"How long do people stay in this place, this purgatory?"

"It depends on how venial their remaining sin was at the time of their death. You seem overtly curious about this issue. Are you concerned about some particular person?"

"I don't suppose," I said. "Like I said. Just curious."

Since I was already in Morgan, I had a thought as we walked back to the cruiser.

"You know about the boy who was attacked off Morris Quick Road the other night?" I asked.

"Yes," he said. "It was terrible."

"He worked at a place here in Morgan called Specialty Tees. I thought I might drop by there and ask a few questions. It occurs to me that I might need a dependable interpreter."

"If you think I might help."

"I'm betting the folks who work there will be less likely to lie if you're interpreting their words."

"I'm flattered."

He didn't say anything more, which I took for assent.

Specialty Tees was in an old building in downtown Morgan that had once been a major department store. When the mall opened on Eisenhower Boulevard, many of the businesses uptown couldn't survive the drain of customers, and shuttered their doors. The department store had been one of them. Some clever developer had come along and figured out a way to make the building profitable by piecing it out in thousand-square-foot parcels.

Specialty Tees was on the second floor of the building. My nose crinkled at the scent of solvents as we trudged up the stairs, and

I marveled that everybody else in the building went home at night without major brain damage.

The shop measured maybe sixty by eighty feet, and every spare inch was crammed with one piece of equipment or another. Young women clustered at tables behind a glassed partition, laboring with sharp blades over screen-printing patterns. I didn't see a white face anywhere.

Within seconds after we walked through the door, a man hustled up to face us.

"Can I help you?" he asked.

"I'm Chief Wheeler, Prosperity Police Department. This is Father Salazar from Mica Wells."

"How are you, Alberto?" Salazar asked, as he took the man's hand.

"So you've met," I said.

"I attend Father Salazar's church," Alberto said. "Is there some problem, Chief?"

"I'm looking for a couple of guys who work for you. Vicente Ramirez and Federico Armand. Have you seen them today?"

Alberto shook his head.

"No. Vicente was supposed to be here after school today, but he never showed up. I haven't seen Rico since Friday."

"How about Jaime Ortiz?"

Alberto shook his head.

"I heard what happened to him. So sad."

"Any ideas who might have wanted to hurt him?" I asked.

"Plenty of people."

I looked around. While the shop was relatively clean and well lighted, it was still a sweatshop. I would have been shocked if anyone in the place made minimum wage. I knew that I could make life rough for Alberto, but I also knew that he was probably as much an employee as anyone else on the floor.

"Maybe we should talk in private," I said.

"Please, step back to the office," Alberto said.

Father Salazar and I followed him through the screen-printing shop. Someone had invested a ton of money on huge Ferris wheel–looking contraptions to mass-produce printed tee shirts. Each spoke of the wooden wheels contained a flat board, onto which the shirt was stretched. With each revolution of the wheel, a new layer of paint was applied to represent a new portion of the image.

I recalled the two hundred shirts worn by the protestors at the football game the previous Friday night, and wondered how much production time had been used to make them. Moreover, I wondered who had paid for it.

Alberto's office was a ten-by-ten-foot affair with windows that looked out over the production floor. He gestured for us to sit, and he took his seat behind a steel and Formica desk that was littered with sheets of paper containing shirt designs.

"You were saying . . ." I said.

"Jaime," Alberto said. It was almost a sigh. "The boy is a good worker. On the other hand, he only has one thing on his mind. That boy is girl stupid. I suppose I can understand. After all, he's a teenager. However, it is distracting on the floor when he constantly hits on the younger women."

I nodded, more to draw him in than in agreement.

"You're saying that he might have been attacked by a jealous boyfriend or husband?"

"It happens."

"Any particular names come to mind?"

He shrugged.

"I only supervise my workers, Chief. I don't get involved in their personal lives."

"I'll bet you don't even know how many of them have green cards, do you?" I asked.

Alberto wouldn't look me in the eyes. Instead, he drew little interlocking circles on the desktop with his index fingers.

"Some do. Some don't. I don't deal with that end of the business."

"Who does?"

"I don't know."

I raised my eyebrows. Suddenly, Alberto looked nervous, which was more than just a little suspicious.

"Really," he said. "I was hired by my predecessor. I worked on the floor for two years. When he left, he told me that I was in charge of the floor. I keep the time cards, deal with little arguments among the workers, and see to it that production doesn't begin to drag."

"What about the tee shirts for Gitana Camarena?" I asked.

"What about them?"

"Who authorized their printing?"

Alberto looked around.

"I did," he said. "It seemed like a good idea. I never met the girl, as far as I know, but it's a bad thing when a Latina gets killed here. Morale is bad enough among the workers. We provide jobs, but not a great deal of money. Most of the workers, me included, are in no position to gripe. If we get angry and quit, there are five more waiting to take each of our places. Everyone in the shop was happy to help on that project.

It showed support for one of our sisters who had fallen to white aggression."

"You're sure that she was killed by an Anglo?" Salazar asked.

Alberto nodded.

"Who else?" he asked.

"Is it inconceivable that Gitana might have had a Mexican boyfriend who didn't like something she did, and decided to take it out on her?" I asked.

"I couldn't say. I didn't know the girl."

"I need some names," I said, getting back to the real reason I had come. "I want to know which girls Jaime was hitting on."

"I can do better than that. I can let you interview them."

"That would be nice."

"Just let me bring them to you one by one from the floor. I have to clock them out while you talk with them."

Andrea Flores looked older than her nineteen years. She was short, even a little squat, with a wide face, work-dulled eyes that flitted nervously around the room, and sweat-soaked hair pulled back severely into a tight bun at the back of her head. She wrung her hands as she looked back and forth between me and Father Salazar. She didn't speak much English. Father Salazar translated.

After I introduced myself, I asked her whether she knew Jaime Ortiz.

"*Si,*" she said.

"You heard what happened to him?"

"*Si.* I heard he was nailed to a tree."

"Really," I said. "Who told you?"

"I heard it on the floor this afternoon."

"Are you married, Ms. Flores?" I asked.

"No."

"Any steady boyfriends?"

She nodded, and averted her eyes.

"What's your boyfriend's name?"

"Corrado."

"Corrado what?"

"Corrado Hernandez."

"Does Corrado like Jaime Ortiz?"

"Corrado does not know Jaime Ortiz."

"Did Jaime ever try to . . ." I turned to Father Salazar. "I don't know how to put this. You translate it as best you can."

He nodded.

I turned back to her.

"Did Jaime ever try to hit on you?"

After Father Salazar made the phrase mean something to her, she nodded and stared at the floor.

"Did you tell Corrado about what Jaime did?"

She shook her head.

"I could not tell him," she said, through

Father Salazar. "Corrado can become *loco* when other men pay attention to me. It is better to forget it and just continue working."

We interviewed two more women, both of whom told basically the same story. Both had been approached sexually by Jaime Ortiz, and neither had told her husband. It seemed that each of the women we talked with felt it necessary to keep secrets from their mates, as much for their own protection as for Jaime's.

"It's a cultural thing," Salazar said to me after the third woman left to return to the work floor. "It's *machismo.* These men truly love their spouses and girlfriends, but it is a paternalistic love. The concept of shared responsibility and equanimity doesn't really compute for these guys. Their wives aren't viewed as independent people. Instead, they are considered extensions of the men, almost property."

"We have people like that here in the South," I said. "We call them rednecks."

"Yes. Also cultural. It is much like the Old Testament admonition regarding rape. If the woman is raped inside the city walls, then she is to be stoned, because if she was truly raped she would scream out, and could be heard. If she didn't scream, then it was adultery rather than rape, and adulteresses are stoned. The woman is viewed as equally culpable, even when she is obviously a victim."

"Kind of a lose–lose situation, for women."

"Twenty-first century American values may be a little slow to filter down to the Third World, Chief."

I gestured out the office window toward the work floor.

"What do you make of this place, Father?"

"It's a sweatshop. Maybe it's a little cleaner and better managed than most I've seen, but these people — most of them — work ridiculous hours for slave wages, and for the most part they are happy to get the work. It's a fact of life among the illegals. It isn't good or bad. It's just the way things are."

I drove Father Salazar back to his church. As I pulled up in front of the storefront, he turned to me.

"I have been thinking," he said. "As I said, I can never, under any circumstances, divulge any information that is communicated to me under the sanctity of the confessional. Neither can I take any direct action based on what I hear there. My role is simply to hear the confession and issue absolution, as a conduit to God himself. On the other hand, people may tell me things outside the box that they wouldn't tell you. Perhaps I could help you in your investigation."

"I couldn't ask you to do that," I said. "This is a police matter."

"It would be of my own initiative. Maybe I'll visit some of my parishioners, ask a few questions. Should I run across a tidbit of information you could use, I'm certain you wouldn't mind if I called you?"

"Not at all," I said. "I'd be obliged."

CHAPTER TWENTY-FIVE

I arrived home around seven that evening. As the afternoon had worn on, clouds had gathered and sludged in from the west, slowly covering the sky with rolling bands of slate. The temperature had dropped steadily, making me sorry I had begun the day by donning my short-sleeved shirt. Indian summer was drawing to a close.

In a land where spring lasts only a couple of weeks before giving way to blistering, sauna-like heat, the slow slide from summer to winter can skip autumn altogether. We had been privileged this year to enjoy a comfortable transition from the oppressive inferno of August to the moderate winter months, but I now had a feeling that the party was over. Daylight Saving Time would end the next weekend, and bring with it the short days and inevitable drag on my increasingly weary body clock.

I walked into the house to find Craig

lounging on the couch, reading his History text.

"Feels like our porch days are just about over, sport," I said.

"I was thinking the same thing."

"Have you eaten?"

"Not yet."

"How's chili and a salad sound? I have some corn muffin mix left over from the other night."

"Sounds like you're storing fat for the winter hibernation. I could eat chili, though. Sure."

That was what passed for communication, I had discovered over the last year or so. There was something that happened between men and boys as the boys edged on toward their own manhood. I was certain that the tension I felt had been shared by many a silverback gorilla as some young buck came along and tried to assert his own dominance. Like the silverback, I could probably fling Craig into the middle of next week if sufficiently riled but, also like the silverback, I recognized the emergence of the next generation, and realized that my time in the sun was drawing nigh.

Fathers and sons, Dostoyevsky had written. The great circle.

Nothing, of course, I reasoned, that

couldn't be overcome by some steaming Texas red and a few sweet corn muffins.

After changing into my civvies, I popped a beer and set about making dinner. I was watching *Jeopardy* on the kitchen television as I waited for the chili to come to a boil, when Craig walked in.

"What is a dodecahedron?" I said, providing the question to an answer on the show.

"That is just spooky," Craig said.

"What?"

"You're a cop. What in hell business do you have knowing what a freakin' dodecahedron is?"

"Education is its own reward. And don't cuss in your mother's house."

"I heard you had a tough day."

"Are you really concerned, or are you just fishing for juicy details?"

"The talk is that Justin Warfield got his clock cleaned."

"I wouldn't make light of it. He's seriously injured. Even if he recovers, his football days may be over."

"Big deal."

"To him, yes. His father, too. In case you aren't already aware of it, Justin isn't going to graduate with honors this year. With his grade average, football was probably his ticket to college."

"So some college will have to deal with one less dumb jock. I thought the concept of student-athletes was intended to stress the *student* part first."

"Those days are long gone," I told him. "Sad to say. Even in my day, though, it was rare to find someone on a sports scholarship who saw it as a golden opportunity to attain knowledge. It's a different set of values. A set of values, I might add, that I am very happy to see you don't share."

"Well spoken, football hero."

"That was a long time ago," I said. "And it paid my way through college. I got in on arts and letters, though, not just sports letters. Guys like Justin Warfield counted on their one strength to carry them through. In Justin's case, I'm afraid he just got sacked for the Big Loss."

"What are you saying?"

I thought for a second.

"I guess I'm just happy to see you taking your own path. I'd hate to think you would do something because it would fulfill *my* dreams instead of yours."

He looked away for a moment, at nothing in particular.

"Okay."

"Which," I added, "should not be construed to mean you can do whatever you want under this roof. If you don't go to college, I'll kick your ass. Now set the table . . ."

Maybe it was the fatigue. Maybe the days of sleepless nights finally caught up with me. Maybe the incessant intrusion of things best left unremembered wore me down to the hubs, and I lost the strength to fight it.

That night, when my nightmares came, I couldn't force them away, or force myself awake . . .

"Chief, this is Wylie Ford at the fire station. We just got a rescue call. Sounds like a coupla cars went head-on near Six Mile Creek . . ."

"Ten-four," I say. I stow my Monster Guzzle soda in the cup rack and drop the gearshift into Drive. I peel rubber as my car jumps from grass to asphalt, and do a couple of little fishtails before the rear end stabilizes.

My cell phone rings, and I instinctively yank it from my belt. I see the number on the display. I recognize it immediately, and I switch the telephone off. I don't have time to answer it right now.

The siren is like a crying baby as I blow down the Morgan Highway toward the Six Mile Creek Bridge. It's a lazy late afternoon, the sun red and huge just above the fortress of trees in the distance, and I can smell the honeysuckle entwined with kudzu along the roadside through the open window of the cruiser.

I round the last corner, just a quarter mile past the high school, and I see the flashing lights ahead of me. So many lights. So many rescue vehicles. This is going to be a bad one.

I pull in right behind one of the Prosperity Volunteer Fire Department trucks, and shut off the cruiser. When I get out of the car, everyone stops. It's really weird. It's like I get out of the car and time freezes, because everyone just stands still and stares at me.

"What?" I ask.

Slim gets to me first. He tries to push me back toward the cruiser.

"Don't go down there, Judd."

"Why?"

He looks back toward the edge of the road. I can see the earth churned up where a car has left the highway.

"One of the cars," he says. "It was Susan."

"Susan?"

"Your Susan."

I don't understand what he's saying.

"What do you mean, it was my Susan?"

I try to push past him, but he holds me back with strength I never knew existed in his skinny body.

"She was coming from Morgan. There was a transfer truck coming from the other direction. It apparently crossed the centerline just before it got to Susan's car. They went head-on, Judd. It crushed the front of Susan's car and flung it down the embankment into Six Mile Creek."

"I have to see her!" I say.

"Wait!" Slim says. "Just wait a minute!"

I realize that the State Patrolmen and firefighters and Rescue Squad members are gathered around, but at a short distance, as if they are afraid of catching some of the shrapnel from my shattered life.

"Why aren't they down there?" I ask Slim. Then I turn to the crowd. "Why aren't you helping her?"

I already know why, but I'm in denial. This can't be happening. Things like this happen to other people.

"She's dead, isn't she?" I say to Slim.

He won't look me in the eye. Nobody will look me in the eye.

I push him away. I stand, unsteadily, on rubber legs, and will myself to walk to the embankment. The car is a crumpled hulk, lying at a crazy angle on the bank of Six Mile Creek. I can see the steam still wisping from the ruptured radiator. The earth leading down the hill is ripped and gouged, as if the car

316

plowed its own furrow to the creek. The rear suspension lies against a water oak fifteen feet from the rest of the wreck.

There's a rescue worker standing next to the car, staring helplessly into the driver's-side window. He stands aside as I walk up. He says something to me. To this day I can't recall what it is.

I can't touch the car. Touching the car will make it too real to handle. I have to be detached, professional. I can lose my shit later, but right now I have to be strong.

Then I see her face. The airbag erupted when the cars collided, and now it has de-flated, and I can see the horror. The steering shaft, snapped by the impact, drove through the end of the steering wheel and pinned her to the seat. But for that single mechanical malfunction, she probably would have sur-vived.

Her empty eyes stare out at nothing, pupils fully dilated.

One hand grips the shaft protruding from her ribcage, as if to stanch the life that flooded from her in such a torrent.

The other hand grasps her cell phone.

The phone she tried to use to call me.

The call I didn't have time to answer . . .

"On one level, it's good to see you again,"

Dr. Kronenfeld told me the next morning, as I settled onto the loveseat across from his office chair.

He was a portly man with a thick salt-and-pepper moustache that only accentuated his prominent jowls. His hair, thinning precipitously in the middle of his skull, fell otherwise in shaggy clumps around his ears and the collar of the sport shirt he wore year-round, no matter how hot or cold it was outside. His voice, as always, never rose above a mellifluous, calm baritone.

"And on the other, you know that it means I'm having . . . problems again."

"I was wondering when you would call. After that business in Prosperity the other day. That poor girl."

"You knew I would call?"

"It was a matter of time. You have post-traumatic stress disorder, Judd. When I read the reports of the murder, I knew you would experience an emotional reaction sooner or later."

"Maybe you should have warned me."

"If you will recall, I did. At our last session, three years ago. I advised you that any stressful situation that involved Six Mile Creek would probably spur some unpleasant recurrences of your symptoms."

"When you're right, you're right," I said.

"Tell me about it. What have you been experiencing?"

I shrugged.

"Sleeplessness. Irritation. Flashbacks. Some nightmares, when I allow myself to sleep."

"Yes. The flashbacks. Tell me about them."

"It's the same as before. I replay the accident that killed Susan over and over. It's like I go into some kind of spell, and it's all happening again, right in front of my eyes."

"The waking dreams."

"They're worse than before. More frequent. One moment I'm fine. The next moment it's like everything around me dissolves, and I'm back on the banks of Six Mile Creek, looking into Susan's dead eyes. It's spooky."

"The death of your wife was horrible."

"You kind of had to be there."

"Don't try to be witty, Judd. Not here. We're trying to do a tune-up on your recovery. The death of your wife was horrible, but what really haunts you is the cell phone, and the call you didn't take."

"Okay. You're right. I thought I could handle myself. I'd seen the worst, man. Everything you could see at a traffic accident or a shooting, or in a domestic disturbance. I'd seen people with their heads cut off, limbs amputated, I'd seen babies left in cribs for days on end. I thought I could handle it. Then I saw the telephone."

"You remembered that she had tried to call you."

"The number on my cell phone. I knew it was Susan. I figured she wanted me to pick up something at the store on the way home. I thought I could call her back later. How the fuck was I supposed to know there wouldn't be any *later?*"

"That's just it. You couldn't know."

"If I'd taken a second, just a moment or two. . . . You know what I think about? I wonder what she was going to say. She had so little time left. She couldn't have said much. Was she going to tell me she was dying? Or was she just going to say she had called to tell me she loved me? Or that I should remember to pick up Craig at school that afternoon? I sit up awake at night and go over and over the *if*s. What would she have said, if I'd answered the phone?"

"Tell me about the last time you did talk with your wife."

"We've been over this."

"Humor me."

"It was that morning. I skipped breakfast, because I had overslept. I had a meeting first thing in the morning with the Town Council, to go over some budget requests for the next fiscal year. I told Susan that I'd pick up a sausage biscuit or something at the Stop and Rob on the way in."

"That's it?"

"No. We had a rule. Nobody was allowed to leave the house without telling the person they saw on the way out that they loved them. It was a rule she'd insisted on when I took the job as police chief. She had heard stories, you know. Cops sometimes left in the morning and never came home. She was afraid that I might be hurt or killed on the job, and our last words to each other might have been something like *Pick up some milk on the way home.* What kind of way is that to remember someone? *Pick up some milk.* Jesus."

"So you told her you loved her as you left?"

"Of course. She insisted on it."

"And she told you she loved you?"

"No," I said. "I was in a rush. She was eating breakfast. She had a mouth full of cornflakes and milk. I had to go. I told her I loved her, and I bent over to give her a kiss, but her mouth was full, you see? So I kissed her on the cheek, and she mumbled something with her mouth closed, and it might have been that she loved me, but who can say? I winked at her, and then I went out the door. The next time I saw her, she was dead."

"With her cell phone in her hand."

"All I can think is that she wanted to say whatever it was she couldn't get out at the breakfast table. She wanted to make sure I knew."

"I think maybe she knew you knew."

"Of course she did. She insisted on saying it, though. It was important to her."

"I see. Tell me about the murder last week."

"I'm way ahead of you. In fact, a lot of people are. As soon as we found Gypsy Camarena's body lying along Six Mile Creek, everyone started acting strangely around me. She was lying in the exact spot where Susan's car came to rest on the creek bank. One of my officers told me I should stay away from Six Mile Creek."

"Why did he say that?"

"I came into the office and my shoes were muddy. I'd gone back down to the murder scene to try to get a feel for what had happened."

"What did you find?"

"A lot of bad memories. I sat on a rock and tried to reconstruct the murder. It triggered a flashback."

"You went down there to find answers," he said.

"Clues. Leads. Anything I could use to help find the guy who killed Gypsy Camarena."

"You presume it was a man."

"Her neck was snapped."

"It isn't so hard. One of nature's little design flaws. The seat of our consciousness is supported by one of the weakest links in our body armor."

"You think a woman could have killed her?"

"I think the important issue is that you don't. You have based your investigation to this point on the premise that she was killed by a man."

"She had sex shortly before she was murdered."

"So a man had sex with her. It doesn't mean a man killed her. But let's leave that for a moment. What did she look like?"

"At the scene? She was a mess."

"When she was alive."

"She was pretty. Dark hair, dark eyes, high cheekbones. Good teeth. Her nose was a little broad, but not disagreeably."

"Was she a tall girl, for a Latina? Long-legged?"

"I suppose. About five-seven. She was a pretty girl."

He nodded, and clasped his hands in front of him.

"As I recall, Judd, your wife was a dark-haired, dark-eyed woman around five-seven, with high cheekbones. A pretty woman."

"What are you saying?"

"I'm laying groundwork. Bear with me. When we last spoke, several years ago, you were starting to date again. How's that going?"

"I'm pretty settled at this point. I'm only seeing one woman. Her name is Donna."

"Describe her."

"She's a former tennis player, considered turning pro. Short, tightly built, athletic."

"Dark," he said.

"Okay, dark. Very dark wavy hair."

"The way you like it."

"Let's not get personal here."

"There is nothing more personal than what we do. Yet, she isn't exactly the kind of woman you have gravitated toward in the past, is she?"

"Not exactly."

"It's interesting, how our sexual scripts work. We are attracted to certain features, even when we try not to be."

"Are you suggesting that I became interested in Donna because of those things in her that were different than Susan?"

"What do you think?"

"Come on, Doctor. No shrink tricks here. Is that what you're saying?"

"I think it's interesting. Research suggests that our sexual attraction, which is the foundation of our love relationships, is scripted at a very early age. People who are initially attracted to freckled redheads, to use an example, tend to remain attracted to freckled redheads throughout life. You were attracted enough to Susan, a fairly tall, dark, long-legged, high-cheeked woman, to marry her. By all your reports, your marriage was a happy one."

"I'm with you so far."

"Yet, after your wife dies — tragically — your next intense love relationship is with a woman who is her rough physical antithesis. She has the dark wavy hair, but everything else is different. You have a good relationship with this woman, Donna?"

"Very good. She urged me to come here today."

"She cares for you."

"That's what I just said."

"I'm sorry," Kronenfeld said. "Poor choice of words. I didn't mean to say that she cares for you in the sense that she likes you or even loves you. I meant that she *takes care of you.*"

I thought about this for a moment. I had always presumed that the relationship between Donna and me was mutual. She had her career and interests, and I had mine. We tried to share, but neither of us had tried to impose our lives on the other.

Yet, it did seem lately that she had become more nurturing, even if it did take the form of a sort of tough love. I had told the doctor that she had urged me to come to the session, but hadn't it in fact been an ultimatum?

"I suppose you're right," I said.

"So tell me, how long have you and Donna been together?"

"A year or so."

"Really. A year or so. Interesting."

"Oh, come on. What now?" I said, a little irritated.

"I have been with my wife for exactly eighteen years, four months, and five days. I have not been with her eighteen or nineteen years. I know exactly how long we have been together. So is it a year, or two years, or what?"

"I don't know. Let's see. We met at a Christmas party, two years ago this coming December. So, that's what? Twenty-two

326

months?"

"Much more precise. Twenty-two months. And yet, you have to work it out in your mind. How long were you and Susan married?"

"She died just before our twelfth anniversary."

"Your wedding anniversary?"

"No. We had two anniversaries — one for our wedding, and the other for the day we met. She died two weeks before the twelfth anniversary of the day we met."

"Didn't have to calculate that, did you?"

"What are you suggesting?"

"You're a cop. You know how to ask questions about inconsistencies in suspects' stories. You tell me. This is your therapy."

"I don't know. I know precisely how long Susan and I were a couple, but I had to calculate the months since Donna and I met. Maybe I don't care how long we've been together?"

"I don't think it's a matter of caring," he said.

"Then I don't want to know."

"Why, do you suppose?"

"Why? I guess . . ."

"Don't guess."

"Okay. Maybe it's because I don't want to make comparisons?"

"You sound unsure."

"No. Not really. As a matter of fact, I said just that to Donna last week. *'I'm trying not to make comparisons.'*"

"How did that come up?"

"It was just after the flashbacks started again. I mentioned that I had told Susan before she died that if anything ever happened to her, I would never remarry."

"Why?"

"Because it wouldn't be fair to a second wife to constantly make comparisons, to hold them up to each other as some sort of test of happiness. It would be better not to remarry, and simply enjoy . . . *being* with another person."

"Other than your dead wife."

"Yes."

"And then you told Donna that you were trying not to make comparisons."

"Yes."

"Maybe you tried to avoid comparing by choosing a person who was as different from your wife as you could manage. Yet, the sexual schema is still there, controlling our initial attractions. Try as you might, you couldn't find someone who was completely different from your wife. There was a common feature."

"Coloring and hair," I said.

"Yes. Then this poor girl was murdered and placed next to the bank of Six Mile Creek, in the exact place where your wife died."

"Yes."

"And you described her as, and I quote, *'Dark hair, dark eyes, high cheekbones. Good teeth. Nose a little broad, but not disagreeably.'* You also said she was tall, and long-legged."

"She was."

"Just like your wife."

"Yes."

"Your flashbacks didn't start again until her body was discovered on the creek bank."

"No."

"I see."

He made some notes on the legal pad in front of him. It reminded me of the pad I had been using to plot the timeline for the last three days of Gypsy Camarena's life.

"What?" I asked. "What do you see?"

"Think about it. Your wife dies before you can get there to save her, and all you can do when you do arrive is gawk at her dead body and ruminate over what she intended to say to you on the telephone. Then, six years later, you're called again to Six Mile Creek, to the exact spot where Susan died, and there's another dark, tall, exotic-looking dead girl. Once again, you've arrived too late to save her. What did you think about as you stared at her corpse?"

"I . . ." I said, trying to remember. "I had a flashback. I thought about Susan."

"And when did the nightmares begin again?"

"That night."

"Now, you tell me what I see."

"I don't know. Something is blocking it."

"Your own reluctance to admit is blocking it," he said. Then he leaned forward, and his voice dropped almost to a whisper. "What . . . do . . . you . . . *want?*"

"I want it to stop. I want to stop seeing Susan's dead eyes everywhere I go."

He nodded, and leaned back.

"You know what I think?" he said.

"No."

He smiled, and ran his hand through what was left of the hair on top of his head.

"I think your flashbacks and nightmares about Susan will go away when you find out who killed Gypsy Camarena."

CHAPTER TWENTY-SIX

I still needed to interview some of the high school students who hadn't made it to first period the day before, but since Dr. Kronenfeld's office was so close to the Bliss Regional Hospital I decided to drop by and check on a few loose ends.

First I went to the basement to look up Carla Powers.

"Nothing from the Camarenas?" I asked.

"Not a peep. I hope Father Salazar can track them down."

"If he can't, I think we've solved the burial problem anyway. St. Ignatius has a section of one of the local cemeteries set aside, so a consecrated plot won't be an issue. Local statutes require a concrete crypt, and he's working on obtaining a donation. All we'll have to worry about is the casket."

"It's sad," Carla said.

"What?"

"It seems there are more people working

on this kid's behalf now that she's dead than there were when she was alive."

"It often works that way. If you have to release the body to the Committee on Anatomy tomorrow, do let them know that burial arrangements are being made privately, and give me a call."

I took the elevator from the basement to the Intensive Care Unit on the sixth floor. The shift nurse supervisor there told me that both Jaime Ortiz and Justin Warfield were still unconscious. Ortiz was being kept in a diabetic coma, but signs of brain swelling were decreasing, and it was possible that he could be brought around by the end of the day.

Warfield, on the other hand, had incurred some nasty closed-head injuries, and it was possible that he would be out for some time.

I saw Fred Warfield sitting in a chair outside the ICU, reading a copy of *New Republic*. Three seats away, Jaime Ortiz's father sat, reading a local Hispanic throwaway newspaper. I walked over and sat in an easy chair between and facing them. The ICU, unlike other sections of the hospital, provided recliners in the waiting areas, because it wasn't uncommon for the families of ICU patients to take up lengthy vigils, waiting for their loved ones to awaken, get better, or die.

"Any word?" I asked Fred.

He folded the *New Republic* and stuffed it between his thigh and the arm of the chair. His eyes were set deeply in his sallow, drawn face. His hair looked greasy. I wondered how long it had been since he had been home.

"A little. He seems to be responding to touches and pinching, and he has good reflexes. He just won't wake up. The doctor said . . . well, he said that maybe Justin will be able to play football again . . . someday. Not this year, and certainly not for quite a while. They'll know better once he wakes up, and they can do some more extensive brain scans."

"Concussions can be rough."

"Yeah, but Steve Young QB'd the Forty-Niners through — what? — ten or twelve of them."

Nobody worked Steve Young over with a baseball bat, I thought, but I didn't say it. Instead, I just nodded sympathetically.

"Have you made any progress finding out who did this to my boy?" he asked.

"We're narrowing the field. If it was done by one of the students at the school, then we have five or six suspects. I hope to talk with all of them today. If it was someone from outside . . ."

I hoped he understood. My best bet was that another student had wiped Justin's slate because, if it was an outsider, I'd have to start all over again.

"Excuse me," I said, and turned to Mr. Ortiz. He had already put down the copy of *Noticias Locales* he had been reading.

This was going to be difficult without an interpreter. I tried to recall my high school Spanish.

"Ah, *como . . . estas . . . Jaime?*" I asked.

Mr. Ortiz shrugged one resigned shoulder.

"He is breathing on his own, the doctor says," Fred Warfield interrupted. "I overheard their conversation. Mr. Ortiz and his wife have taken turns waiting here. They've been praying for him all the time."

"I just spoke with the nurse," I said. "She tells me that they hope to bring him out of the coma later this afternoon."

"May I tell him?" Warfield asked.

"You speak Spanish?"

"Enough."

He turned to Mr. Ortiz and repeated what I had said. The man's eyes brightened a bit. He said something back.

"That would be wonderful, Chief. I hope you are able to find the criminals who hurt him," Warfield translated.

"Could you tell him that I think it will be important to talk with Jaime when he's awake," I said. "The girl he was with, Anita, couldn't identify the attackers. We're working on it. I'd like to say something, though."

I made a point of looking at both of them, as Warfield repeated my words.

"You two can be of great assistance to me, and to the police department. I want to stress that, at least for now, there is no evidence whatsoever that these two assaults were connected. I'd hate to see any more people get hurt because someone is out looking for some kind of retribution."

"Do you think that could happen?" Warfield asked.

"I think there are people in this town who would jump on any excuse to take out some frustration, and I don't want your two boys giving them the reason. It looks bad, first an assault on one of the white boys, then the murder of a Mexican girl and near-murder of a Mexican boy, and now an assault on another white boy. There's a troubling pattern here, but I'm not ready to pin it all on racial tension, at least not yet. I would be mighty appreciative if the two of you would tell anyone who'll listen that we're keeping an open mind on who might have committed these crimes."

Warfield nodded and had a brief conversation with Mr. Ortiz, who looked skeptical at first, but seemed to drop his defenses as Warfield continued.

"He says that you can count on him," Fred Warfield said. "He wants to find the people who hurt Jaime as much as anyone. If you say there's not proof it was an Anglo crime, he will support it."

"Good," I said.

"What if it turns out you're wrong?" Warfield said. "What if there is a real racial problem in Prosperity?"

"Then we'll get to the bottom of it. Right now, though, let's just focus on getting these boys healed up. I'll take care of the investigations and — when it comes to that point — the accusations."

Cantrell, the Homeland Security guy, sat in the waiting room of the Prosperity Police Department when I got there. He wasn't making any small talk. When I walked in, he was just staring at Sherry, giving her the creeps.

"Can I help you, Mr. Cantrell?" I said.

"I wanted to know if you'd found that dead girl's parents."

"Step into my office."

I held the door for him as he walked by.

He smelled like he bought his aftershave on sale at a discount store. It had been a long time since I'd gotten a good whiff of British Sterling.

He took a seat across from my desk.

"Coffee?" I asked.

He shook his head.

I really wanted a cup, but I wanted this fed hack out of my office more. I could live with a minor caffeine jones for a few more minutes.

"Gitana Camarena," I said.

"What?"

"Her name. You keep calling her *'the dead girl.'* She had a name. Gitana Camarena."

"Okay. Have Gitana Camarena's parents shown up?"

"No. Why? You have a couple of coach-class plane tickets for them in that suit of yours?"

"I think you have the wrong idea about me."

"I'll bet you say that to all the small-town cops."

"This doesn't have to be an adversarial relationship."

"You want to make nice now? Okay. Tell me why you're so interested in Gitana's folks."

He stared at me for a second, giving me

the same willies he had given Sherry, and then he opened his briefcase. He pulled some papers and a couple of pictures from it, and placed them on my desk.

"After the inauguration in 2001, the new presidents of Mexico and the U.S. met in Washington to hammer out some agreements. Mexico, for the first time in modern history, had elected a president who was a true conservative."

He waited for me to acknowledge that I knew this. I think he wanted it to be the most important fact I had learned in years.

I nodded.

"The Administration wanted to encourage good relations with a conservative head of state just across our borders. After a meeting at the White House, the Mexican president addressed a joint session of Congress, where he pledged to put a stop to illegal drug traffic across the border from Mexico, and then he returned to his own country.

"That was less than a week before nineteen terrorists flew planes into the World Trade Center and the Pentagon. The borders were temporarily sealed, and all air traffic was halted for almost a week.

"Even while the borders were sealed, the U.S. Customs Services seized almost nine thousand pounds of illegal narcotics at the

San Diego border alone, drugs destined for the United States. A large part of that drug seizure consisted of brown tar heroin. Given the extreme security along that border following the attacks on New York and Washington, can you imagine how much of this junk must have been flowing across the border before?"

I couldn't, so I just shook my head.

Cantrell leaned forward and tapped the picture on my desk.

"That man is Francisco Luis Armando Machado. He was a favorite son of the former Institutional Revolutionary Party administration, and one of the largest tar heroin producers in Mexico. Shortly after the Mexican elections in 2000, Machado was assassinated in an attack on one of his homes on the Sea of Cortez. His operations were temporarily thrown into disarray, until they were eventually taken over by a man named Cruz Pomodor."

He reached over and slid the picture of Machado aside, to reveal another picture underneath.

"That's Pomodor. Roberto Camarena is Pomodor's first cousin."

He sat back again and crossed his arms, looking a little smug and a whole lot triumphant.

"And?" I asked.

"And what?"

"So Gitana's father is this guy Pomodor's cousin. Does that mean something?"

"We're talking about one of the biggest heroin producers in Mexico, Chief."

"And his cousin, a guy who couldn't even keep his telephone bill paid. I get you, Cantrell. I know what you're thinking. Camarena is a first cousin to this Mexican drug kingpin, and he's in this country illegally, so he must be up to something rotten, right?"

"When you consider that he's disappeared, just as soon as the public spotlight falls on him."

"Because of his daughter's murder, yes. Probably because he is afraid of being sent back to Mexico. I met this man. I looked into his eyes, and the eyes of his wife. They were scared to death when they came to my office. The fact that you're here tells me that their fears were probably justified."

Cantrell steepled his hands, a body language gesture I had learned long ago in a college psychology class meant that he felt superior to me. For the life of me, I couldn't figure why.

"I can appreciate your position," he said, slowly. "You're the chief of police in this little burg. You have to keep the peace. You have all these little factions — farmers, businessmen, blacks, Mexicans — and you have to appear to treat all of them equally. I understand that. I'd also suspect that even the most evil man of all time would be devastated by the death of his daughter."

"Don't forget his son."

"You mean the one who died crossing the border? Yes. We know about that, too. I have a job to do, though. I work for an agency whose job is to see that the attacks we suffered never happen again. In the process, we also have to see that the ongoing attacks on this country that have taken place for almost a hundred years, in the form of illegal drug imports, are brought to a screeching halt. If the cousin of one of the biggest drug kingpins in Mexico is in this country, I kind of think he should be sent back."

"Guilt by association."

"If you like it that way."

"Where there's smoke, there's fire," I said, challenging him.

He placed his hands on the arms of the chair, and leaned forward.

"Chief, have you given any thought to the possibility that maybe Gitana Camarena was murdered *because* she was Roberto Camarena's daughter?"

CHAPTER TWENTY-SEVEN

I sat in the Resource office at the high school, looking over the list Hart Compton had assembled for me, but I couldn't get my mind off Cantrell's assertions.

As much as I disliked Cantrell, his question had struck home. I had allowed Gypsy's involvement as a town pump for the local football team to dominate my theories on her murder. Had I inadvertently failed to take other factors into account? Was it possible that Roberto Camarena really was somehow involved in illicit drug trade in Bliss County, and that his involvement led to the death of his daughter? It would explain why he and his wife took flight so quickly after their daughter's body was discovered.

Donna's revelation about the sexual antics of her students had come as something of a surprise to me. It made me wonder whether there were other activities going on under my nose that I hadn't noticed.

I picked up the telephone and called the front office.

"This is Chief Wheeler. Could you ask my son to come by my office for a moment? That's right, Craig . . . Thanks."

Several minutes later, Craig opened the door and walked in.

"What's up?" he asked, as he slouched in the chair.

"I just need some background information. I figured you might have some insight I could use, being a teenager and all."

"Okay," he said, but I sensed tentativeness behind it.

"It's about drugs."

He didn't say anything. Maybe he thought I suspected him of using.

"This guy from Homeland Security thinks that some of the Mexican families in town — I can't say which ones — might be involved in drug trafficking."

"Of course they are."

I stopped. I think maybe I blinked a couple of times.

"You know about this?"

"Sure. I mean, I can't give you names or anything, but everyone knows that it's easy to score if you know the right people."

"You can't give me names, or you won't?"

"I can't, Dad. Relax. I'm not into that shi . . . stuff. I don't know the names because I don't know the right people. I don't need the trouble it would bring down on me."

"I see," I said.

"It's not just the Mexicans, though. There are Anglos and blacks, just about all races and incomes. If you decide you want to be an addict, it wouldn't take long to build a connection. I never could, of course, because everyone would figure I'm a narc, being the chief's kid and all. Guess I'll have to put off my drug experimenting until college."

I looked up at him.

"That was a joke," he said.

"That's a relief. Tell me, if I wanted to find out whether a particular family was involved in selling drugs, where would I start? Which kids would I want to question?"

"You mean, who are the major stoners? You don't need me to tell you that. Just ask your girlfriend."

"Donna would know?"

"Of course. Teachers aren't totally stupid. They know which kids are coming to class high. They can see which ones are nodding off at their desks. Ask Donna. She can tell you."

"You can't?"

"Of course I can. On the other hand, these kids already hate the teachers. I'd like to make it through the end of this school year without getting jumped by some head case who thinks I ratted him out. The teachers are *expected* to betray the students."

"Okay," I said, still a hundred miles away in my head. "Thanks, Craig. Hamburgers okay tonight?"

"Sure. You want me to start the baked beans when I get home?"

"That would be nice. I may be detained for an hour or so, but I'll be home by seven. You get on back to class now. Tell Elsie to write an excuse that says you were up here to pick up some absentee sheets."

He stared at me.

"I don't want you getting jumped either. This is just between us, but things are getting messy. I want to try to keep you out of it."

Donna peeked inside my door.

"Did you go to the doctor?" she asked.

"Come on in. Shut the door behind you."

She did, and sat in the chair next to my desk, after turning it to look at me.

"Well?" she asked.

"I saw him this morning."

"And?"

"He says if I want to get rid of the flash-backs, I have to find out who killed Gypsy."

"He couldn't just give you a pill or something?"

"No. This is a head thing, some kind of association between Gypsy and Susan. In order to get rid of one of them, I have to resolve the other."

"I don't suppose he gave you any clues or anything to help you along the way?"

"No. He did say something, though. He was very interested in the fact that you and Susan were so different."

"I know we are," she said. "It's one of the reasons I didn't run screaming from you months ago. I'm not very interested in becoming the second Mrs. DeWinter."

"What about the second Mrs. Wheeler?"

I thought I heard her breathe in sharply, but she hid it well.

"Don't say that," she said.

"I'm not proposing. Especially not now, when my dead wife won't leave me alone. I'm trying to understand you, though. Kronenfeld told me that you take care of me."

"He did?"

"Yes. Are you aware of that?"

"It isn't something I do consciously. You haven't been all that high-maintenance, up until this Gypsy Camarena thing. Keep you lubed and wash the windshield once in a while and you seem to do all right. The last week, though . . ."

"I know. I hope we're getting close to solving this thing. Maybe then things will get back to normal. That's why I wanted to talk with you. There may be a drug connection with this murder, and I need to know which of the kids here in the school are most likely to know who the major dealers are in Prosperity."

She laughed. "You don't want much."

"Just whatever you can give me."

She leaned over and gazed at the floor for a few moments. I heard her sigh a couple of times.

"Nobody can ever know I gave you this. It's hard enough getting these kids to co-operate as it is."

She wrote several names on a pad on my desk, then stood and turned toward the door.

"I mean it," she said. "You didn't get those names from me."

"My lips are sealed," I said. "Craig and I are having hamburgers at the house tonight. Would you like to come over?"

347

"Find out who killed Gypsy, Judd. I'll be there for you when you've put that behind you."

Among the many provisions of the Safe Schools Act that led to the presence of the Prosperity Police Department in the high school was one that stated unequivocally that lockers in the school were the sole property of the school itself.

It took me about five minutes to get the combinations to the lockers of the three boys whose names Donna had written on my desk pad. The school issued the locks, and it was a suspension offense to replace them.

The first locker opened with a repulsive odor of stashed sweat socks and molded sandwiches. A cursory — and well-gloved — inspection yielded nothing of interest.

When I opened the second locker, the first thing I saw on the upper shelf was a sheaf of rolling papers. It took me about thirty seconds to locate the kid's stash, secreted away in the toe of a pair of sneakers on the floor of the locker. It was just half a nickel bag of pot, hardly enough to warrant a possession charge, but it would be enough for what I wanted to do.

I hit pay dirt with locker number three.

There was a half-ounce baggie of pot stashed in the inner pocket of a down jacket hanging on the hook, and two pipes wrapped in another baggie in a small pencil box on the top shelf. As soon as I opened the baggie, I knew from the aroma that I would find a rich deposit of resin on the screens inside the pipes.

"I want to see this kid first," I said to Hart Compton. "And I want you to have the second kid waiting in the office lobby when I finish. I want them to see each other."

"Why?"

"These kids are naturally paranoid, and I have to protect an informant. If they see each other, they will each presume the other ratted. That way, nobody will suspect the person who actually gave me their names."

"Are all cops as devious as you?"

"You should hope you never have to find out."

Seconds later, Compton ushered in Brandon Oakes, the first of the two youths I'd be questioning. He was sullen and pale, with long, thin bangs that hung down past his brow, so that he constantly had to brush them away. He looked a lot like that sheepdog in the Warner Brothers cartoons, pudgy and benign, yet somehow trying to project an aura of confidence and mastery — and failing horribly.

I could tell immediately he didn't like being in the company of the Prosperity Chief Pig.

"You know who I am?" I asked him.

"A cop."

"I'm the Head Cop. My name is Judd Wheeler. I'm the chief of police here in Prosperity. I need to tell you that I'm investigating a crime, and that you are not required to answer any questions I ask without having your parents present. Do you understand?"

He shrugged, staring past me out the window in an apparent attempt at barely concealed contempt.

"I need to hear you say it," I said.

"Yeah, I understand."

"Good."

I pulled his jacket from under my desk, and laid it on the chair next to me.

"Is this your jacket?"

"Sure," he said, but I could see that he was becoming nervous.

"I thought so. I found it in your locker."

"Hey, man, you had no right to go in my locker without my permission."

"You apparently didn't get the memo, Brandon. That locker belongs to the school, which just lets you use it. I can go in there any time I want, especially if I have reasonable probability to suspect that there is illegal contraband in it."

"Reasonable . . ."

"Probability," I said. "That means I have evidence that you may be stashing things in your locker that the law says you aren't allowed to possess."

I reached into the jacket pocket and pulled out the baggie of pot. I placed it in front of him on the desk.

"Hey, that ain't mine!" he said.

"It's your jacket."

"Well, sure."

"I found it in the locker you use."

"That don't mean that stuff is mine. You planted it."

"I suppose that would explain your fingerprints on the plastic. Plastic bags produce excellent fingerprints, you know."

I hadn't actually fingerprinted the bag, but Oakes didn't need to know that. He seemed to shrink a couple of sizes, as he realized that he wasn't going to be able to bluff his way out of the accusation. He didn't say anything, so I continued.

"You've been a busy boy," I said, as I pulled the pipes out of my desk drawer. "I'm certain that the prints on these pipes and the DNA from your mouth will prove rather definitively that these are yours."

"Look. I told you that stuff ain't mine. I was holding it for a guy."

"Possession is nine-tenths of the law. Which is interesting, actually, since that is precisely what I'll probably be charging you with. *Possession,* that is. It's unfortunate. I'm sure you already know that kids over the age of sixteen are charged as adults in this state. It will mean a criminal conviction that will follow you for the rest of your life."

I sat back and waited for him to respond. When he didn't, I sprung the second half of my surprise.

"Wait a minute," I said. "I just recognized your name. Aren't you one of the kids who discovered that body down by Six Mile Creek the other day?"

He looked up, startled.

"I didn't have nothin' to do with that, Chief," he said. "I was just down there with another guy, and we ran across that body."

"You know who she was, though."

"I didn't know at the time, on account of she was so fucked up, you know? I found out later that it was Gypsy."

"So you knew her."

"Sure. A lot of people did. Gypsy was friendly."

"So I've heard. You and Gypsy never did

any . . . *business* together, did you?"

"I don't get you."

I pointed at the baggie and the pipes.

"No," he said. "Why? You trying to pin something on her?"

"Just curious. You know about the big fish and the little fish?"

"Huh?"

"You go fishing. Sometimes you catch a little fish, but you don't want a little fish. You want a big fish, right?"

"I suppose."

"So maybe you're a little fish."

For a second, his eyes clouded over. He was having a hard time with the abstraction. Chronic pot use will do that to you.

"You think I'm a fish?"

"A little fish," I said, trying to be patient. "Maybe if you can lead me to the big fish, I'll consider throwing you back."

Bless his heart, he finally got it.

"So . . . if I tell you who sold me the pot, you might let me go."

"I'd consider it."

He chewed his lower lip.

"I don't know. This guy's pretty mean. If he were to find out I rolled over on him . . ."

"Whatever," I said. "You have the right to remain silent . . ."

"Whoa! You're arresting me?"

"If you do not remain silent, anything you say may be used against you . . ."

"Hold on a minute!"

". . . in a court of law. You have the right . . ."

"Okay! I'll tell you."

I stopped, and looked over my reading glasses at him.

"I got it from this guy in Morgan. His name's Chaney, I don't know his first name, but he goes by the name Trigger."

"Like the horse."

"Huh?"

"Never mind. Trigger Chaney. Okay. Where does this guy hang out?"

"I don't know. I have a telephone number. I figure it's a cell, on account of when I call it fades in and out. I call him, tell him what I need, and he tells me where to meet him. I think he's a member of the Vulcans, though."

"The motorcycle gang?"

"Yeah. Them."

I knew who the Vulcans were, but I wanted to find out how much Oakes knew. About twenty years earlier, the Parker County Police responded to a call about a shootout on July Fourth at a two-bedroom shack north of town, and found seven members of the Tarheel Vulcans machine-gunned. It was a bloody mess. The Outlaws, a rival gang, were blamed for the shootout, but nobody was ever brought to trial. The Vulcans retaliated two weeks later, and the cops in our sister county to the north had a hell of a time putting down the war. Things had been quiet for a long time. It seemed that the two gangs had drawn their turf lines and had carefully kept within them for a couple of decades.

The Vulcans had taken over Morgan and the rest of Bliss County. They were a minor nuisance, for the most part, though they were known to deal in drugs and prostitutes. This was the first time I had run across a high school student who was buying drugs from them. They were known to be branching off into crystal meth, but I hadn't heard anything about them dealing in heroin.

"That's helpful," I said. "And I will look into it. I'm more interested in people dealing tar, though."

"I don't do none of that stuff," he said.

"Who does?"

"You mean, here at the school?"

"We'll start with the school."

"Well, I don't know anybody that's heavy into tar. Just some guys that have, you know, tried it."

"They had to get it from somewhere," I

said. "Big fish, Brandon. I need some names."

"There's Kenny Broome. He told me once that he smoked some tar at a party. Also, Kyle Hawley. I know he uses, 'cause I've seen him shoot up."

"Where?"

"At a party a couple of months ago. He was braggin' about how pot was pussy and he was doin' some real shit. He let us watch while he cooked it and put it in his arm."

"What did you think?"

"It was scary, Chief. I don't think I could do something like that. You gonna let me off for this?"

I gathered his works and the baggie of pot, and swept them into the center drawer of my desk.

"Let's say I'm giving you a reprieve. You need to keep your nose clean. I'm going to label this stuff, and put it in police evidence storage. You get in trouble again, and I'll pull it out and add some charges. You understand?"

He nodded. I thought I saw tears at the corners of his eyes.

I felt like a real jerk, beating up on a kid, but it was the quickest way I knew to obtain the information I needed. I dismissed Brandon, after telling him to leave the pot and pipes at home, then walked him to the outer office, where Tim Crump was waiting.

"Come on back, Tim," I said.

He followed me to the Resource office.

He was a skinny, freckled kid with oily, straight hair and bad acne. He could have benefited from the services of a decent orthodontist. I knew his family, and I also knew that the odds against him getting good dental work were pretty high.

My grandfather would have called the Bliss County Crumps *white trash*. I tried to be a little more charitable, but there was little doubt that when the rolls were called for Prosperity's more productive and law-abiding citizens, the Crumps would be conspicuously absent.

I let him know that he could have a parent present during questioning. He waived the right, so I jumped right in.

I pulled the nickel bag from my desk and laid it in front of him.

"That ain't mine," he said.

"It was in your locker."

"So?"

"So, it's yours. You turned seventeen two months ago. That makes you an adult in the eyes of the court. What say you and I run on down to the jail so I can process you?"

"Ain't goin' to jail."

"You have the right to remain silent."

"We can trade," he said.

One thing about growing up as a Crump, you learned early to respect the fine art of the deal when it came to the police. Tim Crump was a lot more composed under the gun than Brandon Oakes had been.

"That there is about four, maybe five grams," he said, nodding toward the nickel bag. "You wanna run me in, I'll get probation for misdemeanor possession. Ain't worth your time. So what do you really want?"

"Information on who's slinging tar in Prosperity."

He snorted.

"*Slinging?* What, you heard that on some old *Starsky and Hutch* episode, Chief?"

I didn't say anything. I just stared at him with that stony cop gawp that they teach us at the academy.

"You don't want much," he said.

"I need some names."

"Well, tar means Mexicans. The only brown tar heroin I ever heard of came over the border. You want brown, you go to the brown people, you know?"

"Names," I said.

"I'll be honest with you, Chief. I ain't

never done no *cheva,* you see? So I never had no call to buy it."

"You know who sells it, though."

"I can ask around . . ."

"I don't think so. This is kind of sensitive. Who do you know who uses this stuff?"

"You want me to roll over on guys who just like to party? That's cold, man."

"I need to know."

"Sonny Cline. He uses sometimes."

"He's a student here?"

"Yeah, man. He's a senior. He's not like hooked or nothin', but I seen him do some A-bombs once or twice, and I know he's skin-popped a little. I wouldn't give you his name, but I don' like that SOB so much."

"A-bombs . . ."

"Pot and heroin mixed together."

"Okay," I said, making a note on the pad.

"Tell me somethin', Chief. You about to shut down some suppliers in Prosperity?"

"If I can."

"I just wanted to know. If things are about to get thin, maybe I ought to lay in some stuff to tide me over."

I sat back in the chair.

"Have I said anything to you that implies we are friends?" I asked.

"No, Chief, but . . ."

"You think because I'm letting you off the

hook on this nickel bag that we're buddies?"

He didn't say anything, but his freckled face grew redder by the second.

"You think maybe because you're snitching for me that we can hang together, homeboy?" I asked.

I heard the edge in my voice grow keener by the second. I was going to have to watch it, or I was in danger of going over the line.

He shook his head.

"Here's the way it is," I said. "You're off the hook for the time being on this possession charge. If I find out you've lied to me, I'll have you in the slam in about fifteen seconds. If I find out you've gone out ahead of me and warned the dealers that I'm coming, I'll charge you with obstruction of justice, which will mean real time in a real prison. You want that?"

He shook his head again.

"Then we understand each other," I said. "What happens in this office stays in this office. Your reward for keeping to that agreement is that you don't have to eat state food for a while. Get it?"

He nodded.

"Get out of here," I said.

He gathered his book bag and crept out of the office.

It had been a productive hour. I knew a

couple of things I hadn't known before. There had also been a bonus.

Both Kenny Broome and Sonny Cline were on the list of students who hadn't attended first period the day before, when Justin Warfield had been beaten to a stump in the boys' room.

At one level, I couldn't make the connection. Warfield wasn't known as the kind of guy who would be mixed up with a couple of stoners like Broome and Cline. For that matter, it might have been just one of those strange coincidences that pops up when you're investigating multiple felonies.

I don't like coincidences. I decided that Cline and Broome warranted a little harder look than I had intended to give them.

Chapter Twenty-Eight

Before I could confront my two little junkies, I thought I might stoke up on a little information.

I spent a few minutes in Hart Compton's office, checking the school computer records, and then headed out to the student parking lot.

Kenny Broome drove a ratty old Monte Carlo beater, one of the pre–gas crisis monsters that got about five gallons to the mile. The vinyl covering on the roof was coming off in tatters, and the formerly gold paint had gone pale champagne, and was peeling in places. The tires were badly cupped and unevenly worn, so I figured this bulge-mobile hadn't enjoyed a front end alignment since the Reagan administration. It was the kind of car you could buy with a Jose Canseco rookie card.

The air was apparently shot, too, because Broome had the windows cracked about an inch to keep the interior from reaching roasting temperature.

Through the windows, I could see that the back seat was littered with fast-food garbage, escaped and petrifying French fries, and random articles of clothing.

Kenny Broome was a slob, like most guys on the spike, but I didn't see anything overtly suspicious, so I moved on to Sonny Cline's ride.

If Sonny were to buy Kenny Broome's car, he'd be trading up. His car was newer but, being an AMC Pacer, had started life behind the eight ball. I was surprised that any of these little deathtraps had survived the eighties.

The whole left side of the car had been wrapped around something larger and heavier at some point, judging by the foot-high scrape that ran from the front bumper to behind the door.

The interior of the car was about what I expected, since the Pacer was little more than a rolling greenhouse. The dash had canyon-like furrows of cracked plastic revealing hardened, expanded rubber foam padding. The seats were covered with fake lambswool covers, but I could guess what they looked like underneath. There was the usual accumulation of trash in the backseat.

What really drew my attention, however, were the random rusty stains on the seat covers and parts of the steering wheel. I thought I could see another splotch of reddish-brown stain on the gearshift lever. Unlike virtually everything else in the car, the stains looked relatively new and, in what would almost certainly turn out to be a forensic bonanza, I could make out two extremely well-defined fingerprints in the stain on the steering wheel.

I decided I should talk with Sonny Cline first.

Sonny was a drowsy-eyed, slouchy kid wearing a Kurt Cobain tee shirt and the dirtiest pair of jeans I had ever seen outside a barn raising.

His lower lip faded into a feeble excuse for a chin, and the whole facial package rested on top of the most prominent Adam's apple I'd ever seen on a human. His fingernails were dirty, as were the palms of his hands. I felt like I should be wearing a dust mask just to sit in my office with him.

"You turned eighteen in June," I observed.

"Uh-huh."

Oh, goody. Loquacious, too.

"That makes you an adult. That also means I can question you without allowing you the luxury of having a parent present."

"Don't matter," he said. "My dad wouldn't come no how."

I suspected that there was at least one time when he had, and that he now regretted it.

"Well, Mr. Cline, as it happens I've been talking to a number of students today, and your name has come up a couple of times. Here's the way it's going to go. I'm going to ask you two questions. You're going to answer them. If you refuse to answer, we'll just move this little party down to the jailhouse. How's that sit?"

"I guess it's okay. What's this about, anyway?"

"I know you're a heroin user. Don't even bother denying it."

His head seemed to drop a little. I couldn't tell whether it was ashamed, or his neck was just exhausted from trying to support it.

"I've used a little."

"Good. First question. In your career as an aspiring junkie, have you ever bought any tar from a man named Roberto Camarena?"

His eyes narrowed. At first I thought he was trying to think of a way to evade the question. After a moment or two, I decided he was just thinking. It was apparently an exercise to which he was wholly unac-customed.

"No," he said finally. "I don't even know nobody by that name."

"You're certain of that."

"Yeah. I know who I buy from. I never heard of that dude. Sounds like a Mexican."

"Aren't all the people who sell tar in Prosperity Mexican?"

"Well, yeah, but I don't recall none of them having that name."

"So, as far as you know, Roberto Cama-rena has no involvement in the heroin trade in Prosperity?"

"That's what I said, man."

"Okay. I want you to have a seat outside in the main office."

I led him out and had him sit down on a wooden bench just inside the office door, and then asked the secretary to page Kenny Broome and ask him to come to the office.

Several minutes later, Broome trudged in. He was almost a physical mirror image of Sonny, except that he had a little more chin, and a lot less Adam's apple. His oversized pants bagged around his knees and barely stayed positioned on his hips, but I was spared the trauma of viewing his exposed boxers by the extra-long flannel shirt he had tucked into his trousers.

He looked at me first when he walked in the door.

"Kenny Broome?" I asked.

"Yeah."

He looked over at Sonny Cline. His face clouded. I thought I saw something pass between them, a sort of telepathic warning, but I decided that I was crediting them with entirely too much cranial wattage.

"Come on back," I said to Kenny, and led him back to the Resource room.

He took the hot seat and fiddled with his gnawed fingernails. He needed a bath, or maybe a delousing. Stuffing opiates into your body tended to make you forget things like nutrition and hygiene.

"You saw Sonny sitting out in the waiting room," I said.

He nodded.

"Your school folder says you're eighteen."

He nodded again.

I reminded him that he was an adult and not entitled to have a parent present, though he could have an attorney if he wanted. And if he knew one.

"That's okay," he said.

"I'm going to say two words, and you're going to tell me everything you know about them, got it?"

He nodded.

"Roberto Camarena," I said.

He looked up a little, but his fingers kept fidgeting with each other.

"Who's that, some baseball player?"

"The name doesn't mean anything to you?"

"No. Should it?"

"You're on the spike, right?"

He grinned, and I found out what he had eaten for breakfast that morning.

"Shit, no, man. I smoke a little, and once in a long while I'll skin-pop, but I never put it in my arm, man. That's for losers."

"You never bought any tar from Roberto Camarena?"

"Not as I recall. Is that why you asked me up here? Geez, man, I thought I was in trouble."

"You are."

I waited for a moment, to let the words sink in. For all of half a minute, he had seemed to relax, which told me that when he came to the office he was worried about a damn sight more than fingering some junk dealer.

"I already talked with Sonny," I said.

He looked down. His fingers started to move again.

"Now I'm talking to you," I told him. "Sonny's car is a mess. Someone left what looks like a lot of blood on the seat covers and the steering wheel. There are finger-prints in the blood on the steering wheel. Now, you tell me. When we examine those prints, are we going to discover that they belong to Sonny, or to you?"

He didn't say anything. His ears flushed, though, and his breathing became heavier.

"Here's what I'm thinking," I said. "One of you made the decision to beat up on Justin Warfield. The other went along, because it would have been uncool not to. Here's the catch, though. I really don't care which is which. What I can promise you is that the one that rolls over on the other is going to take a lot lighter ride. You sit here and think about that."

I left the room and walked out to the wait-ing room. I crooked my finger at Sonny and beckoned him to follow me into the staff conference room, just down the hall from the Resource office. When we walked in, I let him lead the way, and I closed the door behind him. I actually slammed it a little. He jumped at the sound, just a little. I told him to have a seat.

"This is going one of two ways," I said. "Kenny's going to roll over on you, or you're going to roll over on him. If neither of you rats the other one, I'm going to impound your car, pull every shred of physical evidence off of it that I can separate from your own filth, and then I'm sending you both over for the major slam time. Do you understand what I'm saying?"

He wouldn't look at me, which was every bit as good as a confession of guilt. All I had to do was keep up the pressure, and one or the other was going to break like a dime-store tumbler.

"I can give you one chance," I said. "So far, I know what happened, but I don't have the details. You tell me what happened, and we'll pin the bad stuff on Kenny. If he talks first, you get to do the long stretch. Assault with intent to kill is some major bad juju, kid. Everyone in the yard figures you're some big-time bad-ass, and that cleaning your clock makes them even badder. Whichever one of you draws the thick end of the shit stick on this one is due for some major healing time. Follow me?"

He didn't say anything. A lot of kids would have tried to lie their way out of it, but for Sonny that meant finding enough intact neural connections in his head to think of something rational and believable, and he just wasn't equipped.

It was like fishing with hand grenades.

"Time's up," I said. "You sit here. Maybe

when I come back from talking with Kenny I'll read you some rights or something."

I stood and slid the chair back under the edge of the table. I wanted him to think I was going to be gone for a while.

I had just opened the door when he spoke. "Wait," he said.

I didn't turn around immediately.

I didn't want him to see me smile.

I parked in the reserved police space at the Bliss Regional Hospital and crossed the parking lot to the front door. The cold front that had begun to sweep through the previous night had really taken hold, and I was glad I had worn my long-sleeved shirt. The day had turned dry and crisp, and it hurt my sinuses a little to breathe in the air that swirled around me and lifted the dried leaves in the lot and made them dance on the hospital tarmac. Autumn was on us like a hungry dog.

The elevator took me to the sixth floor. I didn't bother checking in with the ward nurse. Instead, I went straight to the family waiting room.

Fred Warfield had apparently been spelled long enough to run home for a shower and a snack, because he was in different clothes and he smelled a lot better than he had that morning. He was in the recliner, which was pushed back as far as it would go. He was snoring loudly.

I shook him a little. His snore changed abruptly into a coughing snort as he woke up.

"Chief," he said, as he rubbed his eyes. "I feel terrible, dozing off like that. What if something happened?"

"That's all right," I said. "I wanted you to be the first to know. I have a couple of confessions in Justin's assault, and I've arrested the kids who hurt him."

"Oh, my God," he said, drawing his fingers across his cheeks. "That's wonderful news. Kids, you say?"

"Yes."

"Mexicans?"

"No, Fred. The kids who beat up Justin were involved in drugs. They overheard Justin talking with another student in the parking lot about going out that afternoon to buy some speed equipment for his car, and he flashed a wad of cash."

"Jesus," Fred said. "I took him to the bank to get the cash day before yesterday. I'd forgotten all about it. He was going to add a wing to the back of his Acura."

"Well, he should have kept it to himself. These two kids decided their connection wanted the money more than Justin did. One of them had an old aluminum softball bat in the trunk of his car. They waited for him in the bathroom. When he went in, one of them locked the door, and the other went to work on Justin with the bat. When he was out cold, they took his money and left the school."

"Who are these little assholes?"

"I can't tell you, not just yet. My office assistant is trying to get in touch with their parents, and they still haven't contacted attorneys. I have their confessions, though, signed and notarized. They're in really deep trouble."

"What will happen to them?"

"If they're convicted, and they don't plea bargain, they're looking at assault and battery with intent to kill, robbery, and kidnapping."

"Kidnapping?"

"When they locked the door so that Justin couldn't leave, they were in technical violation of the statutes against kidnapping. Add to that some minor heroin possession charges, and they'll be middle-aged before they see a window without bars again."

"Thank goodness. Justin's mother will be happy to hear this. She's been scared to death that it was some Mexican death squad taking revenge for what happened to that poor boy the other day."

"Any word on Justin?"

"The same. He's banged up something awful, but his vital signs are good. He just won't wake up. The doctor told me that he could go on like that for a while, but his brain scan is pretty encouraging."

"You hang in there. Let me worry about pinning these two punks to the wall. You just make sure you're here for your son. Have you seen Mr. Ortiz?"

He looked over at the other chair.

"No. He must have left while I was asleep. He'll probably be back in a few minutes."

I patted him on the shoulder. I thought I saw tears in his eyes.

The ICU charge nurse saw me coming when I opened the door.

"Chief," she said. "The Ortiz boy. They're bringing him out of the diabetic coma."

"Where is he?"

"Room Twenty-Seven. We like to keep the comatose patients in a special enclosed room, because we can access lifesaving equipment there more quickly."

She pointed at a glassed-in room set between two banks of curtained hospital beds. The blinds in the room were drawn,

374

so I couldn't see what was happening inside.

"Is Mr. Ortiz in there?" I asked.

"Yes. We brought him back about a half hour ago. We thought he should be here when his son wakes up."

I walked over to the ICU room and tapped lightly on the door before opening it a crack.

"Is it okay to come in?" I asked.

A nurse pulled the door all the way open.

"Chief, please," she said. "We're waiting for Jaime to wake up."

"That's good news," I said as I walked in.

Jaime was in a hospital bed, the head end cranked up so that he was about halfway to sitting. There was a tube going into his nose, and three or four snaking up under his hospital gown. One of them was carrying some pinkish fluid to a receptacle under the mattress.

Jaime looked like he'd gone the sad end of ten rounds with a wood chipper. His face was lumpy and bruised. His right eye was still swollen shut, and his nose looked strangely out of place. His lips looked like strips of raw liver that had been sewn to his face. His hands were bandaged, but I could see the telltale circles of seepage working their way through the gauze from the nail holes his attackers had left there.

His parents were at one corner of the

room, watching the process the way a trout looks at a television. Mrs. Ortiz sat in the only chair available. Mr. Ortiz stood behind her, his hands on her shoulders.

"What's the word?" I asked the nurse.

"He's being weaned off the insulin we used to induce the coma. As his blood sugar stabilizes, he will slowly come up through the various layers of sleep, the same as if he had been placed under anesthesia."

"Any idea how long it should take?"

"He's still on a little bit of insulin. We can't withdraw it entirely or he'll go into shock. It may be a while. Probably not more than an hour or so, but everyone responds differently. I could page the doctor for you . . ."

"No, thanks. You've been very helpful."

I made my way back out to the hallway.

My intent was to drive back to Prosperity, find Cantrell, and tell him that I had found no information that supported his concerns about Roberto Camarena being connected with the Mexican brown heroin traffic, what little there was of it in town. I was looking forward to wiping the smirk off his face.

My radio chirped, though, and I heard Sherry's voice.

"Chief?"

I toggled the switch, and spoke into my

shoulder mike.

"Yes?"

"I just received a call from Carla Powers at the morgue. She says she's received some test results back that you wanted to hear about."

"Thanks. I'm at the hospital now. I'll head down to see her."

It took the elevator three interminable minutes to reach the basement. It seemed that someone wanted to get on or off at every level. Finally, the doors opened and I trotted down the hall to the morgue. The automatic doors whisked open as I broke the electric eye, and Carla stood at her reception desk, looking over some papers.

"That was fast," she said, as she looked up.

"I was just upstairs. What have you got?"

"The PCR test results came back on the samples I took from the Camarena girl. I thought you'd want to know."

"What did you find?"

"Well, as you know, we found some evidence of skin scrapings under Gitana's fingernails, which could have meant that she at least tried to stave off her attacker. We took those scrapings and the vestigial semen found in her vagina and sent them off to the lab."

"Okay."

"There are statistical properties among the short tandem repeats of polymorphisms on specific portions of the human DNA strand — we call them *alleles* — that are common to Caucasians. Others are common to Hispanics, and still others to Negroids. I won't bore you with the details. I'll save those for the court, if and when you catch this asshole. This I can tell you, though.

"First, the skin under Gitana's fingernails and the semen in her vagina came from the same guy."

"Good so far."

"Second, there's an extremely high likelihood — on an order of thousands to one — that the guy who had sex with Gitana and then killed her was Caucasian."

I sat in the chair next to her desk, and stretched my legs out.

"We're looking for a white guy," I said.

"I'd say it's almost a certainty."

"What are the chances that the skin under her nails was there because she was a back-scratcher during sex?"

"The fact that two of her nails are broken off at the quick — ripped off is a better description, actually — indicates that the event that led to the skin getting under her nails was violent."

"Okay," I said. "I suppose that narrows the field a little. Of course, she had sex with about seven guys that I know of in the last several days of her life, and so far as I can discover they were all white guys."

She had a trace of a sly smile dancing about the corners of her mouth.

"Not like this guy," she said. "The fellow you're looking for has a rare genetic disorder. It doesn't present with any overt or dangerous physical symptoms. It's probably just a holdover from some ancient and extinct virus we had to adapt to a few million years ago, but it is unusual. Only individuals whose parents both carried the gene mutation inherit this anomaly. Again, I won't bore you with the details, but when you do find this guy, we will be able to match him up with the samples from Gitana pretty quickly just by looking for this disorder."

"And it will be conclusive in court?"

"As damning as a fingerprint. Count on it."

"That's good news," I said, slapping a fist into my palm. "Hot damn, Carla, that's the best news I've heard all week. I think we're going to crack this one. Damn good work."

"I think Gypsy would be happy to hear

someone's looking after her, even if it is after she's dead."

"Now if Father Salazar can just find her parents."

She looked at me strangely.

"What?" I asked.

"He didn't call you?"

"No."

"Oh," she said. "Well."

She leaned back against her desk and stared at the floor for a moment, as if deliberating whether to tell me something.

"I, uh, suppose you can tell from the way I'm not saying anything that . . . well, they've already shown up."

"The Camarenas?"

"Yes."

"When?"

"This morning. Not long after you left. I figured Father Salazar had called you. He brought them in, and they signed for Gitana's body to be released to Father Salazar for a funeral and burial. They specifically said they wanted her to be buried in the United States, so she could always be on American soil."

I pulled up in front of St. Ignatius Church in Mica Wells and slammed the door of my cruiser. The front door of the church was open, and I walked in to find Enrique Salazar pulling a white linen cloth over the altar in the apse at the back of the sanctuary.

"Chief," he said, barely glancing at me. "I thought you might be here sooner or later today."

"I'd imagine you did. Do you know what you can get in this state for obstruction of justice?"

"In all honesty, I don't. Why? Is it harsh?"

"You're damn strai . . ." I started, and then remembered where I was. "You should have called me when you found the Camarenas."

"But I didn't find them," he said. "They found me."

"Come again?"

"When I opened the church this morning. I went to the back and made myself a cup of tea, and when I came back into the sanctuary they were sitting in the nave. I can't imagine where they hid, waiting for me to show up. They were frightened. They had heard rumors that their daughter's body would be sold for medical experiments, and they couldn't bear the thought that she might not be given a decent burial. So I took them to Morgan. They signed the papers to release Gitana's body to me, and we came back here."

"Okay, you could have called me then."

"It wouldn't have done much good. They disappeared again."

"I thought you were going to help with this investigation, not harbor witnesses."

"You sound irritated, Chief."

"It's been an irritating week. There's a Homeland Security agent named Cantrell who would like to have a word with the Camarenas. He's not going to be very happy when he hears that they surfaced and then vanished again."

"I know about Mr. Cantrell," Salazar said. "He came by the church."

"When?"

"Yesterday. He asked me whether I could tell him where the Camarenas were hiding. A disagreeable man."

"What did you tell him?"

"Same as I told you. I didn't know. Why is he interested in these people?"

"It seems Camarena is the first cousin of a major heroin smuggler back in Mexico. It made Cantrell nervous that Roberto Camarena was living in Prosperity and he didn't know about it."

"He thought Roberto was smuggling drugs?"

"I think he wants that to be true. I talked

to a few heroin freaks this morning, though, and they never heard of Camarena. I'd say he's probably clean. Cantrell won't be happy, though, until Camarena and his wife are back on the other side of the Rio Grande."

"I see."

"Oh, and one more thing. We found the guys who beat up that kid at the high school yesterday. They were white kids. There wasn't any racial issue involved."

"I'm happy to hear it. How is the boy?"

"Still unconscious. They're trying to get Jaime Ortiz to wake up, though. I hope he'll be able to tell me who nailed him to that tree."

"I'll say a prayer for him."

"You do that."

I started to leave, but thought better of it, and turned back to him.

"When do you plan to hold Gypsy's funeral?"

"Tomorrow or the next day. The funeral home hasn't picked up the body yet."

"You, uh . . . you let me know. I'd like to attend."

"As soon as arrangements are made, I'll call your office."

"One more thing. I'm not Homeland Security, and I don't think Roberto Camarena is a drug dealer. I wouldn't mind talking with him if he surfaces again. He may have some information I can use to find the guy who killed his daughter."

I was halfway back to the station in Prosperity when the radio in my cruiser crackled.

"Chief?" Sherry said.

"I'm here," I said.

"You're very popular in Morgan today. The sheriff would like to see you there. Says it's kind of urgent."

"Tell him I'm on my way."

Don Webb had been one of my teachers at Prosperity High School, but he had always harbored a yearning to be a law enforcement officer. He devoured books on the subject, but never had the opportunity to actually go to the academy, since he was well past their maximum age by the time I took his class.

The sheriff in Bliss County, however, is an elected post. When he punched out of teaching after putting in his quarter century in front of a blackboard, Webb ran for sheriff and — almost to his surprise — won.

He had turned out to be a first-class cop, and a pretty decent administrator. He was on his fourth four-year term. With a year to go before elections nobody had stood up to challenge him for the job.

I parked in the lot across the street from the Law Enforcement Center in Morgan, and took the elevator from the lobby to Sheriff Webb's office on the seventh floor. His secretary and I had been two years apart in school. She pointed at his door as I walked in.

"He's waiting for you, Judd. He has Clark Ulrich and that man from the Justice Department with him."

Clark Ulrich was the CSI worker who had done the investigations at both Gypsy Camarena's murder and Jaime Ortiz's assault.

I walked in and shut the door behind me.

"Have a seat, Judd," Webb said, pointing at a chair near his desk.

"Mr. Gajewski," I said, shaking hands with him. "How you doing, Clark?"

Webb waited for us to finish our small talk, and then took control of the conversation.

"I called you two out here because Clark here has been working on the Ortiz assault the other night. We think we might have something of interest."

Clark opened a file and handed it to me.

"We were able to pull three good complete prints off the trunk lid of Jaime Ortiz's car, along with five or six separate partials. We scanned them and sent them to the FBI to check against their IAFIS registry, since Mr. Gajewski here was convinced it was a federal hate crime. We got the results back a couple of hours ago."

I glanced over the FBI report.

"Parolees," I said.

"Federal parolees," Gajewski said, correcting me. "Jesse Stout did five years at Atlanta Federal Penitentiary for methedrine manufacturing, and this other guy, Ben Seibold, did three at the Butner facility here in North Carolina for trafficking."

"What's the connection?"

"They're both known to be hanging with the Carolina Vulcans," Sheriff Webb said. "The Vulcs, like a lot of the cycle jockey gangs, have discovered the profit potential in crystal methedrine. We think they're setting up some labs in Bliss County, but they're hard as hell to track down. As you know, Bliss has the highest percentage of rental housing per capita in the state. Anyone can come along, plop down a security deposit on a house or a trailer, and set up a lab. That worries us."

"What I can't figure," Gajewski said, "is how Jaime Ortiz was mixed up with these characters. We can be pretty sure he wasn't dealing for them. The Vulcans are clear-to-the-bone rednecks. They wouldn't have anything to do with Mexicans or blacks."

Webb looked at me.

"Is it possible that Ortiz was trying to muscle into their business?" he asked.

"This is a high school kid," I said. "He had absolutely no jacket in my office prior to this assault. I'm a little skeptical."

"Yet, it does appear he was assaulted by Vulcans, and in this case Vulcans known to be involved in meth production and distribution."

"It does seem that way. Do you know where Stout and Siebold are now?"

Gajewski chimed in.

"I'd like to call the FBI in on this case," he said. "We're talking about racketeering and conspiracy to manufacture and distribute narcotics. It's their bailiwick."

"I don't have a problem," Webb said. "What about you, Judd?"

I shrugged.

"I'd prefer not to have a bunch of guys in wingtips and cheap suits crawling around Prosperity. I imagine we'd survive, though."

I turned to Gajewski.

"So you aren't looking at Jaime Ortiz as a hate crime now?"

"No. The kind of working-over Ortiz received is a sort of trademark for the Vulcans. They like to hit hard, make a big mess, and leave a clear message."

"There's more," I said. "We've arrested a couple of high school kids on the beating at the school yesterday. It was a robbery. No racial motive at all, and no connection with Jaime Ortiz or Gypsy Camarena."

"That's good news," Webb said. "All we need in Bliss right now is a race war."

"I think we're a long way from that," I said. "On the other hand, we're pretty sure now, based on DNA reports I received earlier today from the ME over at the hospital, that the guy who had sex with Gypsy and then broke her neck was white."

"He raped and killed her?"

"No. There's no sign of rape. The sex appears to have been consenting. Doesn't sound like a hate crime to me."

"How do you plan to follow up on it?" Gajewski asked.

"I have a list of people Gypsy screwed during the last four days of her life. I suppose I'll have to start with them."

"Could you keep me informed?" Gajewski asked.

"Drop by the station each day. I'll keep you in the loop. If it looks like she was killed as part of some kind of racial violence, I'll be happy to turn you loose."

CHAPTER TWENTY-NINE

I spent the rest of the afternoon making telephone calls from my office in the Prosperity Police Station. I saw to it that Kenny Broome and Sonny Cline were safely tucked in for the evening, and told Stu to stick close to the jail until their lawyers arrived to spring them.

If they arrived. Guys like Broome and Cline were unlikely to have anyone on retainer, and most of the public defenders from Morgan weren't going to drive all the way over to Prosperity to deliver a writ on a couple of kids who — in all probability — were looking at a decade or two on a roadside work gang. We probably wouldn't see any legal eagles in the Prosperity station until at least the next morning.

By the time I finished, it was almost seven in the evening. I locked up my files, cut off the lights in my office, and took the cruiser back across Six Mile Creek to the farm.

I could tell that Craig had been hard at work on dinner when I walked into the house, which was filled with the homey smell of onions and brown sugar and molasses and bacon from the baked beans he had promised to prepare and place in the oven.

I changed into a Pythons sweatshirt and some jeans, and padded in my sock feet into the kitchen to start working on some hamburgers. I had pulled the meat from the freezer that morning and left it in the refrigerator. I dumped the cool ground beef into a bowl, poured in a few teaspoons of Worcestershire sauce, and a little garlic salt and some fine-ground pepper, and then started kneading the concoction to work the ingredients into the meat.

I was just starting to roll the meat into cue ball–sized chunks to flatten into patties when someone knocked on the front door.

"Craig!" I called. "Can you get the door?"

A few seconds later, I heard another knock.

I figured Craig was plugged into his headphones, and couldn't hear the door, or my call to him. I quickly washed my hands, and walked to the front of the house.

Donna stood on the porch.

"Hey," I said, trying to fill it with as much warmth as I could muster. "Come on in. I thought you were going to pass on dinner."

"So did I," she said. "If you're short . . ."

"Nonsense. I have almost two pounds of ground beef in here. There's plenty. Want a beer?"

"Glass of wine, if you have any."

I pulled a bottle of crisp chardonnay from the fridge and uncorked it to pour her a glass. She took a sip, and sat on one of the stools at the kitchen counter.

I was okay with the silence between us. We knew each other well enough that it wasn't necessary to fill each passing moment with conversation. I started slapping the balls of hamburger meat between my palms to form the patties.

"I arrested the guys who beat up Justin Warfield," I said.

"I heard. How is he?"

"Still out. Vital signs are good, though. He should recover. He probably ought to consider some career other than football. They really rang his chimes."

She didn't reply. I kept slapping the patties, my back almost entirely turned to her, until I heard the first quiet sob.

I turned and saw her with her elbows on the counter, her eyes resting on one palm. It didn't take a genius to figure that she was crying.

Now here's the thing with me. When I was an Atlanta cop, I kicked down the front doors of crack dens, chased perps down blind alleys, and even got into a shootout or two with armed robbers, and never had a moment's problem with knowing what to do.

One crying woman, though, and suddenly I am deep in the land without clues.

"Are you okay?" I asked.

"No," she said, though it was actually kind of a *Nuh . . . oh* sound, since there was a Laura Petrie sob in the middle of it.

I washed my hands again, partly out of some kind of sense that trying to comfort her with raw beef all over my fingers probably wouldn't go over, but mostly to buy time while I decided what, precisely, I should do.

I put my arm around her shoulders.

"What is it?"

"It's me being stupid," she said. "Give me a minute. It'll pass."

"What's upsetting you?"

She swiped at her eyes with the back of her hand, and then wiped away the residual tears with her fingers.

"We have tissues," I said.

I handed her a box from on top of the refrigerator, and she finished mopping her face. She crumpled the tissue, but she didn't toss it in the trash. She just held it in one palm, squeezing as if she might wring money from it.

"I didn't like the way I was toward you today," she said.

"I don't understand."

"I've been pushing you. I don't know whether I'm doing it for you or for me. Ever since they found Gypsy's body, Susan has been standing between us like a brick wall. I thought maybe if you went to see Dr. Kronenfeld, he'd find a way to put her out of the way. Then he told you that you had to find who killed Gypsy, and I didn't like the answer. I figured, well, if you had to find Gypsy's killer to get rid of Susan's ghost and those damn flashbacks, then that was what I wanted."

"It's what I want, too."

"Yes, but I wanted it for the wrong reason. I didn't push you away so you could do your job. I told you to go find who killed her so I could get my boyfriend back. I couldn't believe I was being so callous."

She turned to face me, and she put her hands on my shoulders.

"I *liked* Gypsy, Judd. She had her problems, and she could be a little wild, but you could tell, deep down, that she was basically a good kid. When someone you like gets killed, you should want their murderer to be found so that justice gets done, so they don't die without someone being held to account. I don't know. This doesn't seem to be making sense . . ."

"No, I think I'm following you," I said. "You're upset because you wanted Gypsy's killer found, but for what you saw as selfish reasons."

"That, and because I wasn't sensitive to what you're going through. I saw your memories of Susan as some kind of barrier between us. I forgot that you want those flashbacks to go away just as badly as I do."

There wasn't much I could say to that. She was right. If I hadn't wanted to get rid of the intrusive memories, I never would have gone to Dr. Kronenfeld's office.

"Is it okay to say I'm sorry?" she said.

"No," I said. "I don't want you to be sorry. You did what you did, and I've been single-minded the last week, and this murder has just muddied up our lives for a while. There's no foul in situations like this. I'm stressed and you're stressed and under stress people do things they wouldn't do otherwise. Admitting that you're sorry would be the same thing as telling me you're not perfect."

She looked up at me.

"Hell, I already *know* you're not perfect," I said.

For the first time since she had entered the house, she smiled.

"And you're some kind of prize?"

"Booby prize," I said, and I looked down at her.

"Okay," Craig said from the door to his room. "That's it. I want a transfer to a new English class. This is getting just too damn weird for me."

"Shut up and go light the grill," I told him, without looking back. "And set three places at the table, you hear?"

"Yes, sir," he said.

I was pretty sure I heard a smile in his voice.

I still didn't sleep much that night. I was trying to put a game face on it, but my body was rapidly giving out on me. I found myself nodding off, but as soon as I began to dream, I'd see images of Susan and I would jerk up and force myself to waken.

Around three o'clock, I got up and wandered into the den. I turned on the television and watched an old movie on the Turner network. After ten minutes I was bored, so I started flipping through the channels, over and over, looking for something that would catch my attention in the vast wasteland of infomercials, bad old movies, and recycled sitcoms that pollutes the blue-black hours of the airwaves.

Finally, I gave up on it and pulled out my briefcase, extracting from it the evidence pad I was building on Gypsy Camarena's murder.

There was one hour on the chart that I couldn't get out of my mind. According to Anita Velez, Gypsy had left the party sometime just before midnight, but if she was walking she still should have been on the road when Anita and the boy from Allenwood High School — Mitch Biggers — left Kevin Byrne's house around twelve-thirty. Someone had to have given her a lift. I had thought it might be one of the guys at the party, but Seth had told me that they were all wasted, and fell asleep on the beds in Kevin's basement.

Of course, if they were passed out, how could they know if one of their number awoke and decided he'd rather sleep in his own bed?

Also, just because someone gave Gypsy a ride home that night didn't mean that he came back and killed her two nights later. I was just building suppositions in my head, and not getting very far with them.

I was getting foggy. Two weeks earlier, I would have seen the things I was missing now. Too many hours at work, and too few in the sack, were beginning to affect my ability to reason. I had to find Gypsy's murderer soon, or learn to live with Susan's accusing open dead eyes boring through me just to grab more than a half hour of sleep at a time.

"Judd?" Donna called from the door to my room. "Up again?"

"Yes. I'm trying to figure out some things."

She padded across the hardwood floor to the couch, and sank into the cushion next to me.

"Try it on me," she said.

"It's police business," I said. "Technically, I'm not supposed to . . ."

"Oh, bullshit. You think I'm going to remember a shred of this conversation tomorrow morning?"

She wrapped my arm between her own arm and body and pulled herself up close to me. She smelled sweet, and her warmth emanated sensuously through the oversized flannel shirt I'd loaned her for the night. For a moment I responded to her in that primordial way that men do, and I considered picking her up and carrying her into the bedroom for a little taste of the ol' romp and tussle. But that would have made it twice in one night, and I didn't want to appear greedy.

Besides, in my weakened state it probably would have killed me.

"Here's my problem," I said. "I know roughly when Gypsy got home on the night she was killed, which means that she met with her murderer sometime between eight that evening and midnight. I also know that she was out walking by herself on the Morgan Highway late Saturday night before she died, but she had to be picked up by someone because she didn't have time to walk home before Anita Velez would have come across her on the road. What I could really use is someone who saw her in a car either time — preferably on Monday night, since the car she was in that night was probably driven by the killer."

"How can you be sure?"

"I can't, of course. But even if she was in a car that evening, and the owner of the car didn't kill her, he . . ."

"Or she."

". . . *or she* would probably know where Gypsy went, and that would provide one more period of time I could account for."

"And it would get you one step closer to

her killer."

"Exactly."

She leaned her head on my shoulder.

"I see your problem," she said, and accented it with a poor attempt to stifle a yawn.

"And I can tell that it rivets your attention."

"Sorry. Early day yesterday. Early morning tomorrow."

"Today."

"Jesus. Today. I'm going back to bed. If you have any self-respect at all, you'll do the same."

"In a bit," I said.

She pulled herself up and kissed me, then started the long, slow walk back to bed.

"Liar," she said, just before closing the door.

I arrived at the high school around nine-thirty the next morning. I would have come earlier, but I had to wait for a messenger from the courthouse in Morgan to drop by the Prosperity police station.

When I walked by the Bliss County CSI van and into the school, Hart Compton was waiting for me at the front door.

"They're all here, in the conference room, just the way you asked," he said. "Their fathers are here, too. Some of them are hopping mad."

"That's a shame," I said. I had left my sunglasses on, after looking at myself in the mirror while shaving that morning. Too many days with too little sleep were beginning to mottle the whites of my eyes with spidery little scarlet tendrils of bloodshot capillaries.

"They're gonna raise hell if you go through with this," he said.

"Let 'em."

He led me through the main office to the conference room behind the principal's office. Clark Ulrich was there with what looked like a plastic toolbox.

"We ready to go?" he asked when he saw me.

"Ready like Freddy," I said.

I led him into the conference room. Seated around the table were pairs of fathers and sons. At the near corner I saw Kent and Seth Kramer. Elzie Phipps was there with his son Jason, right next to Ron and Eddie Place. Ed Tomberlin had brought his son Gary. Finally, Kevin Byrne sat next to his father, Mike.

"What's this all about?" Kent asked.

"Murder investigation," I said.

I pulled an envelope from my briefcase

and opened it.

"I have warrants signed by Chief District Court Judge Carlton Beam here. There's one for each of the boys."

I handed them out to the students, as their fathers looked on, aghast.

"A warrant? What for?" Mike Byrne demanded.

"DNA samples. We now have conclusive evidence that the person who probably killed Gitana Camarena was white. We also have reason to believe that this same person has a distinctive genetic abnormality that will identify him conclusively. CSI Officer Ulrich here is going to collect samples from each of the boys in the room."

"Why just our sons?" Ronnie Place argued. "There must be hundreds of white teenagers in the school."

"Yes," I said, "but to the best of my knowledge, these are the only five who had sex with Gitana Camarena in the last three days of her life."

It was at roughly that moment that all hell broke loose in the room. The fathers began to argue and raise objections. The students denied steadfastly what they had done. Mike Byrne in particular tried to defend his son, Kevin.

I waited for them to run out of steam.

"On the Saturday night before Miss Camarena was murdered, she and another young woman attended a party given at your house, Mike."

"Oh, that's preposterous. Kevin had explicit directions that there were to be no parties while his mother and I were out of town."

I simply stared at him. I hoped my gaze reminded him of just how naive he sounded.

"As I was saying," I continued, "there was a party at the Byrne house that Saturday night. These boys attended, along with a kid named Mitch Biggers from Allenwood High in Mica Wells, and Justin Warfield, who obviously cannot be with us today. We've obtained a sample from him at the hospital. Gitana Camarena and this other girl attended the party as — you might say — the guests of honor. Each of the boys here had sex with either or both of the girls. Gitana Camarena demanded some kind of payment from Seth Kramer sometime just before midnight, and he refused. She became angry, and stormed off into the night, walking home.

"Mitch Biggers, the fellow from Mica Wells, took this other girl home around twelve-thirty. They should have seen Gitana Camarena walking along the side of Morgan Highway. They didn't. That tells me that someone gave Gitana Camarena a ride home. None of these boys has admitted to leaving the party. I need to rule them out as suspects in her killing. The only way to do that is to take DNA samples. I see that everyone here has his warrant. Who wants to go first?"

"Hold on a minute!" Kent said, jumping up. "I think maybe these boys have the right to have an attorney present."

"They can have Santa Claus present if they want, Kent. These warrants give us the right to collect the specimens Clark needs to compare to the samples retrieved from Gitana's body. There is no higher legal authority in Bliss County than Judge Beam, and he's approved this acquisition. Unless one of you happens to know a good Appeals Court justice, I'd appreciate it if you'd let us go about our business."

"This is a mistake, Judd," Kent said.

"I would appreciate it, when I am working in my official capacity, Mr. Kramer, if you'd refer to me as Chief Wheeler."

"Maybe not for long."

"Be that as it may, I am directing this investigation for the moment. I think maybe we should begin with Seth."

One by one, Clark took swabs from the

inside of each boy's cheek, and secured the swabs in specimen tubes. When he was done, he turned to me.

"That's it, Chief. I'm going to escort these samples directly to the lab, and ask for an immediate PCR to be performed, under the circumstances. I would expect that I can give you the results later today, or maybe early tomorrow."

"Thank you, Clark."

He nodded, and left the room.

"You boys can go back to class now," I told them. "Mr. Compton will give you passes so you aren't listed as absent or tardy. Thank you for your cooperation."

The students filed out. All of the men left without talking to me, except for Kent. As he walked past me, he closed the door, leaving us alone in the room.

"Chief Wheeler? What in hell was that all about? It's always been just *Judd and Kent."*

"I think, for the immediate future, we should consider keeping our interactions strictly professional," I said.

He sat at the table.

"You call what you did this morning professional?"

"It was expedient. Calling each boy in one by one would have taken more than an hour. I think I've wasted enough time on

404

this case."

"It was an embarrassment. Every man in that room was mortified to learn what his son had done, including me. At least I had a little warning. You placed the reputation of your department at risk. You placed the reputation of this *team* at risk!"

"What team? The *football* team?"

"You know damn well what team. Every boy in this room today is being watched closely by the best colleges in the country. Your antics may have cost Seth a shot at Clemson last week . . ."

"*My* antics?"

"You allowed that protest to take place."

"I had no choice, Kent. In case you've forgotten, those students were exercising their rights of free assembly."

"While disturbing the peace?"

"They *were* the peace. They engaged in no acts of aggression or violence throughout the entire time they were there. They didn't break any laws. What was I supposed to do?"

"Maybe you could have started by remembering who pays the bills in this town. Maybe you should have considered who signs your paychecks."

"We've had this conversation. You want my badge, all you and the Council have to do is ask."

He didn't answer for a moment. He seemed to be counting to ten, or maybe he was thinking about whether he actually had the votes to fire me.

"Damn it, Judd, what is it with you? Have I done something terrible to you over the years?"

"This isn't about you and me," I said.

"The hell it isn't. You sat in my home a week ago and told my son that his college scholarship hopes were in jeopardy because he put some goddamn wetback in his place. Then you told me at your station the other day that even if he does get a scholarship, he'll probably bomb out. I just don't get it. Do you want to ruin his chances the way you ruined mine?"

It took me a moment to hear what he was saying.

"What?"

"You know what I'm talking about," he said. "Twenty-five years ago. The Pooler Homecoming game. I was having an All-State season. We were undefeated. Every week, the front page of the Pooler newspaper featured a story about me. Me! Not some shitkicker quarterback from an unknown high school in Nowhere, North Carolina. Me!

"We scheduled *this* high school for Pooler's Homecoming for a reason, Judd. We expected to blast you farmboys back to the Stone Age, to cap off a banner season. Then you guys arrived, and the next thing we knew we're getting the crap kicked out of us by a bunch of hayseeds we never heard of."

"It was a long time ago," I said. "A whole lifetime ago."

"Well, not for me. There's something you don't know about that game. Something I never told you, because I thought we were friends. The Pooler coach was an Alabama alumnus. He had talked Bear Bryant into taking a look at me. Not some scout, Judd, but the Bear himself! That night you and your squad of country boys danced into Pooler Stadium and cleaned our clocks, I was being scouted by the *man* himself. That was the year Bear Bryant took the Crimson Tide all the way to the NCAA championship, and he was looking at *me* as a prospect. You and your goddamned Prosperity High team took away my chance to play for the Tide and for Coach Bryant. He watched me lose that one game, and he decided not to make me an offer. You and I were friends, though, so you never knew."

I shook my head. He was making me very sad.

"I knew," I said, quietly.

"What?"

"I knew about Coach Bryant."

"How in hell could you know?"

I cleared my throat, and rubbed my palm across my face. It felt like coarse sandpaper against my fingers.

"Because he made *me* an offer."

"Bullshit!"

"No. It's true. He and one of his assistants came by the farm the middle of the next week, and they asked me whether I'd like to play for Alabama. Full ticket, with all the trimmings."

"You turned it down?" he asked, awed.

"Yeah, I did. I'd already talked with the people at North Carolina, and I'd sort of promised them I'd go there. I wasn't very interested in going to school too far from home. So, I thanked Coach Bryant, and told him I hoped he'd have a successful season. And that was that."

"You turned down the Tide to go play for a team that hadn't won five games straight in twenty years? Why didn't you tell me?"

"The same reason you never told me you had been scouted by the Bear. After that game, we became friends. I knew he had come to the game to look at you, not me. On the one hand, I didn't want to embarrass you. On the other, I figured it didn't really matter. I never intended to go pro. It wasn't something I wanted. As it turned out, that was a good thing, because I blew out my knee the middle of the second season, and rode the pine the rest of my college career. I got what I wanted out of it, though."

"What was that?"

"An education. Are we finished here?"

He stood and placed his hand on the doorknob.

"Yeah. I think maybe we are," he said. "You might as well know, since we're finished keeping secrets from one another. I plan to call Art and Tommy and Huggie later today. I'm going to ask for an emergency Town Council meeting. I think maybe it's time to review your contract with the town."

"You gotta do what you gotta do," I said. "I have my job, too, at least for the time being. I plan to keep doing it until you guys decide you don't want me to. We see each other clear, right?"

He nodded as he opened the door.

"Clearer all the time."

"Keep it in the road," I said.

He didn't say anything. He just walked out and closed the door behind him.

CHAPTER THIRTY

I got a call from the charge nurse at Bliss County Regional Medical Center an hour or so later. Jaime was sitting up in bed, drinking with a straw, and was able to string a few sentences together. The nurse thought I might want to talk with him. She was right. I asked her to arrange for an interpreter, in case I had any questions for Jaime's parents.

When I got to Room Twenty-Seven in the ICU, I found Jaime's father and mother, and a couple of siblings, along with the nurse. The hospital interpreter stood on the other side of the bed, ready to help us communicate.

"Good news, Chief," Mr. Ortiz said. "They're going to move Jaime to a regular room later today, if all goes well."

"I'm glad to hear it," I said. "Would you mind if Jaime and I had a few moments alone?"

"By all means. We will go down to the cafeteria for lunch. You should have plenty of time to talk."

Mr. Ortiz and the rest of his family left the ICU. I pulled a chair up beside Jaime's bed.

"I'm glad to see you're coming along so well," I said. "A lot has happened since you were attacked Saturday night."

He nodded.

"I know it can be scary when a cop shows up to ask you questions, but I just wanted you to know I'm looking to help you here, okay?"

He nodded again.

"I'm going to say a couple of names, and I'd like you to tell me if you've ever heard them before."

He looked at me, without saying anything or gesturing. He just seemed to be waiting.

"The first name is Jesse Stouts."

He shook his head.

"I don' know him," he said. His voice was a little slurred, and the words passed through his swollen split lips with a lisp.

"How about Ben Siebold?"

He nodded.

"How do you know Siebold?"

"Customer," he said. It came out *Cuthfomer.*

"What kind of customer?"

"At the tee shirt shop. Where I work. He has shirts made up for the Vulcans."

"And that's the only contact you've had with him?"

He didn't respond.

"Have you dealt with Siebold anywhere else, Jaime?" I asked again.

He closed his eyes, almost a wince. I waited. I don't know if he was hoping I'd go away, but when he opened them again I asked him again.

"I've seen him. I really don't want to talk about that."

"One more name," I said. "Trigger . . ."

I didn't even have to finish the name. His eyes grew wide, and he glanced around the room.

"Okay, so you know Trigger Chaney. You want to tell me how?"

He didn't say anything. His eyes told me that he'd rather be just about anywhere else.

"All right," I said. "Here's the way it is. We pulled some fingerprints off your car the night you were attacked. They belonged to these two guys Stouts and Siebold. We're still looking for them. Here's what I'm thinking, though. You're so scared of Trigger Chaney, maybe it's because you know he is one bad dude. Maybe it's also because

412

you remember seeing him out on that cul-de-sac off Morris Quick Road Saturday night. You know Siebold, but maybe you never saw his face that night."

He stared straight ahead.

"We're looking for all three of these guys," I said. "When we find them, they're going away for a long, long time. Before they do, though, they have a lot of questions to answer. If there's something I should know, I'd much rather hear about it from you. You tell me the whole story, and I can see to it that you never have to worry about these asswipes again. What do you say?"

"It was Trigger Chaney, for one," I told Sheriff Webb and Mitch Gajewski, at the Sheriff's Department. "Jaime didn't want to talk about things in detail, but it looks as if he and some of the other Mexican kids from Prosperity thought they could deal a little bit and get away with it. The Vulcans heard about their side business, and decided to make a statement. They confronted Jaime and several other kids in a parking lot in Morgan, and Jaime told them to stuff it. They passed some angry words.

"The rest of it built up from there. Jaime and Anita went to Morgan to see a movie. There were some Vulcans in the parking lot of the mall where they went. One of them was Siebold. He was a little drunk or high — Jaime couldn't tell which for certain — and he started hassling Jaime. Jaime told him to fuck off, and then he and Anita left. Apparently that was all the provocation Siebold needed."

"Can Ortiz identify Siebold?" Webb asked.

"Not directly. We'll have to go with the fingerprints on that one. He did see Trigger Chaney, though. It was Chaney that worked him over while the other two held him in place. Then Chaney had Siebold and the other guy — we can presume it was Stouts — hold Jaime against the tree while Chaney put the spike through his hands. That's the last thing Jaime remembers."

"Sounds to me like the only one we have for certain is Chaney," Gajewski said.

"Based on Jaime's testimony, yes," I said. "But you know how this works. We pull in either Stouts or Siebold, sweat them a little, and one or the other will roll all over the other two. We also have the fingerprints on Jaime's car."

"While we're at it, maybe we can get one of them to tell us where the Vulcans are manufacturing meth," Webb said.

"It's the gravy that makes the flavor," I said.

"Good work," Gajewski said to both of us. "I'm not at all certain that we can make a civil rights case out of this after all, but the feebs will have a field day if we can take down the Vulcans' meth labs. There's a federal case in here somewhere. You pull in these biker dickheads and make them on the assault on this Ortiz kid. We'll take it from there."

I had just gotten back to my office at the Prosperity station when Huggie walked in.

"We need you next door," he said.

"You and the Council?"

"Yes."

"I'll be right there."

He left, and I walked to the back of the station to make myself a cup of coffee. I dropped by the jail, checked on my two prisoners, and then walked around to the Town Hall.

As I had expected, they were all there. Kent had made good on his promise to pull the Council together and try to get me shit-canned. I was ready for them.

"Sorry I took a while," I said. "I've been in Morgan wrapping up the Jaime Ortiz assault."

"You solved it?" Huggie asked.

"Looks like. It wasn't a lynching, at least

not in the traditional sense. It appears to have been a run-in between two groups trying to share a single drug market. Jaime ran afoul of some members of the Carolina Vulcans motorcycle gang, and they decided to take it out of his hide. Sheriff Webb is running down the suspects now. When they're arrested, they should go out of circulation for a long, long time. So, what's up, guys?"

Huggie cleared his throat. In light of the fact that I'd cleared two major crimes in Prosperity over the course of the previous twenty-four hours, he seemed a little uncomfortable with the duty thrust upon him by the Council.

"Uh, Judd, Kent asked us to hold an emergency Council meeting to review your behavior over the last week or so."

I took a sip of my coffee.

"Mind if I have a seat?" I asked.

Huggie pointed to the chair at the head of the table.

"We have a few questions," Kent said.

"Shoot," I said.

"What is the current status on the murder of Gitana Camarena?"

"Unsolved. We've narrowed the field of suspects to white males. There are large portions of the last three days of her life for which I can't account, but I'm trying to fill in the blanks. Her body has been released to Father Enrique Salazar of St. Ignatius Church in Mica Wells. Funeral arrangements are pending."

Kent read some notes he had made.

"Is it standard operating procedure during a murder investigation to harass innocent high school students?"

"Nope."

"Then how do you explain your behavior this morning?"

"It wasn't harassment. Every boy in that room had engaged in a sex act with Gypsy Camarena within seventy-two hours of her death. The person who probably broke Gypsy's neck also had sex with her just before he killed her. That establishes a connection between the boys and the victim. Judge Beam found sufficient evidence to issue a warrant for the boys' DNA samples. I was following the requirements under the general statutes. I will repeat: there was no harassment."

"What about other boys this Camarena girl might have had sex with?" Kent asked. "She was obviously a slut. Who knows how many Prosperity High boys she screwed over the last week of her life?"

"Not me," I said. "I only know about the

boys who were at the party at Kevin Byrne's house."

Huggie cleared his throat, trying to regain control of the meeting.

"Judd, the Council — that is, Mr. Kramer — has raised concerns that you may be responding negatively to stress over the last week. He has made accusations of erratic behavior, periods when you could not be located or weren't in the station, and blatant attempts to thwart a federal investigation related to the murder."

"There are no grounds for a federal investigation. I told Gajewski and Cantrell that, the first day they were here. Gajewski himself just told me in Morgan that he probably couldn't find grounds for a civil rights violation against Jaime Ortiz, though the arrest of his attackers may lead to some federal drug charges against some of the Vulcans, and maybe a few Latinos involved in the trade. Yesterday's arrests proved that the attack on Justin Warfield wasn't racially motivated, or connected in any way with either the assault on Ortiz or Gitana's murder."

"You didn't know that when you met these agents, though," Tommy Keesler said.

"I knew that postulating civil rights and international drug smuggling violations was premature. I told those agents I wouldn't stand in their way. I didn't see that our investigations would be congruent with one another. There isn't much intersection of goals here."

"What about the charge that you allowed Roberto Camarena and his wife to surface long enough to direct the disposition of their daughter's body, but then let them disappear again?" Art Belts asked.

"Someone's been talking to Cantrell. I figured he'd pop a gasket when he found out his suspects had shown and blown again. You want the facts? Neither Cantrell nor I had any idea the Camarenas had met with Father Salazar until they went back underground after they signed for Gypsy's body. I was informed by Carla Powers at the morgue that they had been there. She presumed that Father Salazar had informed me of their return, because he had been at the morgue with me the day before. In fact, I didn't know they had shown up until after they were gone. I had a discussion with Father Salazar about this, and he said he'd try to get in touch with me if and when he sees Roberto Camarena again.

"Let me say one other thing, though," I continued. "Jack Cantrell is after Roberto Camarena because he thinks there is a connection between Camarena and a Mexican drug lord named Cruz Pomodor. According to Cantrell, Camarena and Pomodor are cousins. In the course of investigating the attack on Justin Warfield, I interviewed a number of students who are involved with heroin abuse. Not one of them has ever heard of Roberto Camarena. I think maybe Cantrell is chasing a paper tiger."

Huggie glanced around the table. Art Belts wouldn't look at him. Tommy Keesler seemed to be absorbing what I had said. Kent was still fuming.

"Here's the way I see things," I said. "You can take it or leave it. The only reason we're meeting today is because Kent Kramer is displeased with the fact that I appear to be targeting some of the town's most affluent kids in this murder investigation. I don't think for a second that he'd raise a beef if I were putting the screws to some of the kids from illegal Mexican families, or kids from the farming families that have lived in this town for nigh on to three hundred years, unless those kids played on the football team. Kent and I have been good buddies for almost a quarter century, but my suspicion at this moment is that his priorities are misplaced.

"I don't manufacture suspects, guys. I follow leads as they're presented to me. If I can exclude these boys as suspects, nobody will be happier than me. This has been a stressful week in Prosperity, and I would suggest that I'm not the only one in this room feeling the pressure."

I paused and looked around the room.

"I guess that's about all I had to say," I told them.

"Well, then . . ." Huggie said. "Unless there is any further discussion . . ."

"Oh, let's get on with it, Huggie," Kent said.

"Yes. Of course. Judd, the Council discussed these matters before you came in, and we have — more or less, that is — decided to place you on probation for a period of time."

"No," I said.

It took Huggie's chins a second or two to stop quivering.

"Beg pardon?" he said.

"I don't work on probation," I said. "Being on probation means I have to run every decision I make by a bunch of guys who never carried a gun or a badge for a living. In addition, since you've made this decision *before* conducting a due process investigation, you've violated my rights under the Civil Service code. Finally, if you insist on ignoring either points one or two, I don't work under probation because I don't want to."

I crossed my arms and waited for their next — inevitable — move.

"Well, then," Huggie said. "I guess that leaves us with very little choice. I'm truly sorry it's come to this, Judd . . ."

"Let me make this easy for you," I said.

I pulled my badge off my shirt and tossed it on the table. It made a solid clanking sound as it hit the hardwood. Then I unbuckled my Sam Brown and laid it alongside the badge.

"Satisfied?" I asked.

"Now, hold on a minute," Tommy said. "I'm not so sure I like this turn of events."

"Let him quit," Kent said. "We'll find another chief."

"Don't be silly," Art said. "It would take weeks to replace Chief Wheeler."

"Months, maybe," I said.

"You stay out of this," Kent told me. "We'll just promote one of the other officers temporarily while we do a search."

"I don't think so," I said.

They all looked at me.

"Slim and Stu have both told me they don't want to be chief. They see what I have to do, and they don't want it."

"So we just do a search for Judd's replacement," Kent argued.

I sat and waited. Art looked very troubled. Tommy chewed at his thumbnail, and Kent just sat looking imperious and triumphant. Huggie kept clearing his throat.

"One thing before I go," I said.

They all turned to me.

"If I'm no longer on the job, you're left without someone to complete the Gypsy Camarena murder investigation. In that case, the job rolls over to the sheriff's department."

I pulled an envelope from my shirt pocket.

"I received this from Sheriff Webb over in Morgan this morning. It's a job offer. He's invited me to join the department there as a detective. I spoke with him after I received it, and he told me that he would like to make my first assignment the investigation of Gypsy's murder here in Prosperity."

Nobody said anything.

"Here's my thought," I continued. "The Council's primary concern here today is over my handling of this murder investigation. Actually, if my perceptions aren't too far off base, most of those concerns are coming from one Council member. I think the Council might prefer to have a lead investigator on this case who is at least partly open to their input, rather than an outside sheriff's department detective who doesn't have to give them the time of day."

I nodded toward my badge and gun on the table.

"If you've been listening carefully, I just resigned. I'm going to go clean out my office now. If you gentlemen are interested in rehiring me, you know where I'll be."

I stood up and started to walk out of the room. At the door, I turned back.

"You have ten minutes, by the way. After that I call Don Webb and accept his offer."

Their decision took about eight minutes.

One thing I had learned about small-town politicians over the years — they hate to give up control, even if it's only perceived to exist in the first place.

Huggie knocked on my door and walked into my office. I was sitting at my desk, sipping my coffee and looking over my notes on the Camarena killing.

My badge and Sam Brown belt were in his hands.

"I thought you would be cleaning out your desk," he said.

"I decided to take a break. What can I do for you, Huggie?"

"I . . . that is, the Council . . . well, we

would like you to . . . well, stay on. For a while."

"I can't stay on, Huggie. I resigned, remember? I'm no longer employed here."

"Yes. Well. I suppose, in that case, that we would like to rehire you."

"Oh. I see. Okay."

I placed the pad down on the desktop.

"Make me an offer," I said.

"What?"

"You're asking me to take a job here as chief of police. I would presume that you have some kind of offer in mind."

"But . . ." he said, scrambling for words. "I don't understand. You want us to . . . *negotiate* with you?"

"Isn't that how the hiring process works?"

"Well, I guess . . ."

"Because, you see, I have another offer," I said, tapping the envelope on my desk from Sheriff Webb. "Real nice one, too. Is the Council ready to match it?"

"I don't know," Huggie said. "I don't know the details of the offer."

I opened the envelope and showed him the letter inside. He read over it quickly.

"I see," he said. "Yes. Well."

"So, make me an offer."

He sat in the chair next to my desk.

"You're enjoying this, aren't you?" he asked.

"Not really. I should be out trying to find out who killed Gypsy Camarena instead of in here dicking with you over salaries and benefits, but I didn't deal this play. You did."

He started to argue.

"Okay," I said. "Kent dealt it, but you let it ride. In all honesty, I ought to get aggravation pay for this position. You drop by my house and threaten to fire me, Kent makes accusations he can't back up because his cretin jock son is embarrassed, and I have to pay the freight in irritation and annoyance. I think maybe you should make it worth my time. So, make me an offer."

He made a couple of excuses about needing to consult with the Council, and excused himself.

He returned about fifteen minutes later.

I was still at my desk, working on my second cup of coffee, and reading some more of the book I'd started the previous week at the high school. Huggie stood at my door and cleared his throat.

"Yes?" I said.

"I'd like you to look this over," he said, as he slipped a sheet of paper across my desk. I perused it.

"This is your offer?" I asked.

"Is . . . is there a problem?"

"No. No problem."

I pulled a pen from the cup on my desk and made a couple of corrections, wrote a sentence or two, and handed it back to him.

"This appears to be a request for a larger uniform allowance and an increase in patrolman pay," he said.

"That's right. Our uniform allowance hasn't kept up with inflation, and my officers haven't been given a raise in two years."

"It's been a difficult economy."

"Don't I know it? I took that into account with my counteroffer. I think this is fair. It matches the raise the Sheriff's Department gave its deputies this year."

"I take it, then, that the salary you were offered was acceptable?"

"More than fair. If you can meet those other requests, I think I would be willing to sign back on as police chief."

I met Donna at the high school after the three o'clock dismissal bell.

"How about dinner in Morgan tonight?" I asked. "Someplace ritzy."

"What's the occasion?"

"I quit my job. Then they rehired me. I got a nice raise. Thought you might want to celebrate."

"Somehow, I think I've come in halfway through this story."

"I'll fill you in over dinner."

We decided I'd pick her up at her house at six, and she took off to get ready. I drove from the school to my farm. Just as I parked my car, my radio squawked.

"Yes," I said to Sherry.

"I just got a call from Sheriff Webb. He wants you to give him a ring."

"I'm on it."

I walked into the house and hung my newly reacquired Sam Brown on the side of the couch. I hit the speed dial number on my home phone for the sheriff, and was patched through to Donald Webb.

"Judd," he said. "I'm afraid I have some bad news for you. None of those samples Clark took this morning matched the DNA samples we took from your dead girl."

"That's a shame," I said. "That means I just ran out of suspects."

"On the other hand, the Prosperity football team gets to play Mica Wells with a full roster Friday night."

"Don't you start in, too. I've just about had it up to my nose hairs with football this week. Oh, it also looks like you're still looking for a detective."

"They decided not to discipline you?"

"Worked like a charm. I owe you one, Don."

"I'll collect the day you decide to stop being a hayseed chief in a three-cop town, and realize your true calling is here in Morgan."

"Keep a seat warm for me. I have a feeling I'm still not the best-loved public official in town. Talk at you later."

"Wait. There's more. Are you missing a couple of Mexican boys down there?"

"I don't know. What are their names?"

"Vicente Ramirez and Geraldo Orozco?"

"Shit. What's happened?"

"We're not sure yet. There was some kind of dust-up out on the north side of Morgan this morning. The neighbors reported gunshots. One kid got hit pretty badly. When we got there, we found Ramirez and Orozco trying to plug several holes in a third kid."

"Federico Armand."

"So you do know something."

"Vicente was close to Gypsy Camarena. Vicente, Orozco, and Armand were all absent from school the morning that kid War- field was worked over with a baseball bat by the two kids in my holding cells."

"From what I can gather so far, this Armand kid got into a fight with some Vulcans, and came up on the short end. I haven't figured out what Ramirez and

Orozco have to do with it. We're holding them as material witnesses, but I expect they'll be released by morning."

"That kid who got nailed to the tree the other night had a run-in with Vulcans too," I said. "Two Mexicans in one week get busted up by Vulcans. Sounds like a gang war to me."

There was a short silence on the other end. Then I heard Sheriff Webb sigh.

"Those two kids in your jail? I think you need to talk with them again."

First, I called each of the boys we had tested that morning, and spoke with them and their fathers, to let them know they were in the clear. I called Kent last, because I didn't mind letting him and Seth sweat a little longer, after the shitty maneuver he'd pulled that afternoon.

Then I drove across Prosperity to the station. Sherry had gone for the day. We had a night custodian who kept an eye on things overnight, but he was more of a glorified babysitter than a law enforcement officer.

I nodded at the custodian as I walked through the station, and grabbed a straight-back wooden office chair just before walking into the cellblock.

Being a small-town cop station, our cellblock was not much more than a fortified room with a hard plaster ceiling and bars set deep into the masonry of the walls. There was barely room in front of the cell doors for two people to walk abreast before you hit the cinderblock wall. The cells themselves were only about eight by ten feet in size. Each one had a steel bed bolted to the concrete floor, and a steel toilet without a lid affixed solidly to the wall. In the back corner of each cell was a small sink.

I set the chair between the cell doors and the front wall, facing backward, and I straddled it, facing Kenny Broome and Sonny Cline.

"Hi, boys," I said.

Kenny Broome nodded.

"Hi, Chief," Sonny said. "Are they bringing dinner soon?"

"In a bit. We need to talk first. I want to know who you boys buy your tar from."

"Yeah, right . . ." Broome said, snickering. "That's gonna happen."

"Yes," I said. "It is. I've had one murder and two major assaults in this town. Something's going down between some Mexican kids and the Carolina Vulcans. Now, one thing I've learned in all my years of law enforcement, man and boy, is that if you want to know what the lowlifes are up to, you ask the lowlifes who keep the lowlifes in business."

"What's in it for us?" Cline asked.

I scratched my head, and made a show of looking as if I were thinking it over.

"You boys ever hear the one about the big fish and the little fish?" I asked.

A half hour later, I called Don Webb.

"We have a break," I told him.

"That would be a nice change."

"I had a powwow with my two little sluggers here, and got them to talk about the Mexican tar business in Prosperity. Some of what they told me falls in your jurisdiction."

"Shoot."

"If I were you, I'd stake out Specialty Tees. Apparently the manager, a guy named Alberto Sanchez, has been using the joint as a clearinghouse for heroin and crank. He gets the heroin in from his raw shirt suppliers, who have connections with the textile plants in Mexico. Want to guess who the crank comes from?"

There was a short pause as Webb digested what I'd told him.

"I smell Vulcans," he said.

"Good call. Sanchez has a major operation going right under your nose, not five blocks from the courthouse. He's wholesaling tar and crystal and distributing it through his street contacts."

"This is good," Webb said.

"That's not all. Remember I told you that Vicente Ramirez, Geraldo Orozco, and Federico Armand all worked for Specialty Tees?"

"Along with your kid that got nailed to the tree."

"Jaime Ortiz. Right. All four of them. So, Jaime was assaulted on Saturday night, and today three of his buddies got into a shootout with Vulcans."

"I'm way ahead of you, Judd."

"You still have Ramirez and Orozco in custody?"

"Yeah. Looks like they just graduated from material witnesses to suspects, though."

"I'd like to interview them, if possible. And Federico Armand, when he's healthy enough."

There was another pause. Then Don coughed softly.

"That's going to be a problem," he said. "Armand took a bad turn at the hospital about an hour ago. Something about platelets. He died."

"Damn. You need me to notify his family?"

"We already took care of it."

"Okay. You might want to put in a call to Father Salazar at the Catholic church over in Mica Wells. He probably knew the kid. He'd want to make sure that Armand got last rites."

"I'll see to it. We're still looking for Chaney and his buddies. I have a feeling that when we run them down, we'll find out they were involved in the gunfight."

"Let me know when you learn something. I'll be by tomorrow to talk with Ramirez and Orozco."

"We'll keep an eye out for you."

I showered and shaved, and dressed for dinner for the first time since the one-year anniversary of the day Donna and I first went out. When I looked at myself in the mirror, I wanted to see a dandy, but what stared back at me was this fatigued middle-aged cop with gray skin stuffed into a $200 wool suit. I suppose, in retrospect, that it was the best I could have hoped for.

Donna and I ate at a new Italian place in Morgan that specialized in grilled dishes, as opposed to the usual array of pasta and salads. I ordered a sirloin grilled over a wood fire in a brick oven, and topped with marsala sauce. Usually, I preferred my beef unadorned, but the menu made it sound lip-smacking yummy, which was exactly what I wanted. Donna ordered fire-roasted chicken with cabrino cheese, sun-dried tomatoes, and a basil-lemon sauce. We split a carafe of the house red.

I was about halfway through my salad before Donna broached the subject of work.

"So, you want to tell me about this quitting thing today?"

I ran through the story. By the time I got to Don Webb's letter, she was almost doubled over laughing.

"So you saw them coming and double-crossed them," she said, when I had finished the story.

"More or less. The way Kent went after me at the school, and after Huggie tried to get me to back off last weekend, I could see the Council getting ready to run up the black flag. I figured I needed a little ammunition on my side. It wasn't a trick or anything. Don would love to have me as a detective at the sheriff's department. I'm just not ready to make that huge a leap. And here's our dinner . . ."

The waiter delivered the steak and chicken, and the next ten minutes or so passed with very little conversation, save for the sounds of gustatory contentment that we both couldn't suppress.

Little by little, our appetites subsided, and we became less focused on food and more on each other.

"Any fallout from my arrests yesterday?" I said.

"Hardly a peep. Those two have been absent about fifteen days of school this year, and they're hardly *there* when they do attend. I hate to say this about any student, but they won't be missed."

"Good."

"Word is getting around that you solved the Justin Warfield assault. Justin is a person people *do* care about. Nobody much cares who beat him up, but they are glad somebody closed the case."

"Students or teachers?"

"Both. Why?"

"I don't know. This is probably heresy coming from Prosperity's former star quarterback, but I'm beginning to think the parents and faculty in this town put way too much emphasis on sports — football in particular."

"Sports are very important in any small town, Judd. I should know. I grew up in one. Tightly knit groups of people need local heroes."

"Heroes? You mean like Seth Kramer?"

"For seventeen-year-old high school kids,

yes. For middle-aged men who would like to believe that they could have made the big time with a few more breaks, you bet. Why in hell do you think they don't put trading cards of accountants in bubble gum packs?"

I had to concede. She was right. I didn't like to admit it, but I recalled how easy it was to get dates when I was a high school hero, and how hard it became after I blew out my knee and became a bench jockey in college.

"There's something else," I said, trying to think of a way to broach the subject gently.

She heard the change in my voice, and looked up, concerned.

"We have another dead kid."

"Oh, Judd."

"There was a gunfight in Morgan earlier today between some Vulcan bike thugs and a few of the Prosperity Mexican kids. Federico Armand got shot up pretty badly. He died at the hospital."

"Armand," she said. "I don't know him very well. This is terrible, though. Two kids in a week and a half."

"Could have been three, if Stu hadn't gotten to Jaime Ortiz in time."

"What in hell's going on, Judd?"

"Something to do with a drug war between Prosperity and Morgan. When the

Vulcans are involved, it almost always means that someone stepped on their turf. I'd appreciate it if you kept that part about the drug war under your hat."

We split a huge slice of strawberry cheesecake for dessert, and then drove back to my place. Donna said she wanted to grab a quick shower before bed, and retreated to the bath. Craig had left me a note on the refrigerator to let me know he was attending a play at school, and wouldn't be back until nearly eleven o'clock. The house was quiet, save for the liquid whisper of water running through the copper pipes.

I realized that I was living a quick preview of my future. Craig would head off to college before long. Soon as he did, I'd come home each night to an empty house. It seemed only a short time since the house had been alive with human interaction every night of the week, with me, Susan, and Craig together as a family. Now Susan was gone. Craig had long since outgrown knee time with his old man. Father Time and his black sheep cousin the Grim Reaper had decimated my family.

I shook off the intrusive sense of desperation that began to grip me, and tried to turn my attention to the legal pad on which I was outlining the last three days of Gypsy

Camarena's life. I hadn't filled in many blocks over the last day or so, which was discouraging.

"What are you doing?" Donna asked from the door to my bedroom.

"Same ol' same ol'," I said. "Trying to piece together this timeline on Gypsy."

I looked up at her. She had changed from her dinner clothes to a Pooler Pythons sweatsuit. She smelled sweet, like cucumbers and melon and hyacinths.

"Did you smuggle girl soap into my house?" I asked.

"Bet your ass. That stuff you insist on buying smells like it belongs in a YMCA locker room."

She crossed the heart pine floor and sat next to me on the couch. She drew her feet up under her and leaned over against me.

"Where'd you get the sweatsuit?"

"Picked it up at the MegaMart this past weekend. Want to know what I'm wearing under it?"

"What?"

"Sweat. Want to come back to the bedroom and see?"

Later — much later — we lay in the dark and listened to the wind rustle the remaining leaves on the walnut tree outside my bedroom window. Donna's breath brushed warmly against my neck every time she exhaled. Sometimes it was accompanied by a small sigh of contentment. There were times when I didn't feel so old after all.

"You can't get her off your mind," she said.

"Susan?"

"Gypsy."

"Oh. Her."

"Same problem?"

"It won't go away. She had to get a ride on Saturday night, and someone had to drive her on Monday night. If I could just find someone who saw her on the road either time, and could remember who she was with, I'd have another clue. Right now, I'm fresh out of ideas."

"It would have been dark both times," she said. "You said that Jaime and Anita brought her home from Morgan around six-thirty, right?"

"Yeah. By seven o'clock, it was dark out. She would have had to stop somewhere to be seen."

"That's true. That or maybe someone in the neighborhood could have seen her when she was brought home on Saturday night or picked up on Monday."

"Her parents were gone both times," I

said. "Who else would be awake in that neighborhood after midnight? It's cold outside these days. After dark everyone's pretty much shuttered in for the evening . . ."

I stopped. I felt connections closing in my mind, as pieces of the puzzle that I had fretted over for days suddenly seemed to fall together by themselves.

"Oh, my God," I said.

"What? What's wrong?"

"I just thought of someone. I may know one person who could have seen her both nights."

CHAPTER THIRTY-ONE

The next morning, I made arrangements for Kenny Broome and Sonny Cline to be transferred to the Bliss County Jail to await trial. Both of them had lawyered up, but neither had been arraigned, and managing them in the tiny two-cell jail I maintained in Prosperity as more or less a holding tank had become awkward.

I would have to meet with Fred Warfield after all the dust settled, and explain to him why the two fuck-ups who trashed his kid were going to skate on some of their charges. The information they'd provided, though, could help wrap up a lot of bad business, both in Prosperity and Morgan. They may not have deserved it, but in the big picture they were probably due a break on prosecution.

Sheriff Webb assured me that they would be picked up by a couple of deputies within an hour or so, and faxed me the necessary paperwork for the transfer. I handed it off to Sherry and got to work on my other problem.

I walked down to the Piggly Wiggly and hit the hot food bar, where I selected some eggs, sausage, biscuits, grits, and also picked up a sealed container of orange juice and a foam cup of coffee.

I drove the new cruiser out to Morris Quick Road, to the neighborhood where Gypsy Camarena's parents had lived until they went on the lam.

As I expected, Jake Wiley was sitting on his shameful excuse for a front porch, in his wheelchair, his legs covered with the tartan afghan I had seen on my previous visit.

I parked the car in front of his house, and hopped out carrying my offering of food.

"Johnny Law," he said, as I walked up the concrete steps of his house. "You finally decide to arrest me? I been really bad."

"You taking your meds, Jake?"

"When I can get 'em. I got some now, so I'm feelin' pretty good."

"I brought you some breakfast. Last time I was here it sounded like you had gone a while without a decent meal."

"Right neighborly of you, Johnny. Lemme see what you got there."

I placed the plastic food container in his

lap, and the juice and coffee on a small rusting metal table that sat next to his wheelchair. He opened the container.

"Well, now, don't this look fine. Yessir. Bet they don't eat like this down to the jailhouse, now, do they?"

"Actually, they do. This came from the Piggly Wiggly in Prosperity. We get all our prisoners' meals from there."

"Gotta get myself arrested, then," he said, as he pulled a plastic fork from the wrapper.

"Maybe not. I might be able to arrange to have meals brought out to you."

"Don't care for them *Meals On Wheels.* The food's okay, but one of the women they had workin' for them got all snotty when I pinched her bottom. Me and *Meals On Wheels,* we had us a fallin' out."

"Well, let's see how things turn out. You spend a lot of time out here on this porch, Jake?"

"Pert' near all the time. My TV's shot."

"It broke, huh?"

"No. It's shot, I said. I got all upset because they took my daytime story off the air, so I went after it with my twelve-gauge. These sure are nice grits. Creamy, like my wife used to make. You make these grits, Johnny?"

I decided not to run through the Piggly Wiggly story again.

I also tried not to look at him while he ate. He had left his teeth somewhere other than in his mouth, which he seemed to be incapable of closing as he gummed his food.

"The people across the street . . ." I said.

"The ones who bugged out? Them Spanish folks?"

"Those are the ones. They had a daughter."

"I seen her," he said, between bites of the biscuit. "Pretty little girl, fer one a' those kind."

"Her name was Gitana," I said. "People called her Gypsy."

"Uh-huh."

"Would you recall anyone bringing her home really late Saturday before last?"

"I'd have to think on it. Would you hand me that there orange juice, Johnny?"

I passed him the juice. He peeled back the foil on the top and took a big swig of it. A little escaped and ran out the side of his mouth. He seemed oblivious to it.

"The person who brought her home late that Saturday night might have also picked her up around eight o'clock last Monday night."

He nodded, as he shoved some more grits

into his mess of a mouth.

"Oh," he said. "You mean Mr. Red Car."

"Say that again?"

"Mr. Red Car. Seen him there a lot."

"Why do you call him Mr. Red Car?" I asked

Wiley looked up at me.

"Mebbe becuz' he drives a . . . red . . . car?" he said, a trace of sarcasm on his face. "Now why in hell would I call him that if he didn't? Some cop you must be, Johnny Law."

"So this man in the red car came by around eight o'clock last Monday night?"

"Yep. Jus' like usual."

"Like usual. You mean he came to the Camarenas' house a lot?"

"Pert' near. I figure he'd drop by one, two times a week."

"Can you describe him?"

"Cain't do that. Never really saw him. Jus' the car."

"Because he never got out."

"That's right. He'd drive up, and the girl, she'd either get out or get in."

I thought this over.

"How long did this go on?"

"Oh, I don't know. Mebbe for the month or so before that there family took off. Do you reckon you could take the lid off that

446

coffee fer me?"

I opened the coffee and handed the foam cup to him.

"When you say a red car," I said, "do you mean a big car, small car, or what?"

"It was pert' big, as I recall. Not so big as the car I used to have, of course. 1958 Buick Roadmaster. You could live in a car like that, by God. I reckon Mr. Red Car's car was big, fer today."

"Two door or four door?"

"Oh, it had four doors. Couldn't rightly tell you what make it was. I lose track of that sort of thing these days, 'specially since I can't see TV commercials for the new makes anymore, on account of my TV's shot, you know."

"So you said."

"I do regret killin' that TV. I think mebbe I shouldn'ta gone and done that. Sometimes I just don't think before I do somethin' though."

I decided I had gotten about all I was going to get from Jake Wiley.

"Tell you what," I told him. "I'm going to talk to the people down at the Piggly Wiggly. How would you like it if they had someone bring you a meal out each evening?"

"You'd do that fer me, Johnny Law?"

"I think it could be arranged."

"Why? What's in it fer you?"

"Well, to tell you the truth, Jake, I think you might have just given me the clue I need to solve a murder case."

"Murder, you say?"

"That's right. And if your tip solves it, I'd imagine there might be some kind of reward in it for you."

"Well," he said. "Don't that beat all."

I drove over to the high school, and cruised the parking lot looking for a large red car with four doors. I saw some red cars that weren't so large, some large cars that weren't red, and some four-door cars that were neither red nor large. None of the cars in the student lot seemed to fit the description Jake Wiley had given me.

Next, I walked around the faculty parking lot. I still came up empty.

It was possible, of course, that if Gypsy had been murdered by one of the Prosperity High School students, he might have been driving his parents' car. If that were the case, I could stake out the school lot and never find a suspect. If she had been killed by one of the faculty, it was possible that he had used his wife's car, and I'd strike out again.

There was something about the way Jake

had described the car, though, that tickled a memory for me. For some reason, I felt like I knew the car he said he'd seen parked at the Camarena house. I just couldn't seem to pull the memory together and make it mean anything. Fatigue had just about Swiss-cheesed my brain.

I parked in front of the Prosperity police station and walked into my office.

"Judd," Sherry said. "The deputies came by about fifteen minutes ago and took those two boys over to the County lockup."

"Thanks," I said.

"I left the paperwork on your desk."

I looked down and saw the custody and transfer papers on my desk, and picked them up to file in Cline's and Broome's folders. When I returned to my desk, I saw a handwritten note from Slim Tackett.

Camarenas' house off Morris Quick Road owned by FLN Enterprises, it read.

I vaguely recalled, through the increasing fog that was supplanting the working parts of my brain, that I had directed Slim to do a title search and find out who the Camarenas' landlord was.

FLN Enterprises. It wasn't a company I'd ever heard of. Most of the real estate developers in the area liked to tout the actual names of the owners. I had always figured that it was an ego thing, since most of the developers craved attention. They believed that their success hinged on their personal attractiveness and gregarious natures, and they hung their names on just about everything they touched.

FLN Enterprises, though, left me without a clue as to the owner.

I called the Register of Deeds in Morgan, and asked for Jeannie Klug. I had dealt with Jeannie on a number of occasions, and she had always gotten things done quickly when I asked.

"Well, hey, Judd," she said. "I sure hope you're calling to tell me you dropped that school teacher."

"Sorry, Jeannie. We seem to be attached at the hip. If I want to drop her, it'll take major surgery."

"Then why in hell don't you marry her, and stop filling all us bachelor girls with false hope?"

"I was married once."

She was quiet for a moment. I instantly regretted the statement. When she spoke again, she sounded a little embarrassed.

"Yeah, Judd. I recall. Nothing personal, right?"

"It's never personal, until it is," I said, trying to make it sound like a joke. I don't think I succeeded.

"So," she said, "I guess you're calling on business."

"Uh, yeah. I have a company renting houses here in Prosperity that I never heard of. I was wondering if you could run it down for me and see who the owner is."

"Sure. Won't take a second. We put in a new computer database system last year. Saves hours and hours of rummaging through old dusty log books. What's the company name?"

"FLN Enterprises."

I heard her fingernails clacking against computer keys. They stopped, and then clacked some more.

"I don't think I'm going to be much help," she said. "FLN is a limited liability corporation, not a sole proprietorship. It's apparently owned by a holding company named EsCoMed, another LLC."

"Can you check EsCoMed?"

"I did. They're based out of state. I can't access that database."

"What state are they working from?"

"South Carolina."

"Any idea what city?"

"Well, their zip code indicates Columbia, but that might not mean anything. Since Columbia is the county seat of Richland

County down there, it could be any of the towns in the immediate area, and there are dozens of those."

"Right. I appreciate it, Jeannie."

"I suppose you could contact the Register of Deeds in Richland County, but they might not be as helpful to an out-of-state police department. You might have to file an official inquiry. That could take a week or two to get processed. Even if it is, it might not help you. Whoever owns EsCoMed and FLN appears to want to protect his privacy. I'd bet EsCoMed is owned by a third company, and so on."

"Guess I'll have to try another approach."

"Sorry I couldn't be much help," she said.

I drove into Morgan and parked the new cruiser in a visiting officers' space next to the courthouse. Ten minutes later, I waited in an interview room in the jail complex.

The door opened, and a deputy escorted Vicente Ramirez into the room. The kid was wearing an orange jail jumper, paper slippers, and stainless steel cuffs. His hair looked as if it hadn't been washed in days. I could see traces of what was probably Federico Armand's blood encrusted under his fingernails.

He looked defeated.

"Hello, Chief," he said, as he sat in the steel chair across the table from me.

"Vicente. I can't tell you how sorry I am to see you here."

"Yeah," he said.

"You heard about Federico?"

He nodded.

"They tol' me this morning."

"Have they read you your rights?"

He nodded again.

"Just to be sure, I'm going to repeat them. You have the right to remain silent . . ."

He sat motionless as I recited the *Miranda* litany, and then told me that he understood.

"You have an attorney yet?" I asked.

He shook his head.

"You want one?"

He shook his head again.

"All right then. Let's start with you telling me how you wound up trading bullets with the Carolina Vulcans yesterday."

"It wasn't me," he said. "It was Rico."

"Federico Armand?"

"Yeah. He and Jaime Ortiz were mixed up in some shit at the tee shirt place. Raldo and me, we knew about it, but we weren't dealing."

That squared with what Kenny Broome and Sonny Cline had told me. They had said that their Mexican tar heroin contact was Jaime Ortiz. They hadn't mentioned anything about Federico Armand, though.

"So how did you wind up at the shoot-out?"

"That was about Rico, too. When Rico heard about what happened to Jaime las' Saturday night, he wen' fuckin' nuts. He and Jaime, they been throwin' down with Vulcans for several weeks. The Vulcans think Jaime was tryin' to cut in on their action. Rico tol' Jaime that he'd have his back, but then Jaime got jumped, an' Rico felt just awful. He tol' Raldo that he was gonna take it out of the Vulcans' hides. Raldo, he called me, an' we went out lookin' for Rico."

"When was this?" I asked.

"When Rico foun' out about Jaime. Monday morning."

"That was three days ago. The shootout was yesterday. It took you two days to find him?"

"No. We found him on Monday. We tried to talk him out of 'fronting the Vulcans, but he was out of his head angry. He kept sayin' he was gonna make the Vulcans pay for what they did to his homey."

"So what happened yesterday morning?"

Vicente wouldn't look up at me. He kept his eyes riveted on the tabletop, where he wrung his hands like wet laundry.

"Rico, he got this telephone call. Then he ran out of the place where we were staying, and he jumped in his car. Raldo and me, we took off after him in Raldo's car. He was drivin' like a crazy man. We los' track of him near the fairgrounds, but when we pulled into the parking lot there we heard the shooting."

I leaned back in my chair and thought about his story.

"Vicente," I said. "You have to tell me. Do you know who shot Rico?"

For a moment, I thought he was going to shut down on me, plead some kind of macho code of honor bullshit. Instead, he slowly nodded.

"Yeah," he said. "The same guys Rico and Jaime been shakin' up wit' for months. Guy named Trigger Chaney. 'Nother guy named Seeble, somethin' like that."

"Ben Siebold?"

"Yeah. That's the guy. There was a third Vulcan there, too, but I didn' know him."

Jesse Stouts, I thought, but I didn't say it. Didn't want to give Vicente any bad bright ideas.

"Who did all the shooting?"

"Mos'ly Rico and Chaney. I think maybe that guy I don' know might have popped one or two."

"This is important, Vicente. I want you to think hard. Did any of the Vulcans drive a big red car?"

He shook his head.

"No, man. They was all on bikes. Why?"

"I'm trying to put all the pieces together."

"Chief, are they gonna let me go soon?"

I stood to walk over to the door. I knocked on it twice, to summon the deputy to return Vicente to his cell. Before the door opened, though, I placed my hand on Vicente's shoulder.

"I'll see what I can do," I said.

CHAPTER THIRTY-TWO

Don Webb's secretary had informed me when I arrived that Webb was out in "the field," wrapping up an investigation. As satisfying as it was to know that justice was being done in Morgan, I really wished he would get back to the office so we could discuss my findings, and figure out where to go from there.

Around five-fifteen, he walked into the waiting area carrying a thick sheaf of papers. Mitch Gajewski was with him.

"Come on back, Judd," he said when he saw me. "I have some news for you."

I followed them to his office, where Gajewski and I took the seats that were farthest apart in the room. Sheriff Webb took the seat behind his desk.

"You want to tell him, or you want me to?" he asked Gajewski.

"You go ahead," Gajewski said. "I have a feeling you tell it better than I do."

The sheriff leaned back in his chair and clasped his hands behind his head.

"About four hours ago we received a tip from one of our detectives. An informant of his had told him that Jesse Stout was hiding in a house over off Stone Canyon Road. We put together a strike team of deputies, along with Mitch here and myself, and took a little ride over that way."

"Was he there?" I asked.

"Now don't go runnin' ahead of me, here. You'll miss all the fun. So when we get to the house, we notice there's two or three bikes parked out front, along with a really shitty decrepit old Chevy Impala. Since we can figure there's at least four people inside, we decided to use a little subterfuge."

He glanced over at Gajewski.

"Subterfuge," Gajewski repeated. "Good word."

"Agent Gajewski got himself a clipboard and walked up to the front door, like he's some kind of census taker or canvasser. He rang the doorbell, and one of the dumb fucks inside actually opened the door!

"Now, if it were you or me, and we were engaged in some kind of felonious activity, we'd probably tell Mr. Gajewski to fuck off, right? Not these guys. The fellow who answers the door was Stout himself. The

458

dumbass actually takes the time to answer Mr. Gajewski's questions. Mitch here can tell the guy is high as a kite, so he out of the blue just happens to ask Stout if he has any pot Mitch can buy."

"Don't tell me," I said. "Stout actually said *yes?*"

"He did. Then he went into the house and came back to the front door with an ounce baggie. By that time, one of the deputies and I are at the door, and Stout gets this really stupid shit-eatin' grin on his face and says — get this — *'Oops.'*"

"He said 'oops'?"

"He certainly did," Gajewski said, laughing.

"We stormed the front door and had everyone in the house cuffed and stuffed in a matter of seconds. So who else do you figure is in the house?"

"As happy as the two of you are, I'd venture that you also arrested Ben Siebold and Trigger Chaney."

"Did I tell you he was sharp?" Webb asked Gajewski.

"That you did."

"So what happened?" I asked.

"We've been sweating them for the last couple of hours," the sheriff said. "First I'd work on them for a while, and then Mitch would step in. By the time they started to sober up, we had them convinced they were going down for everything from the Atlanta Olympics bombings to the Lindbergh kidnapping. They rolled all over each other like a dog in fresh cow shit."

"Ben Siebold gave up Chaney and Stout in the assault on the Ortiz kid," Gajewski said. "He's hoping for a lighter sentence. What he doesn't know is that Stout ratted him out for running a meth lab over in Mica Wells. We'll take that place down later tonight, when everyone's asleep. Both Stout and Seibold said they'd testify against Chaney. This is a major bust, Chief. In one afternoon, we may have lopped the head off the largest drug operation in Bliss County."

"That's great. Has anyone told Jaime or his father yet?"

"We'd appreciate it if you'd keep it under your hat until we take down the lab tonight. Tomorrow, if you like, we'll all go over and have a party at the hospital," Webb said.

"That's not all," Gajewski said.

"Oh, yeah, this is interesting," Don said, as he leaned back in his office chair. "We've been running some information on Specialty Tees. We're not ready to raid it yet, but what we're finding is very interesting. I thought it was some kind of coyote sweatshop, but I was wrong."

"Coyote sweatshop?" I asked.

"Yeah," Gajewski said. "Some documented Mexican makes a deal with his buddies south of the border. The buddies bring the illegals across the Rio Grande, and arranges for them to get to Morgan, for instance, and the documented guy puts them to work in a sweatshop for menial wages. When the workers inevitably fall into debt, the coyote lends them money against their next paycheck. It's never enough, and before you know it the coyote is into the illegals so far they're never going to get even. It's the next best thing to slavery."

"Yeah," I said. "I've heard of similar arrangements among Chinese illegals on the West Coast."

"So we figure that's what's going on at Specialty Tees," Gajewski continued. "Only, when we start looking into the company's ownership, it's like slinking down a rat's nest of holding companies and shell corporations. Someone's gone to a lot of trouble to make their ownership of Specialty Tees a major secret."

"That is interesting," I said. "I've run into a similar situation with my investigation into the Gypsy Camarena case."

"Then there's the other thing," Gajewski

said. "Talk about life's little coincidences."

He glanced over at Don Webb.

"Yeah, Judd. I almost forgot. This might be of some help to you should the Town Council over in Prosperity ever give you shit again. We ran a background check on Trigger Chaney. Want to guess who his uncle is?"

CHAPTER THIRTY-THREE

I dropped by the Piggly Wiggly and knocked on the door of the store manager, Howie Stone.

"What's up, Judd?" he asked, as he invited me in.

"There's a guy who lives out Morris Quick Road who's kind of a shut-in. He just gave me a terrific tip, might help me solve this murder case I'm working. I was wondering if we could arrange for someone to put a dinner together from the deli section each evening and drop it by for him."

"I don't know, Judd . . ."

"We'd just put it on the jail tab. The jail goes empty ninety percent of the time anyway, so I figure I can cover the cost. You can tack on a mileage charge if you want."

"I suppose we could do something. When would you like this delivery to start?"

"How about today?"

I didn't need to remind him how I'd collared a kid who had been ripping him off for hundreds of dollars of merchandise a year earlier. He'd made a lot more on stop-loss than he'd ever lose feeding Jake Wiley, even if I didn't cover his nut.

"I'll see what I can do. You want to give me his name and address?"

I wrote it down for him, and then thought of something else.

"You still have those $60 color televisions on sale?"

"We ended the promotion, but we still have five or six back in the storage room."

"Think you could have one of your stock boys bring one up here for me? I'll pay cash here."

He made the call. A couple of minutes later a kid toted a corrugated box up to the manager's office. I peeled three twenties and a five from my money clip and handed it over to Howie. He counted out my change.

"What'cha need the television for, Judd?" he asked.

"Just a little incentive to make a neighborhood safer."

I toted the television back out to the cruiser and drove over to Morris Quick Road, parking in front of Jake Wiley's house.

"War'n't you just here?" he asked, as I pulled the television from the trunk of the cruiser. "Ain't lunch time yet."

I stepped up on the porch and set the box down on the concrete.

"Go get me your shotgun, Jake," I said.

He wheeled inside the house, and reappeared a few moments later with an ancient Remington double barrel.

"Here's the deal," I said, taking it from him. "You give me the shotgun, and I'll leave this brand new television here for you. We'll just call it our limited edition Tube for Guns campaign."

"Just like that, Johnny Law?" he said. "Gun for TV?"

"Just tell me where you want it, and I'll set it up for you."

A few minutes later, I left him watching a game show, and stowed the shotgun in the cruiser's trunk.

I started to drive off, but thought better of it. It occurred to me that if FLN Enterprises owned the Camarenas' house, it might also own other houses in the neighborhood.

I knocked on several doors before I found someone at home. A woman in her fifties opened the front door and stared apprehensively at me. She was Hispanic, but she seemed to have bothered to learn a little bit of English.

"Yes?" she said, her voice heavily accented. It came out *Jess*.

"Ma'am, I'm with the Prosperity Police Department. I'm investigating a crime against one of your neighbors. Would you mind telling me who your landlord is?"

"Land . . . lord?"

"Who is the person you pay to live here?" I asked, hoping that it clarified things for her a little.

"I not pay," she said. "*Mi esposo* pay the rent."

"Do you know who *he* pays?"

She nodded, and told me.

And everything fell together.

CHAPTER THIRTY-FOUR

I called Slim on the radio and told him I would be out of Prosperity for an hour or two. He assured me he could keep an eye on the town.

I drove into Morgan. I had a pretty good idea exactly where I was headed. I drove onto the lot of one of the city's largest new car dealers, parked the cruiser, and walked around the back lot where they kept the trade-ins.

It took me a few minutes to find the car I wanted. My greatest fear was that it might have already been prepped for resale. I was relieved to find it virtually untouched.

After stopping by the dealership office to advise them not to touch the car, I used their phone to call Sheriff Webb.

"How's it goin', Judd?" he asked.

"Better now. I think I've located the car belonging to the guy who killed Gitana Camarena. It's in your jurisdiction. I was hoping you could get a search warrant and send Clark Ulrich and his new partner Sharon over to take possession."

"Hold on just a minute. I'd need to hear a little more about your suspicions before I can authorize that kind of action."

I told him what I knew, and what I thought.

He agreed to request the warrant right away.

Within an hour, a tow truck showed up at the dealership to pick up the car. They pulled it over to the Sheriff's Department garage, where Clark and Sharon were waiting to receive it.

"What are we looking for?" Clark asked.

"Latent prints, mostly from the front passenger seat. Dried semen, either in the front or back. Epithelials, dried vaginal fluid, hair, you name it. Pull the damn thing right down to the frame if you have to. Oh, and pay good attention to the trunk."

"Gonna take a while."

"That's all right. It may take me a few hours to dig out the details, but if I'm right, we can arrest the man who murdered Gitana Camarena as soon as you get your DNA results back. I don't suppose I have to ask you to rush the tests."

"We'll work as quickly as we can," he said.

I pulled out my cell phone and called Don Webb. I knew he was just upstairs, but I didn't want to waste time walking to his office.

"We have the car," I said. "If I'm right, we can close the Gypsy Camarena case as soon as the DNA tests get back. You might want to put the screws to Trigger Chaney. I'd like to know what his connection to all this is."

"You think your case is related to Chaney?"

"In a way. You remember when you told me about all the holding companies and limited liability corporations separating you from Specialty Tees' real owner?"

"Yeah."

"I wouldn't suppose that EsCoMed was one of them."

"Hold on."

He set the receiver down. I heard him walk away, and then I heard the sound of the file cabinet opening and closing. Seconds later he was back on the line.

"You said *EsCoMed?*" he asked.

"Right."

"Here it is. About three companies down. EsCoMed owns the company that owns the company that owns Specialty Tees."

"Hot damn," I said. "It all fits."

I thanked him and drove back to Prosperity. I placed a telephone call to Stu and asked him to come in early. Then I radioed Slim at the high school and asked him to return to the station.

I could feel the adrenalin rushing in my veins now. After almost two weeks of sleepless nights and fruitless dead-end investigations, I could feel the end of the case approaching. I was about to nail a killer to the wall.

At the same time, I recognized a sense of sadness in the situation. In order to catch the bad guy, I was also going to have to take down a friend.

As soon as Stu pulled up in front of the station, I told him where to wait.

I walked next door to the Town Hall. Huggie was in his office, dictating a letter, when I knocked on the door. He gestured for me to have a seat on the couch, while he finished the letter. Then he placed the recorder on his desk and turned to me.

"Sorry about that business yesterday, Judd," he said. "The Council placed me in a tough position."

"You mean Kent Kramer painted you into a corner."

"He's very powerful. He can deliver a ton of votes. Hell, he could be the next mayor of this town."

I nodded.

"I could use a little help," I said. "You handle contracts for most of the businesses in town, don't you?"

"Pretty much. I'm the only attorney with an office in Prosperity. Most of the people in town come to me."

"I've run up against a company I can't trace, and I was wondering whether you might know who owns it."

"What's the company?"

"FLN Enterprises."

He had been writing on a sheet of paper on his desk, but when I said the company name, he stopped.

"*FLN,* you say?"

"Right. They own a number of the rental properties in town, especially over on Morris Quick. I've been able to track them to a holding company in South Carolina named *EsCoMed.* Does that help?"

"Not as I can tell. I don't recall any EsCoMed coming to me to handle an incorporation in Bliss County."

"I never said FLN was a corporation," I said.

"You said it was owned by this company from South Carolina. Usually, when a holding company opens a subsidiary, they incorporate."

"Or maybe you already knew FLN was a corporation before I walked in. Your middle name is Lynn, isn't it?"

"Yes."

"As in Fletcher Lynn Newton?"

"That's right."

"As in *F . . . L . . . N.*"

He settled back in his chair. He tried to present a composed, calm demeanor, but I could tell that I'd rattled him.

"What are you after, Judd?"

"I was hoping you would tell me. Right now, Clark Ulrich and Sharon Counts — those two forensic techs with the Sheriff's Department? — are tearing apart a five-year-old red Cadillac Seville over in Morgan. Seems this Caddy was traded a little over a week ago, for a new Chrysler 300. Maybe you can tell me what they're likely to find in it."

He stared at me, his eyes small and beady, like black pearls squashed into biscuit dough. He didn't say anything.

"Because," I continued, "I happen to recognize this Caddy. I should. It's been parked outside this building for the past five years, up until about a week ago. Then, last Saturday, you drove up to my house in your spiffy new Chrysler 300. Beautiful car.

Loaded. The dealer in Morgan recalls it fondly. He'd hoped to snag it for his wife, but some guy came in last Wednesday in a bull-goose hurry to unload his Caddy, and demanded to take the 300 from dealer's stock."

Huggie still said nothing.

"He remembers you like a photograph," I said.

"So I bought a new car."

"It's not so much the car you bought that interests me, as the one you *sold*. That red Cadillac is famous over on Morris Quick Road. I have a witness over there who recalls it stopping frequently at Roberto Camarena's house. Sometimes Gypsy Camarena would get in. Sometimes she'd get out."

"I gave the girl a ride from time to time," he said. "Her parents rented a house I owned. It was a gesture of goodwill."

"Awful nice of you, Huggie. It was especially nice of you to give her a ride home Saturday a week ago, around about midnight. It's a bad thing for a young girl like that to be out walking along the side of the Morgan Highway so late at night."

His ears reddened, from the top down. I could tell I was getting to him.

"What I can't figure out," I said, "is why

you picked her up about eight o'clock last Monday night. You running a taxi service now? I can understand giving her a ride home, but why would you pick her up? You want to tell me where you took Gypsy last Monday night?"

He remained silent.

"I don't suppose you went anywhere near Six Mile Creek, did you?"

"I think that's enough," he said. "If you want to accuse me of something, maybe you ought to get on with it."

"Okay, how's this? I think you're Es-CoMed, and FLN Enterprises, and about ten other shell companies. I think you own Specialty Tees. I also think you know that Specialty Tees is a conduit for Mexican tar heroin and Carolina Vulcan methedrine."

"That's preposterous," he said, but I had a hard time hearing any conviction behind it.

"Here's what I think happened. We know that Trigger Chaney, a central figure in the Bliss County crank trade, is your nephew. Don Webb found that out after he arrested Chaney today. We also know that the Vulcans run their meth product through Specialty Tees, who then puts it on the street. We also know that Specialty Tees is a clearinghouse for shipments of Mexican tar hidden in boxes of Mexican-manufactured tee shirts. If I dig deeply enough, I bet I'll also find that you own the factory in Mexico that makes the shirts."

"This is a fantasy," Huggie said.

"There's more. I talked to several renters along Morris Quick Road. They all rent their houses from FLN Enterprises. They also know that you come around from time to time to collect overdue rents. I think that's how you met Gypsy in the first place. I'd say you'd been getting it on with Gypsy for about a month before she died. You'd pick her up at the store, or at school, or sometimes you'd actually drop by her house. I think it was too dangerous for you to go to a motel, so you either took her to your house, parked in the garage, and closed the door before getting out of the car, or you just engaged in a little *ménage a Cadillac.*"

"You're disgusting, Judd."

"I think, Mr. Mayor, under the circumstances, you maybe ought to refer to me as Chief Wheeler. If I'm right, you're a damn sight worse than disgusting yourself. So I figure you started having sex with Gypsy. Maybe you coerced her into it — told her if she didn't give in you'd kick her parents out of that shitbox house they rented from you.

Maybe she did it willingly. She was a wild girl. Why she did it with you isn't an issue.

"Here's the way I think it happened. Saturday before last, she was at that sex party over at Kevin Byrne's house. She left angry around eleven-thirty. You picked her up near midnight out on the Morgan Highway. You came on to her, and she told you to stuff it. She'd already been screwed by six white guys that night, and she wasn't in the mood for lucky number seven. She bragged about the football players she'd shagged only a few hours before. Maybe she compared them to you, and you didn't stack up so well. So you dropped her off at her house and drove off to lick your wounds.

"Then, you came by to pick her up on Monday night. I know that Gypsy was very good friends with a girl named Anita Velez. Anita Velez was dating another kid named Jaime Ortiz. Ortiz had a running feud with your nephew Trigger Chaney, something to do with a turf conflict regarding who was going to sell what, and where.

"You were already angry at Gypsy for refusing you on Saturday night. I'm guessing that Gypsy had talked with Jaime in the interim. She told him about you, and he told her about his problems with Trigger Chaney, and about what was really going

476

on at Specialty Tees."

"You can't prove any of this," Huggie said.

"No? Jaime Ortiz is out of his coma. He's already fingered Chaney and a couple of other Vulcans for the beating he got last Saturday. We have forensic evidence that proves they were at the scene. Don Webb is grilling Chaney right now at the courthouse in Morgan. How long do you think it's going to take for him to give you up, Huggie? It's all about the little fish and the big fish."

"Fish," he snorted.

"But back to Gypsy. You figured you'd show her that you were as good as any six-foot high school halfback. She got in the car with you, and you drove her somewhere and had sex with her. This time, though, she demanded money from you, exactly the way she did at that sex party at Kevin Byrne's house two nights before. I'd guess you refused, being basically a tightwad, and that's when she hit you with the real dirt she had against you. I'm guessing that she told you she knew all about your involvement with the Bliss County drug trade, and threatened to blow the whistle if you didn't cross her palm.

"You're a smart guy, though. You knew that if you did pay her, it was just going to be the first installment in a lifetime contract.

Maybe you thought you could intimidate her. You grabbed her, and in the struggle you snapped her neck. You didn't know what to do, so you dumped her by the side of Six Mile Creek, far enough off the road so you didn't think she'd be found for several days.

"You went home and tried to figure out what to do next. You cleaned out the car, and traded it the next day at the Chrysler dealership in Morgan."

"This isn't going anywhere," he said.

"Remember, Huggie, this is all just speculation. On the other hand, every piece of evidence we've uncovered over the last three days points back to you, eventually. Like I said, Sheriff Webb is taking your nephew to town. How long do you think it's going to take Chaney to admit that you ordered him and his biker butt buddies to work over Jaime Ortiz?"

"He can't admit to something that never happened."

"Hell, by the time they're finished with him, Chaney will probably admit to the Lincoln assassination. There's more, though. We really don't need Chaney to get you for Gypsy's murder.

"Let's say you and Gypsy were getting it on — just postulating, you understand. As it happens, Gypsy had sex with someone the night she died. She also appears to have scratched that person defensively when he attacked her. She had skin cells underneath her fingernails. The DNA report from those samples indicated that the person who probably killed her had an unusual genetic mutation. If we were to find that same DNA profile on another person, the odds against him *not* being the killer are hundreds of thousands to one. So, you want me to call Clark Ulrich over here so he can take a couple of samples from you? Could take you off the hook if the profiles don't match."

Huggie crossed his hands against his ample protruding stomach.

"I think I want to talk with my attorney," he said.

"You'll have plenty of time for that, Hug. I have Officer Marbury standing outside this office. He's going to drive you to your house. Don't worry about your new wheels — we'll take really good care of them. With your considerable resources, I'd say you're a fairly reasonable flight risk. Officer Marbury will be joined there by Officer Tackett, to ensure that you don't go rabbit on me."

"That's false imprisonment," he said.

"No it isn't. I'm giving you the benefit of the doubt, sir. If I knew for certain that you killed Gypsy, I'd slam you in my jail so hard you'd leave a grease spot on the back wall. As it is, I have sufficient cause to keep you under protective supervision. As soon as Ulrich gets me the DNA results, I'll either cuff you or offer you my sincere apologies."

For some reason, Huggie was smiling.

"Let me show you something," he said.

He got up, and started around his desk. I unsnapped my holster and laid my hand on the grip of my pistol.

"It's okay," he said. "No reason to get violent. I just want to get some papers from that table."

He pointed toward a circular table on the other side of the room. He walked over, pulled a sheaf of blueprints from under a couple of books, and opened them.

"Come look at this," he said.

Cautiously, I walked over to the table.

"Do the words *eminent domain* mean anything to you, Judd?"

I looked as his fat index finger stabbed at the blueprint.

"This here is a set of plans for the next phase of development for Prosperity. See? Here's Kent's new neighborhood over off Morris Quick Road, where that poor Mexican boy got nailed to a tree. Here, where the Camarenas' house used to stand, is the new Prosperity Commons Shopping Center. That entire block is going under, Judd."

"Can't do it," I said. "The town charter plainly limits commercial development to the plot at the corner of the Pooler and Morgan Highways."

"That's the beauty of this plan," he said. "The Town Council can rewrite the charter. We've been talking it over, and the way the town is growing we think maybe it could stand a shopping center on either end of the town limits off the Morgan Highway.

"We're not entirely mercenary, though. We plan to provide a new park for the entire town, a place where the citizens can relax on a warm spring afternoon, complete with softball fields, basketball courts, plenty of rolling hills for picnics. A thing of beauty."

He pointed at the map. His finger fell directly in the center of my farm.

"What in hell . . . ?"

"*Eminent domain,* Judd. The good of the many outweighs the good of the one, and all that. You and your son are sitting on a lot more land than you're probably due. In the next phase of the town development, we plan to condemn your farm and turn it into Prosperity Park. Oh, we'll make sure you're adequately compensated, of course. I figure that land is worth somewhere between

$30,000 and $40,000 an acre. You'll realize between three and four million from the deal. Makes a cop's salary look pretty skinny, now, don't it?"

I couldn't take my eyes off the plans. Just as Huggie had said, the boundaries of my entire farm now enclosed a mixed-use public park. My barn was destined to become an enclosed picnic and meeting space.

My house — the house my grandfather had ordered from the Sears catalog — was nowhere to be seen.

"Why are you showing me this?" I asked.

"To give you a choice. You can take the money, or I can shitcan the entire plan and you get to keep your farm — though for the life of me I can't imagine why you'd want to. According to the town charter, condemnation takes the vote of the entire Town Council, *and* the mayor. You tell me what you want, and I'll make it work out that way."

"You're bribing me," I said.

"I'm offering you a fair trade."

"I don't understand. What do you get in return?"

"Don't arrest me or hold me until you get the results from the forensic testing. If they don't look good for me, we'll come up with a reasonable explanation for it. Hell, I'll admit to fuckin' that little wetback girl. Between you and me, she was a great piece. I've paid good money for a lot worse. Don't mean I killed her, though."

"What about the rest of it?"

"Oh, I'll probably be arrested sooner or later for that stuff. Like you said, Trigger will probably roll over on me. That damn boy never did have the slightest shred of loyalty."

"You admit it then? All of it?"

"I'm not admitting squat, Judd. Things are what they are, though. You guys want me badly enough, you'll find a way to get me, sooner or later."

"You'd be forced to resign as mayor."

"I *can't* be forced to resign. I have to be voted out of office. There's no initiative and referendum in North Carolina. I can't be recalled in midterm. The only way I don't serve out this term is if I die in office. That gives me plenty of time to make the sale of your farm happen, if you want the money, or trash the whole plan if you want to keep the place. All you have to do is tell me which way you want it."

I'm ashamed to admit it, but for just a moment I considered his offer. It would have been easy enough to let him ride until the forensic results came in. I hadn't told Stu what I wanted him to do. I could have just sent him back home, told him it was a false alarm. I could have ordered Slim back to the school, and we'd just chalk the whole episode up to a misunderstanding.

If I thought my dreams of Susan had kept me awake, though, I knew they were nothing compared to the sleep I'd lose if I let Gypsy Camarena's murderer slip through my fingers. There was the distinct possibility that if I let Huggie off the hook, however temporarily, he'd just take off for the Caribbean and live off some offshore bank account he'd socked away.

What finally made my decision for me, though, was my understanding of myself. If I joined forces with Huggie and helped him to stay in office when I knew he was guilty of killing Gypsy, I might save my farm, but I knew I'd lose my soul. That was a sacrifice I wasn't prepared to make.

Today was today. I'd worry about saving the farm later.

"Officer Marbury is waiting, sir," I said.

"This is a big mistake, Judd," he said.

"Not as big as the one I'd make helping you escape. Let's go."

I escorted him to the front of the Town Hall.

"Stu, I'd like you to take Mayor Newton to his house. Escort him inside. Then I'd like you to stand guard at the house and make sure he doesn't leave until I call or come by to relieve you. You got that?"

"What's up, Chief?" he asked.

"I'll explain it later. Slim will be at the house when you get there. One of you guard the front, and the other can take the back. I have to go into Morgan and meet with the sheriff. If it looks like you'll be there for more than a couple of hours, I'll get Sheriff Webb to post a couple of deputies to take your place. Any questions?"

"Only about a dozen, Chief. You'll let us know what's going on later?"

"I hope so. You get going now."

CHAPTER THIRTY-FIVE

I returned to Morgan, where I sat around in Sheriff Webb's office jawing with him and Gajewski. After a while, he didn't seem quite so obnoxious, for a fed. We were enjoying a fresh pot of coffee after eating dinner at a place next to the courthouse.

"If it helps," Webb said, "Chaney rolled over on his uncle. From what he told me, Newton's been laundering money from the Specialty Tees operation through his other shell companies for five or six years. Chaney said that the mayor came to him late last week, and told him that Jaime Ortiz was talking about the operation. Newton asked Chaney to shut Jaime up."

"Shut him up?" Gajewski said, incredulously. "Damn near killed him."

"According to Chaney, he almost lost control. At one point he thought he'd killed Ortiz," Webb said.

"Did he admit to killing Rico Armand?" I asked.

"He's holding back on that one. Says he'll talk about the shootout if we'll make a deal for him to testify against Huggie."

"Turns my stomach, making deals with guys like Chaney," Gajewski said.

"On the other hand," I chimed in, "if it sews up the case against Huggie, I think we can probably live with ourselves."

The telephone rang.

"Let me put you on speaker," Webb said, after answering. "I have Agent Gajewski and Chief Wheeler here in my office."

He punched a button, and Clark Ulrich's voice came over the metallic speaker, sounding far away and artificial.

"We went over the Cadillac front to back and top to bottom. Apparently Mayor Newton did a thorough cleaning before he traded it last week."

"How thorough?" I asked.

"It was a professional job. I'd imagine he used a detailer. It wouldn't have looked suspicious if he did. A lot of people do that just before trading. They think it increases the value of their car."

"So, were you able to find anything?" Webb asked.

"Well, you can clean a car all you want,

and you'll still leave stuff behind. I'd suspect that, in the long run, Mayor Newton is going to wish he'd opted for the leather seat option. We found dried secretions on the back side of the cloth upholstery in the back seat, and hair samples that had been pushed down between the cushion and the seat back. We also found a few flecks of blood and some skin samples in the trunk of the car, stuck in the taillight wires.

"We rushed the polymerase chain reaction tests, and got the results back about ten minutes ago."

"What did you find?" I asked.

I realized, suddenly, that I was actually sitting on the edge of my chair. Whatever came of these tests would make or break my case against Huggie Newton.

"The hair samples produced two specific DNA genotypes. The first matches the samples we harvested from Gitana Camarena's own skin and hair."

He seemed to pause for effect.

"The second genotype is a match for the semen samples and the fingernail scrapes we obtained from Ms. Camarena during the post-mortem. It's accurate right down to the abnormal allele described by the Medical Examiner. I'd say, at least on the surface, you have probable cause. It might be time to have a discussion with the District Attorney."

"Hot damn, that's fine work," Webb said. "Do me a favor and fax your findings directly to my office. We'll call the DA now and get him over here to bang heads. Thanks, Clark."

I thanked him too, for his fast work and for his results. I sat back in my chair, almost unable to breathe.

"You ever solve a murder before, Judd?" Webb asked.

"Not like this," I said. "The gold shields always handled that kind of thing back in Atlanta. I helped with a couple of murder busts resulting from their investigations, but I never did the actual legwork before."

"Well, boy, anytime you decide to kick out of that puny department over in Prosperity, I'll have a gold shield waiting for you here in Morgan. You did a first-class job."

"There's still the matter of the arrest and the trial. Let's take this one step at a time," I said.

Webb called the DA, a man name Chris Wampler, and asked him to drop by the office for a conversation. He resisted at first, but when Webb told him who the suspect was, he couldn't get downtown fast enough.

By the time Wampler arrived, Clark Ulrich had faxed over the results of the tests on Huggie Newton's Cadillac. I described my investigation into the murder of Gypsy Camarena step-by-step. Wampler reviewed the results of the forensic testing. When all was said and done, he agreed that there was probable cause to arrest Huggie Newton. He was almost foaming at the mouth at the prospect of taking down the big fish.

He made a telephone call to Judge Beam, who agreed to the arrest warrant. A half hour later, one of Webb's deputies arrived with the signed document in hand, and delivered it to me.

I held it up to Don Webb.

"Don't you want to serve this?" I asked.

Webb shook his head.

"It's your bust, Judd. He's in your jurisdiction, you worked the case. I'd say you probably earned the right to take this cocksucker down, wouldn't you?"

I couldn't have agreed more.

I thanked Sheriff Webb for his help, and told him I'd arrange for Huggie to be transferred from the Prosperity Police Department holding cell to the County Jail the next morning. Wampler urged me to call him after Huggie was transferred so he could begin work on the arraignment. He wanted to get Huggie officially charged as quickly as possible.

By the time I left the Bliss County Sheriff's Department, it was well after nine o'clock. As I walked to my cruiser, a car pulled up alongside me in the parking lot. The driver's window rolled down and Cory True, the reporter from the Morgan *Ledger-Telegraph,* poked his head out.

"How ya'll doin' tonight, Chief?" he asked.

"Been better. Been worse," I said. "I really can't talk right now, Cory."

"Just two minutes. Word has it that you've solved the murder of that girl over in Prosperity last week."

"Whose word?" I asked.

"A little voice here, a little voice there. I have my contacts, and the Constitution says I get to protect them. So, is it true?"

"Talk to me tomorrow," I said, as I reached the cruiser.

"Just one more question," he said. "Would you like to tell me why there're bubbletops from both the Prosperity Police Department and the Bliss County Sheriff's Department parked in the driveway of Mayor Newton's house over in your neck of the woods?"

"No comment, Cory. Call me tomorrow."

"I, uh, don't suppose you'd be headed over toward Mayor Newton's house yourself right about now, would you?"

"Tomorrow, Cory. Call me then."

I unlocked the door of my cruiser and climbed in behind the wheel. Cory True chirped his tires as he sped out of the parking lot and drove off toward Morgan Highway.

I had little doubt where he was going.

Huggie Newton lived in a five-thousand-square-foot Georgian revival house right off Morgan Highway, where it intersected with the Mica Wells Road. The house was set about three hundred feet off the highway, and was separated from the asphalt by a half-acre pond and a long split-rail fence painted white. I had never figured out what a single man like Huggie needed with five thousand square feet, though I had imagined that it had something to do with compensation.

He had built a long stamped-concrete driveway that started at Morgan Highway and wound around between the pond and the front porch of his house, and then emptied into Mica Wells Road. A circular spur off the driveway led around to the back of the house, to a garage.

As I drove into the estate, I saw that Stu Marbury had parked the old Prosperity squad car right in front of the porch. Right behind it sat a Sheriff's Department cruiser. Behind that sat Cory True's car.

I pulled in behind Cory and turned off my engine. I didn't bother to cut off the lights on top of my car since I was, after all, on official business.

I looked up at the house, and I thought I saw Huggie peering out at me through one of the downstairs window curtains, just before it flopped back into place. Maybe it was my imagination.

While I collected my papers, including the warrant for Huggie's arrest, Cory walked up to my car and rapped on the driver's-side window.

I rolled it down.

"Thought y'all would be headed this way," he said.

"When you're right, you're right," I said.

"Want to tell me what's going on?"

I shook my head.

"Oh, come on, Chief. Somethin' big's goin' down tonight. I'd like to get an exclusive."

"You can stay and watch," I said. "I can't stop you from doing that, so long as you don't get in the way. If you impede official police business, though, you may find yourself eating breakfast in one of my holding cells tomorrow, and everyone else will scoop you before you can touch a keyboard. Do we understand each other?"

He nodded, and could barely suppress his grin.

I rolled my window back up, and pulled myself out of the cruiser, papers in hand.

Stu stood next to the front door. He leaned against one of the half-columns that had been installed there to offer the effect of two layers, and fiddled with a toothpick in his teeth.

"You get anything to eat?" I asked as I walked up.

"Slim dropped by a little while ago with some barbecue sandwiches for me and the deputy 'round back. You want to tell me what's goin' on, now, Chief?"

I dropped my voice almost to a whisper as I leaned into him, so Cory wouldn't hear me.

"I have a warrant here to arrest Huggie. I hope it's going to go smoothly, but you might want to be ready in case things go south."

His eyes got very wide. In his wildest dreams he probably had never imagined arresting the mayor for anything.

I reached past him and pushed the doorbell button.

Almost instantly, I heard the shotgun blast from inside.

"Aw, shit!" I said, as I pushed past Slim and shoved the door inward. "Keep that damned reporter outside!"

I could smell the acrid sting of cordite hanging in the air. There was something else, too, a smell I'd almost forgotten, and had hoped I'd never encounter again.

I ran through the foyer, and found Huggie in his office, between the living room and the kitchen.

One foot was bare, but otherwise he was dressed to the nines. He had put on one of his best court suits, sat on the floor against the wall of his office, wedged the barrel of a twelve-gauge Beretta skeet gun up under his chin, and pulled the trigger with one fat toe.

Blood and tissue stained the wall behind him, and cascaded down the front of his suit and across the walnut stock of the gun, which still lay in his lap.

He had fucked it up. At the last second, he must have jerked the barrel of the shotgun sideways, and instead of blowing up straight through his chin the charge had blasted away the entire right side of his face. The other side was almost completely unscathed, save for spatter that had blown across it when half his head had been taken off.

"Jesus, Huggie," I said, as I stood in front of him. "What a lousy way to die."

I looked at him for a long moment, and then decided I should do something. Without taking my eyes off his ravaged face, I started to walk toward the desk.

His one remaining good eye followed me.

It rotated in its socket and tracked me as I walked. I stopped in my tracks, and walked back the way I had come.

The eye followed me again.

"Aw, damn!" I said. Then I shouted, "Stu! Call an ambulance! He's still alive!"

I heard Stu grab his radio and call for the Prosperity Rescue Squad. I knelt in front of Huggie and tried to figure out what I could do to keep him from cacking before the medics got there. He was bleeding profusely from the head wound, but I couldn't tell if the major arteries in his neck had been severed. I didn't see any arterial spurt, but that could have been because he was too low on blood to support a lot of pressure.

I ran into the hall bathroom, grabbed a couple of towels off the rack, and dashed back to the office. Without any real understanding of what needed to be done, I wadded the towels and tried to pack the massive wounds on the left side of Huggie's face as best as I could. His lone eye grew wide as I worked. I thought I saw a tear collect at its corner.

His jaw moved a little as I tried to stanch the bleeding. It took me a minute to realize he was trying to talk with his ruined mouth.

I leaned forward and tried to hear what he was saying.

The air coming from his mouth was fetid and wet. I could tell that his lungs were filling with fluid. Still, he tried to make some kind of sound come out.

"What is it?" I asked. "It's okay, Huggie. I'm not going anywhere. What are you trying to say?"

The breath he forced up from his lungs finally found his vocal cords. The sound was raspy and fluid.

"Hurts," he said. "Hurts bad."

"The medics are on the way. They'll give you something for the pain."

"Sorry," he gasped. His remaining eye went wide. His body quaked with one racking spasm, and I saw his pupil go completely black.

I wouldn't be arresting anyone that night.

I leaned back against his desk and stared at him.

Off in the distance, I heard the wail of the Prosperity Rescue Squad sirens.

Hours later, long after the ambulance and the police cars and the television trucks had left, I sat in Huggie's living room, with the note he had left in my lap.

I had found it moments after he died. It had been set upright against a paperweight on his desk, and was addressed to me. He had known that I would be the person who would find him after he shot himself, because he didn't plan to do it until I arrived to arrest him.

I had read the note over and over, and still had trouble absorbing the words.

Dear Judd, it said.

The fact that you are reading this letter means that two things have happened. The first is that you have found sufficient evidence to charge me with the murder of Gypsy Camarena. The second is that I have cheated the hangman's noose by taking the easy way out.

I want to tell you how sorry I am. I never intended to kill Gypsy. It was a horrible mistake, compounded by my irresponsible attempts to cover it up.

It's an old story, I suppose. Like most

people, I started out wanting to change the world for the better. Something's wrong deep inside me, though. Anytime I see an opportunity to grab another wad of cash, it's like putting a bottle in front of a drunk.

The affair with Gypsy started several months ago. Another old story — a middle-aged man and a beautiful young girl, neither with the scruples the Good Lord gave an alley cat.

For the record, you were right about almost everything — the money laundering, the involvement with Specialty Tees, the assault on the Ortiz boy, all of it. The parts you got wrong really don't matter. I don't know how you put the whole story together, and I suppose that really doesn't matter either.

Gypsy was beautiful, but she had a mouth that could etch glass. There was something cold and hard deep inside her, and when she allowed it to come out it could consume you. I let her get under my skin, and then I let her enrage me, with her threats to expose my illegal dealings.

I will say this again — I did not mean to kill her. I just lost control and before I could stop myself she was dead.

I placed her alongside Six Mile Creek, in

the exact spot where your wife died, in hopes that you would be distracted by the coincidence and not be able to conduct a decent investigation. I underestimated you, Judd. I'm also sorry for that.

In the top drawer of my desk you will find a holographic will. I wrote it this evening while I waited for you to come to arrest me. It isn't notarized, but it's completely legal under the general statutes of North Carolina, and supersedes any previous wills I have made. Please see to it that it is delivered to my personal attorney, Mr. Alton Blades, in Morgan. He will see to it that the conditions are carried out. I have made Roberto Camarena and his wife my primary beneficiaries. It's the least I can do for taking away their daughter.

I have also left a little something for you, to be used for your son's education. I know how difficult it must be for you to make ends meet on the pittance the Town Council pays you. Maybe this trifle I've bequeathed will help make up for the way I treated you during this investigation.

There is one more thing you should know. Underneath the envelope containing my new will, there is a folder. You should take it and put it in a safe place. The plans to convert your farm into a city *park are very, very real. No matter how good a friend you perceive Kent to be, he is a dangerous opponent in the political arena, and money always outweighs his other allegiances. Take it from me. This is something I know about all too well. All politics are dirty, but small-town politics are the dirtiest of all. The information in the folder I've provided for you, used judiciously, will stop any condemnation process against your property. Just remember — it isn't blackmail; it's just the way the political process in small towns works.*

I must close now, so that I can go prepare for what I know I must do. I hope that, in the passage of time, you will remember that we were once friends, and that you will come by whatever grassy knoll they place me and visit once in a while.

Huggie

I folded the note and placed it inside my briefcase, and then looked at the folder again.

The information inside detailed construction and inspection payoffs, bribes, and the substitution of substandard materials for those actually specified in home plans. If the contents of this folder were ever divulged, Kent Kramer would be ruined.

There are things you just don't want to know about your friends. The Gypsy Camarena case had placed a huge strain on the relationship between Kent and me. The allegations in Huggie's folder might have put it beyond redemption. If Kent could do the things outlined in this report, he could just as easily yank my farm out from under me, and not lose a night's sleep over it.

I sighed, closed the folder, and placed it next to Huggie's letter and new will inside my briefcase. The next day, I'd drop by the bank and place the folder in my safe deposit box.

CHAPTER THIRTY-SIX

They buried Gypsy Camarena and Huggie Newton on the same day, in separate cemeteries.

The day after Huggie killed himself, I received a call from Father Salazar.

"Chief Wheeler," he said.

"Father."

"I don't know whether to congratulate you on solving Gitana's murder. I can only imagine how much this case has cost you."

"Thank you."

"I wanted to tell you that we will hold Gitana's funeral tomorrow morning at nine, and I would like to invite you to attend."

"I'll be there. Will her parents be able to make it?"

"Yes."

"I need to meet with them," I said. "I have some information they need. Also, you can tell them for me that they needn't fear being deported. I've talked it over with the

Homeland Security agent who's been working with me here, and he's satisfied that Roberto isn't a criminal risk."

"They will be happy to hear it. Nine o'clock here at the church?"

"Count on it."

After they placed Gitana in the ground, I met with her parents and explained what had happened to their daughter. I tried, as best I could, to tell them how their daughter's murderer had felt so bad about what he did that he had left them virtually his entire estate. They were in such shock that I don't think it sank in. I had a talk with Father Salazar, who assured me that he would look after them, and explain it again in terms they could understand once they were ready to hear it.

I had so many things to do with Father Salazar that I was almost late for Huggie's funeral. Given the circumstances of his death, there was no church ceremony, no procession, and no reception. There was just a pitiable graveside service, attended by the Town Council, myself, a few onlookers, and the press.

I hung around after the others had left, and watched as they released the winch ratchet and slowly lowered Huggie's coffin into the ground. I stood over the hole and gazed down at the concrete cap of the burial vault. The cemetery manager walked up behind me.

"We need to inter him, Chief," he said. "We have another funeral in a half hour."

I nodded, as the diesel engine of the backhoe parked at a discreet distance from the grave coughed to life with a plume of blue-black smoke. The operator dropped it into gear, and it began to lumber toward me.

I pulled the envelope containing Huggie's farewell letter to me from the inside pocket of my jacket. I dropped it into the grave, then walked a short distance away and watched as the backhoe shoveled a couple of tons of dirt on top of it.

Sometime around two in the morning, Donna awoke and found me staring at the ceiling.

"Are you all right?" she asked.

"What?"

"You should be asleep."

"I know. I've been thinking."

"About Huggie?"

"Partly. And about Gypsy, and about Susan."

"Oh."

"No. Good things. I've been thinking

about that damned cell phone, and what Susan wanted to say to me. The more I think about it, the more I realize that it's just one of those things that I'll never know. I have to learn to live with that."

"And that's good?" she asked.

"It's a resolution. It puts things to rest. I can let it go."

"You're sure?"

"No. But I'm closer to it than I was before the murder. I reckon that everything we needed to say to each other got said, and whatever I missed — well, I already knew it. I'm going to presume that she just wanted to say goodbye."

"What about the flashbacks?"

"Haven't had a single one since I figured out that Huggie killed Gypsy."

"Do you think she's gone? Susan?" Donna asked.

"Yeah," I said, as I leaned over to kiss her. "I think everything is okay now. Let's go back to sleep."

"You bet, Chief," she said, as she shuffled across the sheets and curled her body up tightly against mine. She settled her head against my shoulder.

"Sweet dreams," she said.

My dreams were sweet.

I didn't wake again until morning.

ABOUT THE AUTHOR

Richard Helms retired after a two-decade career as a forensic psychologist to take a position as a psychology instructor at a college near his home. The author of nine previous novels, Helms has been nominated three times for the Private Eye Writers of America Shamus Award, and has won the Short Mystery Fiction Society Derringer Award twice.

The father of two children who somehow managed to become adults, Richard Helms lives in a small North Carolina town that looks very much like his vision of Prosperity, with his wife Elaine, and an indeterminate number of cats.

The employees of Thorndike Press hope you have enjoyed this Large Print book. All our Thorndike, Wheeler, and Kennebec Large Print titles are designed for easy reading, and all our books are made to last. Other Thorndike Press Large Print books are available at your library, through selected bookstores, or directly from us.

For information about titles, please call:
  (800) 223-1244

or visit our Web site at:
  http://gale.cengage.com/thorndike

To share your comments, please write:
  Publisher
  Thorndike Press
  10 Water St., Suite 310
  Waterville, ME 04901